cohen's control

Crave & Cure

Book Two

daisy jane

Cover Photo | Wander Aguiar

Cover Model | Lachy McLean

Cover Design | Daisy Jane

Editing | Laura Davies

Beta Reading | Karen Quimby, Jes Vaz, Randi Nash

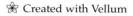 Created with Vellum

content & trigger
warnings:

This book deals with heavy topics not suitable for all readers.

There is no book plot too good to forgo checking these warnings.

Please read the following possible content and trigger warnings and read accordingly: narcissistic ex, emotional abuse, verbal abuse, mention of miscarriage, hurtful language around miscarriage, divorce, death of a child (off page, some description), suicidal ideation/thoughts, depression, anxiety, trauma, characters in therapy, FMC who is an active sex worker.

Please, do not continue this book if those topics are disturbing to you or your reading experience.

foreword

"Somehow, even in the worst of times, the tiniest fragments of good survive. It was the grip in which one held those fragments that counted."

Melina Marchetta

prologue

· · ·

scarlett

…TWO MONTHS AGO

"You can't spin in jeans, you know. You'll get wicked thigh burn," I tell the handsome but somewhat cold looking man who perches on the bike adjacent to me.

He smooths a hand through his hair, the color of night, silver sparking on the sides. He's good looking and well dressed, and honestly, a bit too tall and built for the bike.

"I'm not spinning," he says, his eyes pinched on me since he sat down. And now I'm starting to feel… uncomfortable.

"Look dude, I have mace in my bag, and I have a taser, and I have used both." I fold my arms over my chest and narrow my eyes at him. He doesn't intimidate me, he doesn't know who I live with.

"I'm not gonna hurt you, I just want to talk," he says, peering around conspicuously, keeping his voice low. "Lucy."

The hairs on my neck rise.

"Lucy?" he questions.

"Yes," I reply cautiously.

He draws his hand to his chest. "I'm Augustus Moore. I'm the director and CEO at Crave & Cure." He waits a moment for this information to settle. I recognize the name Crave because for the last two years all the other girls at Jizzabelle have been going on and on about the lead star Tucker Deep, and how they wish he was signed to Jizz. I also recognize Crave because… they're the Starbucks, while Jizzabelle is the coffee corner inside a gas station. I've heard of him, but I've never seen Augustus Moore until now though.

"I've heard of you," I say, relaxing my shoulders, putting in a few lazy revolutions on the bike.

"I'll cut to the chase. I know Pete Bryson is your partner, and I know you're in contract at Jizz. But I want you at Crave."

I shake my head. "He'd never go for that. Ever." A chill rolls through my spine just thinking about what Pete will say when he hears about this conversation. I edge away from him, leaning uncomfortably off my bike. "You know what, Pete will hate that you're doing this and honestly, I just don't have it in me to be his emotional punching bag for three days over it." Brutally honest but again, I'm too tired for this. I have to save my energy for *him*.

Augustus doesn't look surprised by my sighed admission. Instead, he captures my eyes with a heavy, pointed look. "You leave him behind, I'll get you on your feet in a new place with a new contract, all dictated by you. Your terms plus the best medical and mental health care, pension and a 401K."

I blink, completely taken aback by what he's floating. Because he didn't know—he couldn't—but that's everything I need. A way out, and a way to take care of myself.

Pete's promised me things that Augustus Moore can't give me though. Things I want with all of my marrow.

"Listen, let's go get a coffee and talk. Okay? I'll sign an NDA just for the coffee, so you don't have to worry about Pete finding out."

My legs slow until the bike stops. "Why do you want me at Crave? Because I'm the top star? Or is this some dick measuring contest with Pete? Are you two like, enemies or something?"

He blinks at me with an expression of sheer confusion. Pulling a hand down his face he slips off the bike and stands before me, imposing but not intimidating. "I want you because they have you and they're wasting all of your beauty and potential on scenes you're clearly not enjoying. I think you would enjoy your job at Crave, feel safe in your scenes, and still be at the top."

I swallow, a lump forming at the back of my throat. "How do you know I'm not enjoying scenes?"

Aug taps the center of his chest as he punctuates his words. "Because *I* make movies based on the importance of sexual empowerment and *respect*, and my gut can tell when someone is trapped and miserable." He steps even closer and rests his hand on mine, still gripping the bike. "Please have coffee with me. That's all I ask."

I'm frozen on the bike, too scared to move. Because if Pete finds out I had coffee with a competitor, another man, *fuck*, if he found out I so much as blinked without his permission, we'd have a fight.

I'm tired of fighting. I'm tired of Jizz and being their toy, their show pony, their money making puppet. I'm tired, period, and right about now, I feel like I might finally be prepared to risk it all for a chance at something better.

"Alright," I say, sliding off my bike, grabbing my bag off the floor. "I can't make any promises, but I'll listen."

As we walk next door, I begin to fantasize about quitting Jizz and leaving Pete.

I keep my fingers crossed under my leg the entire time.

one

· · ·

scarlett

Because that's what I'm good at.

Three minutes can sometimes be a life changing amount of time. It can feel like an eternity when you're waiting for two pink lines, but when you're rushing around your former home trying desperately to stuff the most important items you own into a garbage bag, three minutes is nothing.

I skip the phone charger and laptop, too. Those I can replace. I don't want to buy a new computer and new cables, but I can. *Grab only the most important things, Scarlett*, I whisper, trying to keep myself calm. Growing up, my mom was always talking to herself and it took me being an adult to realize that was a self-soothing technique, and I hate that like her, I need it.

"The photo album, your passport and social security card,

then the jewelry box. If there's time, clothes," I hum the orders to myself as I fly through the apartment, padding down the hallway, fingertips dragging along the wall as I bounce from one spot to another. In the small office, I push junk around in a drawer, my mind moving so fast I skip past my file twice. Sweat beads and slides down my spine, and beneath my arms, my t-shirt clings to my damp skin. "Breathe, you're fine," I remind myself, knowing I've already wasted a precious minute I don't have.

I didn't want to cut it this close. But he stole my key and it took me much longer to get inside than I'd planned. I finally convinced the apartment manager to let me in, but that left me with less than five minutes.

He has come home for lunch at the same time every day for the last two years. Despite the fact that there's one huge change in his life—*me leaving*—I still expect him to be home for lunch.

That's why I need to get my stuff and get the fuck out.

I freeze in my tracks, arms above my head clutching a storage box in the office closet. From the open window, more than a soft breeze drifts in. Pins and needles warm the back of my neck, and I twist to face the dirty torn screen, listening intently. "Your wife lost her key. I let her in, I hope that's okay, Sir."

I hate that he's referred to me as his wife.

Fuck. Fuck, fuck, fuck!

I let the box topple to the floor and grab one of the albums out, shoving it deep inside my garbage bag before hooking it around the corner, down the hall to the bedroom. Panic has my head flying from side to side, desperate to locate my music box. I keep all my favorite jewelry there but truthfully, it's the box I want. I got it from my mom when I was a little girl, and she got it from her mom. It's one of the only things that means something to me anymore.

The front door swings open, slamming against the drywall, making the entire apartment shudder. I look to the dresser, where my things used to sit, spaced out nicely on a glass tray. That is, before we got into an argument last night and Pete swept his arm along the surface, sending all of my things across the floor. My perfume shattered. The room smells overly floral and sweet, it's acrid and I've never felt so sick. I leap across the bed, dragging my bag with me. With one hand, I feel around under the bed, then run my arms beneath the heaps of clothes but I can't find it. Heavy foot-steps stalk down the hall, toward me, and that's when I know... I'll never get it back.

"You couldn't even make it 15 hours without me," he sighs, his voice unwavering and calm. It's so eerie to be with someone so full of anger and hatred, and have them be so fucking calm. It's terrifying, because he's done and said some of the most cruel things to me while wearing the same stoic expression he's wearing now.

I hold up the bag. "These things belong to me." I refuse to let my arm tremble the way it wants to. The way my spine is already shaking. I wouldn't say I'm brave, but I left last night. After two hours of screaming and fighting and being held to the wall and made to *think* about my actions.

I won't go through that again.

I left, and I intend to stay gone. But these are my things, and he doesn't own me. Or my things.

Not anymore at least.

When he was gone yesterday morning, a few of my colleagues from Crave helped move me out. He came home shortly after they left and caught me trying to leave. That's when he stole my key.

"Those things are in *my* apartment, so I disagree." He stalks toward me, his gaze searing me so intensely that my stomach sours, my mouth grimacing with sickness.

How did I get here? How did my judgment become so clouded that I let myself be with a monster for so long? Why did it take me years to leave? Why am I so weak?

I swallow around the vomit, around the emotion, around the self-loathing and pain. Holding the bag to my chest with both hands, I leap across the bed as he approaches, and without a second look back, I run.

I run as fast as I can until I'm out the front door, my bare feet taking the cement steps two at a time as I fly downstairs. With the sun burning my eyes, I tip my face toward the apartment, my feet cooling in the grass. My chest heaves with adrenaline and my whole body trembles with… relief.

I didn't get the music box but I got my documents. I got a photo album. That's better than nothing, and that will have to be my big win.

I got out, and that's all that matters.

He appears at the railing, leaning over casually like he isn't the most terrifying human. The biggest monster. The slickest thief. "You're acting like a fucking idiot, Scarlett," he says casually, shaking his head from above.

All I had to do was get downstairs, where people are. Currently oblivious people, but we both know he won't say or do a single fucking thing if people are around. Because he's one of those monsters that exists just for me. *Only* for me.

I see the moment he realizes I've effectively silenced him.

A vicious grin travels across his face and he disappears. A moment later he returns, my music box in his hands. The fading pink flowers along the back make my heart race. That box is important to me. It's special. Just seeing the aged print and dark spots on the edges where I held it for hours as a young girl—tears well in my eyes.

"Pete," I call his name, but his gaze never leaves the box. He lifts it in the air, far above his head, and that's when he finds my eyes.

Still wearing a cruel smile, he lets go. I scream but for what, I'm not sure. The box is old, and while that means it's made well, it also means it's been man-handled for the better part of forty years. It's rickety, and as soon as he releases it, I know it's gone.

It can't survive a two story drop onto a pillow, much less concrete.

It doesn't happen in slow motion. Rather, he releases it and the box shatters almost immediately in front of me, the tiny little pink-velvet lined drawer ricocheting off the concrete across the lawn, landing next to my foot. The music dies softly in the air as the tiny ballerina sits in the mechanism, now broken and free from the box. She spins one last time, with no music, and stops. The lid with the adorable gold latch is separated from the box, and rests in a puddle of sprinkler run-off. The main box, which held a few gold necklaces and a ring from a former boyfriend, is completely split in two. The gentle velvet and tulle that once lined the inside is now torn, exposing the wood core of the old box.

He relishes every ounce of pain etched on my face, laughs and then turns on his heel, slamming the apartment door shut behind him.

With tears stinging my cheeks and snot bubbling at the end of my nose, I suck in a breath and wipe my face with the back of my hand. Moving quickly, I collect all the broken pieces and stuff them into the bag. I make my way to my car, parked at the back of the complex, and get inside.

As soon as my keys are in the ignition, my phone rings.

I know it's him without looking at the screen. I answer the call, out of habit I guess.

"Where are you going?" he asks, his voice rattling. "You have nowhere to go without me, Scarlett. Quit being a dramatic, selfish little bitch and get back here. You forced me to make a huge mess last night because you don't listen. You need to get back here and clean up *your* fucking mess."

"No," I say, my chin suddenly bobbing.

He laughs, as if I'm an actual idiot for no longer letting his narcissistic gaslighting control me. "Where are you going to go, Scarlett? Hmm? You gonna live in your car?"

"No," I say again, and though I know I shouldn't answer him—I should leave him to wonder, and let that wondering make him fester and stew and grow miserable and achy at all the unknowns. But I don't. I want a little win. I deserve a win, no matter how small damnit, so I spread salt in the wound. Which is a stupid move, but I deserve to inflict misery on him. "I have an apartment. Believe it or not, Pete, *I'm able to exist without you.*"

He snorts, the sound vile and disgusting. Every noise he makes turns my stomach, boils my blood, wears me down. I should have done this last year but it doesn't matter. I've done it now. I've left. And he can't get me back.

This time is different. I have an apartment. I have a new job. The exit strategy is no longer just a strategy, it's a plan I've set in motion. I've actually done it this time.

"Keep telling yourself that. But you'll see very quickly, Scarlett, that I was the one keeping you paid. Keeping you fed. Keeping you at the top. Without me, you'll realize you're nothing more than a useless, washed-up *whore.*"

His words shouldn't cut me like they do… Maybe he's right?

No! He's fucking not. "I'd rather be a whore than your

anything," I hiss, my pulse hammering in my throat, my anger palpable at this point.

"Where the fuck are you living?" he asks again, this time unable to temper his rage, unable to keep up the facade of control. "*Tell me, Scarlett!*"

I end the call, and wipe my cheeks again. I have more makeup on my hands and the collar of my shirt than my face. With the car in drive, I head to my new job, where I'm expected on set in less than an hour.

Windows down, I use the fresh air to my advantage, letting it dry my cheeks and refresh my face. The whipping breeze swirling through the cab helps me collect myself. I don't want to show up to my still kinda new job looking like I just had a massive fight with my toxic ex. I don't want *anyone* at Crave & Cure to know how messy my past is.

All I want is a clean slate. A vast road stretching ahead with endless possibilities. No looking back. No bringing the past with me.

By the time I arrive, my cheeks have completely dried and the pink flush has drained from my cheeks. I grab the sandals in the passenger seat—I'd been barefoot before in an effort to persuade the apartment manager that I'd just locked myself out—and slide them on. Standing next to my car, I pull on my hoodie and look down at myself. I wasn't able to get many clothes out last night, just what I had on. So as of now, I own a pair of yoga pants, a tank top and a hoodie.

Looks like I'll be shopping online tonight after filming is through.

With the stress of the last fourteen hours weighing on me like a ton of fucking bricks, I hold my head high as I pass through the back security door at Crave, lifting a palm to the cameras. With a soft smile, I duck into the building, my eyes taking a moment to adjust to the muted lighting.

"Hey, Lucy!" A bubbly, sweet voice reaches through the darkness, and I look up to see Vienna smiling at me, her hands stuffed in her overall pockets. She wrinkles her nose as she smiles, her glasses slipping down her nose a little.

"Hey, Vienna," I reply with a smile I wish I felt. Vienna is about to start casting me for a line of for-men sex toys. Pocket pussies. We'll be working closely together and already have been a little. I adore her. She's so sweet and genuine.

But I'm empty, and there isn't even a molecule of energy to scrape out and serve up to my new colleagues. They are the people who deserve my focus and kindness, and yet here I am, showing up with the bare minimum to give.

I hate myself for it.

"Gotta go change," I tell her as I motion down the hall toward the dressing rooms.

"Oh, of course! Have a good scene today!" And with that, she nods, waves me goodbye and is off to the craft services table to talk to Maxi. She calls all of the actresses and actors by their stage names, even me, despite the fact I've urged her to call me Scarlett.

Quietly, I pad down the hall and slide into my dressing room. We're on an afternoon shoot today, so not many actors are still here. Confident that no one will be looking for me, I lock the door.

I sink into the chair in front of the large mirror and catch my reflection; blonde hair tangled in a knotted heap on top of my head, darkness pooling beneath my weary eyes, my lips cracked and dry.

Alone with ten minutes to spare, no one here to speak to me or look at me, I let my head fall back against the chair, and my face tips to the side as one deep ugly sob after the next leaves me, steady and powerful. The chair becomes slippery beneath my face as I cry uncontrollably for a solid five minutes. I cry so hard my chest aches like I'm ill, I bawl until my eyes hurt, and I don't stop until Lance taps at my door, giving me my five minute warning.

Then I pull it together and get ready to put on a show.

Because that's what I'm good at.

two

. . .

cohen

Why should I get to breathe?

I keep my eyes shut tight, nearly grazing the bottom as I make my way to the other side. My chest burns with the breath I didn't take, the one I needed to take when I reached the end.

By the time my fingers graze the shoddy cement wall, my lungs burn so fiercely that my body jerks to the surface, gasping and pleading for breath.

It's hard to force myself to stay down. I *want* to stay down. But I always rise up. I always steal that breath I don't believe I deserve.

Keeping my eyes closed, I take in just enough air before sinking into the cold water again. Pushing off the wall, I head back to the other side for the fiftieth time at least. I don't know for sure because I haven't been counting. I come here and do this to feel the pain, not to count laps or calories.

I'm here in this pool every fucking day to immerse myself in misery. Call me a glutton for punishment but the mental anguish isn't enough. I need pain to physically eat me from the inside out, at least a little each day.

In my heart, it feels like she still exists—as long as I'm constantly bathing in grief and agony. She's still fresh in my mind if I punish myself daily. And I don't want to forget her, so I choose pain.

My lungs burn, the familiar sear of elapsing time extinguishing the air from my lungs. My fingers collide with the cement as I reach the other side, and instead of surfacing, I stay there. Hovering in the darkness, my chest so tight that the growing emptiness creeps up my throat. My body is starting to panic, starting to become desperate for relief. For breath.

I open my eyes and blink through the discomfort. There are lights dotted around the pool's sides so I close them again, like I always do, immersing myself in complete darkness. My heartbeat overtakes all my other senses, pounding relentlessly in my ears, telling me *you need to take a breath, you need to breathe.*

I ignore the way panic clutches my chest, and I pay no attention to the fuzziness filling my head. This is the part where the painful lack of oxygen kisses the sweet relief of giving up the fight. Where, with one mouthful, one swallow, that enticing, detached fuzziness will win out, and bliss will take over before the final darkness comes. Before lasting relief takes over.

I hover there, aching. Aching fucking everywhere.

There was an accident.

Four words, six syllables, but so much goddamn weight,

15

so much fucking power. How many people have those words absolutely decimated? How many lives have been altered, irrevocably changed, made forever dark by those words?

I'm not alone. I know I'm not. I have a television. I use Reddit. I'm aware that tragedy doesn't discriminate, and it's everywhere.

I place a palm over my chest, my heart thudding heavily against it, like a prisoner beating on cell walls, begging for a breath of fresh air. I loathe the weighty thumps, I loathe the way I can't hold myself there much longer. My breaking point is coming and I'm too fucking pathetic to stay, open my mouth and feel what she felt. Fill my lungs just once with cool, icy damnation.

As I settle into that sliver of painful comfort, the surface ripples wildly next to me, and my eyes shoot open to see a little boy floundering next to me. His hand comes down on my shoulder, stubby fingers sinking into my muscle. He opens his mouth, sending a stream of bubbles to the surface as he shouts unintelligible words underwater.

I push off the bottom and break the surface, choking and gasping for air. The boy surfaces, rubbing his brown eyes with his wilted fingers. "Are you okay?" he gasps, pushing dripping strands of hair out of his face. He blinks at me with panic and confusion.

He looks to be about ten, and I remember what ten felt like. At that age, you can't possibly fathom knowing a pain so great that drowning is relief. I force a small smile to calm him.

"Yeah. Just seeing how long I can hold my breath," I lie, though to be fair, I don't know if it is a lie anymore. Because I've been swimming laps in this gym pool for years, playing chicken with myself almost daily.

But every time the pressure builds and I'm at the point of

no return, I can't do it. I always rise to the surface, sputtering and gagging but breathing.

Why should I get to breathe?

I force a bigger smile on the boy to get him to smile, and he does. "Okay, well, that was a long time, Mister," he says skeptically.

"Yep," I say, smoothing a hand through my wet hair before clutching the edge of the pool, hoisting myself out onto the concrete. "That was my longest yet, but don't try it. I'm—"

"A pro?" he offers as he bounces on the balls of his feet, arms splashing gently.

I can't help the sadistic snort that leaves me. I'm far from a pro. In fact, I'm a failure at drowning. I've been trying for years but can't bring myself to do it. "I have experience in the water," I finally say as I snatch my towel from the ground and shimmy it along my back.

He seems satisfied with that answer, and a moment later, his father is calling to him from the other side of the pool, standing at the edge in a sweaty t-shirt.

"I'm done with my workout, son," he calls, lifting a hand to acknowledge me. I wave back to him.

"Your dad wants you to get out," I tell him, extending a hand to the boy.

He shakes his head. "I'm gonna swim back to the other side. That's where my towel is."

"Smart."

Then he's thrashing and kicking his way back. I watch his dad help him out, wrapping him in an oversized Lego beach towel. They walk off together, and I hear promises of pancakes with chocolate chips.

All of me hurts.

I stand beneath the gym shower for a few minutes before

stepping out, pulling on some black jeans and a henley. I shove my socked feet into lace-up boots, sling my bag over my shoulder and make the drive to work.

I like my job, and I like the people there. I have tasks. I have things to do that are very detail oriented. I have things that have to get done or people are at risk of getting hurt, or work can't get done. I'm focused and driven, and most importantly, completely fucking distracted from everything else when I'm there.

I arrive at Crave, ignoring everyone and the hello's that flank me as I make my way to the back, where I've carved a little office out for myself. I shove my bag under the desk and grab my utility belt, hooking it around my waist. With my lanyard looping around my neck, I make sure I have all my access keys, my light meter, and everything else.

Back on my feet, I head out and get to work. The only place where I can comfortably ignore my pain, at least for a few hours.

three

· · ·

scarlett

I feel like the lucky one

Chewing the inside of my cheek, my knee bounces as I busy my hands with the cuffs of my oversized hoodie sleeves.

He'll stop. *He will stop.* I mean, he's not going to harass me forever, right?

If anything, he'll stop sooner than later. After all, narcissists like control and once he realizes he can't control me anymore, he'll quit harassing me to maintain appearances. He can't risk his reputation.

Pete's greatest skill is keeping the monster hidden. Then when it was just us he'd let it out to play. I'd get to see what was behind that CEO and director mask he wore so many hours of the day.

A hand comes down on my shoulder, pulling me from my worry. It's not pure worry, it's worse. It's a dark, soul-scraping worry that assaults me in waves, bringing an undertow of anxiety that threatens to pull me out to sea and consume every last bit of me.

"Hey," Aug says softly, shaking me only a little. He crouches in front of me, capturing my eyes.

I blink at him, and his presence is a reminder of why I'm not giving up. There is kindness out there, there are people who want what's best without tethering favors to promises—Augustus Moore being one of them. He reminds me that I want more for myself, and more than what I had with Pete.

"Scarlett, are you okay?" he asks, concern etched into the furrow of his brow. His dark eyes squeeze me as they narrow, studying me like he's got the answer key. But the truth is? Augustus does know me. In the last few months, he's made it a priority to not just get to know me for the sake of Crave, but get to know me for me. I think from the first time we met—when he tracked me down at my cycling class—he knew I was struggling. Whether my fractures were visible or he's just intuitive, I don't know. But I can honestly say he's a safe person in my life, and genuinely cares.

I swallow the clog of fears in my throat, and wipe at the evidence of my anxiety forming on my upper lip. "Hey Aug," I force myself to say in the most normal tone I can muster, even putting on a small smile. "Just... talking myself down right now." I shrug, letting my eyebrows rise and fall. "You know me."

He drops his hand to my knee now, and squeezes with the same affection a father might show his daughter. "What's he doing now?"

I sigh. "Calling me non-stop. I wouldn't tell him where my new place is, and he's furious. He called me one-hundred and two times yesterday."

Aug shakes his head. *"Jesus Christ."*

"Right? So right now I'm just feeling freaked out and overwhelmed while telling myself that eventually he'll quit. Because it will be too damaging to his ego and at some point, he will leave me alone for good." I rest my chin in my palms and my elbows on my knees. "I just wish some point was now, you know?"

Aug nods slowly, patting my knee as he studies a spot on the ground, clearly in thought. But I don't want him to feel obligated to fix my whole life. He's already done so much. I open my mouth to assure him everything will be fine, and that he doesn't need to worry, when the art and set director walks by, fiddling with the carabiner on his work belt. His eyes flick to mine only briefly, but for some reason, my gaze follows him all the way out of the room.

He looks at everyone with the same impassive, almost soulless gaze. Though he's never been friendly with me, nor have I seen him really come alive in conversation with anyone here, his continual stoicism makes me feel safe and secure because it's predictable. And predictable is the desire of every woman who's been in a relationship with a volatile man.

He's also incredibly handsome. Meeting an extremely good-looking, well-mannered, quiet, respectful man in the adult film industry isn't an every day deal.

But, I guess I meet a lot of men like that now that I'm with Crave & Cure. But at Jizzabelle, with Pete, there wasn't a single *good* man on the roster.

I can't pinpoint a singular thing about him that intrigues me. I guess it's everything. Or maybe my sore, aching brain looking desperately for a diversion from reality.

"It's not your worry," I say, recentering myself in the conversation with Aug. "Honestly, you guys helped me move after you helped me find the apartment. You brought this job to me, and the line with Debauchery. You've already done so much," I say, every word genuine. This man walked into my life like a fucking blessing, the deus ex machina of my story, my canon event, saving me from a world where I'd cornered myself into seemingly inescapable toxic misery. "It isn't your worry," I repeat, demanding his attention, eyes pinning him with serious intensity.

I do not want to be pitied. I've accepted his help, but I won't be the studio's wounded bird. I need to move past this and show them I'm okay. Them obviously being code for me.

"One-hundred and two times is restraining order territory," Augustus offers, rising from his crouch, running his hands down his thighs. From somewhere not far, Lance appears at Augustus's side, his trusty iPad in his hands.

As if he's been sitting in on this conversation, Lance says, "I can get Dante in legal to get a restraining order in the works if you'd like, Scarlett."

My eyes veer to Aug who leans into my questioning gaze with a subtle bob of his head. "Lance is—" he glances over at Lance, who I already know is Aug's right-hand man. In the last month and a half I've been here, I don't think there's been more than a few times I've seen Aug without Lance. He's the assistant director or something, and while I admit to having liked Nickelback at one point in my life, I'm not a complete moron.

Whatever connection they have extends beyond this studio. But the same way I desire privacy around my embarrassing personal life, I pay Augustus the same respect. I don't ask him about things that don't concern me.

"I get it. He knows and it's safe for him to know," I say, tossing Lance a scrap of a smile. In truth, I assumed he knew based on my assumptions about the two of them. I guess what's more surprising is the instant, unquestioning way Lance has come to my aid.

"And I can help you. I'm here to do that," he says, his gaze steady and chin high, eliminating any possibility of sarcasm. He is here, despite the fact I'm a stranger to him.

I'll never get over how different Crave & Cure is compared to Jizzabelle. Hell, not just Pete's production company which, in hindsight, is of course incredibly toxic. But I've heard things about Finger Fun Films, Daddy's House and Cumplex Studios. So many actors are being mistreated, stuffed with performance enhancing drugs, diet pills, shot up with injectable ED drugs—none of which they need in the first place. Health, safety and the well-being of the actors is not in the top ten priorities at those places. In truth, the only concern of most film companies is money. We're their show dogs, their cattle to be branded and prodded then milked for all we're worth until we're cast out.

Crave is the opposite, and sometimes it's hard to believe.

"It's okay. I really think his ego will bruise and he'll stop. Plus," I say, smoothing my fingers down my hair, finding myself nervous being treated with this level of consideration. I'm not used to how it feels to have someone look at you and care about you and expect nothing in return. "I think a restraining order would only make things worse."

Aug nods. "Okay. But let me know if he does anything else besides just call you." His dark eyes are serious. "Scarlett, tell me."

I nod reluctantly. "I would tell you, I promise." It almost sounds like I believe it myself but in truth I hope I never have to ask for their help.

He tips his head to Lance. "Or Lance. I trust him, for whatever that's worth to you."

I caution a glance at Lance. He stands with a straight

spine, lips in a line as he blinks at me. But his pulse. At the base of his throat, his pulse bobs, and before I face Aug again, I swear his color is a little… pinker than normal.

"It's worth a lot." I smile, still stroking my hair. "I can't believe people like you exist."

He smiles, tempering his sadness as another gift to me. This man is so kind yet brimming with a feeling of uncharted power. Lance is lucky. I think.

"You're in your after. And good people exist in your after," he says before leaving me with a shoulder squeeze.

I look at Lance who surprisingly hasn't followed after Aug just yet. "I owe him more than I'll ever be able to repay him."

"Thrive. That's the greatest way to repay him and also, the best revenge." And with that, he goes, leaving behind a cloud of teakwood, sweet tobacco, and wisdom. Maxi edges over to me.

"Hey Luce. I'll take your hoodie? Put it in your dressing room?" She smiles widely and it reminds me I'm about to film. I reach behind me and yank it off. Folding it, I pass it to her.

"I'm sorry. I know I should've come out in a robe. And it's totally not your job to take my stuff. I'm sorry," I repeat, feeling sweat slide down my back as I rise to my feet and step out of my yoga pants. "It's been a long…"

"Day?" she offers sweetly, clutching my folded sweater to her chest like I'm Taylor Swift. Again, the people at Crave have this enthusiastic and bold energy. I can't get over it.

And I was drug tested and so are they. It's all *natural* charm.

Shit's crazy.

"More like years," I say drily, shimmying into the outfit laid on my chair. I think it's an— "Am I an ice skater?"

Maxi nods, her eyes gleaming as she takes in the glittery bodysuit. Ice blue ombre into snowy white, rhinestones and sequins sporadic throughout. Behind me, Alexa the hair stylist appears. She puts her hands on my shoulders, forcing me gently into my seat.

"You're getting a bun. Give me five."

She gets to work, and Maxi continues on. "Years? Oh Lucy, I'm sorry. For whatever's happened, I'm sorry." She gives a pout but again, it's not playful or invalidating. It's... genuine. "We're all so glad to have you here though. Seriously." She steps close as Alexa sprays something in my combed hairline. "Lucy Lovegood at Crave?" She flushes, shaking her head in genuine wonder. "We're so lucky."

"I feel like the lucky one," I admit. "Everyone here is so nice. Sometimes I feel like it's a joke, and I'm just waiting on the punchline to realize... this isn't real."

Alexa yanks back on my ponytail, sending a shock of pain down my neck. "You're real. You felt that, right?"

I laugh and rub the back of my neck as she rolls my hair into some bun contraption. "Oh I felt that." *I have no problems feeling pain*, I think as she finishes up. Maxi excuses herself, and I hate that she's likely putting my things away for me. Tomorrow I will do better.

I face the mirror and think about what's ahead, trying to get my mind right.

I'm in a solo scene today. My contract is pretty specific and rare for porn, I think. But Aug was the one to suggest it, the one to make me feel like it was okay. I realize he saw just how broken I was before I even did.

He knew traditional scenes, no matter how respectful, would break the fragile thread holding me together. I'd reached the point where I just couldn't be touched that way anymore.

I still can't.

I haven't since the last scene I filmed at Jizzabelle over two months ago. And the more time that passes, the more I think I don't ever want to be touched again.

After finding my mark on set, I browse the script laid out for me. I'm a figure skater who has fallen in love with her partner. We've just won a gold medal on ice, and I'm realizing my needs for him.

That's…I can do that. I mean, I can't actually masturbate and bring myself to orgasm. But I can stand on my mark, focus on the story, and perform a beautiful and believable scene.

There will be no longing, no heat, no orgasm. I can't.

I take my spot, and blink toward the set light to spot Aug behind the camera, Lance at his side. "Light check, then we're ready," he calls to me, and I nod, smoothing my hands along the sides of my head, making sure my skating hairstyle is intact.

From the inky corners of the set, where reality blends with the scene, Cohen appears. His big hands fiddle with a device as he steps next to me. Without a glance my way, he lifts his meter then checks the screen, passing a single nod to Aug across from him.

He steps past me again, making his way off the painted floor to the plain concrete. Lance begins to count, and I can't take my eyes off Cohen and his solemn indifference.

"Three," he counts, and right then, Cohen's sharp blue eyes lock to mine. My breath hitches, my chest tightening.

"Two," Lance calls.

I've looked at Cohen many times. I even asked Tucker about him. It's not often a tall, handsome (gorgeous, really), well-dressed man works on a porn set and is respectful, quiet and reserved.

I mean, he's as good as a leprechaun riding a unicorn in my book.

But he's never ever looked at me. Not once.

The slates clatter and my focus moves jarringly to the small mirror in front of me. I collect my breath and rattle off some lines, all the while wondering why?

Why did he look at me today? And why did it make me feel seen?

Reaching up, I release the band from my hair, letting the bun free, sending waves toppling down my back. With a gentle shake, my blonde hair falls like a curtain of silk across my shoulders, partially covering my breasts. That's important as I'm supposed to seductively unzip the bodysuit, and have my breasts only somewhat exposed initially.

Shimmying it down my hips, I place my heel in the crotch of the unitard and step out easily. Finding my reflection in the tiny prop mirror, I let my hands fall to my breasts. Something about your hair down and wild all around you, holding yourself, yearning—it's powerful in solo scenes.

It's meant to put both the performer and viewer in the mood.

But I'm not in the mood. Touching myself, seeing my naked body, being under the lights—none of it feels right. Even with safety all around me, all of me itches to cover up and... disappear.

But that is for therapy later today. Right now, I'm in scene and need to honor the man who rescued me from my hell by being present here and now. Giving this scene everything I have.

"I wish it was your hands," I murmur softly, rolling my neck slowly. My long hair slides off my shoulders as my head falls back, my palms skating down my bare belly. The cool studio air nips at me, making my nipples harden. Contrastingly, the bright light above sears my closed eyelids, and I drop to my knees on the small couch in the "dressing room" set, lessening the effects.

"Your hands all over my body, holding me, helping me fly," I groan, my fingers exploring my groin as I slowly reposition on the couch, allowing for a camera on a boom arm to cut in close to my face.

No genital close up in solo scenes for me at Crave. And for that, I couldn't be more grateful.

I bite my lip as I spread myself apart, dipping the tips of my fingers inside. "I wish it were you," I repeat, keeping my eyes closed to sell the fantasy, to deliver the dream.

Aug calls cut. Maintaining my body position for angle integrity, I only lift my head enough to meet his gaze. With his head, he motions to the caddy sitting on the edge of the set. "Alexa, get that tangle out of her hair and bring her some of the lube."

That's the thing about faking. I can't force myself to get wet. At least here I'm not shamed for it. Not called a *dick eater with a desert cunt.*

Alexa appears with a tiny brush, passing me the lube before she detangles me quickly. I squirt some onto my fingers and pass the bottle back.

"Get comfortable before we roll," Aug advises, which means *fuck that lube into yourself so it looks like you're wet.* I get the subtext, and I'm grateful he cloaks the orders in respect.

I nod and as my gaze wanders around the set while plunging my fingers inside myself, I find Cohen and he's looking at me.

And not where my hand fucks myself, not how my tits sway with the movement, not at all the long hair spilling down my back. That's what they usually look at first. All of those other things.

But quiet Cohen holds my eyes and before I can fully process it, he looks away, and disappears into the off-set fray.

"I'm good to go," I say softly to Aug, my gaze wandering over the lightless spot where Cohen just stood. I don't know why he grabs my interest. I have no business being interested in... anything... or anyone. I don't even *want* to be interested in anyone.

Still, my mind wanders. Where did he go? And when is he coming back?

four

. . .

cohen

I'm ready to be underwater.

It pierces your soul when it happens. That nighttime ring. No one ever calls with happy news at night. No one. Not ever. The sound of an incoming call is something that normally piques interest, but at night, it's something completely different. It's a monster, waking you up clutching your throat in an icy grip, a sharp cry in your ear, a punch to your gut.

Ring, ring. Hello, it's me, life-changing news. Something so vile and rotten I had to grab you by the throat and tear you from dreams to destroy you.

Tonight, I'm trapped in that singular moment from that night. I'm in bed, the bed I slept in back in Michigan. I haven't seen it in years but it's always as clear as glass in my dreams. What I can escape in daylight always finds a way back in at night.

The ring drones, running on loop, my anxiety clawing higher and higher each time. I reach for my phone but as dreams go, I can never quite answer it.

And that's it. That's the dream currently assaulting me, jolting me from sleep. I sit up covered in sweat, my shirt drenched, overcome with anguish and dread.

I run a hand through my hair and take a moment to breathe. I bring my hand in front of my face, exhaling to feel my breath, to remind myself it was a dream and I am awake, no longer there.

The part that keeps me jittery, that has my stomach tight in acidic knots is the truth of the dream. That familiar ring yanked from my memories, from the worst night of my life.

I breathe in and out, calming when I remind myself that this dream is *good* compared to what I know is hiding in my brain. There are *really* bad dreams, ones that take place further into the timeline of that night. Ones that bear sounds more painful than a fucking phone ringing.

I blink into the darkness until the pattern on my comforter is visible, then brave a look at the clock on my bedside table. Red numbers taunt me; 3:43 am.

Goddamn it. It's too early for anything meaningful except sleep, but now that I've woken from that nightmare, I can't go back to sleep.

Unsurprisingly, I don't sleep much.

Swinging my legs out of the warm comfort of the bed, I suck in a deep breath through my nose as my body adjusts to the cool air stinging my bare skin. They don't use the heater and while it's not winter, San Francisco gets pretty cool at night in the early Spring.

I like it. I like the shocking reminder. The instant pain of discomfort. It helps me remember. It keeps *her* fresh in my mind.

On light feet, I move across the room to my closet, and collect my bag. I grab my things and layer them in; my trunks, a towel, and my carefully folded work clothes. I always leave my boots in my car. After dressing in sweatpants and a hoodie, I slip my feet into sneakers, draw the hood over my head, hook my bag over my chest and go.

The old house is already humming, despite the early hour. The aged appliances and single-pane windows create a symphony of white noise at all hours. It's something I like about this place. It's never quite quiet.

I close and lock the back door behind me, walking between cars until I get to mine. Then I drive to the gym, thankful they open at three for the early risers. I'm ready to be underwater.

The little boy and his father aren't here today, then again, it's only ten after four by the time I'm lowering myself into the chilly water. I swim mindlessly, unable to track time when I'm beneath the surface. I go back and forth, holding myself under for as long as I can every few laps. Finally, when fiery strain seizes my lungs, and when my fingers are so pruned they split against the cement wall, I drag myself to the edge and clamber out. My knees slip along the wet bullnose edge of the pool, and I fall against the concrete, bracing myself with my palms.

Then I just lie there, cheek against the wet cement, water dripping into my eyes from my sodden hair, my chest heaving from the laps, from holding my breath, from my perpetual fatigue.

I lie there until my breath steadies. I lie there until my back is dry. And I am in no hurry to get up until there's a poke in the middle of the back.

"Are you okay? Do you have low blood sugar or something?"

I recognize the voice. The little boy is back. I push off the ground to get on my feet, aware of the strange scene he's just stumbled upon. Grabbing my towel I wrap it around my waist and sling my bag over the shoulder.

"I don't have low blood sugar," I reply, forgoing the response of *I'm okay* because whether he's eight or eighty, his eyes are knowing. He sees I'm off. He's just trying to understand *how* off.

"Did you hit your head?" he tries again, desperate to make it make sense. I'm sure *his* father has never slipped while getting out of a public pool then proceeded to lie there for thirty minutes, contemplating his worth.

From the other side of the pool, his father appears, this time in swim trunks. "Laps before work, am I right?" he shouts across the water, but his words ping pong off the empty walls, echoing a little.

I nod. "Right." I look back at the boy. "I didn't hit my head." I force a smile. "Have a good swim."

I head toward the locker room, somewhat anxious I'll be followed and questioned by his father. Worried that this kid is too empathetic, that he'll be worried and pass those concerns to his dad.

But I get through a scalding shower and dressing completely alone, and don't see them again before I head out.

At Crave, I slip into my cozy office, arranging my schedule on the computer. Aug pops in to notify me of a last-minute set change, explaining the outdoor scenes we'd had scheduled later today were postponed due to the spitting weather. We rearrange shooting schedules often, as it's always one swift wind away from raining here in San Francisco. The irritation clouding my mind isn't from Aug or the reschedule. Days following nightmares are just like this.

I wish I could disappear.

Instead, I give Aug a polite smile and nod of acknowledgment and proceed to thumb through the daily printed scene schedule, readying myself for what's ahead.

The first shot is the new actress, Lucy Lovegood, in another solo scene. This time, she's a Hollywood actress from the 1920s, and she's performing for a director *off-camera*. She's in the spotlight. It's Jessica Rabbit without the overdone everything and I dig the vibe Aug is going for. He's got a great vision.

I grab my waist harness and some ropes, in addition to a few more carabiners. I'll be hanging one large light next, so after collecting the rest of my safety gear, I grab the light canister from our prop room and head to the set.

My focus pinches on the task at hand, riding a small lift up to the beams then hanging the wireless spotlight. I grab the walkie on my hip and call Lance, who is on set below.

"Position check," I call, adjusting the angle with my level out, to get the perfect forty-five degrees. My hands begin to tremble around the bar, and though the light emits warmth, a cool shiver wraps my spine, my core full of insecurity and fatigue.

Fucking nightmares. Every fucking time I have a dream about her, about that night, I'm ruined the next day. Pair it with the usual inability to get back to sleep and I feel like complete shit. Impatience claws at me, but I make it a point to tame myself. To keep control. Always.

There was a time when I didn't, and my inability to hold my tongue cost me everything. Or, what was left of everything.

Lance moves to the camera and paces to the marked spot on the floor. I radio down to him. "Thanks." He waves me off, calling to Aug. "Roll in three."

It takes me three minutes to collect my shit and move the lift, and right as I'm out of the way, the production team moves in. Alexa curves around me to blot at Lucy's face, while Lance directs a new camera man on what shots to take and when.

"Hold," Aug calls out, leaning back in his chair as Maxi scurries toward him. She cups a hand to his ear and when she's done, neither of them look happy. Maxi wears concern while Aug's features twist angrily.

Like a voyeur, I watch as he relays Maxi's message to Lance. The two of them gaze out at an unknowing Lucy Lovegood, the latest procurement by Crave. They hold a private discussion with something clearly important in the balance. I follow their gaze, finding the blonde actress perched on a stool at her mark, a glittering red ball gown hugging her. Alexa finger combs the ends of Lucy's hair, and my chest tightens when my eyes find Lucy's subtle smile.

It's wide and toothy, lifting the corners of her eyes with genuine happiness.

I've seen her a few times. And I've never seen her smile. Not like this.

My chest goes concave for a moment, crushing my lungs, stealing my breath.

The unbalance I felt on the lift returns, and my legs tingle with unease. The corners of my vision bleed into an ombre of darkness as my heart hammers, scalp tingling, sending an erratic pulse through my veins. I can't look away. I swallow, and my ears thud.

It's been years since anything has earned my attention. And I can't remember a time when I've been this captivated, felt a roaring current of electricity moving through my body as if... *no.*

I finish duct taping the ground where a loose electrical cord rests, and make my way to the back of the room, letting my back fall to the wall.

I usually stand on the perimeter of the set, lying in wait for anything Aug or Lance may need.

The laces on my boots are all I can focus on. Fuck, it's all I'll let myself look at.

Her laugh, gentle and inviting, filters through everyone, making it to me. The delicacy in her tone lifts my chin, and my eyes are on her again.

I have no right, no fucking business staring at her. I feel guilty that my body is reacting to her, but I can't fight my racing heart, I can't combat the awareness prickling through me.

I place a palm to my stomach as I stare at her. I'm queasy, but queasy with something I haven't felt in ages.

Possibility.

My body is pulled to her. My body is reacting to her. And

not to her naked or dressed scantily clad, or her scene or her role.

Her laugh. Her sweet smile and gentle voice.

Padding across the dark film-ready space, I shoulder tap Lance to let him know I'm stepping off set for a moment. I'm in my office with my back to the door in less than thirty seconds.

My mind spins.

That feeling in my stomach... they're... *butterflies*.

five

. . .

scarlett

"Please let me take you home."

"Tremendous work today, Scar," Aug says, poking his head into my dressing room.

I didn't want to come off as the Mariah Carey of porn, but when I signed with Crave, I had a few non-negotiables. And it isn't because I'm a top earner, or the most desired female star in the industry.

The non-negotiables were all about reclaiming my strength. Starting somewhere new with boundaries set. And privacy. I never had privacy before, so here, I bathe in it.

The way Jizzabelle, *namely Pete*, put me on display, pushing me into scenes and roles I wasn't comfortable with—it left me covered in scars. The worst kind of marks, the kind invisible to everyone around me, but have forever changed me. Scars that have me shut off from feeling if I even *attempt* intercourse.

Thus, the no male penetration stipulation in my contract.

And the private dressing room is so I can break down and sob without eyes on me.

It's important to me that I'm more than my past, and that all the amazing people at Crave go on unaware of my scars. I need a clean slate, and some distance between myself and the overwhelming feeling of shame. Why didn't I leave sooner?

"Thanks, that was a fun one this morning," I admit, recalling the solo scene where I embodied a sultry singer. I got to strip from a beautiful sequined dress, and take things slow with my body. I still found myself faking the orgasm as it's been ages since my body has actually made it to the finish line—but nonetheless, I loved and appreciated the creativity and artistry of the scene.

"That was gorgeous. You were perfect. But the lunch shoot and afternoon shoots were just as good. I'm liking that promo Debauchery suggested," he says, looking a little surprised. I've learned that Crave is at the helm of promoting Debauchery and Crave partnered toys, but this time, Debauchery had a strong hand.

"I think that was Vienna," I say with a smile. In my pre-casting sessions, I've gotten to know Vienna pretty well, and one thing she told me is that Debauchery really listens to her. I remember that she told me that, because it gave me hope. Hope that these companies I'm now with actually have my best interest at heart.

Because again, at Jizzabelle with Pete, shock and awe were traded for cash and views on the daily. I was a cog in the studio's machine, a whore for Pete to use, a pretty face and a well groomed pussy to be presented to men as a prop to use and abuse.

Panicked heat blankets me at the briefest of memories, and I reach for my bottle to take a cooling sip. It does nothing to soothe me, so I take another few drinks as Aug nods and closes the door behind him, leaving me alone.

Panic and anxiety attacks are part of my normal life now. Granted, they've started to decrease the last few weeks since I'm no longer with Jizzabelle. But they won't go away until *he* goes away. Of that I'm sure.

I dig my phone out of my bag and find that I've missed several text messages as well as *forty-eight* calls. All from Pete.

He needs to let me go so I can be free. *He has to.*

Though if I really peer into the complex mixed bag of my emotions, the truth is, I realize he's not the only problem.

It's also my mind. It's a battlefield of self-loathing, anxiety and hatred. And according to my shrink, Dr. Evans, a battlefield I'm currently working through.

Crave has mandatory mental health care. We have to meet with their shrink once a month. But we have access to the doc as much as we need.

I've been seeing her once a week for two months, and it's helping. God is it helping. And I don't know what I did in a previous life to deserve being scooped up by Aug and given these opportunities, but thank God for him. Thank God for Crave.

I swipe through my text messages, glancing at them. My read receipt is off, so he'll never know.

PETE

> You need me. I just hope you realize that before it's too late.

> If you stay gone a week longer, you'll be on Jizz's blacklist.

A whore is fun at first, but once the novelty wears off, whoever it is you've run to won't want you anymore. Trust me.

The phone slips from my hand into my open purse as a dull, nagging ache eats at my head. A knife prods the nerves behind my eyes, and I bring my hands to my temples in an effort to massage away what I know is a stress migraine.

"Fuck," I mutter, immediately lying down on the small couch, curling up as to not knock my purse off. I cover my face with my hands completely, and go completely still, willing the headache to leave me so I can go to my new apartment, take a hot bath and crawl into bed and cry myself to sleep.

Yet the migraine doesn't obey, and my head vibrates with extreme pain. And I guess being here in pain is no worse than being at my apartment in pain.

I stay still, breathing slowly, waiting it out. I can't drive home with my head like this, so, I'll wait.

Blinking, I find the dressing room dark and cold. My head pulses with residual pain, but the stinging nerve pinching is gone, leaving me with a headache hangover. Slowly, I sit up and find my phone in my bag.

Shit, it's nearly eight. I hope they didn't lock the gate.

How do I even get out of the building if they set the alarm? Panic that I'm going to have to disrupt Aug or Lance already and be *that person* has me on my feet, reaching for the doorknob.

But I'm sitting as quickly as I stood.

"Fuck," I moan, my fingers coming to my temples to massage the unrelenting pain that reappeared simply from standing.

Just as the panic returns, and I'm wondering how the hell I'm going to get out of this building and the parking lot with no one here, there's a gentle tap at my door.

Immediately my chest hollows as I sigh out in relief.

Okay, *Aug is still here*. I'm not trapped nor do I have to make a tail-between-my-legs phone call and ask him to come rescue me. Thank goodness.

Another soft rapping at the door.

"C-come on in," I say, finding my voice a little rocky from the turbulent waves of agony rolling through my brain. Fucking Pete, and fucking migraines from anxiety attacks. I hate this life.

The door slowly opens, but the face that pops in isn't Aug or Lance.

It's Cohen.

He blinks at me a few times before dropping his gaze to my feet. I look down to find myself in a hoodie and sweats—my head had me forgetting what I threw on after the last scene. Yet Cohen diverts his gaze after a moment, as if I'm naked and he's uncomfortable.

"It's eight and I was going to head out but I saw your car was still here and I don't want to lock you in."

"Th-thank you. I was worried about that. I got a migraine and dozed off..." My sentence wilts. I find myself wanting him to look at me. So I stay silent until he does. It only takes a few moments of quiet before his gaze slowly returns to mine.

He's incredibly handsome, but his eyes are absolutely intoxicating. Deep, rich, with shades of blue I've only ever seen in a cloudless sky.

"I... I was about to leave but when I stood, my head..." Again, my sentence dies as my throat grows tight. He's so beautiful, and this is the first time he's spoken directly to me. The rocky timbre of his voice has bumps erupting from my flesh, making the back of my neck warm. "I don't think I can drive. Let me just call an Uber and I'll be out of here. I'm... I'm so sorry," I stumble, my hands delving into my open purse to find my phone. I don't want to keep him here.

"No," he says, the word rooting me to the couch with its certainty and power.

I blink up at him, surprised to see he's still looking at me.

"I can drive you," he says, stepping a little further inside the dark dressing room, keeping the door wide open. "I'll drive you, as long as you're comfortable with that." He reaches behind him, bringing his wallet out. He flips it open and shows me his driver's license.

Cohen Steele.

I never knew his last name until now. He returns the wallet to his pocket.

"I'm Cohen Steele, I've worked here for four years. I'm the Art and Set Director."

I can't help but smile at him, warmth eating up my chest. "I know who you are. I've seen you around here."

He steps in again, the door resting against his backside as he shoves his large hands deep into his pockets. "Well, if you want an Uber, you can call one. But... I can and will drive you and make sure you get home safely."

I give my answer quickly and eagerly. "Okay."

Bracing against the couch, I push to my feet, discovering my balance is a bit off, my legs unsteady as I collect my bag.

Cohen's hand comes out of his pocket, and he reaches out, but doesn't quite touch me. Instead he seems to offer his palm as a safeguard for a moment before his gaze falters. Crisp blue eyes pinned on his own outstretched hand for a moment, he brings it slowly back to his side and instead offers an ushering arm to the hall.

We walk silently—though not uncomfortably—through the dark studio. Something about the set in the evening, with nothing but stray shafts of moonlight glittering off the camera lens. It's beautiful. I blink at the stage, a singular bed with the covers turned down, band posters covering the bedroom wall.

The scene prepped for tomorrow is a discovery scene, and I'm playing an eighteen-year old discovering masturbation. The set reflects a bedroom at that age, and I turn to find Cohen waiting patiently for me, eyes on his boots.

"You're excellent at your job, the set is… well, it's always perfect."

Slowly he lifts his head, eyes glittering as they dance between mine.

"You know what," I say, suddenly feeling embarrassed for needing help. "Either I Uber now or tomorrow morning," I say with a soft smile. "I'd hate to put you out, and I don't think I should leave my car. I'll drive. I'll just… go really slow. Thanks for the offer though, but it's too big an inconvenience."

Cohen's head droops forward as he brings one strong hand from his pocket to his jaw, dragging it down his face. The scratch of his palm along his evening stubble has my stomach tightening, and my face hot. He turns his head, and my breath hitches at the intensity of his gaze.

"I'll drive you home in your car and I'll walk home." He declares without hesitation, every word brimming with sincerity.

"You can't," I protest. I don't know where he lives but even ten blocks in this city can equate to over an hour of walking, accounting for the steep streets. "You can't walk home, or even back to your car at this hour. I can't let you do that."

The idea of being a burden to someone, having someone help me because perhaps Aug has coached them or Aug has told them I'm some wounded-winged bird flies through my mind. Anxiety flourishes through my veins again, achingly familiar, and my hands tremble as nervousness and self-loathing threaten to pull me under. All in a matter of seconds.

Nervously attempting to snatch my phone out, my purse falls to the ground, sending a tube of lipstick and a can of mace to the concrete floor.

Without hesitation, Cohen closes the distance, crouching at my feet as he carefully collects my things, putting them back in my purse. Before he rises, his gaze lifts to mine. With my purse strap laced through his hands, he swallows. A sudden numbness grabs hold of me, and my anxious rumbling settles a bit as I stare down at the man at my feet.

"Please let me take you home?"

I extend a hand down to him, not for my purse but for him, and for a moment I worry he won't understand. But his piercing eyes flick to my outstretched offering before coming up to my eyes again.

"Will you let me drive you home?" His voice is as unwavering as the rigidity in his spine. From this close, despite the low light, I notice crows feet at the corners of his eyes, and some wear on his forehead. But his hair reflects youth and time spent in the sun. This man has been through shit, I can see it in his face. His sweet and handsome face.

"Yes," I whisper, suddenly feeling weak under his loaded gaze. The pounding pain in my temples makes its presence known, and I clutch at the side of my head as I reach down for the purse. Instead, he places his hand in mine but uses his own body weight to rise.

I look down at our linked hands and up at him.

"I'm going to hold your hand until we're in the car, to keep you steady."

My mouth is dry, but I manage, "Okay."

Being led out of the studio, through the parking lot and into the passenger seat of my car with Cohen's big hand wrapping mine is the first time I've felt cared for in… years.

He ducks into the cab, reaching for the belt then leaning over me to click it into place.

No one has done that for me since I sat in a booster seat as a kid.

Through the melting moonlight, he dips his head into the cab again, one strong arm slung up over the car. "Plug your ears."

I cup my hands over my ears and watch as he grabs the handle and, keeping a palm on the door, closes it silently with his body weight. Through my earmuffs I hear the metallic click of the door engaging, and know it's shut.

He didn't want the door closing to make my headache worse.

When he's in the driver's seat and clipping his own belt, I find his eyes across the cab and hold them. "Thank you," I say, tipping my head back toward the door without breaking eye contact. "That was thoughtful."

He nods, then faces forward, assessing the windshield.

After starting the car, he twists the defroster knob and asks, "Where do you live?"

I reach out and access the GPS on the touch-screen mounted to my car. It's not a great car but after moving to the city, I knew I needed GPS or I'd be stuck in the maze of uphill streets for the rest of my life.

Tapping the button that says "Home," the GPS begins spouting off directions as a list floods the screen.

With a careful look at the screen, he returns his focus to the windshield, waiting patiently for the icy windshield to dissipate under the heater. Once it's clear, he backs out and follows the robotic female voice directing him to my apartment.

I keep my eyes closed most of the ride, trying to avoid the bursts of brightness from bold street lamps and traffic lights. He drives slowly, and I don't know if that's how he usually is or if it's for my head, but some deep part of me really believes it's the latter of the two.

Tuck sang his praises, telling me what a kind and talented man he is. I smirk to myself in my clouded reflection of the passenger window. He isn't interested in me, he's just... a true gentleman.

"Thank you again for driving me. I hope you don't live far. Can I call you an Uber?" I ask as he turns the car into the small parking lot behind my apartment, where the GPS guides him. There are only a handful of parking spaces here, and he idles between them as he turns slightly to face me.

"Which number are you?"

"One."

He blinks at me, and for some reason, a flutter takes off in my belly, making my arms and fingers tingle. "I'll walk. It's not far."

"Are you sure I can't—" I want to offer the Uber again, in

hopes that he takes it. How can he do something so nice for me and ask nothing in return? But I guess this is what Tuck meant when he called Cohen *solid.*

"No Uber. But I will be making sure you get inside," he says after steering the car into the center of my parking spot. He unclips my belt then his. "Stay there."

When he appears at the passenger door, I move to push the door open but he opens it for me, before I can. He extends a hand to me, and I stare at his palm for a few seconds. This is the second time our hands have come together, and it rocks me to my core. It's kind and nurturing and everything I could wish for. It's a startling contrast to the touch I have felt for so long from Pete.

I take his hand, and he gives a gentle tug, helping me to my feet. My head whirrs and I clutch Cohen's forearm to steady myself. Waiting, he looks down at me. It's then I realize just how tall he is, hovering at least six inches above. "You lead," he says, his words slow and quiet.

I nod a little, and move us toward the stairwell.

"Apartment 1 is actually upstairs," I tell him, still holding his hand with one hand and clinging to his bicep with the other. My head hurts as we take the stairs like an elderly couple, I'm glad I have him to hold until we're at the top.

On the landing, his head swings between the two apartments, located directly across from one another. "Which is it?"

It occurs to me now that they aren't currently numbered. I point to mine. "They're being repainted externally so they took the number plaques down. That one's mine. The other is actually empty."

Cohen releases my hand before slowly sliding my purse down my arm, placing it on the ground between us. He motions to the contents of my bag as he crouches to access it, looking up at me.

"May I get your keys?"

Asking permission before going through my things. I blink down at him, registering the fact that men like him even exist. "Y-yeah, please."

In response I get a single nod, then watch him carefully sift through my purse until he plucks a ring of keys from it, passing them up to me. I can't look away as he rises and brings my purse with him.

I fumble the key at the lock, which earns more concern from Cohen. "Can I help you?" he offers.

"I got it." The key trembles in my shaky hand but finally, I make contact and manage to unlock the door. I step inside but immediately spin to face him. "Thank you for the ride. I genuinely appreciate that."

I smile but he doesn't. He just does this small dip of his head.

Cohen is tall and strong. I felt his disciplined muscle as I clung to him coming upstairs. He's handsome with a full head of sandy blond hair, and eyes meant to get lost in displaying an endless sea of emotion. And he's standing here, in the dark, with me. Not trying to barge in and claim restitution for the ride, not looking at my tits over my sweatshirt.

"Well—" I start but he lifts a big hand and motions to the lock.

"Lock your door. I'll stand here until I hear you lock it, Lucy."

Lucy. In the dark corridor outside my new apartment, Lucy feels so wrong.

"Scarlett," I correct softly. "My real name is Scarlett."

His lips part like he's trying the name out in his head. He motions to the door again. "Lock your door, Scarlett."

"I will. And thank you again for coming to my rescue."

He nods slowly as I close the door, immediately I press my eyeball to the peephole. He's there. I watch through the peephole as I twist the lock and add the chain. He stays one moment longer before turning and heading down the stairs.

With my back to my front door, I look around my tiny, practically empty dark apartment. Head still aching, and my phone now ringing loudly from my purse, I stalk through the narrow hallway toward the bedroom, quickly sweeping the curtain back.

There in the faint streetlight is Cohen, white puffs of breath in a wake behind him as he heads down the street, disappearing from my sight in twenty seconds. I can't believe he's walking home.

I let the curtain go and it blocks the glow of the street light. My phone continues to ring from the spot on the floor near the front door, but I'm tired. I'm so incredibly tired. Instead of retrieving it to check and risk being thrown into another anxiety attack or even intensify my migraine, I kick off my shoes, take two steps, and faceplant into my bed.

Tomorrow is yet another day on the other side. *The after.* Tomorrow is another day to try to not let Pete get to me. To not check his messages. To stay strong and be positive.

To move forward.

I realize as I'm dozing off, the nap didn't ease my anxiety. Maybe it helped take the edge off my migraine, but it didn't squelch my anxiousness and panic.

But Cohen did.

He chased away the thoughts threatening to overwhelm me by simply helping me and wanting nothing in return. I'm in no place to have more than strangers in my life right now, but I can't deny the fact, I'm more curious about Cohen than ever before.

six

. . .

cohen

I haven't returned a sweet smile in… years.

I run my curled knuckles down my chest, attempting to push out the feeling lingering there. Everything behind my ribs feels full and uncomfortable. Up and down I drag my fist, eager for the sensation to go away.

For so long I thought I wanted to regain feeling, then at some point in the years of listless misery, I started to believe I just… couldn't. That losing *her,* irrevocably broke me and I'd never be right again. And I learned to be okay with that because it's what I deserve.

The sound of that lock engaging. The metallic slide of the chain. Those noises, those two minor fucking noises.

I rub my chest again, but alas, the feeling remains. Because it's not something extinguished with pressure or a massage or an antacid.

It's an undeniable twist, an awakening; part of me came alive knowing she was safe last night. And that I had some part in that.

In truth, part of me awoke when I heard her laugh. Because nothing has sounded so sweet in years, nothing at all. My favorite Al Green album on vinyl, the sound of a crowded baseball stadium after a grand slam, the slow drip of coffee percolating—not even so much as a flutter or twitch anywhere inside me.

But her laugh. Soft and sweet. Her laugh slid down my spine like the jets of water from a hot shower, reminding me, *there is good left, there is happiness out there.*

I swing my legs out of bed, enjoying the cruel nip of the cold on my bare skin.

I pad across the small space to the open closet, collecting the things I need for the day. Filling my bag, I get dressed in sweats and make my way through the quiet, sleeping house until I'm outside. Last night I made sure to book an Uber for this morning so I could get to Crave early and grab my car.

The driver is waiting in a compact blue car, waving against the rolled up window. I duck into the backseat, taking care to close the door as quietly as possible. The family is still asleep.

"Morning! Early riser, huh?" He grins at me in the rearview as fresh brewed coffee comingles with the smell of his car's heater. "Where to?"

"Lower Haight, before the Painted Ladies," I reply, settling into the seat with my bag at my feet. I could say Crave & Cure, but in truth, I'm not sure too many people realize what goes on inside of the brightly painted building. It's easier to give him the exact address.

"Alrighty," he chirps, tapping his GPS until the location is pulled up. I tip my head back against the seat and close my eyes, trying to focus on the swim. How I'll drag myself along the bottom, holding air in my lungs until I almost can't, surfacing just in time to choke and gasp, my head and eyes throbbing. A familiar tingle spreads through my limbs, the dull anticipation of pain rolling through me.

I look forward to these punishing swims in the early morning.

The driver pulls up outside the locked gates of Crave, and I hand him a ready wad of cash from my pocket.

Typing in the passcode, I unlock the gate and close it behind me, making my way around the back of the lot to find my car. Tossing my bag across the seat, I get in and head toward the gym, peering through a frosted windshield, my only focus is on breaking the cool surface and suffocating my thoughts. At least for an hour.

The shower scalds my skin, stripping it of not only the chlorine, but also any visible traces of my anguish. These early mornings are the only time I allow myself to think about her—*to think about them*—but I make a promise that after I leave that tiny shower stall at Globo, I'm all about Crave and the work I do there.

I do not bring it with me.

I moved to California to start over, and though it's been four years, I'm still in the same state I was in when I left

Michigan. No matter how far I've traveled, I still carry them with me.

I'm trying to move ahead, like the first therapist advised me. He also said punishing yourself forever doesn't change the past, and that it would serve me better to work through the pain and move ahead than tread water in it daily, even if it's only mental.

I never went back to that guy. He doesn't understand. I can't escape the past in my mind.

Once I'm back in my car, I realize I must've cut the swim short. I have twenty minutes to spare before I usually arrive at Crave—and I'm there an hour before everyone else as it is.

I drum my fingers over the steering wheel, watching a homeless man push a stolen shopping cart full of tin cans up the sidewalk in front of Crave.

She was weak last night. That headache made her shaky and she was clearly in pain. Does that go away with sleep? I run my hand through my still damp hair. Fuck, I don't know. But she could need a ride to work. She could need... *something*.

I sit in my car, chewing the inside of my mouth, stroking my hand through my hair, clutching the back of my neck, touching everything because I'm suddenly riddled with nervous energy. Why do I feel the need to make sure she's okay? In fact, why do I feel uneasy and anxious at the idea of her *not* being okay?

Scarlett.

That's a beautiful name. And she's... she's fucking gorgeous.

Something happens in my stomach at that realization. A hollowing followed by an uneasy spinning. My head even grows a little woozy. My uneasiness urges me to check on her.

I've worked at Crave for four years. I've been around

beautiful naked women having and giving orgasms for most of that time. And Lucy Lovegood is the first woman to ever steal my focus. The first human being to ever take my thoughts away from my shame for more than a few moments.

I drive to her apartment, not really sure how I'll explain myself if she asks why I'm there. If she questions why a coworker who has spoken less than fifty words to her is checking up on her. I don't have an answer. But the idea of going straight to Crave without knowing if she woke up feeling okay or whether she's well enough to get here... it drives me mad, so I drive to her instead.

Her car is still where I parked it, which brings a strange sense of relief or... I don't know, satisfaction? I scratch at the side of my jaw as I stand at the bottom of the cement stairs, peering up at her apartment door while early morning chills my ears and nose.

Should I be doing this?

I take two stairs.

Why do I care so much about this woman when I don't even know her?

I climb three more stairs.

What could it hurt to check on her?

I move the rest of the way up, my hand gliding against the metal railing, chilled from the San Francisco morning.

Standing in front of her door, anxiety floods my veins and my heart pumps like I ran those stairs instead of taking them with weighty hesitation.

This is fucking weird, Cohen, I think, ready to turn around and ignore all these feelings I'm having out of nowhere. Putting myself in her goddamn shoes, why would I show up here again? I have no business here so I retreat the way I came.

But I stop on the top step and turn around, blinking at the closed door.

A phone is ringing, and it sounds like it's near the door. Is she standing by the door holding her phone, looking out her peep hole, waiting to call the cops and tell them some fucking loser is standing outside her place at 6am?

I look down at the descending stairs, unsure of what to do. But the phone rings again and then again, so I make a choice.

Gently, I knock at her door with a closed fist, hoping to God she's awake so I don't scare her. Being woken up to a phone ringing off the hook is one thing, paired with someone pounding on the door… Well, that's a whole other trauma. I fucking know.

With one palm on the doorframe and the other against the door, I lean and call for her, as soft as one can while still pene-trating a door.

"Scarlett," I call, "it's Cohen, from work. Are you okay?"

Just as I'm starting to feel completely asinine for coming here—hell, she could have company, she could have a man in there with her—footsteps sound from the inside. Nervously I step back, feeding a hand through my hair as I wait.

The sound of the chain sliding open followed by the lock twisting has my heart fucking pounding. The door swings open and Scarlett is there, wearing the same clothes she had on last night. She blinks lazily at me, and I know then I've woken her up. Through a yawn she catches with the back of her hand she says, "Cohen. Is everything okay?"

The phone rings again and at the same time, our eyes drop to the purse on the floor at her feet. She looks back to me, holding the door with one hand, smoothing her other along her forehead. After she acknowledges the ringing phone, she seems bothered. Anxious, even.

I don't like that.

"I wanted to make sure your headache was gone and that you're OK getting to work."

A soft smile curls her pouty lips and I'm close to returning the expression but the phone rings again. I haven't returned a sweet smile in... years. I look back down at the phone then study her uneasy expression, which she's trying to mask by fiddling with a stray strand of honey hair, then touching her neck.

"You aren't answering?" I question, not sure if that's exactly what I want an answer to but knowing I have the right to nothing. I likely shouldn't even ask.

But the phone rings again and she shifts on her feet, so visibly uncomfortable that it spurs me into action.

"May I come in?"

She blinks at me, brows cinched in confusion. But she pulls the door open, giving me her answer.

I step past her and as she closes the door, I hook my hand in the straps of the bag, lifting it to set it down on her bar counter.

"May I?" I ask, motioning toward the bag where the phone rings relentlessly. Clearly, at this point, she's intentionally not answering. And when someone doesn't answer the first time, you don't call back.

Whoever is calling her is rude and disrespectful, and

though I have no claim to it, anger bubbles inside me that they're continually calling. *Harassing* her.

She nods, and a wave of happiness washes over me for just a minute. I don't know why she makes me feel things, but I reach into the bag and embrace the feeling.

I swipe the call, noticing the number is programmed into her phone as *PB*.

"Scarlett, *you little fucking*—"

I do not let whoever the fuck this is finish his sentence. My neck fills with strain as my jaw clenches, holding back a slew of obscenities that fill my mouth. But Scarlett drops to the ground, wrapping her arms around her legs as she rocks in a ball, pressing her face into her knees. And if I'm angry and loud, I will make her worse, even though the man on the line deserves my anger.

She's trembling as I think, but I don't know her well enough to pull her into me and give her any comfort. But the way she cowers and shakes at just the vibration of this person's voice through the receiver—I don't fucking like it.

I don't want to make the anxiety attack she's likely experiencing get any worse. Not because of me, at least.

I exercise control, and keep calm. For her.

I keep my voice low and my eyes on her as I say, "She isn't answering, which means she does not wish to speak with you, so stop calling."

The man on the other end snorts. "You my fuckin' replacement? Jesus fuck, that who—"

Scarlett's trembles amplify, so I end the call. I slide the phone onto the counter and take a seat on the old linoleum floor of her entryway. Keeping five feet between us—because everything about her screams wounded—I clear my throat.

"Are you okay?"

Three words, yet they clearly canvas so much terrain. I'm

not just asking about her headache anymore, and we both know it.

Her glassy eyes find mine, and my stomach seizes uncomfortably at the tear that slides down her porcelain cheek. I don't make a move to comfort her physically, but my finger taps the edge of my boot as I watch that tear disappear, her hand swiping it away.

"Can you please just... go," she meekly pleads, dropping her eyes to her toes. She remains in a ball, still rocking gently. I glance around the apartment, and even in the early morning darkness, I can see there's not much in here. A few boxes are stacked in one corner, but aside from those, a side table and a television, the place is sparse.

"Please go," she begs again. My visit and unwillingness to leave is upsetting her more, I can hear the anguish in her words. My eyes connect with hers, and the silent pleading I find there sends a jolt of pain through my chest.

I get to my feet, unable to take my eyes off her. Opening the door, I step outside but before I close it all the way, her gaze lifts to me. "I'm sorry," she whispers. "I'm fine. My head is f-fine. I'll be at work. Just... *please*... go."

Then she turns her head, dropping her cheek to her knee, and resumes her gentle rocking.

I pull the door closed and wait, hoping to hear her lock the door. I realize it's no longer night, but threats exist during the day. And if the despicable human on the line knows she lives here? I lay my palm on the closed door and bring my mouth as close to the seam as possible.

"Scarlett, I'll go, but I need to hear you lock the door." I don't know why it's become important to me that she's safe, or why after years of nothingness and depression, I'm hyper fixating on her.

The lock twists, and my core unclenches, settling back

down. I take the stairs two by two and get into my car, frozen behind the wheel.

Who the fuck was the on the phone?

I drive to Crave, and tell myself I don't need to know who was calling her. I wanted to make sure she's fine and she is. Because knowing anything about her... that's none of my business.

seven

. . .

scarlett

He waited to hear the door lock.

When I have therapy, I usually go after work, or on my lunch break. But today, I had to come in the morning since Dr. Evans is going out of town this afternoon, and she didn't want to miss our appointment. Truthfully, as much as I dragged my feet to get into therapy, I now look forward to it.

Because it is helping. I am feeling better. Slowly. But Rome wasn't built in a day and all that.

My phone vibrates in my purse, sitting between my feet, and I peer down to see those same ten digits dance across the screen. I look up and find Dr. Evans' eyebrows have risen high on her forehead, and she's tapping her pencil against her notepad.

"He's *still* calling?" She shakes her head, disapproval and disdain rolling off her in waves. "Have you revisited the idea of a restraining order like Augustus suggested?"

I assume Dr. Evans sees Aug, too, as she's the Crave & Cure staff therapist. But she mentions him now because I've told her about everything Aug has done for me. And that he knows about Pete and Jizzabelle. That he's the only one at Crave I told.

I snarl one nostril as I shake my head. "No point. If I did that, he'd only get angrier."

She jots something down on her notepad.

"And I still believe he will stop calling," I tell her, resting my arms on the chair.

Dr. Evans bobs her head. "And how have your interactions with Cohen been since the morning you asked him to leave?"

I let out a sigh. I hate that I pushed him away when he was only trying to help, and even though I've already apologized, I still feel shitty. "Well," I exhale, nudging the purse under the chair to mask the unending vibrations of Pete. "I'm interested in him, but... I don't mean that the way you're thinking. I just... I don't know. He's a gentleman, and it's intriguing." I shrug, picking invisible lint from my thigh. "It's been so long since I've been intrigued, in any way."

Finally I wager a glance up at Dr. Evans whose lips are tipped up on the edge in a curious little smile. "I think it's a good idea to have a friend." She glances at her notes then looks back up at me, determination in her eyes. "Cohen seems kind, and you're platonically intrigued, so why don't you make Cohen your first new friend?" She leans over her lap, narrowing her eyes at me. "And I mean real friend. Not the way you are with your new colleagues. I want you to actually befriend Cohen, and for the two of you to get to know each other. I think talking through things with someone not holding a notepad would be good for you."

I wrinkle my nose. "How?" I'm not just skeptical, but I also would rather do anal without lube than tell that handsome man just how fucked up and broken I really am.

At one point in my life, I was happy. I had goals. I even dared to dream a little. I was going to be a computer programmer and then I was going to marry a man I love and become a mother.

Now I'm being advised to make a friend so I don't have a mental breakdown and the stark contrast between then and now sets off a painful ache in my bones, one that radiates through every nerve ending, infecting me from the inside out.

"Human connection," she says as I sit and silently ache. "And not just from coworkers. You need human connection, and since you're not ready to date, you need a friend. Cohen clearly wants to be your friend."

I study my cuticles as the collar of my sweater heats. "I wouldn't say *clearly*."

"He walked home after driving you and came back in the morning to check on you. You know who does that? A friend," she says simply, reaching back to drop her pen back in the holder on her desk.

"And don't be afraid to share with your friend. Sharing helps us work through residual trauma," she advises, scooting to the end of her seat to better peer at the clock on the table behind me. I veer away from it and she nods. "And since we're out of time, I'd like to leave you with this."

My stomach clenches into a tight ball. I hate final thoughts and assignments from Dr. Evans. Because while she's always right and they have whatever effect she'd intended, they're always challenging and uncomfortable. That's how growth always is.

"If you tell him about Pete, make sure you tell him everything. Without all the details, it's hard to understand why a sharp, beautiful woman like yourself would've stayed with Pete," she says softly, wrapping up her point in tissue so as to not upset me.

I know she's right. I know I was a fucking idiot to stay with Pete, but I was a confused, lost, heartbroken and abused idiot. One that desperately, utterly, completely, with every ounce of energy in her soul—wanted *one thing* above them all.

She ushers me out into the muted waiting room. Before taking her next client, she faces me, taking my hands in hers like a grandmother would a granddaughter. Somehow, it feels kind instead of clinical. Her gray eyes soften as they flit between mine.

"Cohen or not, make a friend. And *tell them.*"

She's vague with those two words but we both know exactly what she's saying.

Tell them about the baby.

"Are you nervous?" The whisper is meant to avoid me, but makes it to me regardless. I continue tugging my tights up my leg, pretending to be oblivious to the fact that I can hear them.

"A little, I mean, it's freaking Lucy Lovegood, you know?"

Maxi's voice is rich with shock, and a warm tingle worms through me.

At Jizzabelle when I overheard people discussing me, it was never a confidence-boosting conversation. Here at Crave, though, everyone is excited to work with me, honored even. And it's genuine.

Like most things, it gives me anxiety.

And on the heels of a gritty session wherein my therapist and I discussed my need for friends, I am feeling down.

Collecting a deep breath, I twist my torso and glance back at them, over my shoulder.

"I'm so excited to work with you too, Maxi," I interject awkwardly, seeing an organic moment to bond and not wanting to miss my opportunity to take Dr. Evans' advice. And more than that, I know I won't have the courage to do it without an organic opening.

God I used to have so many friends. More than I could keep up with. More than I knew what to do with. But Pete managed to scare them away, convince me they were toxic, and make me believe I was better off without them. All in under a year.

It feels strange to make friends as a twenty-three year old woman. It shouldn't feel clunky and foreign, but it does. But Maxi makes it easy, getting up to sit next to me, bumping her hip to mine.

"Oh my gosh, that's so nice of you to say," she beams, blinking at me with her wide dark eyes. She's beautiful, but it's not her eyes or curves that caught my attention. All of the actors here at Crave are healthy. No one has track marks from injectable performance enhancing drugs, no one seems like they've taken an anti-anxiety drug to help them through the job, and I've never caught a whiff of booze on set. It's amazing.

"I mean it," I add, moving to my other thigh to tug the fishnet up. It snaps around my leg as I release it. "I watched some of your movies this week, in my dressing room, and I have to say, I think we're a great pair on camera. We complement each other."

It's true. Over the last week, I'd asked Lance to drop some movies in my dressing room so I could get a feel for the actors I'd be working with this week. I like to do that, and I'll do it until I've officially worked with everyone here.

I can't deny that watching the movies gave me a reason to stay in my dressing room. And staying tucked away in that room alone made it very easy to avoid Cohen.

I don't even want to avoid him but... I feel so bad for asking him to leave. I just, I don't want him to know about Pete and all the humiliating things I tolerated. The way I was treated, the things that took place at Jizzabelle... It's mortifying and I don't want *anyone* at Crave to see me that way.

Especially Cohen, which I know is ridiculous because we're virtual strangers. People who pass by one another daily and don't even exchange eye contact.

But he drove me home. He cared enough to wait for me to lock the door—twice. It doesn't matter. Whether his intentions are kindness or more, none of it matters because I'm in a million tattered pieces. As it is, I'm working myself up to making friends as if I'm at my first day at kindergarten. And this task is almost too much.

Caring about Cohen is a fool's errand, and one I won't let myself go on.

"I think so too," Maxi says finally after being shoulder tapped by Lance. "And I know that's flattering myself because hello, you're you, but still, I do think we'll totally be fire together on camera."

I nod, pushing the stiff curls Alexa left me with behind my

shoulder. Today, we're competitive dancers after the big competition. We're in the locker room together, reminiscing on training and how we've felt about one another.

I'm going to touch her, and she's going to touch me, and it's the first scene I've had since being at Crave to explore this part of my contract—the contact same-sex scenes. Until now, Aug has been easing me in with masturbation or dual masturbation. But today, I'm *giving* an orgasm. And I'm receiving one, too. Or at least, pretending.

"Ladies," Lance interrupts again. "Come take your spots for a lighting check. Then we're going to roll." His gaze veers up and down our bodies after we stand, and he nods his head approvingly. "I like the costume change. This is much more realistic."

Maxi and I are both in thigh highs, wearing glittering unitards with mini skirts attached. The first outfit was literally dance recital outfits for a third-grader, complete with a bonnet and skin-colored tights.

Maxi and I chat about how we'd like the scene to go, as this one has the dialogue completely left to us. We take our spots on the X's marked with red tape on the floor, then the lights flicker on. Large and bright, they immediately warm us and in tandem, the studio air conditioner kicks on.

"Test," a gruff, deep voice radiates from the radio on Lance's hip. Heat forms beneath my cheeks, dripping down the back of my neck.

Tipping my face up, I raise my gaze to *him*. His eyes are on me already, but I think I knew that. He doesn't smile but gives me a subtle nod. No warm arms looping my waist, no soft lips against my cheek or soothing words melting into my ear but still—Cohen's attention feels like an embrace.

"Fine," Lance calls up, and then Cohen's back is to me, taking the lift down, and disappearing into the ring of darkness bordering the set. Suddenly, as I align myself on my mark, I have the urge to explain to him that I did appreciate him checking on me. I did like the care. It's just, I'm not keen on anybody witnessing my train-wreck of a life.

"In three," Aug says, and I snap my focus to Maxi, bringing my hand to cup her shoulder.

She smiles, her lips shiny with a fresh coat of strawberry-scented gloss. "I'm so excited for this," she whispers, shimmying her shoulders a little. I return her smile.

"We're rolling," Aug calls, and the quiet murmurs around the set fall away as I feed my hand through Maxi's dark hair, pushing it off her shoulder.

"You were great out there," I say softly, keeping my voice light.

Maxi reaches out, taking my opposite hand, weaving our fingers together. "Gosh, you were too. Everyone did really well." She leads me to the bench, a couple of the lockers doors behind us spread wide, coats and bags exposed to the camera.

I drape a palm on her knee, running my hand up, exploring the etches of the fishnets, curling my fingers into her thigh. We face one another, and a thrill rolls through me at the pure excitement in her eyes.

She brings her hand across my body, cupping my cheek. Leaning in, we meet halfway and share a soft, slow kiss. Her tongue moves into my mouth, and I caress hers with mine. Her soft moans cast a light echo across the set, and a moment later, we're pulling apart.

She touches her bottom lip, eyes wide with vulnerable excitement. "I've wanted to do that all season," she breathes, eyes flicking between mine as if the moment were real.

That's another thing about films at Crave. The actors have sex on camera, yes, but they're *actual* actors. The feeling that we all care about our performances outside of the sex makes me feel so much pride. I never felt proud of my work at Jizz.

"Me too," I whisper, biting my bottom lip as we lock gazes, our hands beginning a journey of discovering each others' soft curves and smooth valleys. Then my lips are on her neck, and hers on mine, and the cameras are changing position, getting ready for the next scene.

We peel off our dancer's garb as the non-primary cameras lock their new position, and from the corner of my eye, Aug is nodding.

Maxi lies down on the locker room bench, arching her back as I straddle the seat, taking a spot between her spread legs. With one hand pressed low to her belly, I use the other to stroke down her thigh. Her glassy eyes hover over my hardened nipples, and as she whispers her lines about not telling the coach, I find my head lifting slightly. Just an inch or two, I reposition myself, bring my mouth to rest just above Maxi's naked pussy. And then I see Cohen.

Not just see him, but he sees me back. He holds my eye contact, and I don't know if he continues to watch, but I break away, looking back at Maxi. This is work. Even when I worked at Jizzabelle with Pete, in the beginning when it was good, I was never distracted. Ever.

As I bring my lips to Maxi's soft, wet ones, I think if Cohen looked at me like that every time I was on set, I'd be fired in under a week. Because those gorgeous eyes, that molten stare, and his completely stoic and unreadable demeanor—I suck in a breath, playing it off like raw pleasure as I move my tongue through Maxi's softness.

I want to know about Cohen, because *he waited to hear the door lock.*

He checked on me the next day.

And when I looked at him and found him already looking

at me just now, he wasn't looking at my naked body, or the way my mouth hovered above another woman's naked cunt. His eyes held mine.

Maxi's long nails push hair from my face, and I look up at her, over the mountainous range of her full breasts. I blink and moan against her as she bears down on me, her hand on my shoulder.

"Yes," she moans, her hips reverse grinding the bench as she finds her orgasm against my mouth and prodding tongue.

I wrap my hands underneath her thighs and hold her steady as she writhes, delicate moans of release pouring from her lips. From the edge of the set, as Maxi reaches for me, moving the scene to the facesitting phase, I see him.

My heart flips, the way it did in junior high when I went to the movies with my crush, and he put his hand on my thigh. It was the first time I'd ever been touched, and though he was harmless and had no idea that I was soaking my panties, my body jolts with heated urgency, the way it did back then.

I thought I was too old for fireworks and butterflies, but just his eyes on me have my body thrumming. Positioned over Maxi's mouth, her lines float around me, nothing more than a hushed cue to move the scene forward. Because for once, I'm not *in* the scene. I'm somewhere else entirely, with this man whom I don't even know.

But I have to look down, so I drop my gaze to Maxi's eyes and take my breasts in my hands. "I can't believe you're actually tasting me. I've touched myself thinking about your tongue exploring me so many times," I whisper, rocking my hips against her face. Her nails drag down the small of my back, tracing the steep curve of my hips and ass. She finds my clit amidst the slow stroking of her tongue, and sucks it into her mouth.

The cameras rotate, and from the edge of the set, Cohen clips the purple flag to the front of an abandoned chair, where I can see.

I need to come, because the scene needs to be wrapped up. We're filming a shower scene later, but for now, oral orgasms are all we're doing.

Maxi's good and gorgeous as hell, and it's not her—in the past, I've received some of the best orgasms I've ever had from beautiful women in the industry. It's me. I just can't orgasm. My mind won't let me go there.

But I can act, so I grind my hips and squeeze my breasts, wondering what Cohen's large hands would feel like against me. Would his skin be rough and calloused, or surprisingly soft and tender? Or both? Would he want to pinch my nipple, or would he be the guy who likes to cup, squeeze and drive a woman wild with a breast massage? Would he bite my nipple? Would he suck at it until my eyes rolled into my head and my cunt was clenching all around whatever he'd give me?

My insides coil, and pressure builds, and even with Maxi's skilled tongue and lips doing everything that worked before, I can't do it. I tip my head back, and envision his body swallowing mine in a protective hug as he drives his hips back and forth between my spread legs. I moan my *release* , and Aug calls cut.

"Perfect. Nice work, Maxi. Great, Lucy. See you both at next call time."

I shimmy off Maxi and help her up, giving her a damp cloth from nearby to wipe her mouth. Alexa appears, tapping Maxi on the shoulder with irritation written on her face. "Maxi, I need to touch you up in five minutes. I have Tucker and Otis to do after that." She casts a pointed glare, the implied *don't be late* hanging between them before she walks away.

"Lucy," she starts, dragging the terry cloth along her chin and down her throat. "I don't want you to get mad or offended or anything," she continues, drawing her words out slowly, cautiously.

But I already know.

"It's ok Maxi, it's not you. It's been a long time since I've been able to orgasm. Months. Maybe even a year."

She cups a hand to her gaping mouth, her eyebrows shooting up to her hairline. "Lucy," she breathes, her disbelief palpable. "Why not? Wait—didn't you and your ex break up just a few months ago?" She's doing mental math.

I nod my head with a sad smile pulling at my lips. "Yeah, two months ago. I actually broke up with him the day before my first day at Crave."

"Oh-oh," she stutters, clearly having solved the equation.

"It wasn't a good relationship. And Jizzabelle," I start, unsure of where I'm taking this. It's better to not get into a lot of detail, because starting fresh requires not a single crumb of the past. "Jizzabelle was not at all like Crave," I say, deciding those words are perfect and truthful, yet not too descriptive. She bobs her head as she drops the towel in the laundry bin near us. They're kind of everywhere around here, and it's so much better than wet spots all over the floor, like at Jizzabelle.

"I'm sorry. I hope you find it again," she says, pouting her plush bottom lip. I smile and slide into the robe I'd draped on the chair before the scene.

"Thanks," I smile, unsure of how to respond to that comment.

The idea of being intimate, having someone inside me in those ways again, comes with a plethora of various emotions.

Excitement, because sex is the ultimate way to be connected to someone. And when you care about them, it's goddamn magic.

Fear, because what if? There are so many, my brain spins at the notion: *what if.* Because I've been taken down by the what if's before.

And *nerves.* Nervous to be vulnerable to heartbreak and abuse. Nervous that it's too soon. Nervous that I'm undeserving. Nervous that I attract the losers. Just plain nervous.

I didn't think I'd want to share that part of me ever again. I thought I'd ruined it, used and abused myself in getting orgasms and handing them to undeserving partners—and Jizzabelle. I've accepted I will never be able to mentally get myself to a place where I could orgasm again.

I've kind of made my peace with it.

I still like sex. I still enjoy my job. There's just no *finale* for me. I can live with that.

I don't need to figure out an explanation for her though, because Maxi turns and waves me off as she heads to makeup. I have casting with Vienna today—our first day, and my focus should be there. Focused on the great deal Debauchery and Crave made me, and all the opportunity stretched before me.

Orgasms can wait.

"And that's how casting works. Pretty cool, right?" Vienna nods excitedly, bumping her glasses up her nose with a curled knuckle. In her overalls—smeared with all sorts of hues of clay—and Crocs, she beams at me, completely unphased by the fact that I'm spread eagle in front of her.

I nod with a smile, because even with a ton of shit on my mind, her happiness is infectious, even if only slightly. "Yeah, it's very cool."

She takes a rubber glove—one so big I think it's got a full sleeve attached—and shoves her arm in with a snap. "Now, you coconut oil up and I'll grab the mixture. Your body chemistry and natural resting heat will be different than Tucker's, and that's what this formula is based off of, so don't get concerned if we have to do this part like, twenty times." She smiles. "It's just part of the process."

I nod as I nab the bottle of coconut oil and squirt a healthy amount into my palm. After distributing the oil to both palms, I coat my labia and groin, spreading some of the warm liquid up my thighs.

Vienna turns around with compound in an injectable syringe, her molding cup out. She seals it around my vagina, injecting the warm mix from the top. It fills in around me, rough and heavy, and I take a deep breath to steady the ripple of discomfort that wriggles down my back.

"You feel like you have to pee?" Vienna questions, though clearly rhetorical. "That's normal. It's the weight of the clay and the heat. It made Tuck feel that way, too. Of course," she smiles, talking now more to herself than to me, but I'm grateful for the distraction. "He didn't tell me that until after. If he would have, I could've told him it was normal."

"You two make a great couple. Are you excited to be engaged?" Even I know the question is dumb as I say it, because of course she's happy to be engaged to the man she loves. That's normal. But I'm so awkward around relation-ships now, because it's been so long since I've experienced a healthy romantic one. Even speaking about one feels like cautiously tiptoeing around shattered glass.

She's so overtly happy that she doesn't pay attention to how stupid the question is. "Yes," she beams, eyes shiny. "I'm so excited. Vienna Eliot sounds so nice, doesn't it?" she asks, and I nod because it absolutely does.

"So good," I continue. She asks me to hold the molding cup as she peels off the glove and replaces it with a dispos-able one. Vienna sets the egg timer and returns to my vagina.

"Tucker told me you asked him about Cohen," she says suddenly, her tone low and private, despite the fact the door to the work room is indeed shut.

Sweat immediately surfaces along the length of my back, and I look down directly at the mold being made between my legs. "He's just so reserved," I say after a moment, because that's a good answer, too.

I like Vienna, and I hate that a lot of our conversation today has consisted of things I'm not saying.

"He's a really good guy, though. Quiet but kind. Tuck says he doesn't know him well but says he's always known Cohen to be good, but very private." The timer ticks and I chew the inside of my cheek, thinking about her words.

He is private. Even Tuck, the number one star here who's friendly with everyone, doesn't know Cohen well.

Yet Cohen gave me a ride. He came to my house. He checked on me.

"Is there a reason you were asking about Cohen?" she questions as the egg timer dings. She runs a finger along the seal, popping the dried compound free from my body. Slowly, she shimmies it free.

I asked Tuck before this, but I use it anyway. "He gave me

a ride home the other night when I had a migraine. He was very polite. A gentleman."

She smiles at me as she slips the completed mold into a bag. "Entirely unsurprising. He's got total Sandor Clegane energy." Her head tips to the side, then enlightening me, "He's a loyal tough guy from Game of Thrones. Like a knight."

I shrug with nonchalance, but my stomach twists uncomfortably. I don't like acting off set, and more than that, why am I having to act? Eye contact and a ride does not make a romance.

And anyway, romances include penetrative sex. And I can't do that.

I wipe up as Vienna cleans her work space, telling me all about the castings she did for Tucker, and how many times they failed before they got it just right. I force my mind back to Vienna.

The final scenes with Maxi went well, and I enjoyed myself. No orgasm, but I had a good time and more importantly, I felt safe the entire evening. And I realized after the scene, as the crew chatted around the set and all of them kept respectful eye contact, this studio is healing me.

Crave is curing what Jizzabelle took, Maxi and the women

are returning to me the things the men at Jizzabelle stole, and I'm repairing the erosion inside me.

And knowing that not all hope is lost makes me... happy.

I wave goodbye across the building to Lance, who barely nods, and push open the heavy door into the new moonlight. It's only eight, but still, the sky holds gray clouds pregnant with a storm, and the street light flickers, leaving me in a purple dusk.

I'm pulling my car door open when I hear my name. My *real* name. Soft and slow, but the rocky timbre flushes my cheeks. Tingles give way to bumps rising up on my neck as I turn to see Cohen.

"Y-Yeah?" I reply, tossing my purse onto the passenger seat, stuffing my hands in the kangaroo pocket of my hoodie.

"Are you safe?" he asks.

I don't presume to play dumb. He heard my phone ringing off the hook. Pete no doubt said horrendous things when Cohen answered. And he saw my apartment, barren and lifeless. We both know he's asking because I do come off like the victim in a crime show podcast. Seriously.

I smile. "Yeah, Cohen. I'm okay." I like saying his name, much more than I should. I hold my smile in place until he dips his head, turns around, and disappears around the corner. A moment later, headlights shine in the distance, and I know he's in his car now, too. I get inside of mine and start it, sitting a minute to let the windshield defrost.

I wish he wasn't so nice. Because all that kindness slides into all the deep crevices in my heart, and I have no business catching feelings. I'm in no place.

My phone rings in my bag, and I peer down at it, two ugly letters staring up at me. A heavy sigh leaves me, and I drive to my empty apartment.

eight

. . .

cohen

I forgot about myself. I'd only thought of her.

"Hey Mister," the little boy's voice prods at me as I clutch the bullnose edge of the pool, gasping for breath, choking for a lungful of life.

That one was close. The closest I think I've ever come. I almost blacked out under the surface today. And for the first time in a long time, I was *grateful* to surface. Eager to suck in chlorinated, heated gym air.

With one arm still draped on the edge of the pool, I turn halfway to blink at the little boy treading water just a few feet from me.

"Yeah?" I breathe, my chest still pumping steadily as I struggle to normalize my breathing. I blink one eye as a chlorinated drop rolls over my lid.

"Why do you do that?" He swims for a minute before

grabbing the wall next to me, settling in for early morning conversation. I glance around the underground pool area, looking for this kid's father.

"He's working out," the kid offers, noticing.

I smooth a hand through my hair, sending rivulets of water everywhere. "And you're allowed to swim alone, huh?" I wouldn't let my child—*as if I have a right to judge.* I clap a hand against the surface. "Nevermind."

He nods along. "So why are you still doing that? You still trying to see how long you can hold your breath?"

I continue fishing a hand through my wet hair. "Yeah," I eventually reply.

"Well you should wait for me to get here. What if you passed out? If I wasn't here, you'd die, Mister," he says, nodding with wide eyes. He's so young, he doesn't know that there are worse things than death. And for the last few years, surfacing has felt like one of those things.

"I like swimming alone," I counter, trying to get him off my trail. *Let me play roulette and leave me the hell alone, kid,* I think to myself as he repositions himself on the wall, kicking his feet a little.

"I could count for you, you know," he offers. "I taught my little sister how to count, I'm really good at it. I can go up to 600 if you need me to but really, I don't think you can hold your breath that long anyway."

I snort. "You're right—I can't hold my breath for 10 minutes. But I count for myself," I say, disappointment washing over his features at my response. I get out of the pool, and for whatever reason, he does, too. Like he's not done with me yet.

"I told ya, I taught my four year old sister how to count," he says somewhat indignantly, if a kid his age can even be indignant.

Then I process his words. He's got a *four-year-old sister*.

My chest seizes as if I'm trapped below the surface, holding my last breath. My hand falls from the back of my neck, and I find myself clutching at my bare chest as I blink down at this kid. His eyes study my hand and come back to my face, brows pinched quizzically.

"You okay, Mister?"

"Cohen," I say, my tone sounding foreign as I fight and struggle against the anxiety wrapping around my spine. "My name is Cohen."

He offers me a pudgy hand. "Dad says you shake hands when you meet another man," he says, wiggling his hand to get me to shake it. "And my name is Albert Jr."

I shake his hand, all the while focused on not passing out. "Nice to meet you Albert Jr."

He loops his towel around his neck like a boa, and nods behind him toward the far off locker room door. "I have to go. If you want me to count for you next time I'm here, I will."

I smile, albeit a small, crooked and forced smile, as Albert Jr trots off and disappears behind a blue steel door. I look around the indoor pool space. Old butter colored tiles checkered with light blue ones, rusting steel on the fixtures, cracks in the concrete, and from the ceiling condensation drips.

Swimming laps has always been my punishment. I've never looked around here until now. Never noticed the dilapidated state of things. This morning, I see this place for what it is, and it feels more like a prison than ever before.

The potent aroma of ground and brewed coffee beans wafts around my head, permeating my focus. I flip the switch on the soundboard and wait for the corresponding light to flicker.

The coffee smells good. I haven't enjoyed the smell in so long.

Yesterday, Lance made coffee.

The day before that, Lance made coffee.

Everyday for the last four years that I've been here, Lance has made the coffee.

Today, the aroma nestles into me deep, making me long for things I haven't had in ages. With my hand hovering on the soundboard switch, I let my eyes fall closed for just a second, the smell of the roasted beans taking me back.

I can hear my ex laugh as if it was yesterday.

The metallic clink of the glass carafe against her to-go mug. "I need extra coffee after last night," she says, wiggling her brows. She dragged her nails along my belly, in the space between my jeans and shirt. Rocking to her toes and placing a coffee-infused kiss on the corner of my mouth.

I don't miss her. We ruined each other with sharp words and painful emotional jabs. But I miss the closeness. Sharing habits with another person, knowing another person like you know yourself but being excited by their presence nonetheless. I miss that.

My eyes jerk open, my heart racing, the smell of coffee roiling in my stomach, making my palms damp and my throat itch.

"Black," I hear her say, "Just black."

I don't turn, but I know it's Scarlett. And now I know she takes her coffee black. The rumbling in my veins seems to settle as Crave moves on all around me, preparing for a scene, unaware of the dark memory that threatened to sink me on dry land.

Another minute of tinkering and the soundboard is functioning, so I duck behind the set as Aug counts down to roll.

As soon as the slates clatter, there's a loud sneeze.

"Cut," Aug calls, and then there's shuffling. I peer around the set to see Alexa center stage, trusty Q-tip in hand.

"Give me five," Alexa sighs over her shoulder toward Aug and Lance. "The sneeze smeared her mascara." She looks down at Uma, the actress. "Need allergy meds?"

Uma nods, and as I'm about to shuffle down the hall to my office and reorder the LED bulbs for the prop makeup desk on set, Aug claps a hand over my shoulder.

"Cohen," he greets, "How are you?"

I cast my gaze around the room, but come up empty. The set is full of people, but I don't see her. Lance appears, sliding his iPad into Aug's hands. He faces me with steely blue eyes that mirror my own. "She's in her dressing room, taking a phone call."

I furrow my brows as my gaze darts between them before Lance takes off, cupping his hands to his mouth to shout at the caterer coming in the building.

"On the concrete! Do not roll that cart over the wiring!"

I face Aug, and he shrugs. "He's very... intuitive."

I don't deny that I was looking for her. "I gave her a ride

the other night. I get the impression that someone's bothering her, and I'm concerned."

It's all true, but I omit that I don't *want* her to be bothered. I leave out how despite the fact I hardly know her and have no business inserting myself into *anyone's* life, I like her. Something about her softness on set, the sincerity in her voice. She's real but wounded, and maybe she sticks out to me because I see myself in her. Alive but emotionally a little mangled.

I hope that's not the case. I hope I'm wrong and she's fine. But the way Aug doesn't rush in with soothing words, or doesn't immediately laugh and throw his head back like it's crazy, that has my hands balling into fists at my sides.

"Is Scarlett safe?" I ask, my voice deliberately small but also unintentionally gruff. There's a dull ache in my chest as I wait for Aug's response. He drags a hand over the top of his shiny dark hair, the overhead lights making a few silver strands shine.

"You know Pete Bryson, right? The head of Jizzabelle Films."

I narrow my eyes, thinking back to the last event mixer held at The Fillmore for our industry, put on by Debauchery. A tall, thin man comes to mind, a heap of greasy brown hair falling over his forehead, gold ring shining on his pinky finger. When he slipped his hand in mine, it was limp, and he only held my fingers. Never trust a man with a bad hand-shake, my dad always said.

"The limp handshake guy?" I ask Aug, though I'm sure it was him.

Aug dips his head in acknowledgement. "Yeah, that's him." He surveys the people around us before lowering his voice. "She was in a relationship with him for two years. He's how she got started in the business."

I know how Aug found Tucker, but something tells me Pete Bryson finding Scarlett wasn't quite as wholesome. And Scarlett with Pete? That makes no sense. She's beautiful and sweet, and he's...Pete fucking Bryson. A guy who'd screw over his own blood to get ahead.

"What about him?" I ask, but I know what's coming. I think of the unrelenting ringing from her purse that morning. The voice on the other line. Hairs rise up along the back of my neck and all down my arms. That was Pete.

"Like I said, he's both her ex boyfriend and former boss," Aug says, an obvious discomfort clouding his normally clear eyes. That makes me nervous, because Aug is so solid. For him to be stirred or shaken must mean Pete Bryson is more of an asshole than even I know.

I just stare at him, trying to control the unsteady breaths that wrack my chest and cause my shoulders to lift with every concerned inhale.

"I'm glad we have her here at Crave. Pete was doing a lot of shit at Jizzabelle that would get the entire place shut down if anyone reported him."

"And that would be a bad thing?" I question, still clenching my fists at my side.

Aug pulls a hand down his face before motioning something to Lance behind me. With his focus back on me he drops his voice to a private tone and says, "We have her here now and that's what's important."

"Tell me more," I say, gripping his wrist as he moves to walk past me. He may be done with this conversation but I'm more interested than ever.

He looks at where I'm gripping him then up to my eyes. He's clearly conflicted as to how to respond, but something he sees in my stare prompts him to answer. "Pete forced her into scenes, and other times, wouldn't even tell her what was in the scene, but he'd tell the male actors and she'd just get... *surprised.*" He puts air quotes around that word, and I feel sick. "She had no real say in things. Pete treated her like shit, at Jizz *and* at home."

"They don't have contracts?" I may not be an actor, but I know how Crave works. Everyone and everything is contracted, for mutual benefit and protection.

Aug straightens, taking the slates from the chair where he rested them. "They do have contracts but they were in a relationship and..." his voice grows distant as he chooses his next words, as if he's trying not to lie while also not telling the whole truth. "Pete is not a good man, and what happened at Jizz is just the tip of the iceberg," he says.

From the hall, Scarlett appears, robe wrapped around her torso tight. Alexa has stopped her, and is assaulting her face with a brush and powder. Aug turns his focus back to his job.

"We have less than two minutes of filming, guys, okay? No hiccups, no sneezes. Let's get it done," Aug calls, and as the slates smack closed and he calls action.

Pete is not a good man. Aug's voice rattles around my brain as my heartbeat intensifies. I swear I can hear that phone vibrating, the indignance in his voice. With my head down, I move quietly off-stage until I'm completely out of sight of everyone else, heading down the hallway.

I push the door open to the men's room and turn around, locking it. Chest heaving, heart racing, I make my way to the sink where I turn on the water, twisting it to ice cold. I roll up my sleeves, lower my cupped hands under the faucet, and bury my face in the cool water.

Over and over, I splash water on my face, even holding my nose and mouth in my cupped hands. But the water slips through my fingers, and suddenly I miss the pool at the gym. Where I can fill my lungs with pain in privacy.

I blot my face with paper towel, and run a hand through my hair. We're strangers. She is not mine to protect. But that doesn't stop me from timing my exit from Crave to align with hers.

In the parking lot, as she walks to her car, head down as she scrolls through her phone, I come to her side and say hello.

It's only one word but heat bands my collar and fills my chest as she glances up, stopping in her tracks. "Hi Cohen." I stop walking, too, and we stand there in the center of the parking lot, street lights throwing glowing rings around our feet.

"Would you like to walk down to Rise and Grind and get a coffee?"

A neutral space. In public. Near work. And cameras will see us walk off the lot together. I don't know how else to make her feel safe while I talk to her.

She glances over her shoulder then back to me, as if considering my offer. My blood stops pumping as I wait for her response.

"As long as I can get my car out when we're done, sure." She smiles and knowing that she wasn't hesitant to say yes to me but merely wanted to make sure her car didn't get locked in, makes me happy.

My toes curl in my boots and there's a faint tick at the corner of my mouth. The anxiety I felt at the sink earlier all but disappeared.

"Don't worry, I won't let them lock up until you get your car."

She blinks at me, her eyes smiling. "And yours."

I forgot about myself. I'd only thought of her.

I've missed that feeling.

nine

· · ·

scarlett

I'm... enjoying myself.

I think when most people have out of body experiences, they're doing something monumental. And I don't mean that in a good way. I mean life altering ways: Witnessing a motorcycle accident, sliding down a ravine while harmlessly hiking or getting bad news that forever changes you in a split second.

I can honestly say I've never had an out of body experience. Not until now. And it's from something so simple; being asked out for coffee.

I don't consider it a date, but still, a man asked me for coffee. It's been well over two years since I last hung out with anybody simply to spend an hour talking—to have a drink and enjoy their company.

I forgot what it feels like to walk next to a stranger, to have your arm graze theirs and wonder if they're feeling the tiny pinpricks of electricity through their veins too, to talk over each other awkwardly because you don't know their cues, to say you hate something they like and share a laugh because you're both just so new to each other.

I forgot those simple pleasures are out there, and as I walk next to Cohen out of the Crave and Cure parking lot, they rush back to me. Every last one of them. It's almost dizzying, the amount of potential happiness out there with the right relationship. Cohen asks me how my day went, and I answer, masking the sudden disappointment running through me.

I can enjoy the buzz of a proper not-date, but I can't let myself get excited—I can't date. I can't give a man what he needs any more.

"It was good. Pretty standard today, but I guess you know that. You've been at Crave longer than me," I say, tucking a strand of wavy hair back into my loose ponytail. Ahead the sign for Rise and Grind appears, a neon red open light flickering in the window.

"I have, that's true," he says, stopping in front of the antique store next door to the coffee house. I look up at him, taking in the slope of his nose, the perfect set of his eyes and the crisp shave on his chiseled jaw. My eyes drop to his chest, covered in an emerald and navy blue plaid button up, but I see the way his clothes hang off him, clinging to his pecs and biceps, falling loose in other places. He looks both fit and kind of gaunt, but I don't have time to overthink it because his eyes are back on me.

"Mind if we go in, just for a second?" he asks, holding my eyes and really studying them.

I nod. "Sure."

I expect to follow him inside, to traipse around after him

in silence until he's ready to have coffee. Instead, he pulls open the door and keeps his eyes on his feet. "After you."

We browse the antique store, with Cohen quietly greeting the owner. After a few minutes, he turns to me and asks me if I'm ready to leave.

My eyes burn at the question. It's so simple. The same way being asked out is so simple. But Pete never asked me what I wanted. Ever.

I swallow and manage a nod, hoping my face isn't flush. A few paces down and Cohen is pulling open the coffee house door and waiting for me to enter. Once we're inside, he places his hand on the small of my back. His fingers don't stray—no pinky grazing my ass or anything like that. It's meant to guide only, to offer comfort even maybe.

We blink up at the menu and after a moment passes, he looks down to me, eyes flitting between mine. "What would you like? I can order and you can choose whichever table you like."

I stare at him a moment, his blue eyes patiently on me, awaiting my reply.

"Um, I like my coffee black, and a lighter roast. And virtually any baked good. I have a huge sweet tooth."

He tips his head in a half nod. "Okay."

Turning, I survey the little coffee house. I've not been here before but mostly because I'd been a little afraid to venture outside Crave, especially alone. The few close friends I had—well, it turns out I didn't have them after all. After I left Pete and quit Jizzabelle, they never returned a single call. I had no one to get coffee with, no one to peruse stores or pick out candles I don't need, buy throw pillows I'll never use. And I'd been too anxious to do it alone.

I pick a small table with only two seats across from one another, and take a seat. Plants line the windowsill nearby, and I reach out to feather a leaf between my fingers. This place is brimming with life—between freshly brewed caffeine, a sea of plants and sweets—it's a perfect slice of happiness, inside these four walls.

A minute later Cohen appears, lowering a big white styrofoam coffee cup to the table. Next he sets down a pink pastry box.

"I bought a few things, so you'd get something you wanted. You can take the rest home," he says, taking a seat across from me after getting his own coffee from the counter. The barista perches on the counter, engrossed with her phone, leaving us in the quiet shop. Alone.

"Thank you. Thank you for breakfast and also, thank you for driving me home and checking in on me. And I know I said I'm sorry for asking you to leave but I just want you to know, I am sorry. I was frustrated with... well, myself I guess, and I took it out on you." I pull the pink box open so the apology doesn't seem like a big deal. My mouth waters at the array of assorted pastries resting inside. My nose fills with sugar and heaven as I assess the goodies. A bear claw, a cinnamon roll, a glazed donut, and a large blueberry muffin. Plucking the bear claw from the box, I take a bite and finally meet his eyes.

"You don't have to keep thanking me or apologizing," he says, pulling some napkins from the metal dispenser on the table. He reaches forward, placing an unfolded napkin beneath me just in time for a slivered almond to plunk down on it.

"Thanks," I say, which earns me a hint of a smile from Cohen, and his tiny smile makes me grin. "I mean for the napkin."

He takes a sip of his lidless coffee, and I notice he takes his black, too.

"My therapist says I'm used to people pleasing as a trauma response, so, yeah." My cheeks burn with my stupid admission. And starting a sentence off with "my therapist says" is not the vibe. I bite into the bear claw again, just to fill my mouth.

I'm about to go in for another bite when I stop, bear claw hovering close to my lips when he simply asks, "Are you in danger?"

Carefully, I set the pastry down and take a slow sip of my coffee. I don't hate that he asked that, more so, I hate that he's known me a singular fucking minute and already has valid reasons to ask.

"I asked Augustus about you, I want you to know that. I don't want you to hear that from someone else—I asked him about you because the man on the phone—"

"My ex," I interject, head a bit woozy from the fact that this man whom I barely know has shown me more kindness in two weeks than my ex did for two years. And it has nothing to do with what sex I can give him, or what scenes I'm willing to do, what deals I'll make nice and fat with my name and popularity.

"I asked Augustus because he seems to know everyone thoroughly and... I wanted to make sure you're not in danger," he explains, twisting the button beneath the collar of his plaid shirt. "I kept thinking about your phone ringing, and the tone in Pete's voice."

My throat goes dry at the mention of his name, and like most poisons, as soon as I process that he knows Pete is my ex, my insides roil with sickness and shame. My defenses rise, because that's what I do when I feel ashamed; I defend and deflect.

"I'm at Crave now. And I'm single. I want to leave the past in the past." I take a sip of my coffee through a locked jaw, trying to temper my reaction. Everything about Cohen is candid and real, from the eye contact to the respect he shows me and all the small things in between. He's not trying to snoop. But it's embarrassing, having been with Pete.

"Understood," he says simply, not meeting my attitude with anything but kindness.

He cares. And he barely knows me.

My fingers stroke down the cup over and over as I study my hands, willing the flush and heat in my neck and face to die down. To prove to us both that the mention of my ex and the past won't throw me into some emotional tailspin.

Cohen clears his throat. "How long did you work at Jizzabelle?"

"Two years, give or take a few months."

He nods. "I've been at Crave nearly four years."

"What did you do before Crave?" I'm grateful he's steered us easily from the bumps, that he picked up on the fact that I needed a diversion.

I hadn't realized how large and dominating his hands are until he wraps one around his cup, dwarfing it. Something low in my belly awakens, a familiar sizzle I haven't felt in some time as I hold his gaze.

"Same kind of job just... across the country."

"Yeah?" I ask, eager for specifics. "Where?"

His eyes drop to the steamy surface of his coffee for a minute, before coming back to me. We're still across the table from one another, but there's a great distance in his gaze as he says, "Michigan. I worked as a set designer and electrical engineer at a theater there."

Something tells me there's more to the story than that. Maybe he got fired? Maybe he started a relationship with an actress and it went wrong so he moved to California to start over? Though there are theater and production companies everywhere, not just California. Hmm.

I don't peel and poke his answer, but instead, move on. The way he did with me moments ago.

"That sounds fun. And you do that at Crave, too, so you must really like what you do." I take another bite of bear claw and nod to the open box next to me. After I swallow I say, "You don't want one?"

He shakes his head. "They're for you."

"Thanks," I reply, feeling my cheeks go rosy again. I take a sip of the coffee, wishing I could fan myself. Cohen isn't dirty talking, yet something that flutters in my belly reappears at his words. "You like it at Crave then, I take it, since it's been four years."

He nods. "I do. Do you?"

I pluck a piece of slivered almond from the pastry. "I do. It's so different from Jizzabelle," I reply, braving the topic only slightly, trying not to come off as *tantrumy* as before. "And there are so many great perks. I love having a quality therapist. Though I think I need a few actors to not use her to balance out just how much I see her." Laughing a little awkwardly, I meet his eyes. They're soft but serious and that does something to my stomach, too. Why do I keep bringing up the fact that I have a therapist?

"That is a nice perk." He looks at the surface of his coffee then back to me. "I see a therapist but I'd already started seeing him before I started at Crave, so I've stayed with him."

Comfort washes over me at his words. I was worried he'd think I was… damaged? God that sounds stupid, I know that sounds stupid. But I *was* worried.

Pete always said therapy is for people who want to wallow in their issues. While I know that's asinine and untrue, still, it surfaces in my brain on days where I feel like a hopeless wreck. There's comfort in knowing Cohen goes too. That he understands the value and importance of recognizing you can't always handle your own shit. Sometimes you need a professional.

"I have to admit," I say, feeling like the truth feels so much different with Cohen than any other man I've met. Even Augustus, who is arguably one of the nicest men I've met. Still, Cohen looks at me like he'd accept and understand anything I have to say. "I didn't expect you to be in therapy."

He takes another drink of coffee and I try not to look at the way his Adam's apple bobs, at the tiny triangle of chest exposed at the top of his button up, at his huge hand cupping his drink. I lock my ankles together under the table.

"Most people need therapy, they just don't realize it," he deadpans, giving me a tiny little smile. Small and fleeting, but his smile radiates through me, leaving possibility simmering in its wake.

"I agree wholeheartedly," I laugh, because I really do. "I like that the therapist at Crave is on location, too. Everything about being here is better for me. My apartment isn't too far, either, so that's nice."

He nods, stroking a hand through his hair. For a moment, I feel his hand resting on the small of my back all over again. I shift in my seat, trying to get comfortable. "I'm not too far away either."

"Where's your place?" I ask, finishing the bear claw in three ambitious bites. Once I hit that marzipan filling, I can't be stopped. I take a drink of my coffee.

"Near the Painted Ladies, not far from where you're at, actually."

I quirk a brow. "Wow, you were able to get into that area? Most people who own homes over there hang onto them forever, or rent them out."

He lifts a finger as if to say that's me. "I rent."

"I think when you work in show business, it makes sense to rent. You never know where the job is going to take you."

Something about the way his expression grows serious for a moment before volleying back to casual has me intrigued.

"I rent a room. In one of those big houses, I rent a room. I just have some clothes and books, so I couldn't justify renting a place in the city." The way he looks around the coffee shop, emotionally diverting from the topic, hits me. I do that—I know I do because Dr. Evans calls me out on it all the time.

I don't call him out, I only want to know more.

"That makes sense. Who are your roommates?"

He laughs. It's deep, with a low timbre. His laugh brings a smile to my face, and I even laugh a little too. It's a beautiful laugh. "I wouldn't call them roommates," he says, pulling a hand down his jaw as he settles forward over the table, getting comfortable. I like the hair on his forearms, and how his sleeves are rolled up just a little. I like that he's getting comfortable. "It's actually a family. They rent me their down-stairs room. Their children are in high school and I think they're saving my rent money for college funds."

He lives with a family. In a room. By himself.

"You've rented that room for the last four years?" Surely not. Surely he had a place of his own then downsized or something.

"Yes."

A singular room. For four years.

That likely means he hasn't brought many—or any—women back to his room and for some strange reason, that information trickles through me, warm and heady, like the first sip of bourbon.

He *could* live with a bunch of equally handsome bachelors

but he doesn't and something about that hits different. His priorities are so different.

"I don't know why I like that, but I do," I tell him, my admission a little quiet, feeling private for some reason. I don't have a right to like or dislike anything about the choices he's made, and I'm ready to amend my statement and possibly walk it back out of embarrassment but I can't, because he speaks. His response is quiet, too.

"I'm glad you like it." The littlest bit of pink circles his cheeks, and he looks from the inside of his empty cup back to me. "Scarlett, why don't you get the restraining order?"

I blink at him, knowing this information came from Aug. I can't imagine Aug telling anyone things about someone that he knows in confidence, but then again, it's not exactly a well-kept secret that Pete is a piece of shit, and that my phone has been ringing off the hook for weeks. It's not rocket science putting those together.

"You sound like my therapist. She keeps telling me to do that, too. But trust me, it would only make things worse." I circle the top of my empty cup with one finger tip, steadying my breathing. I can't get worked up anytime someone mentions Pete. He's in the industry, I have to move forward. And Dr. Evans told me to make a friend and Cohen is the only one at Crave who has shown below surface level interest in being my friend. "I appreciate your concern, though, I really do."

His brows pull together and my thighs clench. "I don't want you to hurt."

Not *get hurt*, not *hurting*, but a broad *to hurt*, as if the idea of me being in any kind of pain at all troubles him.

"I'll be okay. He'll stop calling. And he doesn't know where I live now and I think we both know he'd never get into Crave so... it's okay."

Cohen doesn't look convinced, but he nods to my response anyway.

"In the meantime," I say, switching gears. "My therapist tells me I need a friend. I think she eventually wants me to trauma dump on said friend. She says sometimes getting things off your chest to a friend is better than therapy."

"Do you think that's true?" he asks, sounding like a therapist himself. I smile and wag a finger at him as I call him out.

"You sound like a shrink." The smile that sweeps his face positively hardens my nipples, so I fiddle with the pastry box in front of me so he doesn't notice. "And I don't know. It was hard for me to have friends before. Pete always had an issue with them. He scared them off, and I let him. It'll take some getting used to, having a person I can trust. Trust is kind of like a winning lotto ticket, a unicorn, or a perfectly cooked burger. I've heard about it but never experienced it for myself. But I need to have a friend I can trust. I think she's right, I think it would really help."

"I'll be your friend," he says, collecting our empty cups. He takes the napkin I was using and tosses everything in the trash before sitting back down. "And I'd like to get to know you better." He smirks a little, and it's so sexy, it stirs me up as he leans over the table just slightly. "And I can cook a perfect burger."

I tuck my hair behind my ear with a laugh. "Good to know about the burger and… I'd like to get to know you better, too." And the truth is, I do want to get to know him better. And that's what friends do, anyway, they get to know each other.

"Let me give you my phone number, and then you'll have it in case you need help."

My lips twitch. "Okay, but I won't need it for that. Trust me, Pete is… he's a real piece of shit, if I'm being frank with my *new* friend," I smile, "but he doesn't have a pair of balls big enough to find me." I pinch a piece of blueberry muffin off and eat it. "Also, he's lazy."

Cohen's phone sounds and I quickly do the thing that everyone does when they're with someone new and their phone rings. I try to busy myself to allow him time and privacy to take his call.

But he silences it and smiles. "That's just the alarm for us to get back before the gates close." He takes the pink box then pulls out my chair. "I'll walk you to your car."

I rise and dust crumbs from my lap, raising a palm over my shoulder to say thank you and goodbye to the barista. Once on the sidewalk and headed toward Crave, I ask, "You're not leaving, too?"

His strides are long, like his legs. I watch his worn boots eat up the sidewalk as we head back. And even though I've said Pete's name too many times in the last thirty minutes, I'm not depressed. I'm not drained or weary.

I'm... enjoying myself.

"No, I've got some stuff to take care of."

"Do you always work late?" I ask, because now that I think about it, Cohen is always there when I leave. Even on some of the late shoots.

He nods. "Yes."

Then we're back at Crave, and I'm almost annoyed the distance is so close. I wanted to know more about my new friend.

"Thank you for the coffee and the pastries," I tell him as he pulls open the car door and places the pink box on the passenger floorboard. He circles the back and opens my door, too. "Thank you for that, too."

He smiles. It's only the second real smile of his I've ever seen. I want more. He's gorgeous.

"Can I take you to coffee again?"

I'm eager, and I don't mask it. "I'd like that"

He closes my door and I try to hide my eyes in the rearview as I peer back, taking a mental picture of Cohen standing in the parking lot, watching me drive off.

ten

. . .

cohen

Use it or lose it is a saying for a reason.

It's been six days since I took Scarlett to coffee. Since we exchanged phone numbers. There have been a few times where I almost sent her a text message. My fingers were hovering, thoughts spilling out of me as I nearly typed them up.

Then I remember *her*. I remember *them*. I remember all the ways I failed my family. And I put my phone down.

Though we haven't shared a text message thread, and we haven't spoken too much at work, we shared a moment. I don't know if she felt it, too, but with my whole chest, I felt it.

She was preparing for a scene, discussing it with Aug and Lance. I was nearby, replacing the foot on one of the prop barstools. I wasn't trying to listen. But when she speaks, I hear it, I swear.

"I don't know. The authoritative role just… isn't one of my strengths," she'd said to Aug. It pained me hearing how nervously she spoke the words. So much uncertainty inside of such a beautiful soul. I couldn't believe that she could be uncertain or insecure about her performance. Before she was even officially here at Crave, I must've heard a hundred conversations between actors, sharing their disbelief that Lucy Lovegood, the number one female adult film star, was coming here to work with them.

I did something out of pocket for me, but necessary for her. Stepping outside of my comfort zone, I moved forward onto the set under the guise of adjusting electrical cords running adjacent to the rolled out carpet. Scarlett, still looking nervously through the script pages, didn't seem to notice I was kneeling at her feet.

Looking up at her, the spotlight for the scene already on and in place, shone brightly behind her. A sort of ring rounded her profile, and my plan wavered momentarily as I committed her image to memory. The light caused her hair to glow, as shadows lapped at her sides. She was truly a sight.

Blocking out my hesitance, I reached out, placing my palm over the top of her foot. She startled a bit but didn't move except to look down where I was crouched at her feet. I watched her throat bob in a nervous swallow, and then I took one more chance.

"People tremble in your presence, you're that good."

She stared at me, her eyes glossy and wide. I couldn't believe she looked surprised, and I didn't know if it was my words of affirmation or the fact that I was touching her. I took my hand back and tucked the cords under the carpet, rose, and disappeared into the off-set fringe.

While coiling the extension cords in the very back of the studio, I kept my eyes on her during the scene. I've never done that before, not even once in four years. As someone with almost no sex drive, the movies being made were simply something happening around me, nothing more.

But that day, it felt wrong not to watch.

She was filming promotional material for her new toy, Loved by Lucy. I don't know what was intended, but I watched her guide Otis into the toy with one hand, the other hand tenderly stroking down his flexed bicep. Each time he'd groan his pleasure, she'd pump the toy up and down his shaft, earning more growls and grunts from him. She repeated that process on Dallas, using the replica toy to masturbate him slowly, keeping him on the edge of his seat. Then she produced a second toy, and finished them off at once. The tagline, *more pleasure with Lucy Lovegood*, was slated to roll across the screen post editing. I'd overheard that part.

When Aug slammed the slates, and the piece was done, a set hand approached the guys with towels, like usual. But Scarlett put her robe on, and it occurred to me then that I hadn't even taken in her bare naked body. I'd been so focused on her eyes and trying to understand what she was feeling, why she'd been nervous, and if my words had helped her.

But there were no retakes, and she walked off set wearing a huge smile, heading into the workroom with Vienna.

And even though I didn't have any more answers than before, she seemed happy, and that brought me inexplicable relief.

While in my office looking through our inventory spreadsheet on my computer, there's a knock at the door. With my back to it I call out, "It's open."

Another few clicks and I'm highlighting all the specialty bulbs we need. "What's up?" I ask, only partially looking back, waiting for Aug to interrupt my work. He always does. A nice knock followed by a slew of one-sided conversation is his MO.

As I highlight the LED field, a hand comes down on my shoulder and gently squeezes. The touch is both soft and strong, and my eyes fight closing to bask in the touch. Fingertips dip into my shoulder as her voice melts over me, sticky and hot. "What you said to me a couple of days ago, on set."

It's not a question, but my voice is hoarse nonetheless. "Yes."

She strokes her hand along my shoulder and I fight the feeling of comfort and keep my eyes open.

"Thank you. I got through it because of you."

My eyes glide over the same number in the cell on my spreadsheet about fifty times, but I have no clue what I'm seeing. All I can focus on is her admission that I indeed made her feel better. I did it for her, but I can't deny that a bit of selfish pride runs through me.

She takes her hand back and a moment later, the door clicks shut. I spin in my chair and face the wooden grain. My heart is racing, my thighs flexed against my chair. I grip the arm rests and stare at the door, chest rising and falling with fatigue and urgency. As if I've just surfaced after a cruel swim.

It takes me a minute to quantify the pulsing, heated feeling coursing through me. It's been four fucking years after all. *Use it or lose it* is a saying for a reason.

I look down at my lap, finding my cock hard, running down my thigh. I stare at it. Reaching out, I *almost* drop my palm to the head. I *almost* feel the length of my erection.

Almost.

Panic barrels through me.

My eyes veer between the computer screen—what I should be focused on—and my lap. I can't stop looking at my engorged, thick erection.

I have an erection.

And it feels fucking good.

I don't just mean in my cock, either. Everywhere, my chest and my head aren't angry, they don't fill me with guilt and remind me what I don't deserve. I just sit there, with my hard cock, feeling good, for the first time in a long time.

Because of Scarlett.

That night in my room, lying in bed, watching the small ceiling fan rotate in lazy circles, I can't sleep. I glance at my gym bag and consider getting up and going for a swim, but I know if I do that, I really won't sleep.

I force my eyes closed, because sometimes that works.

Tonight, it doesn't. Tonight, with my eyes closed, I feel her hand on my shoulder. I feel the heat her words inspired, the vulnerability of her tone. It washes down my back, through my veins, into my limbs—everywhere.

Reaching under the covers, I slip my hand beneath the elastic waist of my sweats and underwear. A rush of hot breath surges past my lips as I grip my cock.

It's been ages since I've touched myself with the intent to do more than fucking take a piss. I haven't had those urges, not since *before*.

Until today.

Fanning out my fingers underneath my cock, I hold myself loosely as I harden. Poor guy hasn't been man handled in so long, a simple touch has him turning to stone.

I stroke my finger tip along the thick vein running up the underside of my shaft. It feels… good. From somewhere above me, maybe the second floor, could even be the third, a cell phone rings. It's not uncommon to hear a phone ringing at this time—teenagers, after all.

But it rips me back to reality.

Pulling my hand out of my pants, I let my cock tent the bedsheets for a few minutes before my erection wilts away. I can't bring myself to touch it again.

I know I should jump on this opportunity considering I'd convinced myself two years ago that I had become fully impotent.

But I don't just think of Scarlett; I also remember them. That night. The ringing phone. The high pitched screaming. The promises to God. The disbelief.

I finally fall asleep, though when it happens, light is already streaming in through the old Victorian window.

Bags line my eyes and my entire face feels heavy. I miss the leg hole of my jeans twice and nearly topple over. I've yawned enough that my jaw burns and when I snatch my gym bag off the chair, I realize… I don't have the energy for a swim.

I don't know if I'll be anxious all day without the energy spent in the morning, because swimming is part of my normal routine and has been for years. But I'm groggy and yawning and—

My therapist always says, *the worst lie you can tell is the one you tell yourself.*

I'm not going to swim this morning because I'm eager to get to work. Something roils in my gut telling me that I need to see Scarlett. I collect my phone from the nightstand and open a new text message, type S to populate her name. I only have a few contacts, so my phone knows just who I'm searching for.

In the body of the message I type and delete things, sweat beading along my neck. I finally go with simple.

Cohen

How are you?

I hold my phone, screen unlocked, and watch the

message. No blue dots appear, and no read receipt materializes. I glance at the top of the phone and see that it's only six in the morning. Somehow when I try to tell myself that she's just asleep and hasn't seen it, I can't bring myself to believe it. But I don't know why.

There's stirring in the house, and in order to not make small talk or get roped into a playful family discussion that leaves me remembering what I lost, I throw on my jacket and head out the back, ducking into my car as quickly as possible.

After nightmare nights, I get to the gym extra early, and after I get to Crave early, too. I'm used to finding things to do around the set, so when I key in the security code and stuff my things into my office, I get to work.

Seven approaches, and Lance and Aug wander in, holding matching stainless coffee tumblers. They head to their office, or Aug's office—I've never been quite clear on who it belongs to—and close the door. Around eight, actors start to filter in, starting with Maya and Chanel, who come to work together because they're neighbors. I check the time around half past eight because she's usually here by now.

Next, I check my phone and there are no replies to my message. Anxiety builds, so I head over to the wall of monitors hosting the security camera feeds. I scan the first monitor which faces the side parking lot. My car is there, and another which I recognize as one that belongs to Uma.

On the next set of monitors I see the front of Crave, a steady stream of morning commuters filling the street.

My heart plummets into my belly when my eyes lock to the next monitor, the grainy black and white clear as fucking day to me.

Otis is laughing, his head back as if he's just heard the funniest joke. Next to him, talking away wearing a shit-eating grin, is *Pete*. My hands ball into angry, tight fists and I'm temporarily rendered useless by my overwhelming rage. Why the fuck is Pete here? And where is Scarlett?

Pete claps a hand onto Otis's shoulder, and turns, walking away, out of the gate. I flip through all the security screens until I get the shot of the sidewalk off the gate. I watch Pete until he's gone, and stomp toward the door, catching Otis the moment he walks in.

"Why was Pete here and why are you talking to him?" I bark, speaking more words to Otis than I ever have in the last four years. He shirks back a little, eyes wide with surprise.

"Who?" Confusion takes over his surprise, and my anger only grows.

I tip my head toward the closed door. "Pete Bryson. The man you were just speaking with. Why was he here and why were you speaking with him?"

Otis looks no less confused. "Who the fuck now?" He scratches his jaw and the noise needles into my brain. "That was my friend, Brian Peterson."

Aug, likely attracted to the situation from the sheer fact that there is a situation involving me, strolls up, eyebrows to his hairline, waiting for answers.

"Pete was here, talking to Otis. Otis says it's his friend, Brian," I tell Aug, who immediately recognizes the situation for what it is. With a tone much calmer than mine, Aug faces Otis.

"How do you know *Brian*?"

Otis's eyes morph into a panic mode, and bounce between us like a child caught red-handed. I realize, though, that Otis has in fact been played.

"I, uh, I met him at Rise & Grind. He ordered the same thing as me." Otis shrugs, still looking confused. "Who's Pete?"

"How long have you known Brian?" Aug asks as my chest fills with anger, palpable, seething, raging anger.

"A couple of months I guess." He looks between Aug and I one more time before asking, "what's going on?"

"That's Pete Bryson, he's the director and head of production at Jizzabelle," Aug says, and Otis's eyes widen.

"You think he's trying to poach me?" he asks incredulously, but Aug shakes his head before Otis can get too carried away.

"No. He's been using you to find out information about Scarlett."

"Scarlett?" Otis looks genuinely confused and knowing that he doesn't know Lucy's real name alleviates some of the pain in my chest, some of the rage boiling inside me.

"Lucy Lovegood," Aug sighs, frustrated with the situation. He waves Lance over. I scan the monitors one more time, looking for her car. I've never wanted to see a granular black and white feed with her car more than now. I face Lance.

"She's not here." An idea overwhelms me and my body tenses. I turn to Otis. "Do you know where her new apartment is?"

"We helped her move. Lance, myself, Aug, Maxi... a few others. Why?"

"Fuck," Aug grumbles. "Tell me that you didn't tell him where she lives?"

"Yeah," Otis says slowly. "I mean, I didn't say *Lucy Lovegood's address is*. He asked me last week if I knew of any good apartments in the area for rent. Any places I've seen recently that looked nice. And I remembered Lucy's complex had some for rent. So I told him we just moved my friend Lucy in and he should check it out."

Otis looks between the three of us, his face finally growing concerned. "Why can't he know where she lives, anyway?"

"Because he's her abusive ex-boyfriend who's been harassing her for months. And let me tell you, the harassment doesn't hold a candle to the way he treated her at Jizz," Aug says, anger throttling his tone.

I don't like hearing that he treated her like shit at Jizzabelle, though I could've assumed. I swallow, around a lump of discomfort in my throat.

My gaze moves between Aug and Lance, who look equally as concerned as I feel. She's not here, she hasn't answered my text, and now we know that Pete knows where she lives.

I look at Aug, who nods, and says, "Go."

eleven

. . .

scarlett

Please let me inside

I study my toenails, the imprint of the carpet burning my ass. I've been in this ball of self-preservation and tears in the corner of my apartment living room for hours. Sun spills in the sliding door on my balcony, so I know it's morning. I knew it was morning when the birds started chirping some-time ago.

But I can't move.

I've made so much progress with Dr. Evans, and Crave has reinstated a base level of safety and security in me when it comes to making adult films. While I can't say I'm ready for any male-female roles, still, I've been feeling and performing like my old self, slowly but surely.

All of my progress feels washed away with one singular wave of *Pete*.

I want to get up, wash my face, brush my teeth, pull my greasy and tear-heavy hair off my face, and go to work. Soak in the friendliness and comfort of my new studio.

I want to but I can't. Anxiety and fear overwhelm me.

He knows where I live.

A yelp breaks past my lips as a quiet thudding comes down against my door. I wrap my arms around my knees and blink at the door, waiting for it to be pushed in, waiting for banging, anticipating yelling. My heart jumps up my throat, nausea spreading through my insides.

Another blunt knock at the door has me tugging my knees closer to my chest.

"Scarlett, it's Cohen. I'm alone. Please... open the door." His voice is thick with concern, loud and heavy to penetrate the door, but quiet enough to lower my hackles.

"Scarlett, please let me inside," he says again, desperation lacing the strength of his tone. I blink at the door, remembering Cohen's palm against my foot, and find myself scrambling to my feet. First the chain then the deadbolt, and after I've made quick work of both, I pull the door open.

Cohen stands there, looking exhausted with dark crescents beneath his eyes. Without words, I move aside and he steps in, taking the door from my hand with gentle care. He closes it quietly, slipping the chain into the groove, locking us in.

When he turns to me, his sky blue eyes soft and tender, I break. Trembles wrack my shoulders and knees, and I crumble to the floor in a sea of tears and unintelligible words. Cohen lowers his large frame to the worn apartment floor, and slowly, cautiously, wraps his arms around me. He pulls me into his lap and presses my head into his chest, keeping his hand on my cheek.

With my ear pressed to his heart, I hear it beating, rapid

and irregular. The longer I sit in his lap with his arms around me and his hand on my cheek, the more my crying slows, and the more regular his heartbeat becomes.

After a few minutes he drops his mouth to my ear. "Come on," he says, somehow standing while keeping me in his arms. He takes me down the hallway, nudging my room door open with his boot. A moment later, he's lowering me to the bathroom countertop, turning the light on to immediately dim it.

His voice is steady and calm, and though he asks hard questions, my pulse never quickens.

"Did he get inside?"

I shake my head, a tear rolling free. "H-how did you know he, he came by?" I snuffle the words.

"He came to Crave. He befriended Otis, that's the only way he figured out where you are," he says calmly, and I watch his large hands move through the stream of water, soaking a washcloth.

"Oh my god," I cry, "he came to Crave?" I hold my head in my hands, a million things running through my mind. I don't want to be associated with him. I don't want Crave associating me with him.

"Don't worry," he says, voice a bit stern. "He didn't come inside. I saw him on the monitors and he left before we had a chance to speak." His large hand comes to my face, hovering over me before he touches. His eyes claim mine, wordlessly imparting safety and care. Then he places his hand on my cheek, pushing the hair back. He repeats on the other side, then brings the washcloth to my face. Slowly, he strokes the warm, soft terry down my tender, tear-stained cheek.

"He... he wouldn't stop calling and knocking. He knocked on the door, he beat on the door—" I correct, because what he did wasn't a knock. He kicked, he screamed, he smacked his flat palms to the door. Over and over and over. "He did it for hours. I don't even know how long."

Cohen dips the washcloth beneath the running water again, squeezing the excess out before bringing it to my other cheek. He softly wipes away the tears, soothing the sting of my swollen flesh.

"I feel stupid," I say, now that my nerves are calming. So he came here, he beat on the door. So what? A lot of women have it worse. He didn't break in. He didn't rape me. "I'm sorry to scare you, I just..."

"You were triggered by his behavior because he's traumatized you," Cohen states, moving the cloth over my forehead. His thick fingers slide into my hair as he holds me steady. I like the way it feels.

"Yes," I whisper, loathing the truth of it. "I don't like yelling, I don't like aggressive behavior. I never have. So that's why he uses it. He knows it makes me anxious."

Cohen nods, sweeping the cloth around my jaw before tracing the curve of my throat. It's warm and it feels so good.

I don't know if it's his soothing demeanor or just him in general, but in the dim light of my 1960's apartment bathroom, I spill.

"We were happy the first year. I didn't feel bad about temporarily dropping out of college for this, because it was *temporary*." I put air quotes around temporary with my fingers for good measure, because I never thought I'd quit. Truly. "Then when I started to get a lot of success, he made it harder and harder to go back to school. My schedule filled up, he'd approve me for movies and scenes I hadn't consented to, and that's when things got *really* bad."

"Has he ever been physically violent with you?" Cohen asks, his grip on the washcloth a bit tense at the weight of the question.

"No," I tell him honestly. "Just classic emotional abuse." I crack a weak smile. Cohen pulls the shower curtain back, and pushes down the stopper in the tub. He retrieves a bottle of body wash from the window sill, and squirts it under the running water.

He's running me a bath.

"What was that emotional abuse like for you?" he asks, sounding like Dr. Evans, but feeling more like... a friend.

"I'd have hard lines on scenes," I tell him as he feeds his hands under my armpits, lifting me from the counter to set me on my feet. "Anal," I say without meeting his eyes. "I never wanted to do that on film. You know, I explained some things I wanted to leave for my personal life. *Our* personal life. But then we'd be on set of a high-budget production, Pete would yell at everyone to get the take right, no cuts, and if we had to cut, he'd take the production value out of our paycheck. And he did it before, I know for a fact he did. Then he'd advise the male actors to penetrate me, telling them that part of my kink was acting like it hurt, acting surprised."

Things can get blurry but one thing that's always clear to me is consent, and it's vitality to any sexual act. "A lot was done without my consent, and I know I can press charges for that. But... I just want to move on. That's why I'm in therapy."

Cohen listens as he turns me toward the tub, lifting my arms slowly. His fingertips smooth down my raised arms, sending a hot vibration rattling through my belly. Gripping the hem of my shirt, he slowly lifts it up and over my head. From the corner of my eye, I see him place it on top of the hamper. Next his solid fingers are dipping into the sides of my waistband, tugging my pants down.

He never looks at my nude body, only my eyes and his feet.

"I know what you're thinking. Why wouldn't I just stop and say, *I don't want this*," I say with so much shame weighing down my voice that it comes out as a whisper. "But there's more to it. He... held things over my head and I was weak."

He stills. "You're not weak, Scarlett."

I lick my lips as he tugs my pants down and I step out. His hand extends out in front of me as he stands behind me, and I slip my palm into his to steady myself. Stepping in, I sink down in the tub and look over, finding Cohen leaning against the wall, eyes on his boots.

"What are you thinking, then?" I whisper the question, afraid to know the answer.

He lets out a breath, dragging a hand down his jaw. "I want him to leave you alone."

I want to ask, *why do you care?* I want to remind him that we hardly know one another.

But the truth is, I like someone showing up for me, I like feeling cared for versus hearing empty promises. And I'm starved and selfish, and I want to soak up his wholesome attention for as long as he'll give it to me.

"When did he finally leave?" Cohen asks, looking over at me, his serious gaze capturing mine as I settle into the bubbles. He doesn't try to look at my body under the surface or through the soap, and I've noticed at work when I catch him watching me, he's looking at my face.

"I don't know. The birds were chirping, but it was still dark. Maybe three or four?"

He nods but I don't miss the strain in his neck as he keeps his jaw shut. "And he showed up at what time?"

"I guess eleven or maybe midnight. I was asleep."

He isn't angry when he says it, but I feel bad nonetheless. "You call me next time, okay?" He reaches for a towel from the stack outside the door—I still have no furniture or anything—and places it on the closed toilet seat. "I won't be loud and I won't get violent. But you call me if he comes back."

The way he knows that shouting and violence would send me into a trauma state has something inside my chest swelling.

He nods to the towel before I can answer. "Take your time, get out when you're ready."

Panic clutches my throat. "Are you leaving?"

Cohen shakes his head. "No."

After pulling on some clean black yoga pants and a hoodie, I gather my wet hair and put it on the top of my head, too tired to comb it. My body is vibrating with exhaustion, the only thing keeping my feet moving is adrenaline… and the smell of food.

In the kitchen, I find Cohen, arms above his head. His shirt has lifted from the top of his jeans, and wisps of blonde hair fall in a line down his pants. I'm not sure what he's doing, but I envision dragging the tip of my tongue through his happy trail, down to the gold at the end of the rainbow.

When I turn the corner, my fantasy catches fire as I spot Cohen replacing a light bulb above my kitchen sink. I glance behind me at the light in the dining nook, and it's been replaced, too.

"You didn't have to do that," I tell him. "But... thank you."

"You didn't have much to work with, but I made you something to eat." He nods to the counter where a bowl of mac 'n' cheese rests, a cut up apple next to it. My stomach aches with hunger.

"Thank you." I pick up the bowl and take a bite, letting my eyes close to savor the warm sustenance. "You're so kind. I really... just, thank you, Cohen."

He doesn't acknowledge the praise, but washes his hands at my sink. "How are you feeling? Better?" he asks, inspecting me, from my face to my bare feet.

"Better, yes. Thank you. I'm just... tired. And I feel weak," I admit. Something about admitting weakness to Cohen doesn't make me feel like a failure. Being around him is so easy and comfortable.

"The food will help. But extreme fatigue is usually caused by prolonged periods of adrenaline."

I take a seat on the floor and watch Cohen disappear down my hall. What's weird is that I don't question what he's doing. I just eat my mac 'n' cheese, and relish in how much better I feel now compared to just two hours ago.

He returns... with my hairbrush. "You're too tired, I understand, but it will give you a headache to sleep with it up like that."

I blink at him, and his knowledge of ponytail headaches. He's clearly been in a relationship with a woman for some time in his past if he knows this. Jealousy creeps into my consciousness at his knowledge. Which is insane, so I shovel in the rest of the pasta as he drags out a folding chair from the kitchen.

He sits in it, behind me, and carefully lets my hair down from the wet bun. And slowly, as I eat slices of apples, Cohen combs out my hair.

When he's done, he extends a hand to me and helps me to my feet. After placing my bowl in the sink, he disappears into my bedroom, telling me to stay put. I stand in my apartment, wondering so many things.

When he returns, he gives me a partial smile. "Sleep. Don't worry about Crave. Aug knows you're taking the day."

My eyes fill with warmth and I smile up at him. "Thank you. I didn't know I needed that, but I did."

His hand falls away, and my bones feel empty.

"I'll stand outside until I hear it," he says, tapping the locks. Pulling open my apartment door, he steps onto the doormat. At the threshold we stand, looking at one another before Cohen leans in and pulls the door closed...

A fisheye and distorted view of Cohen is there as I press my eye to the hole, and there's a skip behind my ribs when he says, "Let me hear it lock, Scarlett."

I lock the door, and watch until he's so far down the stairs that I can no longer see him.

When I go to my room, I find the bed turned down, my phone plugged into the charger, my dirty clothes put inside the hamper, and the blinds and curtains closed. Sliding my legs under the sheet, I lie back against my pillow and stare up at the ceiling.

There's a stirring between my legs, brought on by all of Cohen's care. And for the first time in a really fucking long time, I realize... that stirring is arousal.

And I don't just want to touch myself.

I want *him* to touch me.

twelve

. . .

cohen

That fulfills me, and that's fucking terrifying.

After leaving Scarlett's apartment, I went back to work and explained things to Aug. I'd relayed to him that Pete showed up and essentially fucking harrassed her all night.

That's when he'd started to share with me some of the horrendous things Pete had done.

Let actors enter her bare when she was in bondage scenes and couldn't physically or verbally say no.

Cut her pay if she cried on set.

I stopped Aug there. These revelations angered me, but the reason I cut him off wasn't to abate my anger. It was for her. They're *her* stories to tell, her trauma to share. If she wants me to know, I should hear it from her. Not from Aug.

Scarlett showed up on set the next day with a toothy smile

and shining eyes, and it floors me that anyone would have this beautiful woman and treat her that way.

You're supposed to protect and honor what's yours, at all costs.

I don't even know if I can move forward, but I can't deny that she's awoken things in me. The desire for a connection, the want for more. And she's the first, so even though I've got no idea what I'm even capable of, I ask her to coffee again. And she says yes.

I tap the dressing room door. "Lucy?" At work, it feels too personal to call her Scarlett. And it makes using her real name that much more special when we're together. At least, that's how I feel.

The door swings open, and her perfume engulfs me, making me... tingle. "I'm ready," she smiles.

It's been so long since my body yearned for a specific physical place, to be anywhere, to even *be* at all. And now, as we walk down the sidewalk toward Rise & Grind, I realize, logical or not, I'm aching to be near her when I'm not. And when I am? She's all I can see.

We stop in front of the antique store, and she peers in the window. "Can we pop in here again for a second?"

I nod; I'd go anywhere with her, I'm realizing very quickly. "Looking for something specific?"

She pushes her long hair behind her back, as if preparing for something serious. "A music box. I had one as a little girl, the last thing left of my childhood. Pete destroyed it. And I know what you're thinking, you can get a music box anywhere. But this one was made with a pink satin interior and a tiny spinning ballerina wearing a tiny tulle skirt." She brings her hands to her heart and shakes her head, eyes brimming with sadness. "I can hardly talk about it without getting emotional."

"Lets go look for it then," I say, pulling the door to the antique store wide open. We go separate ways, Scarlett disappearing down an aisle while I sidle up to the owner at the front desk. I let her know what Scarlett is searching for, and leave her my phone number in case she finds one. Scarlett turns up after a few minutes, shrugging.

"I'll never stop looking," she says. "But alas, it's not here. That would be incredibly convenient, right?" Her smile is full of hope despite the disappointment. I'm learning that hope is contagious.

We go next door, and I get her settled in at a table near where we sat before while I order her coffee and sweets. This time I opt for an old fashioned glazed donut, a blueberry scone, two mini cupcakes, and a slab of carrot cake. When I return with the coffees, then with the pink box, she looks like I brought her the sun, moon and stars.

"I'm not even going to act like I didn't just get super excited by the sight of that box."

I smile and it earns me a pointed finger over the table. "You smiled. I've hardly seen you smile."

I've gone a long time without a lot of things, so I change the subject and flip the lid of the box open. "Do you like carrot cake? I guessed."

She makes a show of licking her lips as she pops the lid off her coffee, and it's fucking cute. Sunlight trickles in around the leaves consuming the window, leaving phosphorescent orbs along half her profile. It's beautiful. She's beautiful. "There isn't a sweet I don't like. Even brownies with walnuts. Walnuts are gross, but in a brownie?" She shakes her head with a teasingly smug smile. "Don't even care."

"Let me get you a fork," I say, realizing my mistake. She reaches out, wrapping her hand around my wrist. It's one of those moments where you can't believe it's true—the things you've seen in movies. There is an actual electric touch that fills your body with sizzling energy. I know now that it's not made up. My gaze falls to where she's holding me, and then across the table, discovering her wide, sapphire eyes.

"No," she says, and the single soft word has me back in my seat, as if an army general had commanded me.

It's that precise moment that I realize no matter how hard I fight against my past, I want to make her happy. Every part of me comes alive at the idea of serving and pleasing her. With her hand around my wrist, I see myself at her feet, worshiping everything she is and what she does for me. She's saving me, I can feel it, even though I don't want to give it credence, give it hope. I know I'm changing, and after being vacant for so long, I think I want it. Even if I still feel like I don't deserve it.

I want her to be mine to protect, love, serve and adore.

Pleasing her fulfills me, and I'm fucking terrified by this realization.

"Can you sit in the other seat?" she asks, pushing the box across the table. I move to the seat next to me, and my pulse zips when she sits where I was, right next to me. With one hand, she plucks the glazed donut from the box and the other drops beneath the table, resting atop my thigh.

She eats her donut leisurely, talking about all the blooming fern plants on the opposite side of the shop, and how she's never had a green thumb. I stare at the way her slender hand looks on my thigh, and out of nowhere, I put my hand on top of hers, and weave our fingers together.

She turns to me, a piece of glaze on her bottom lip. "That's nice," she says, wiggling her hand.

"I think so, too," I say, my voice unusually husky, the gravity of my feelings settling in, twisting up my chest.

"Cohen," she says quietly, setting the remnants of the

donut back in the box. "Will you tuck my hair behind my ear for me?"

With my other hand, I nudge a silky lock off her shoulder, my heart racing. There are spots of green near her pupils in both eyes. I'm noticing now. And her lashes are so long, her lips so full.

"Kiss me," she whispers, moving our linked hands up my thigh just a little. "Because if I'm ready, it would be with you."

I glance around the shop. Beautiful plants growing all around us, the slow, hypnotic drip of a fresh brew, sugar and cinnamon hanging in the air. I look down at Scarlett, the beautiful, strong woman that's pulled me out of my depths while treading water on her own. She's been scarred and marred by undeserving men, but she's here, risking the potential for pain again… for me.

I wrap my hand along the curve of her neck, my thumb under her chin. I bring her mouth to mine, fusing our lips. Her mouth parts with a breathy moan, urging me to do the same. The flavor of glazed donut floods my mouth as her tongue sweeps mine lazily. She leans toward me a little, putting a little weight on our joined hands on my thigh. When she breaks the kiss, she runs a finger tip along my bottom lip, smiling.

"Was it too soon for you?" I question, feeling a little out of control. From just one kiss. She doesn't realize, I'm asking us both, because I haven't kissed anyone in so very long.

She shakes her head, smoothing a fingertip over my bottom lip, eyes holding mine. "No," she breathes. "That felt really good."

I smile, unsure what to say. It felt good for me too, and as I suspected, that little high is tethered to guilt.

"I almost called you." She leans back and returns to eating

her donut, keeping our hands linked. "Last night, I almost called you. But... I felt..." she sips the coffee after her last bite, wincing a little like it burned her.

"Hold the cup," I advise. She grabs it as I use my free hand to pop the lid off, then slide the cup my way, and blow the steamy surface, cooling it down.

After a minute, I pass it back to her. "Try it now."

She takes a sip, smiling at me with wet lips. "Perfect."

"It's okay that you didn't call." Then, because it's so true, I say, "You're very strong." I mean those words, but I don't like how they make her eyes wet, so I grab her hand a little tighter, this time adjusting us so we're palm to palm. My heart jumps a little at the contact, and warmth rises up the back of my neck. Our hands being pressed together, her taste still in my mouth, goddamn it, I've missed this feeling. And shit do I like Scarlett.

"I'm not strong, though. A stronger person would've left a long time ago."

I take a moment, carefully mulling over the question on my tongue. But I don't get to ask, because she adds, "But that's a story for a different day." Tipping her head toward the window where plants eat up the space, she jokes, "Don't wanna kill the plants with my sadness."

Just knowing she thought of calling me has me sitting a bit taller.

We walk back to Crave together, and I watch her car fade into the sherbet horizon, and head back to my room at the house.

There is an unshakable, big, bold move swallowing all of my other thoughts as I lie on my back in bed, watching the old ceiling fan.

She almost called me. What if next time she doesn't even

get the chance to almost call? I think about that kiss as I settle in my bed that night, and while I don't touch myself, I want to.

And that's new, too.

thirteen

· · ·

scarlett

I'm beyond ready to finish what I started when I woke up.

Today is the first day since dropping out of school and starting to work for Pete that I have woken up with hope. I'm not gonna go so far as to say I woke up smiling, because I still feel off. But Cohen. He makes me feel like me again, he makes me feel like a healthy normal woman, but also feel special and seen. He gives me hope, but I'm nervous, gaslighting myself by reminding myself, *all beginnings are good.*

And I can't lie and say I didn't think things were good with Pete to begin with.

But even so. A part of me then knew something was off. He was always pushing for a little more even after I'd asked him to stop, always egging me on when I got frustrated, and never quite hearing my preferences when it came to scheduling my scenes.

I lick my lips as I stretch my feet through the sheets, trying to find the taste of Cohen's kiss. It's gone, but I close my eyes and play it back. Imagining his fingers beneath my chin has my body shuddering. I've never been with a man that touches and speaks to me with so much tenderness and care.

Blinking up at the streaks of light dancing across the ceiling as early morning kisses day, I let my hand wander beneath the covers. I find my pussy. It's warm, and with my fingers splayed over the cotton fabric, I can feel I'm swollen. Neediness rolls through my belly, seeping into my groin just from replaying that kiss. While I have no clue what will come of it, I slip my fingers under the elastic.

"*Ohh.*" I let out a soft moan as I spread myself with two fingers, slickness immediately coating them. It's been so long since I've been aroused for real so I lie there, playing with the discovery for a minute, remembering the enjoyable things about intimacy, the happy things about good sex. Even at Crave, there are times where I want to be aroused, where an erotic scene really does speak to me, but I just... can't get there.

Now, though, with the memory of those thick fingers curled beneath my chin, the imprint of his lips against mine— I think it's possible; I think I could have an actual orgasm.

I find my clit, swollen and tender, and begin to stroke it. The pads of my fingers barely graze as I tease and pleasure myself.

With my other hand, I push my long hair away from my neck as my body begins to heat, and lift the hem of my old t-shirt until my bare belly and breasts are exposed. Looking over the terrain of my nearly nude body, heat tears through me at the sight. My nipples, stiff peaks, my belly coated in a thin layer of sweat, my hand stashed between my legs, kneading an ache—I feel sexy.

I squeeze my eyes shut as I take one of my breasts in my palm, kneading the way I love when I'm with a partner. I've always liked my tits played with, my nipples sucked and teased. I squeeze, moaning at the delicious pressure, imagining it's his hand... not mine. Slowly, I push my fingers inside, my cunt immediately tightening around the intrusion. Panting, I alternate between plunging inside and massaging my clit, the combination of the two my absolute favorite.

I'm so wet that my tiny empty bedroom echoes with the sounds of my arousal, my moans bouncing off the walls, surrounding me, intensifying everything.

My toes curl and my legs straighten, the start of an orgasm creeping up my spine. I keep my fingers over my clit and play with the sticky wetness, tapping and stroking, grabbing my other breast.

What would that strong hand feel like on my breast? What would those lips feel like sealed around my areola? Would he keep his eyes closed as he worshiped my breasts? Does he talk during sex? What are his grunts like?

The unknown has my hand working faster, and the disbelief that after everything I've been through, I'm actually turned on again... it has the orgasm coming quickly.

I push up on my elbow, loving the sight of my knees spread, covers bunched at my ankles in passionate urgency, my hand swaying back and forth beneath the cotton.

Bang. Bang.

My hand freezes, and my heart leaps into my throat.

Bang. Another loud thud from outside.

Panic swims through my veins, but I think of Dr. Evans' advice and take a deep breath. Sitting up, I yank my hand out of my panties and wipe my fingers on my t-shirt as I pull it down. Getting to my feet, my orgasm shriveled and gone, I pad down the hallway, saying a silent prayer it's not him.

But as I near the door, I realize... the noise isn't someone hitting, knocking or pounding my door. Rocking to my toes, I bring my eye to the peephole, and at the sight, gasp.

Unlocking the door, I open it and take a few steps outside onto the landing between my apartment and the vacant one. On the ground, crouching in front of me with a roll of duct tape and a torn box, is Cohen.

Still in just panties and an oversized t-shirt that sits right above my knees, my hair tangled and messy around my shoulders from sleep, I blink down at him.

Slowly, knowing it's me hovering over him, he brings his gaze up to mine. His hand falls from the box, coming to cover the top of my completely bare foot. He squeezes a tiny bit, his voice hoarse as he says, "I couldn't sleep not knowing if you were safe."

My eyes heat as I etch the vision of his hand on my foot into my memory. Crouched before me, he drops the duct tape, bringing his other hand to my leg. Slowly, he drags the backs of his knuckles up my inner ankle, other hand still covering the top of my foot. "I'll keep you safe," he says, and before I can even register all the things this moment has me feeling, he takes his hands off me, collects the splitting box in his arms, and rises. Nudging the apartment door with his hip, it flies open, exposing an equally bare space, a few boxes already inside.

He moved in across the hall from me.

He moved for me.

After placing another box inside the threshold of the apartment, he smooths his hands down into his pants, and my eyes gravitate to the thick curve along his thigh. The unachieved orgasm pulses in my belly, my clit throbbing and swollen. I glance down, knowing the length of my shirt but eager to verify my panties are indeed covered.

When I look at him, he's studying the tops of his sneakers, gaze respectfully pointed away from my partially nude body.

"I, uh, I have therapy this morning. And then I need to get some groceries," I tell him, a quiver in my voice I wasn't expecting. Butterflies spread their wings inside me, and I get a little hit of happiness at the way I feel around him. Excited, nervous, eager. This is what the beginning of relationships should feel like.

"But when I get back, would you like to... have dinner? We can uh, christen your place." His eyes lift to mine, and I amend my statement. "You know, cook the first meal."

His smile sends flutters through my clit as he replies, "I'd love that."

"I'll text you when I'm home and we can work it out from there. Does that sound okay?" I ask, a smile lifting my lips, even the corners of my eyes.

He nods. "Sounds perfect. I'll be here, waiting for you."

As soon as I'm inside my apartment, with the door closed, I press my back to it, fingers blindly tracing the seam as I breathe in and out heavily, working to steady my labored breathing.

He moved across the hall to make sure I'm safe but I had to ask him to kiss me.

I'm beyond ready to finish what I started when I woke up.

Slipping into the now sun-warmed sheets, I close my eyes, plunge my hand beneath my panties, and in less than thirty seconds, my toes are curling and I'm moaning his name as I have the first orgasm I've had in... a *really* long time.

Because of Cohen.

"How is pursuing friendship going?" Dr. Evans asks as she uncrosses and re-crosses her legs.

She's wearing a pencil skirt the color of a stormy sky, and a ruby colored blouse, with her hair in a fancy bun. The idea of wearing fancy clothes day in and day out to a job does not sound pleasant. Sliding my feet in and out of my Birkenstocks, playing with the hole in the thigh of my jeans, I tell her the truth.

"Good. But… and I don't know how this happened… but it feels like more than friendship." I chance a glance at the Doc, and find her smiling knowingly.

"I can't be ready for this yet, can I?" I ask, all of it seemingly impossibly true, and shockingly too soon. Yet here I am, smiling back at her just thinking of Cohen.

"I'd be cautious of the pace—" she starts, and I tug at the loose strands on my jeans nervously as I interject.

"We're going slow. Really slow. In fact, I had to ask him to kiss me when we had a coffee date yesterday."

She tilts her head a degree or two, enough to throw me off my axis a bit. "And how was it?"

"The kiss?" My hands stop playing with my pants and my feet stop their incessant sliding. I've never been asked about a kiss in therapy. Reading my confusion, Dr. Evans repositions herself in her leather chair, setting her notepad and pen down next to her.

"Did the intimacy bring with it any feelings of anxiousness or, perhaps even fear? With your past, in being essentially forced into sexual acts you were not privy to or on
board with, some residual trauma is to be expected. Even if it
were with a partner you love."

I snort. "I'm not in love."

She bats her thick lashes at me. "No, but you've expressed
that Cohen is kind, and he clearly cares for you. Whether
you're in love or not, how was the kiss? How did it feel?"

I know what she's asking, and it's not about lip softness or
anything else. My voice is quiet and a bit weak when I reply,
"I felt safe. And important, and I've never felt those two
things at once. Ever."

"Where do you see things going from here?" she asks,
picking a piece of fuzz from her skirt. I think part of the
reason I'm so comfortable with Dr. Evans is how she
doesn't focus on me intently the entire session. She allows
for my gaze to uncomfortably sneak away from hers, and
she also focuses on other things to bring me ease. It's
perfect.

"I don't know. I like him, but I don't know." Why does
that truth sour my stomach?

"And you don't have to know. All you have to do is move
through each day, honoring yourself and your newfound
strength." She picks up her notepad, and jots things in it.

"There's something else." A knot ties in my throat.
Whether I'm a porn star or not, talking about your self-love
habits is slightly awkward.

"Oh?"

I clear my throat, push my braid back behind me, and sit
taller.

"I had an orgasm. The first one since... Well, the first one
in a long time."

Her brows cinch. "You've still not had one at Crave, despite the fact everyone is professional and safe?"

I shake my head. "No, not even close. I mean, I enjoy the other actors and the scenes, but it's still all been acting. I mean, at one point I thought whatever synapses in my brain that are connected to my ability to have orgasms were shot, and that maybe I'd never feel that type of pleasure again."

"And how did it feel to achieve orgasm?" she asks, focused on me.

Understanding that she isn't asking how the actual orgasm felt, I take my time formulating my answer. Because it is hard to put into words how complex that orgasm was.

I give it a try. "I really didn't think I could so it was... it exceeded any pleasure in any previous orgasms."

She smiles. "You're not broken, Scarlett. And that orgasm should prove to you that you still work. All parts of you. You're just rebuilding your heart to love and trust again. That's all."

Our time comes to an end, and I collect the appointment card for the session later this week, and head out.

I drive to the organic market a few blocks away, parking in a spot under a crooked "NO PARKING AFTER 6PM" sign. Closing my eyes, I relive the orgasm, I relive the kiss, I relive the feeling of his knuckles softly grazing my inner ankle. Beneath my white crop top, my nipples are hard, and my breasts actually ache when I envision Cohen.

Was that orgasm the flood-gate opener?

Bringing my thighs together beneath the steering wheel, I clench them once, sending a pulse through my groin. I'm wet, I can feel it sticking to my cotton panties. But I'm in public, and I'm not the girl rubbing one out in a parking lot, so I take a steadying breath, grab my purse, and head off to get some groceries.

Inside the store, with my cart full of essentials, I head to the produce section to collect items for a salad. If I'm heading to Cohen's for dinner tonight, I'm going to help make a really good dinner. I want to show him I'm not just needy.

I gather ingredients for a salad, snag a bottle of the clean label dressing I like (and only discovered recently at a cast party at Tucker and Vienna's apartment) and head toward the meat department. Telling the man at the counter just what type of steaks I want, I wander around as I wait for them to be cut and trimmed.

Down one aisle are self-care items, like tampons, PMS pills, and an elaborate assortment of body washes. There's a new one that catches my eye, the word rainfall scrawled across the baby blue bottle in fancy cursive. I don't know what rainfall smells like, and I've never heard of the brand, but I can't take my eyes off of it.

The bottle is tall and bears a rounded cap. The girth of a thin can, with no external label, as the words are printed directly on. It's an undeniably *familiar* shape.

Leaving Pete so suddenly, I took the bare minimum. I left a lot of things because I had to, because I wanted to. And there were many things I didn't need to take. I hadn't thought to use them in years and I didn't want the reminder.

I push my cart a little further down until I'm standing right in front of the rainfall body wash. Heat sears between my legs as I pluck the bottle from the shelf and drop it into my cart.

Maybe I'll go to Cohen's smelling like my new body wash. Maybe by the time I get back to my place I'll feel a lot differently, and I'll laugh at myself as I unpack the bottle onto my counter.

Maybe.

"Miss," a deep voice calls, and I turn to find the man in

the white and bloodied smock holding the white Kraft paper wrapped steaks. "Your steaks are ready."

I head back to him, flames licking my cheeks, and a part of me wants to reach into the cart and drag a loaf of bread over the body wash, to hide it.

"Thank you," I tell the man as he lowers the steaks into my hand over the glass counter. "Have a good day."

"You too, sweetheart," he says, returning to his display of jumbo prawn.

I pay for my groceries, trying hard to focus on the meal I'm planning to make with Cohen. But as I unload the brown bags into the passenger seat and hop into the driver's seat, the blue bottle of body wash sits on top of my other toiletries, taunting me.

I drive a little faster than normal back to my apartment, squeezing my thighs together the entire time, dying to relieve the pressure settled low in my belly. The door to Cohen's apartment is closed when I walk up with my bags, but I notice the large window adjacent to the door is bare. There used to be a dingy curtain covering it, the same as the one currently hanging at my place. I jump a little as his door swings open, his hair damp, gray t-shirt marked with dark spots.

"Hi," I say, a little breathless at the sight of him again so soon. Each time I see him, I notice something new. There's a small scar near his hairline, and when he smiles, a tiny dimple appears in his cheek.

"Hi," he returns, walking to me with his arms out. He unloads my bags into his arms and waits patiently for me to unlock my door. Following me inside, he sets them on my kitchen counter, driving a muscular arm down into one of the bags, unloading.

His large hand cradles the bodywash, and his other hand

holds a box of cereal, and my face grows hot and my knees shaky. "It's okay...I can... you're unpacking. I can unload these. Really," I say, and I don't have to explain it again or say more.

Cohen listens, lowering the two items to the counter. "Okay then," he says, then smiles. He's not angry that I don't want his help, he's not frustrated. He just listens, and does, then smiles.

It's wild.

"I'm going to have a shower and take a nap. I had therapy so I always need to recharge after," I tell him as I walk him out to the breezeway between our places. He stands in his doorway and I stand in mine.

"I do too. I sleep best on my therapy days."

I like that he knows and understands what working through trauma is. And while I still don't know *why* he goes to therapy, I find myself more attracted to him because of it. A man proactive about his mental health is a sexy man.

"I'll text you when I wake up?" I offer, letting my eyes slide down his body. Aside from the sweat-marked t-shirt, he's wearing black sweats, the same thick curve against his thigh. I swallow and blink up at him, unsure he realizes I just totally checked him out.

"Come over when you're ready. I'll be here."

My eyes dart to the exposed window and back to him. He pulls a hand down his face, now veiled in blonde growth. "I want him to know I'm here," he says, and my heart flexes beneath my ribs. He's sacrificing his privacy for my safety, and *now it's time to find the fucking rainfall.*

I look back to him and smile. "I'll be over later. I'm bringing the food."

He nods and watches as I slowly close my door. A moment later I hear him faintly say, "The locks, Scarlett."

I lock the door and turn around, chest heaving, cunt pulsing. I kick off my shoes, snatch the body wash from the counter, and head down the hall. The rest of the groceries can wait.

I can't believe I'm doing this. Well, I can't believe I'm *going* to do this. I'm surrounded by a full plate of beautiful humans every day at work, not to mention all the toys in the world.

But I don't have those toys here. And I don't want those people.

I want to feel something plunge deep inside me, I'm hungry for that sated, fullness that comes only with being fucked slow and deep.

I'm not ready for that with anyone, even Cohen.

But I can simulate it. He's making me miss it, yearn for it even. And the fact that I can even think about doing this is a victory in itself. One I feel strongly is attributed to him and the slow, tender kindness he's shown me.

I wash the bottle off in the bathroom sink, watching suds swirl around the basin. Leaving a trail of my crop top and jeans, I slip into bed and wiggle out of my panties. Reaching down with my empty hand, I spread myself, finding heat and moisture spilling from between my thighs.

Moans long trapped in my chest slip free, and it's never felt so good to feel myself wet and starved. Spreading my legs wide, I look down at my naked body, ends of my blonde hair curling beneath my full breasts, nipples in stiff peaks. My belly trembles with nerves as my breathing grows shallow. Notching the bottle at my entrance, I slowly push inside, and my knees pull to my chest in reaction.

It's thick and spreads me, even more than anticipated since it's been a while.

Burning halos my opening as I push the bottle deeper and deeper, until my stomach whirrs and my groin tightens, and

I'm to the hilt. My eyes close as I imagine Cohen's hand on my foot, his knuckles sweetly grazing my leg, imparting security and closeness, and confidence, too.

He makes me feel protected without feeling babied or pitied, he turns me on without really even handling me at all —oh god. I move the bottle in and out, panting, orgasm already building.

He doesn't even look at me when I'm on set. He treats me —and the other actresses—like professionals, speaking to us while maintaining eye contact and never turning a casual conversation into anything overtly sexual. It's a stark contrast since every man at Jizz did.

I fuck myself faster and harder with the weighty bottle, my cunt hungrily gripping it. My breasts jiggle as I pick up my pace, and I imagine Cohen bringing his mouth to my nipple for the first time. Guiding him to taste and touch me just the way I like—making sure he traced my areola and the hardened nub with the tip of his tongue.

I can almost feel the soft swish of his hair between my fingers as I thread them through, holding his head to me as he licks and worships everything that brings me pleasure.

My knees snap shut as I twist my torso, rolling onto my side as hot, abundant pleasure wraps my entire body, my pussy shuddering around the bottle as my orgasm grabs hold.

"Oh my god," I whine, "holy shit, *oh my god*," I breathe, over and over, my vision dark, mind spinning with pleasure a hundred miles an hour. I push the bottle in and pull it out slowly now, my wrist practically pinned between my knees. Still, I imagine him inside me as I shatter to a million pieces in the best way possible.

Lying on my side, catching my breath, late afternoon painting pinks and purples on my old carpet, I pull the bottle from between my legs and set it on the nightstand adjacent to me.

Glistening and sticky, I stare at that bottle. I don't think even the people who made the damn rainfall body wash have gotten to know it as intimately as I just did. But I think about how, a year ago, after Pete and I had sex—or, rather, after Pete had sex with me—I tried to find pleasure in it. I tried to tell myself that even though I couldn't orgasm during the act, maybe I could finish after and make myself believe that was okay.

Only, my brain stopped allowing me to experience that kind of pleasure. And then work became impossible, and my body hadn't reverted until this morning.

He's the reason I can do this now. The reason my mind can even go anywhere but panic when I'm aroused. Cohen, it's all because of him.

I close my eyes, tired of staring at the bottle, tired of thinking. We're having dinner tonight, and I'd like to cook him a nice meal.

Feeling excited for the first time in a long time, I forgo the post-therapy nap and instead get to my feet, putting away my groceries and wiping down the kitchen. I have energy unlike I've had in months, and I'm eager to have a perfect night with Cohen, *my new friend.*

fourteen

. . .

cohen

She sees through the veil

I hit the gym after moving my stuff over. Swam laps. Lots and lots of laps.

I went much, much later than my normal time and in turn, was met with a pretty populated pool.

I don't know if it was the group of elderly women with floral swim caps huddled near the stairs. I don't know if it was the twenty-something guy doing the breaststroke, or the two women in the spa adjacent to the pool. Maybe it was all of them, the crowd of people inadvertently steering me away from my bad habits.

But for whatever reason, I didn't hold myself under. I didn't test the strain of my lungs, the limits of my mind—not even once. I swam beneath the surface, from one end to the other, rising up to collect air before dunking down, turning and doing it over and over again.

Probably just the crowd.

After my swim, I stop by a small deli, eat a sandwich and pick up sweets for Scarlett. By the time I get home to receive my mattress and box spring delivery, I'm ready for a nice shower. I check my phone as I turn the water on, grabbing a towel from my open suitcase. I only own two, and suddenly that seems... nomadic.

SCARLETT

> Shit. I forgot to ask—do you have a pan? Cast iron ideally but anything would do. I got steaks.

> No. Do you want me to run out and buy one?

I glance at the time at the top of my phone, realizing if I have to drive to a department store in the city at nearly 6pm, we won't be eating until well after 9. Closer to ten if she likes her steak well done.

> No! Shit. I'll be over in ten, if that works?

I stick my hand under the falling water, which is now pretty hot.

> Perfect.

In the shower, I think about what it was like dating *her*. Before things were serious and they were still new and exciting. I'd jerk off in the shower before every date, giving myself a leg up on a long, lazy night in bed.

Soaping up, I reach down and cup my balls, getting them sudsy. I don't know how many showers I've taken where all the elements are there, the stars have aligned and yet... I do not touch myself. I've told my therapist this plenty of times but it all started because I didn't feel worthy of any pleasure, and eventually, I didn't even feel worthy of anything at all. Only guilt, with a side of easing grief.

With close to three minutes already spent soaking up the hot water, letting it run through my hair and down my shoulders, I know I don't have a lot of time. When I take my cock in my palm, I look down to confirm what my hand already knows—I'm hard. Very fucking hard.

My arm works as my fist clenches, and my head tips back as a roar of a groan leaves my chest hollow.

It feels good.

And I could finish. *I could.*

It's there—release—creeping through my sack, burning my groin, making my stomach clench. There have been plenty of nights waking up with this feeling melting away from me, my sweats sticky, or my belly damp. But right now, awake and by choice, I would be able to orgasm, and though I drop my cock, smearing my soapy palm over my chest, *I could have.*

That's not something I could have said truthfully for years.

As I hop out, I pull the towel through my hair before looping it around my waist and add toothpaste to my brush. But then there's a knock at the door. I glance at my phone, which unsurprisingly has no new messages. I spit out the toothbrush after a few quick but powerful swipes, and hustle toward the front door, leaving a trail of water behind me.

Her eyes sweep my chest the moment I open the door,

then her brow pinches. "Oh no, I'm early," she steps back toward her place but I reach out quickly, taking her wrist.

"It's fine," I say, releasing her wrist. "I was running late. I stayed at the gym too long," I explain as she timidly comes through the door, sliding off her shoes. With one hand gripping the towel, I close and lock the door with the other, turning to find her rosy cheeked.

She's staring at her bare feet. My vision catches on the wall, and my chest flexes at seeing her sandals lined up with mine. "I'll just wait right here while you... put a dress on." She slaps her palm to her forehead, shaking it. "Get dressed, not put a dress on." She waves a hand up and down my torso without looking. "Not gonna lie, your semi-nakedness took me off guard."

I cock a brow that she can't see is cocked. "That's... interesting," I comment, walking past her toward my room. The apartment is a two-bedroom, and I chose the one that is closest to the door. I pop in and grab a clean pair of sweats—because it's either sweats or jeans and since she's wearing sweats and a tank top, sweats it is.

Feeding my hand through my shirt, I call to her. "You're around and work with nude people all day. Do you need time to adjust to them on set, too?" I ask, genuinely curious. I don't pay close attention to the scenes and the actors' interactions.

Appearing in the hallway, smoothing my fingers through my damp, uncombed hair, I find her leaning over the kitchen counter waiting for me.

Her eyes come to mine across the apartment as I make my way toward her.

"No," she says, her answer low, her voice brimming with subtext. "Just you, Cohen," she says even softer, making the hairs on my neck stand up. "And hey," she adds, changing the mood immediately, straightening her spine as she looks around my empty kitchen. "I wasn't thinking straight when I picked up the stuff for dinner. I don't really have anything beyond a pot with a lid and a tiny, single-serve coffee machine. And by the looks of it, you don't have much either."

She crouches, opening my cabinets to unsurprisingly discover they're bare. "We won't be cooking," she says flatly.

I reach for my phone, and pass it to her because I notice she came over here with only the keys to her apartment. "Call your favorite place for delivery, and we'll stay in."

Because I have no furniture, she drifts toward the far wall, putting her back to it, sliding down into a puddle. Long, lean legs stretched before her, soles of her feet exposed, she pinches her attention to my phone, fingers moving fast over the screen.

She seems so comfortable, and her comfort satisfies me. Dialing the phone, she cups her hand to the receiver and asks, "Do you think they'll deliver wine?"

"Where'd you order from?" I ask, knowing that in the city, many places will.

"The Italian place around the corner from Crave." Her face falls. "Is that okay? Do you like Italian?"

My stomach clenches, hunger tearing through at just the mention. "I love Italian."

"Yes," she says happily, returning to the phone. A second later she sighs, "sure."

Looking back at me, she says, "We're on hold. But I guess that's good because I should tell you... I'd planned on ordering a few of my favorites, and us splitting them all. But now that feels weird and selfish and—"

"Do it," I say eagerly, anxious to know what her favorite Italian dishes are. And I'm excited to share a real meal with her, despite the fact neither of us really have tables or chairs to have a proper meal. Still, chairs and table or not, even if we use plastic cutlery, food with Scarlett, just the two of us, is… a perfect date. "I can't wait."

She keeps her eyes on me, the maître d' clearly taking her order. She speaks clearly, ordering bolognese, spinach lasagna with ricotta, tortellini with brown butter and sage, and a large caprese salad. She orders tiramisu and two bottles of red, asking them to please bring plastic utensils and styrofoam cups.

When she ends the call, she gets to her feet and walks my phone to me. Her fingertips graze my palm as she places my phone there, eyes still holding mine. "Pete ordered for me. He never let me choose. He always said, *you'll get something you won't like, you'll complain and it'll be a total waste.*"

Though she doesn't draw the parallel, I know why she's saying this. I close my hand around the phone. "I want you to have exactly what you want."

She sighs as her eyes flit between mine, the oxygen between us thin, the apartment shrinking. "Somehow, I believe that, Cohen."

"I hope you do." I take her hand, and lead us back to the wall where she sat, and we sit adjacent to each other in the corner of the room, our backs to the walls. Her bare feet graze mine, and she does it over and over, dragging the ball of her foot along mine, and it's so private and tender. But she talks as if the gentle movement isn't a big deal to her, so I ignore the clutching in my chest reminding me how good it feels to have this type of casual intimacy.

Reminding me how much I've missed it.

"So tell me about Michigan," she says, wrapping the end of her hair around her finger, smiling at me. I like that she came over here in sweats with no makeup.

But I'm not ready to talk about Michigan, so I give the question a wide berth. "I grew up there, lived there my whole life, but needed a change of scenery and... well, needed a fresh start."

"I get that," she comments.

"I came out here, met Aug—"

She interrupts, so interested in soaking me up that she can't wait. My cheeks tingle a little. "Where and how did you meet Aug? I feel like everyone has a crazy story about meeting Aug."

I smile. "Do you?"

She untwirls her hair, tucking it behind her ears on both sides at once, leaning forward, her foot still grazing mine. "Yes, definitely. And when I retell it, it kind of sounds like a movie or something." Her gaze snaps to her foot stroking mine, as if she's only just now realized, and she stops, crossing her ankles, moving her foot away from mine. "Sorry," she says quietly.

Leaning over my lap, I reach out and take her by the ankle, gently replacing her foot where it was. "That was soothing to you," I tell her, because clearly it was. "And I liked it, too." I have to work to ignore the buzz in my cock when she again drags her foot along mine. Gooseflesh rises up my legs beneath my sweats, but I keep my eyes focused on her, not on all the new things she's making me feel.

"Well, I was in spin class and he came in. He asked if I'd go next door with him to get coffee, so I did. He told me he was aware I was working at Jizzabelle, aware that I was in a relationship with Pete Bryson, and wanted to know if I'd be willing to come to Crave under an entirely different structure and system. One where adult films are safe, and the production company is family." She shakes her head, her vision unfocused as she relives it. "I laughed at him. I didn't think that was possible. And I also told him to fuck off."

I'm surprised by that. "What did he say when you told

him to fuck off?"

A tiny smile curls her lips. "He put a hand on my shoulder and said, that's one thing that will be different at Crave. One of many. And I asked what he was talking about and he said, you will be able to trust that people mean what they say. Because everyone at Crave is quality."

"He's right."

Her glazed eyes come to mine. "I know." She swallows, and her foot grazes mine again. "Anyway, he knew Pete from industry events and apparently, heard from actors that had defected from Jizz that Pete had... gotten worse."

She drops her hands to the floor, splayed against the carpet around her, as if steadying herself. Pushing off the floor, I take a seat next to her, and place my hand over the top of hers before sliding my bare foot beneath hers.

I want her to know I'm here, and selfishly, I needed our hands to touch again. I needed that subtle connection. She turns her palm up to face mine, and at the same time, we curl our fingers, interlocking our hands.

"You want to be a programmer still?" I ask, remembering how she'd said she dropped out of school.

She nods. "I really do. And I never planned on quitting school but... Pete kept telling me how big I was getting and how much money I was making and... I kept thinking, if I just do it a few more years, I can pay for school outright, you know? And the truth is, I have always been sex positive. Initially, I liked making movies."

"Initially," I repeat slowly.

She stares at our linked hands. "The beginnings of things are always good, right?"

I nod. "Relationships, yes, war documentaries, not usually."

She giggles and smiles up at me, and our heads tip against

the wall. Her eyes veer to my Adam's apple then to my lips before she rolls her head to face forward. "I quickly learned that Pete was the problem, but we were already living together, I still had a year on my contract, and I hadn't made all the money I needed to go back to school." She swallows thickly, pain etching her features as she turns to face me. "There were other things I wanted, so I can't lie and tell you Pete was the sole reason I dropped out. Something happened, and I had some big realizations about what I wanted in life. And he promised it to me, but instead, held it over my head like a fucking carrot to a horse. So yeah, it was bad there and Pete was a complete asshole, but I chose to stay. He never forced me."

"The contract forced you," I add, trying to alleviate some of her guilt.

She nods. "Yeah, but that was secondary to other things that happened."

Other things bobs between us, ominous and foreboding. The oak tree outside swishes, and the setting sun dips below the horizon, taking the remaining orange glow with it. She hops to her feet and turns on the light, returning to her spot on the floor next to me.

"People have it wrong, you know?" she muses, in what I hope is a rhetorical question that will lead me to better knowing her. I stay quiet, but link our hands again, more for me than her I think. She curls her fingers into my knuckles as she holds my hand tightly, and I cross at the ankle to divert the buzz running up my legs.

"It's not the industry. It's not porn. They're just... scapegoats." She twists to face me, blonde hair framing her face. "It's people. Bad people hurting and taking advantage of other people, plain and simple. Aug asked me if I associate porn with my trauma and my answer was no. Because porn at Crave is beautiful. It wasn't the act of on-camera sex that traumatized me. It was Pete's direction, what the actors did. It's *people* that ruin things, and each other."

It's people *that ruin things, and each other.* That sentence echoes through my mind as a hard knock comes down on the apartment door. I jump to my feet and snatch my wallet from the kitchen counter fringing the front door.

"Can I pay?" Scarlett asks from her spot on the floor. I blink at her, remove a few bills from my wallet, and hold them out to her.

She laughs. "Not with your money, with mine."

I blink again. "Never."

Then I open the door, feeling her eyes on my profile as I exchange money for bags of food, and two bottles of wine, leaving the delivery driver with a generous tip.

After locking the door, I turn to Scarlett, lifting the bags. Her eyes are wide, and I swear she licks her lips. "That smells so good."

I nod, realizing one crucial mistake. I look in the bags, then up at her. "Bad news."

"The Italian food has arrived and bad news are not two things I like in the same sentence," she says, rolling the waistband on her sweats after getting to her feet. She peers in the bags and looks up at me, our faces just a few inches apart.

"Wine bottle opener," she says, blinking at me. I can't help but smile.

"Yep."

She makes her way to the door, sliding her feet in her sandals. I place the bags gently on the floor and grab her hand, waffling our fingers together.

"You set up on our floor-table, I'll go to the corner store for a corkscrew," I say, sliding my sneakers on, nabbing a baseball cap from the counter. I only own one, and I rarely wear it, because it's from my other life. I couldn't bear to toss it, and it's the only thing I kept. I tug it down over my still damp hair. "Lock the door, I'll be right back."

She peers up at the emblem on the hat, then back down into my eyes. "Okay."

I stand outside of my own door until I hear the chain slide into the grooves, locking the door. Then I shove my hands in my pockets, take the stairs two by two, and head down the street.

"Siblings?" she asks, holding out her styrofoam cup for me to refill. We've already killed a bottle of wine. I haven't drank in so long, just two glasses has my veins buzzing.

"None. And my parents passed away when I was fourteen."

She lowers the cup, her lips stained ruby from the booze. "Oh my god, Cohen, I'm so sorry. What did you do? Where did you go?"

I pass her the styrofoam clamshell with the lasagna. We decided to open each course, one at a time, and take a few bites until we were ready for the next. We started with the salad, which was good, and now we're on lasagna.

"I stayed with my grandfather until I was seventeen, but then he died, too."

"Jesus, Cohen," she drawls, draping her hand on my inner

thigh. We haven't touched since we stopped holding hands earlier, and even though she's not making a move on me, her hand on my thigh tells my brain otherwise, and my cock begins hardening. I don't have a pillow to place on my lap, and I've already passed her the lasagna, so I sit there, willing my growing erection to stop. But she keeps her hand on me as she takes a bite, and my cock has been starved for so long, he doesn't listen to me.

If she notices, she doesn't let on. She squeezes my leg, eyes wet, and says, "I'm sorry that happened to you."

My stomach roils with sickness at her words. She has no idea who she's apologizing to. The things I've done, or haven't done. What my past is really like.

Her kindness stings me, but I try to focus on my therapist's words. That I deserve happiness. That I have to stop punishing myself.

"I lived on my own from there on out. Fortunately, I inherited my grandfather's house and money, so I got through college just fine." I take a drink of the wine. "What about you?"

She stares at the spinach lasagna for a moment before bringing a forkful to her mouth. I reach out, pushing her hair behind her shoulder so it doesn't get into her food. When she's finished her bite, she looks at me. "My parents, well... I think they're doing good." Her smile is sad. "They kind of cut contact when they realized I'd dropped out of school to... act."

"You told them?" I ask, somewhat surprised. I've overheard plenty of the actors at Crave say they tell their parents they're extras in mid-grade films. I don't fault them for lying; I understand wanting to preserve a relationship, even if you're going about it in all the wrong ways.

"No," she says, her tone snarky as she passes me the clam

shell. I take a bite, and holy shit is it rich. The ricotta is in the lasagna is smooth and buttery, the noodles the perfect mix of soft and al dente, the spinach fresh. I've been eating sandwiches and soups from the deli near Crave for... years. "Pete told them. Once when we were in a fight, he texted my dad and..."

I nearly choke on the delicious lasagna. "He *what*?"

She nods, taking a long pull of red wine. "Yep," she says after a loud swallow. "And yes, I stayed with him for another year after that." When she looks at me, I see the booze coloring her cheeks, weighing down her eyelids. "A story for another day. Or a story for a day where there's more wine, I think. Because it makes me sound way too pathetic to tell you about this sober."

"You're not pathetic." I smile at her. "Or sober."

She points at me. "That is true." Extending her arm, she wiggles her empty cup. "And I have no plans to sober up. Fill 'er up."

I pour us each more wine, and we sip slowly as we start the next course. Bolognese and holy shit, my lips actually tingle at the rich flavors. She watches me as I eat, and I try not to moan like a creep but Jesus. I forgot food is also enjoyable, not just to ease the growling.

As if attuned to me, her voice is quiet when she asks, "What do you normally eat?"

I finish my bite, and drink from my wine, calculating my response. "Soup or a sandwich for lunch, from the deli down the street from Crave."

"What about dinner?" she asks, twirling her fork in the noodles.

I stare at the unmoving surface of wine in my cup and look over at her. "A protein bar. Sometimes another sandwich."

She blinks a few times, confused by my answer. Probably confused as to why I eat the same thing every day, or sometimes hardly eat at all. "Do you ever go out to eat?"

"Only with Crave," I admit.

"Do you love sandwiches and soup?" she asks, eyes flitting between mine, her focus unspooling all of my tightly wound secrets. I want to spill, to tell her every fucking thing kept locked deep inside me, but I know that's the wine, so I stick the simple truths instead of the entire saga.

"No."

She nods, trying to make all of the complicated pieces of Cohen fit into place. "You're fit; are the sandwiches and soup part of a health regime or something?" She asks like she already knows the answer, but I respond anyway.

"No."

Holding my eyes, she leans over me, bringing her fork spun full of pasta to my mouth. "Open," she whispers the command, and I obey easily. She slips the loaded fork into my mouth and I close my lips around it. "You deserve good food," she says plainly, completely unaware that she's nailed the trauma right on the fucking head.

Deserving.

I've not felt deserving of anything for so long.

She slowly pulls the fork from lips then presses her mouth to mine in a short but sweet kiss. I chew and swallow the bolognese, my heartbeat going a million miles a minute, and lean down, taking her mouth with mine. We taste like wine and pasta, sadness and hope. I like the way we taste, I love how her lips fit against mine.

"Tell me more about you, Cohen Steele," she breathes, her sweet breath flanking my senses, causing another stirring below the waist.

"I'm thirty," I tell her. "I'm from Michigan, which you

already know. And I like baseball, documentaries, and swimming."

She glances over to the counter when I left my baseball cap when I returned. "Big Tigers fan?"

I follow her gaze to the faded cap. A momento from another life; I kept it to remind me that at one time in my life, I really lived. Even though it ended in flames licking at every ounce of happiness I had left, burning me down, leaving me a pile of ash, I did live. And love. In a different life.

"Not really," I admit. "But it meant something to me before, when I lived in Michigan."

She sighs. "I know what that's like. That's how I felt about my music box, the one Pete destroyed. It was the only thing I carried from my past, when my parents still loved me and I didn't know what true darkness was like." She smiles sadly at me, her blonde hair glowing from the bright light overhead.

"You're so beautiful, Scarlett."

Her lips part, and she leans in, but stops herself. "When you're ready, I'm here," she says, sending a shiver down my spine at how aware she is of my wounds. How I've spent so many years hiding them, hiding myself—yet in just a couple of hours with her, she sees through the veil. She knows pain when she sees it.

I nod, but say nothing. She reaches for the wine and refills our cups. We pass the other dish back and forth, taking small bites, when she lets out a sigh. "We need furniture."

I know what she means. She means both of us, independently, need to furnish our places. But for a split second, I envision us picking couches and lamps for a home we share together. For *our* place.

Another first poured into my lap courtesy of Scarlett.

"We do."

She pulls her hair into a messy bun, securing it with an elastic from her wrist. The soft slope of her neck calls to me, making my lips tingle and again, my cock thick with need. My mind whirrs from booze and excitement, and it's almost too much to handle.

Right when panic is clutching at my throat, and all of this is about to become too overwhelming, and I start to question why I thought I could protect and take care of her when I'm so fucked up, she tips to the side, resting her head on my thigh.

"Stroke your hand through my hair, Cohen," she says softly, her eyes closed. "When you touch me, my world feels safe and right. And you're the first to make me feel that," she says, her words slurring softly.

My chest tightens with her truth. That's exactly how I want her to feel, and her admission alleviates the panic that held me by the throat just a moment ago.

I stroke my fingers through her hair, and a moment later, she snores softly, the wine getting the best of her.

She's comfortable enough to sleep in my lap, and that fact has me pushing through the discomfort of fighting. Fighting to make myself believe this could be possible, that I could have what I once had, again, and deserve it.

I stroke her hair and look at her body next to me, enjoying her warmth. After a few minutes, I pull her entire body into my lap, rock forward, and rise with her in my arms. She doesn't even stir.

I didn't get a chance to buy new sheets for my new bed—and all the sheets at the other house, along with everything in the room, were theirs. I do, however, have one large fuzzy blanket and a matching pillow. Darla, the woman whom I rented the room from, didn't let me leave without it. She and her husband never knew my story, but she sensed pain in me I think.

I agreed to take the blanket and pillow and now I'm glad I did.

I lower Scarlett to my brand new mattress, sliding the fuzzy pillow beneath her head. Then I pull the blanket up over her, and smooth her hair out on the pillow behind her so it doesn't tangle. I rinse out her wine cup and fill it with water, placing it on the floor next to the bed.

After cleaning up the food, and turning off the light, I settle onto the old carpet in the living room using a balled up sweatshirt as a pillow. Scarlett's drunken snores echo through the empty apartment, and the floor nips at me, sending an ache through my hips.

Still, this is the best night I've had in years.

And I sleep well.

I'm handing a wad of cash to a delivery driver in the doorway when Scarlett wakes, sauntering out of my bedroom in a way that makes me envision her doing this every fucking day. My eyes widen at the fantasy, and through a yawn she asks, "Why the eyes?"

"Ah, nothing." I lift the bag. "Breakfast is here."

She rubs her palms together. "Not gonna lie, I could get used to being taken care of like this."

Before I can think about it, I say, "I wish you would." Quickly, I pull clamshells from the bag and set them on the counter, flipping them open.

"Eggs," I say. "Pancakes," I add, then opening the last one, she swoons, "Bacon."

"The perfect antidote to two bottles of red wine," I say, grabbing a paper plate from the bag. I asked the guy to bring paper plates, disposable cups and utensils. "Tell me what you want, and I'll make your plate. Have a seat, I'll bring it to you."

She looks at me like I'm suddenly speaking gibberish.

"You okay?"

Nodding, she reties her hair as she moves across the apartment, sitting exactly where she sat last night. "I've never had a partner serve me, or want to serve me," she says. "I mean, you're not—we aren't—" She shakes her head, messy bun sliding around the top of her head. "You know what I mean." With a nod, she adds, "And I like all of that, so fill me up."

I freeze over the containers, the comment lighting a fire beneath my skin. Out of nowhere, I envision myself over her, inside of her, pumping, groaning, eating up her sweet and soft moans while I flood her with years of pent up release. She takes it, she loves it, she presses her hand to her lower belly and moans of her sated fullness. Of the life I leave inside of her.

I make her plate and take it to her, not meeting her eyes. But she takes my wrist, and forces me to find her gaze. "Thank you, Cohen," she says. "I appreciate it."

"Of course," I say with a smile. I make myself a plate and this time, I sit across the room with my back to the opposing wall. What I feel for her, what I see with her… it's currently overwhelming me. I take bites of warm eggs and think of the pool at the gym, and how much I want to go for a swim right now. How much I need to sink below the surface and keep myself there to sort out my head. Because beneath the surface, the truth is always clear. *You belong here, with nothing but memories to haunt you. You do not deserve another chance at it.* The water practically whispers that, I swear.

"Thank you for taking care of me last night. Buying dinner and putting me in your bed, all of it," she says before biting the end off a crispy piece of bacon. She licks her fingers, and my previously dormant dick twitches a little. I cross my legs at the ankle, subtly telling him to back down.

I'm not ready for that, and I know she isn't either.

I get to my feet and collect the sweets I'd picked up yesterday, and bring them back. "I got these for you yesterday, thought you'd like them today."

She grins. "Why Cohen Steele, that's mighty presumptuous of you. Thinking I was going to spend the night."

I hand her the box and love how her eyes go wild and wide at the sight of gourmet cupcakes. She lifts the Oreo one from the box and licks the frosting. Her tone serious, her face soft, she says, "Thank you Cohen."

The two of us eat and discuss our plans for the day, and Scarlett tells me she's going to meet Vienna at Crave, even though it's a Saturday, because they're still working on the final prototype of her sex toy. I like knowing she'll be at Crave, because the place is teeming with security cameras and gates, and now that Otis knows Bryan is Pete, she'll be safe there.

She kisses my cheek before she leaves, one palm splayed against my pec as she does. I know we're not a couple, and that she'll be safe at work, but still, panic rises inside me as I watch her unlock her apartment door and step inside.

"Text me when you get to and leave Crave, so I know you're safe," I blurt out.

She turns on her heel, smiling at me. "Thank you for giving a shit."

I don't know what to say to that, and she closes the door, leaving me with the memory of her smile, and the scent of her hair all over my apartment and in my bed.

I'm thinking things I shouldn't, so I grab my still-packed gym bag and head out. Swimming will clear my head and bring me back down to reality.

It always does.

Two hours. That's how long I was in the pool at the gym. And for two hours, I swam laps and tried desperately to stay under, to find that panic and darkness that usually has no trouble locating me.

But the entire time, all I wanted to do was keep swimming. My brain kept telling me to rise up and grab a breath, the exact opposite of all the other things it'd been telling me for years.

So after too many laps, my skin pruned and my feet sore from the rough bottom of the pool, I got out. I rinsed off in the gym shower, driving home in a daze.

I swam without wanting to drown.

I swam without punishing myself.

I swam, like a normal human being. And I have yet another hard-on, too.

fifteen

. . .

scarlett

Things are getting better. I'm fucking manifesting that.

"Really?" I ask Vienna, who is busy sliding pocket pussies into plastic bags, the cooler door held open by her hip. She says two more casts and she should have the official, final prototype. I'm actually looking forward to it, more than before.

She nods. "Yep. He wants to be a stay at home dad when the time comes. Can you believe it?"

I shake my head. "That's awesome, Vienna." I always imagined myself staying home with my children, the ones I've dreamed about in my future. That dream now seems further away than ever before. And I thought with Pete I was getting so close to *having it all.*

"How about you?" I ask, knowing that I'd be the one to

stay home with the kids. I'd want that. I've craved that. "You think you'll ever want to trade places and stay at home?"

She considers the question, and answers honestly. "No. I mean, I will love my children to bits and pieces, that much I'm positive of. But I also know myself. I'm better working in an adult atmosphere. I'd be way too on edge otherwise." She lifts her pitcher of Earth colored mix, pouring it into the top of her molding cast. "What about you? Do you want to be a stay at home parent some day?"

"I want to be a mom," I reply quickly, because those are words I haven't been able to say aloud for some time. Those words were the rocky, unstable base of many terrible arguments between me and Pete. The word *mom* still feels like it's bad and I don't have the right to speak it. But Vienna nods, and I realize, Pete can't soil this anymore. "I want to be a mom so bad," I say again, feeling a surge of confidence as it occurs to me that I'm free to have, be and do whatever I want now. Vienna's eyes come to mine in the mirror across from us, her mixture slowing down as she nears the end of the pour. "But I do think I'd like to work still."

She smiles. "Same, I think I'd go stir crazy."

"I'd want to stay home while they're young, but then when they get older, go back to work."

She grins, nudging her glasses up her nose as she wipes the spout of the pitcher, ending the now trickling stream. "Them, huh? How many kids do you want?"

I sigh, considering her words. Having one felt nearly insurmountable, nothing more than an impossible dream I was unwilling to let go of. But now I can honestly consider it. "At least two but maybe even three."

Vienna nods as she rinses the pitcher. "Where's the ceiling?"

"Four, because five gets to the point where you need a special vehicle and one's left out," I say easily, as if I've planned this out before. I haven't, but it's so exciting to even talk about it, I get a little giddy.

"I think Tuck is wired like you," Vienna admits. "He wants like, endless children. I told him, my uterus isn't a high-capacity hotel. A few guests, then we close it up."

I laugh at Vienna. She always makes me laugh and honestly, I'm so glad Aug introduced me to her before a lot of the others. She's sweet and quirky, and her off-beat personality brings my walls down. I know whatever I say or share, Vienna will never judge.

"So," she starts, twisting the faucet, waiting for the water to turn warm. She wears gloves but her arms still manage to take a healthy dose of compounding material. "You asked about Cohen the other day," Vienna starts, and immediately I tense.

Asking about him then felt silly and embarrassing, but talking about him now, with Vienna, doesn't necessarily feel right. But I like Vienna, and cutting her off at the knees with a cold *I don't want to talk about this* doesn't feel right either.

"We've been..." I consider saying hanging out, but that sounds so immature and completely devaluing of the time we have been spending together. "Spending time together," I say instead, watching her face closely for a reaction.

Her brows lift as her glasses slip down the bridge of her nose, a mile-wide smile on her face. "Really? Oh that's so great, Cohen is so sweet."

"It's not like, anything though," I quickly add, because the idea of Cohen walking in this room and overhearing me describe him as my boyfriend is so cringe it makes me want to tear my skin off.

"What do you guys do?" she asks, her focus on the metal rack loaded with bagged pussies. This building is full of shocking things, and it's funny to me that a locking chest full of pocket pussies doesn't even garner a second glance from either of us.

"We went to coffee twice. He's come to my place once. And we hung out at his place a couple of nights ago." I smile at her, the back of my nose suddenly burning. "He bought me cupcakes. He makes sure I lock the door. He hasn't made a move on me. He's just... so sweet and kind."

Vienna smiles, the ends of her hair curling around the button on her overalls strap. "Just because he hasn't made a move yet doesn't mean he doesn't want to." She unties the apron at the back of her neck, and then again at her tailbone, then slips it off over her head. "It was hard for you at Jizz-abelle, right? I mean, I'm sorry—" she winces a little, like she's spilled the beans. But the truth is, I always assumed the gossip made it here. "I was just gonna say, I've heard that Jizzabelle and their director really mistreated you."

"Pete Bryson is the director and my ex. He was very trau-matizing on many levels, yes," I say, making sure my voice doesn't give over to a waver. I keep my chin high.

"Well," Vienna says, returning her focus to the sink where she turns the water back on, plugging the bottom of the basin. "Maybe Cohen is moving slow because he knows—"

"I'm damaged?" I interject, laughing a little, silently wincing at the truth.

"Not what I was going to say!" Vienna giggles, flipping a dark braid over her shoulder to her back. "I was going to say, he's likely moving slow because he knows Pete is your ex and can assume since Pete's a total shithead, that he treated you like shit, too."

"You know what," I say, my words vibrating with raw truth. "I hope you're right. And I can't believe I'm moving on already. I didn't expect this to happen. But I'm feeling things I really thought I'd lost forever."

"I love that for you so much," she beams, wearing a genuine smile.

The timer sounds and while we wait for the mold to set, Vienna cleans up the entire work room. Putting a new pair of gloves on, she comes between my spread legs, running her finger up and down the sides of the devices. Pretty soon, it suctions and releases me, and she pulls the toy off, leaving a towel in my hand.

I clean up while she double checks everything is cleaned up and turned off, and we head out into the hall together.

"I need to grab my stuff from my dressing room," I say, hooking my thumb over my shoulder in the other direction.

Vienna peers up and down the hall. "I don't think anyone is here. Want me to go with you?"

I shake my head, waving her off. There are cameras surrounding this place, and you need an ID card to get in. And minus the twenty minute stint yesterday morning, Pete's calls have slowed down some.

Things are getting better. I'm fucking manifesting that.

"No, it's fine, seriously. Go home, tell Tuck I said hi," I say, having not seen Tucker in a few weeks. Because I do so much solo work, I often film in the pocket hours, the time between core takes.

She pulls me into a hug, and right then it occurs to me.

"We're friends," I say, waving a finger between us, probably looking completely insane, bouncing a little on the balls of my feet, eyes wide.

But Vienna matches my energy, shaking her head. "Yes!"

she squeals, "Of course we're friends. I think of you as a friend."

I pull her into me, practically smothering her. She laughs with me, and I totally see why Tucker is so completely enamored.

Letting her free so that she doesn't start to wish she had someone to walk her out, I explain myself. Because, she is my friend after all.

"My therapist said I needed to make a friend and open up to them. And I thought I was doing that with Cohen. And… I was, I mean, I am. But it feels very controlled with him. Like I'm choosing when to share, what to share. You know? But in there," I motion to the space we just left. "I told you how I feel about Cohen. I told you I'm seeing him. And I didn't really measure words. It just… came out. Easily." I sigh as she beams back at me, clearly clued into the subtext. "I made a friend, I'm not damaged and Pete was most certainly wrong," I say, hearing the words I've said to myself a million times, but today, feeling them with my whole fucking chest.

Vienna leans in, her eyes narrowing in intensity as she snarls, "Fuck Pete."

I stick out a closed fist, and we bump knuckles. She heads out, and I hear the door chirp as it locks behind her. After getting my bag from my dressing room and throwing on my favorite hoodie and sweatpants, I slip out into the hall, eager to leave. Eager to go home and… see what Cohen is doing.

But I stop in my tracks at the end of the hall, hypnotized by the neon light in the corner of the studio. In front of it, a beautiful silhouette of blurred darkness, Cohen stands, arms up, tying off a cord that swings from a boom arm.

I look around at the stagnant life around us; the untouched set with a bed ruffled from sex, cameras with shiny lenses exposed, screens dark, waiting for a story to be told. Everything in this studio is on pause until tomorrow. Except us.

"Hey," I say, my quiet voice carrying through the empty space easily. Cohen falls to his heels, letting his arms lower to his sides as he faces me.

"Hey."

I feel it. Standing fifteen feet apart, in the empty studio, no one here, no one but us. *I feel it.* The buzzing between our bodies, the invisible tie that binds, the thing that makes me fall asleep in his lap and want to touch myself again.

Whatever it is, the hard to hold, difficult to explain, and even more challenging to find… I've found it. And it bounces back and forth, wrapping around us, tying us together each moment that passes.

It's terrifying. My cuts haven't healed, and there *will* be scars. Scars that need aftercare, and things I'll need to do for myself before I can belong to anyone else, trust anyone else.

But maybe two great things can exist at once.

Maybe healing and great love can coexist. Maybe they can feed off of each other or even coil together, merging to create something so full of depth and complexity that it supersedes any other fears or challenges. Experiencing those canonic moments simultaneously, maybe that can happen. And we'll survive it, richer in character, stronger in soul, happier in heart.

I'd risk it for him. Even if I don't think I'm ready, my heart pounds as his feet move toward me. It chants to me, whispering, echoing through my veins; *trust him, take him, heal him, own him, love him.*

"About to call it a day?" I ask, noticing that his eyes veer to my mouth just once, and my stomach drops in response. I live now to gather his crumbs of interest, to exist in them and bask in the feeling of being cared for by him.

There's no question if I want him; I do. But what man, gentlemen or not, is going to start a relationship with someone who isn't quite sure if they can be intimate?

I want to touch myself, yes, but that's not the same as giving myself that way.

I'm afraid. Of what, I don't know. But nonetheless, I'm afraid. And I want him, but my fears scream in my ear that wanting is not enough.

"Yes," he says, unclipping the utility belt slung on his waist. He walks toward his office, but not before linking our hands together. Wetness spills from my center as his solid fingers wrap my palm tightly. I love that he doesn't just weave our fingers together. He actually holds my hand.

Beneath my hoodie, my nipples harden, and I'm sure they're hard enough to pierce even a sweatshirt at this point. I want him. But being horny and turned on after a long spell of believing I couldn't orgasm doesn't mean I can actually give myself that way with a man this soon.

They forced their way inside me when I didn't give my consent, and sometimes, I wake at night, legs thrashing. Fighting back the way I wanted to but couldn't then.

He pulls the chair out from his desk and motions for me to sit. I hadn't intended we stay in his office long enough to need to sit, but when he sticks his arm out that way, chivalrous and silent, a loyal knight at my beck and call, I sit.

Hanging the belt on a silver hook behind his desk, his fingers work the length of his shirt, popping open each button. He peels the blue and emerald flannel off, exposing a fitted black t-shirt, clinging everywhere just perfectly.

I'm almost concerned I'm going to leave a wet spot on his office chair at this point. I clench my thighs to send pulses through my pussy, hoping to egg on the tingling or bring it to a stop. But this continual buzzing inside me is torture.

"How was your day?" he asks, pinching the collar of the stripped shirt under his chin, bringing the arms together, folding it. He unzips his open bag and layers the shirt over something else black inside.

"Good," I reply, my voice hoarse, my pulse throbbing in the hollow of my throat. "I'm tired, though. You know, a lot of standing around today for casting and promotional shots."

He blinks, scratching at the side of his jaw. Then he lowers to a knee, taking one of my feet between his hands. Slipping my sandal off, he rests my heel on his kneecap and proceeds to softly knead my sore, tired feet. Beneath my sweats, I'm soaking wet, my sex clenching and pulsing each time his thumb slides up the top of my calf.

"How was your day?" I ask, my voice husky and thick. I know my cheeks are flush, but his eyes hold mine like he's none the wiser.

"Good. But the days here are always good."

God, that response isn't helping. A few minutes of comfortable silence and he switches to the other foot. "Do you want to go buy couches after this?" My heart is racing and I'm about one deep tissue knot away from coming, right here, right now.

"We do need furniture. I was thinking a dining table is a priority, but you're right, a couch would be good, too." He lowers my foot to the floor after a few more minutes, and slides my sandals back on. "Yes," he says, "if that wasn't clear, I want to go with you."

Unsure if the moment is right or if it's all wrong because we're at work, unsure if he wants me this way, unsure if I'm ready, unsure fucking period—I stand and step to him, looping my arms around his neck.

"Cohen, you need to kiss me now," I tell him, and his lips are against mine within a moment. My mouth opens for his tongue, and despite the denim he's wearing, I press my body to his and feel a distinctly hard ridge pressing deep into my thigh.

My sex pulses and contracts, and as I'm teetering on uncharted orgasmic territory, he steps back, his head falling to one side.

"Let's go get a couch, and then dinner." He outstretches his hand, and the warmth in my belly goes from delightful to incinerating as I slide my small hand into his big one.

"I think we should consider buying pans and plates. Probably cups, too. We're kind of fucking the environment out of our laziness," I say, letting my head fall against his bicep as we stroll through the building toward the exit.

"That's always how it happens, out of laziness," he agrees.

We decide to leave his car there, then he drives us in mine. I pass him the keys with ease, and wonder how l got so lucky to have this amazing man under my nose.

I get more excited when I realize we're about to spend an entire evening together.

So excited.

We opted for dinner first, with Cohen asking me to pick the top three places I wanted to eat. Because I wanted to get to the couch shop, I chose a little takeout corner eatery, one that sells gyros—the best fucking gyros ever.

We went back and forth about our favorite and least favorite restaurants, a lot of our likes coming down to the comfort of the chairs and the kindness of the wait staff. "But I'll get treated like shit for a good plate of fries," he'd said, and something about that made me a little dizzy. Like I could have him between my thighs, in control of his orgasm and mine, and he'd be just fine with that.

Hope makes you heady, kind of drunken, too. So as we peruse furniture store number two, we're laughing, hands intermittently linked.

He runs his hand along the headrest of a large sectional. "I think we need to find the two to three seater section," he says, peering down at the massive couch.

I lift the tag from the couch and read it aloud. "Sits twelve comfortably." My mouth falls open. "I don't think I could find twelve people to come over at the same time. That's so many people."

He smiles, his eyes lifting over the couches, searching for something closer to what we need for our smaller spaces. I flop down on the mega sectional, rolling and cracking my ankles as I sink my head into the cushions.

Cohen comes around and sits next to me. "It's soft."

I bounce a little in my spot. "Yeah, pretty good." I lean forward and look across the length of it again. "Maybe it's for a big family. You know, a household with lots of kids." I lean forward, realizing that this couch sits a little lower than the rest. "Probably for people that have small kids, too. Because little arms and legs, you know? They're not great at reaching and grabbing, so the shorter the couch the better."

I sit up and face Cohen, and everything in my diaphragm tightens before freefalling like bricks to my stomach.

He's pale, white, a sheet in fact. His mouth is parted, eyes on me but also distant, lost almost. I put my hand on his knee. "Cohen, what's wrong?"

He pops up to his feet, and walks away, circling the couch. From behind he says, "I'm going to look at the couches for our apartments." And then he's on the other side of the store, talking to a different sales clerk.

After I cross the store to him, I curl my hand around his bicep, but he raises his arm to motion over a salesman, breaking the contact. Dejected, aching, I question everything. We were on the best date ever. We were connecting.

I replay the last five minutes in my head. I run through the things I've been mentally pinning, completely aware that Cohen has more complication beneath the surface, just like me. But I've never known what, or who, or...

What did I say? I tune out Cohen's conversation with the man in the gray suit and rerun everything, pulling it apart, scrutinizing every syllable.

I was talking about kids.

I look up at Cohen, knowing no more now than I did a moment ago. Did he have a sibling he lost? He said he was an only child, but did he mean now? I worry, chewing the inside of my cheek as I wonder *what* is happening.

Because the idea of him hurting physically hurts me.

"If you like this one," the salesman says to me, and I glance over at the couch opposite where Cohen stands. It fits three. It's blue. It's fine.

"Great, yes," I say, digging my wallet out, face burning from the way I've hurt him and because of it, been discarded.

I have to know what's going on with him. I'm not even angry. He's helped me so much. All I want is to make him feel good, too. Make him happy, too.

I don't push when the salesman disappears with both of our credit cards. I sit with him in silence, and then nod in silence when we make small talk about lamps and television sets. And we drive back to Crave where he picks up his car and we drive home separately. And God do I feel the distance between the two cars, even though we end up parking side by side.

We stand in the breezeway between our apartments, and my mouth falls open, ready to spill so many things, but instead, I say, "Thanks for everything tonight Cohen."

He nods, and I step inside. He stops the door with a palm, and my pulse quickens, believing for one moment that he's going to pour himself out right here and now for me to see. Finally.

"Lock the door, Scarlett. Right now. I need to hear it."

Disappointment crushes me, but I force a smile. I refuse to give up or get disappointed. "I will. Goodnight. Sleep well."

I close and lock the door, and watch through my peephole as he does the same at his place.

Unsurprisingly, I don't sleep well that night.

"I'm so happy," Dr. Evans comments after I tell her all about Vienna, and how I formed an organic, pure friendship without even realizing it. "That's wonderful."

"She's so great, too, Dr. Evans. I feel like she's the first real girlfriend I've had. Everyone at Jizzabelle cut me off."

"Do you suppose your ex had anything to do with that?" she asks, peering at me over her readers.

I sigh. "I know he threatened them, that's totally his style. But still. Threats or not, you like to believe friends and human beings are more important than jobs. Jobs are replaceable."

"People are shitty," she says with a shrug, catching me off guard.

She cracks a slow grin, knowing she's just thrown me, and as I laugh, she steers me into a more serious topic.

"And how are things with Cohen? Still friendly?"

I sink into the armchair. Actually, I melt into it. I am part of the fabric now. Linen, acetate, Scarlett. That's the official label.

"Uh oh," she tries but I sit up and shake my head.

"No, I mean, they're good. It feels like we're more. And not in the physical sense, either. I just mean, I feel like he and I together could be everything, the real deal. But... he's holding something back from me. I can feel it."

"We always can," she says, shaking her head. "Communicate with him. Tell him how you're feeling, that you see a future, but that he must show his cards for things to work."

I swallow hard, hating that I have to ask the question, but knowing I do. "Am I even ready to be in a relationship?"

She smiles, taking me in for a second. Her voice is low and steady when she says, "You can heal and love at the same time." An actual shiver wriggles up my back, slithering inside me. "If you wait until you feel safe and comfortable, you'll never take the risk, because part of great change involves existing with fear and discomfort, but pushing through. Succeeding, not letting it claim you. And you, Scarlett, can absolutely do that. You're strong."

"He says I'm strong, too," I tell Dr. Evans, and not in a way that makes me come off eager to make people like

175

Cohen. I did that a lot with Pete, reworking his words, shining them up, promising to whoever would listen that he's just different, he's not a jerk.

Uh, yeah he was. Still is.

"So talk to me about what you believe is going on in Cohen's world. You mentioned you feel there's an event or perhaps a piece of his history you're unaware of but one that you think is intrinsic to his sense of identity," she says, getting comfortable in her chair as she remains focused on me.

"Yeah," I agree, "though you made that sound way fancier. But yeah, I think something's up with him. Because I get that he can be respectful and a gentleman and everything but... there's something keeping him from really being with me, you know? And like I said, I don't just mean in bed. I just mean..." I sigh, my head pounding from the discourse. But I'm here, and I want Cohen, and if she thinks I can do that, then I have to fight for it. Collecting a breath, I hold it a moment, steadying my mind. With an exhale, I say, "I think we both are falling for each other, I really do. But I need to know what is keeping that final piece of him from me."

"Communication," she deadpans. "I know it must feel like a get out of jail free card on my end. But it's true. Communication gets to the root of most problems."

I grin at her. "I'm really feeling better."

She looks at her notes then back up at me. "Did you fill the Zoloft and Lexapro prescription I wrote you?"

I swallow, shame and guilt pounding in my ears. "I didn't," I admit, wincing in preparation for a scolding I deserve. I should have filled them. I should have taken them. Because they would have helped me, I know she's right.

Hazarding a glance at her, I'm relieved and surprised to find her nodding, writing something mid-paper. "Okay, that's good."

I sigh, pressing my palm to my chest. "I thought you'd be mad."

She takes her glasses off, resting them in her lap. She's never looked more motherly, and for a moment, I miss my mother. That doesn't happen often, as she was cold and unloving most of my life. When I was excommunicated from the family, I can't say I was shocked. It felt like they finally had a reason to be rid of me.

Their awful, porn star daughter.

I've met my first real friend in the porn industry. I've connected with a lot of seriously intelligent people at Crave, Aug and Lance being just the tip of the iceberg. I've experienced a positive workplace and earned very good money, and my online fan base has grown and increased my popularity in my field.

I am successful.

When I held those paper prescriptions in my hand, something in me told me I didn't need them. Having them felt like all the security I needed. So I didn't fill them. Just having talked to someone, it started to alleviate some of the depression. It gave me a sense of accomplishment. It felt like my first step to recovery.

"But I still have them. Just having them makes me feel better," I breathe, still surprised to see her smiling. "I know you wanted me to take them."

She shakes her head. "I wanted you to feel better, whatever safe avenue you took."

I swallow. "Thank you. I know we're not friends, you're my doctor. But still, thank you."

After a smile, she glances at her wrist, blinking. "We ran over," she says, rising, placing her notes facedown on her desk. We shake hands like we always do, and I leave there feeling enlightened.

She didn't say she wanted to stop seeing me because I didn't listen to her. That's not how real relationships function, and fearing that was... silly. On top of which, Dr. Evans believes I am ready to be in a relationship. And she thinks I need to talk to Cohen about everything between us.

I drive home, silently plotting my next move. A first step into the new me, one who has total control.

sixteen

. . .

cohen

But I'm selfish and I want you anyway

With time to kill and my body full of energy, I head to the gym to swim some laps. I discover late evening at the pool looks a lot like early morning, and I'm relieved to be alone. After hanging my bag in the locker room, I clutch my towel at my side and head out. The concrete is warm beneath my feet, and instead of bringing comfort from familiarity, I ache to get off of it. To dip my feet into the cool water.

I toss my towel on a seat and grab the metal railing with each hand, slowly lowering myself in. The water is warmer than normal, maybe a result of a high-traffic day. But as I sink beneath the surface, feeling water bubble in between my ears and all through my trunks, there's a shift.

Pushing off the bottom, I gasp for air as I break the surface. Blinking through watery eyes as I watch the slow splashes fade, rejoining the still surface. Small ripples of water lap at the sides of the faded tile pool, and as everything grows still and stagnant, I just stand there, staring down through the hazy water at my blurry feet.

Every time I've come here before, it's felt necessary. The same way I felt staring at my feet in a church pew as a kid, then later with my grandfather; it felt like it had been etched into my grand design, and that I couldn't deviate from the ritual of it. That it was part of my story, and I couldn't veer from this course.

Swimming those laps, holding myself under water, punishing my mind, testing my body—I thought I owed them that. I thought I deserved that. That no matter what, that was the path for me forever. To repent and feel that pain and loss every fucking day.

My therapist has always told me it's unhealthy. Always. But when you've made your mind up about something, therapy can be a waste, because you have to want to be different... to be different.

His words echo through my mind as I stand in the still water.

Torturing yourself doesn't change the past.

Ceasing to live your life has no bearing on the things that have already come to pass.

And lastly, the words I still am not sure if I can believe, but am willing to accept that I could be wrong about everything—*it was out of my control.*

That's the point I think I've struggled most with, beyond the loss, the last few years. Why couldn't I have been there? Why didn't I do something? How could I have changed the way things happened?

It was not in your control is perhaps my therapist's favorite sentence. I've given it no credence over the years. None. I assumed part of his job was to make sure I didn't collapse in on myself in pain and misery, and take my own life. Good advice and hard truths sprinkled in with pep talks—that's what I assumed therapy was about.

A crazy laugh erupts from my chest, bouncing off the tiled, mildewed walls of the gym. That little boy weeks ago thought I was fucking strange, and I told myself he didn't understand what I was going through. That a little boy could never know exactly why I held myself under, tested my limits and hoped that I'd have the courage one day to stay under.

But he was right to find me odd. He was right to question me.

What the fuck have I been doing?

"Jesus Christ," I breathe, panic pushing the walls in around me, making me hyper aware of the heated room, and the warmth of the water. I need to get out of here. I need to get the fuck out of here.

I can't get to the edge fast enough.

My hands wrap the cool metal poles and her face flashes behind my eyes. I freeze for a moment, water sloshing around my hips, and I close my eyes. I can feel her soft body in my arms. In slow motion, her curls dance as I toss her in the air, loving the squeal that erupts from her when she's in my arms again.

That was a good moment. A good memory. I look back at the water. I can trap myself here, in the pain of knowing I lost something so good and perfect, or I can rise from the pain and keep the memory.

I can move forward with the good and understand that bad happens, has happened, and will happen again.

I pull myself from the water and drape the towel over my head, chest heaving and not from exertion. My thoughts run so fast my breathing intensifies. I fall onto a bench near the pool, clutching the sticky wooden edge of it, curling my fingers beneath.

I don't know if I can, that's the thing. I don't know what I can be for Scarlett, or what it will look like, but I want to try.

I'm fucking terrified. But I want to try.

I force myself to my feet, feeling woozy like I've taken a couple of shots on an empty stomach. Maybe that's the effect of emotional revelation, maybe that's what it feels like when you realize your therapist has been right for the last four years but you've been too fucking dense to realize.

I skip the post-swim shower, eager more than ever to get back to my new apartment, to get back to her.

We're meeting this evening. I came here to swim, because I envisioned holding myself under for some clarity. And now I realize, I have clarity without the pain. And I know exactly what I need to do.

I'd say I hate myself more than ever right now, but I can think of a few distinct memories from my past where I definitely hated myself more.

We had a fucking great date. And I fucking freaked out, and I've essentially been ghosting her since. It's only been a few days, but still, I feel like shit.

I've tapped on her door, making sure she's okay, she doesn't need anything, and asking to hear her lock it. She doesn't call me on the new distance, and I don't know if that upsets me as much as it does make me angry. Angry with myself for putting her through additional strife when she's currently bloody fingered from clawing her way out of a fucking horrendous situation.

I pace back and forth in the small kitchen of my apartment, sweat breaking out along my spine. I couldn't even focus in the goddamn shower. I got out, water is everywhere, I think there's soap in my hair, and all I can do is pace and worry.

I'm pacing, worried to fuck that I ruined the best thing to happen to me in years. That before I had her, I lost her; the woman to pull me out of myself, to make me see what my therapist has been telling me—life is worth living, even when it scares you, even when it hurts.

I texted her today, telling her I *needed* to talk to her. The positive is that she agreed, but she also added, *I wanted to talk to you too.* I told her I'd come to her place when she got home. I wanted to ask where she was at, since I know she's not filming at Crave tonight, but I don't have that right.

Fuck, I may have ruined my chances at having it at all.

Her sandals shuffle against the cement stairs as she climbs up. The gold rings on her left hand clink against the steel railing. My stomach drops.

It's now or never. Live my life or die simply existing. Having to continue existing in a half life is miserable.

I want to live.

I yank the door open, startling her with my suddenness. My chest heaves, water gliding down my shoulders, the chill of the night reminding me I am dripping wet. I step once, then another, and drop to my knees at her feet, not even feeling the scrape of concrete I know is inevitable.

"I don't know what I can give you," I breathe, nostrils

flaring as I work hard to temper the passion roaring through me. "But I'm selfish and I want you anyway."

She reaches out, sifting the tips of her lithe fingers through my hair, her nails skimming my scalp. Quickly, she smooths her hand down my cheek, taking me by the chin, squeezing. The intensity of her grip, the way she angles my face up to hers—my cock is throbbing, tenting the damp terry cloth pinched only loosely at my waist.

"I'm fucked up," I breathe, enamored with the way her gaze pierces mine. "I've been celibate for four years. I don't even know…" I trail off, embarrassed by the words. Embarrassed I'm a man who may not be able to *do* what she needs. I'm hard now and of course I want her but when it comes down to it, fuck, it's been so long.

"Cohen," she says softly, though her touch is still sharp, gripping my chin tight.

"I'm fucked up, and I'm sorry that I am. But all I want to do is make you happy. And keep you safe." I swallow on that last one, knowing I will not make the same mistake twice. "I want you to be mine, even though I don't know what being with me would be like." There, the honest truth. I gave her all the pieces and now she will decide for herself.

Her thumb drags over my bottom lip. My belly clenches and my cock throbs, precum beading at the tip, smearing against the terry cloth as I inch a little closer on my knees. My face is at her groin, and she's wearing those gray sweatpants she wore the first night she came to my place. With her hand still in my hair, she nudges me forward, and I press my mouth to her pussy, over her sweats.

Her hand slips to my neck as she squeezes me, moaning my name in the softest tone I've ever heard. I close my eyes, nudging her with my nose, inhaling the scent of her aroused, sweet cunt. Before I can bask in it, she's cradling my jaw, pulling me back.

"Do you trust me, Cohen?" she asks, velvet and smoke. A rumble knocks free from my chest and I roar my response.

"Yes, I trust you."

She traces my earlobe with the tip of her finger, and my nipples harden. The tucked towel moves a little, reminding me that as I dry, it does too and I'll likely lose it in a minute. But she's my focus.

"Do you know that you can stop me at any time?" she breathes, running the pad of her finger down the bridge of my nose, a line of fire eating up my back in response.

"Yes."

"If I ask something, if I touch you in any way that feels too soon or not right, or if I do anything—you can always say red."

She lifts my face, and I see her again, eyes soft, grip firm. It's a confusing, heady mix, and it makes my blood pump like crazy and my cock hard. It gives me hope.

I know she's setting parameters, for both of our safety, and I fight the urge to nuzzle into her palm. I keep her safe, but she brings me so much peace, so much fucking comfort.

"I want you Cohen, but before I can have you, *I have to know.*"

I blink, and the towel releases, falling around my calves behind me. Her eyes stay on mine, and I groan when her mouth parts, and her breathing slows. She's turned on. I recognize it.

"What?" I ask, rounding back to her statement while also realizing I'm now naked outside for the world to see. Granted it's dark and we're upstairs but I don't fucking care.

The idea that I almost ruined this has me melting at her

feet, giving myself to her. I *want* to make her happy for as long as I possibly can. She's my light.

"Whatever it is," she hedges, "I have to know."

"What do you mean?" I ask, but I don't know why. Scarlett's smart and I clearly have not concealed my pain very well.

She hooks her thumb in my mouth, her eyes hooded as she rasps, "Whatever it is, I have to know. That's what will make me happy. Knowing. And then we can move forward, whatever it is."

I can't deny her anything.

I think I'd die before I'd tell her no.

She steps back. "Come on," she says, motioning to her place. I grab my towel, heart still racing, and go to wrap it around my waist. Scarlett's face is somber as she yanks the towel from my hand. "I'll keep my eyes on your eyes, the way you do for me."

She noticed.

I follow her in and lock the door, promising myself that the next time I go back to my place, she'll be mine.

I have a lot of talking to do.

seventeen

. . .

scarlett

We'll go slow

I hadn't planned for Cohen to fall to my knees and hand himself to me this way. I thought I'd have to edge around hard topics and pull things from him and maybe I still will but hell, just knowing he wants this, knowing I was right about that feels so good.

The way he needs me to have control right now, it gives me so much pride. I'm so happy to be able to do something for him for a change. He's always filling my cup, one way or another, and returning it feels so good.

I will gladly take control, and show him he's worth belonging to someone. Inside the apartment, I lock the door, taking my time as I replay his shattered tone and messy words. *I don't know what I can give you but I'm selfish and I want you anyway.*

He doesn't know what he can give me? It makes my head spin, and it breaks my heart a little, too. He already gives me so much, I can't believe he isn't aware of that.

And the celibacy. A lump tightens in my stomach as I remember the curve of him pressed against me in our embrace, the sight of his soft cock pressed to his thigh in his sweats. His shirt kissing the disciplined curves of his body. His arms overhead at work, bearing strength and skill.

He's so incredibly beautiful and sexy. Hell, if someone pointed out Cohen to me at Crave, I would have assumed he's an actor, too.

Celibate. For *four* years.

I want to tear into that and explore every morsel, but I know we have to move slowly. I feared moving slowly would push him away, and now I see that he needs it as much as I do.

Maybe our traumas share no common ground, but our pain and the fallout clearly does. We're wounded. Trying to heal while cautiously… falling in love.

"We'll go slow," I tell him as I lead us to the brand new couch that we picked out together, that awkward night.

I sit but he stands, and I pat the spot next to me.

"I'm wet, this is your new couch, I'd prefer to just kneel at your feet," he says while he seeks permission in my gaze. Above my collarbone, my pulse hammers, excited and nervous.

I nod my permission, but know he needs to hear it, the same way I'd need to hear red to know to stop. "You can kneel."

It's work to keep my eyes on his, but I manage. "I want you to know, at any time, you can put the towel on or go across the hall and get dressed."

He drops his chin to his chest with a nod.

"Can you take my sandals off?"

Red-rimmed, hazy eyes meet mine and then his hands are on my foot, sliding the sandal free. He repeats on the other side and rests his hands between his knees, waiting.

"I need to know, Cohen."

His swallow is so thick, it pains me. I feel his fear, I feel his insecurity. Everything he's feeling radiates off him, filling my pores, sinking into my heart.

"We'll bare ourselves to each other, and we'll feel better. We won't be stuck in limbo anymore. Do you believe that, Cohen?"

I lean forward, stroking my hand through his soft hair, appreciating how his eyes close for a moment to savor the touch. "Yes," he says finally when I take my hand away.

I stroke my palm down his face, shivers running up my arm at the coarse stubble growing. He's almost always clean shaven, and he came over here out of the shower, dripping wet.

He's going through something, same as me, the only difference is, he hasn't worn it on his sleeve the way I have. He's silently suffered, but no more. No. Fucking. More.

I'll have to start. To show him there is room to grow on the other side of discomfort, but we have to traipse through it to get there.

"Two broken pieces can come together. We just need to be aware of each other's sharp edges."

My thumb slides between his lips, and I find his mouth wet and warm. He turns his head, kissing my hand as I pull my thumb from his mouth. My belly rumbles with need, because despite being on the precipice of tearing down emotional walls, I still want him. In fact, I want him more and more each passing day.

That's where I start.

"I don't know if I'll be able to make love to you right away, Cohen, and that's one reason I've told myself we're only friends. Because I don't know that I can give you what a partner needs, romantically, for a while."

He reaches out, kneading the tops of my feet. "I understand. And because of that, I'd prefer it if you led. Show me, tell me, make me aware of exactly what you want and need."

"You won't get tired of never being able to act off impulse? You won't hate being told when and where?"

He blinks at me, grooves of confusion vertical on his forehead. "I want to make you happy in all ways, Scarlett. And I want you to feel safe with me."

"One day I could be normal again. One day you could take control, but I can't promise that. Can you be with me if I can't promise that?" I make my voice strong despite the fear rattling in my diaphragm. It's a big ask, and I would understand if he can't do it.

His palms come to one ankle, cupping it, sliding up my calf, pushing my sweats up. His big, warm hands feel so good on my body. "You are normal," he says, "and I don't need to control sex to be happy, Scarlett." He looks at where his hands are on my body, and it takes everything I have to not look at his naked groin. I want to, I want to see him fully, to know every inch of him.

Not right now.

"My shut down is a mental block manifested in the physical," I explain, paraphrasing Dr. Evans' smarter words.

"What does that mean?" he asks.

I nudge him back by the shoulder, and get to my feet. "Take my pants off," I tell him, and watch as his lean arms lift, and his solid fingers wrap my waistband and start to tug. His knuckles grazing my inner thighs drive me wild, but I hold it all in, every moan, every shudder, everything.

Sinking back into the couch, I watch as Cohen folds my sweats and sets them on top of my sandals, carefully aside.

"It means that while despicable things happened to me at Jizz, I recognize that those things were at the hands of Pete. What Pete did to me emotionally has created a physical block, where I'm fearful of intimacy because of what he put me through." I trace the lobe of his ear, and heat slides down my spine like water as he traps my hand between his face and shoulder, soaking up my touch, keeping me there.

Cohen's face is etched with concern as he blinks up at me, and I watch him drop his palms to my knees, running them up and down my calves. It's simple but intimate. Yet he doesn't interrupt me with his own story, so I continue, hopeful I'm nudging him closer.

"I wanted to have a baby," I whisper, and his head snaps up, eyes dancing between mine, pupils wide, the blue dark like a deep sea. "I wanted to be a mother as much as I wanted to be a programmer. And when we moved in together Pete assured me I could have both of those things, that he would give me those things."

He's captivated by my words, or me, I'm not sure which. But he blinks up at me, his hands motionless on my knees. "As time went on it was always later. After. Soon."

He releases my hand from his face, straightening his neck. I place my hand on his shoulder, and the heat of his skin flutters between my thighs.

"When things were bad on set I'd threaten to report him for what he made the actors do to me. For the scenes he'd shoot without my consent, knowing if I was bound and gagged, I couldn't do anything." I take a breath, realizing my hands are now trembling, I place my other hand on his shoulder.

He reaches up and drops his hands over mine, and my

trembling ceases. His focus pierces me. "He'd gaslight me. Tell me it made a more powerful scene if I didn't expect it, if I went outside my comfort zone. Then he'd say, if you report me, who will father your baby? Who will get you back into school?"

I swallow hard, embarrassment settling in my cheeks in the form of crimson heat. "It sounds ridiculous now, but when you have the beauty of being on the outside, looking in, there's much more clarity than when you're trapped in a snow globe, you know?"

"I know," he says, voice gravelly and raw.

"My entire life the one thing I knew for sure is that I wanted to be a mother. Always. And when Pete and I got together, he shared my dream of being a parent. He said he wanted to be a father. At some point, I realized I didn't want him to father my child, but I also believed that if I could get pregnant, I could create my own happiness, fulfill my own dream, and that having the ideal partner or being in love was less important."

Cohen squeezes my hands and twists his face to press a kiss to each of my wrists. "He knew the one thing I wanted more than anything else, and he held it over my head. Used it against me to keep me silent, to keep me in check." I smile at him. "Then Augustus found me, and he saved me." I swallow hard at the unexpected emotion burning the back of my nose, wetting my eyes. "And now you're saving me, Cohen. Did you know that? Did you know that before I met you, I couldn't orgasm. In a scene, alone, nothing. My body was shut off to that kind of pleasure, or maybe it was my mind all along. I don't know."

I take a breath, and a moment to sort through what I've said and what I still need to say. I want to lay it all out there, to show him how getting through the difficult things will make us stronger, together.

"You fill places in me I didn't know were empty. I got so used to a cold, unloving childhood and a cruel and sadistic boss and partner, I didn't realize what *could be*. And then I met you." Leaning down, I bring my lips to his, placing the softest of kisses against his lips. "I matter when I'm with you. My thoughts, my opinions, my preferences, my needs. Everything about me matters when I'm with you."

"That's how it should be," he says quietly. "A man exists to serve and worship what's his."

I smile at him as I lift my sweatshirt and tank off in one pull, dropping it to the floor near his neat pile of my things. "Tell me, Cohen," I say, unclasping my bra, his eyes still only on mine.

I rise and shimmy off my panties, and fall to my knees in front of him, his equal. He can be my protective man, the man who lives to serve, but in this moment, we are two lost ships at sea, coming together to rescue one another.

Reaching up, I take his worn face between my hands and I wait. I wait for his words to come, for his pain to spill, for me to pull him back together after it does.

Tears slide down his cheeks, going unacknowledged as he speaks, slowly, voice weak. "I was married. And I was a father, too."

Was.

My thumbs sweep over his cheeks, but I refuse to react. I hold him there, pushing down the pain and agony rising up inside me like a rapid tide, determined to be his strength in this.

Tears slide down my cheeks as the word *was* loops in my brain.

"Ten years ago I married my college sweetheart," he says, an invisible weight of his trauma clearly resting on his shoulders, his posture slouching as his breathing intensifies. "Eight years ago, we had a baby." His bottom lip tremors. "I had a daughter."

Had.

My nose burns as tears slip freely and easily down my cheeks, but I continue ridding his face of the pain, swiping his tears with my thumbs. "Oh Cohen," I breathe, my voice weak, my entire body aching with second hand pain.

He's lost a child.

There could be nothing worse, in all of life and existence, than losing a child. This is a huge, cruel, unfair circumstance, one so unnatural and painful that it can't be topped. There is no loss as big as losing the person you love more than yourself.

"My wife went to her sister's. She lived in Cheboygan. We lived in Mount Pleasant. It's a couple hours drive, but feels longer with a young child."

I don't nod. I don't speak. I only stay there on my knees, tears still streaming freely as I listen. Listening is often the greatest and most underrated gift to give someone you love.

"I couldn't go. I had to work. I had this... We were working on a bigger production set at the theater. And she'd taken her up there a few times before, so it wasn't unusual."

His eyes unfocus from me for a moment, and actual pain clutches my throat because I know what's going on.

He's remembering.

"She wanted her to see her cousins, and experience the lake before winter. Her sister lived right on the lake."

My heart beat slows, growing heavy with anticipation. His face droops, but I hold him there, giving him the strength he doesn't have.

"They swam. She had a life jacket on. But the kids were

194

wild, and," he shakes his head, letting a sigh break free. "I know that things happen fast, I *know* that."

We kneel there together for a few minutes as he gathers the energy and courage, and I wait as if no time has passed. I press my mouth to his, and hold his gaze, imparting on him in all silent ways that I am here, I am here and I have him, the same way he has me.

"Valerie called me at dinner time. She was crying, all shaken up. And I knew it had to be bad, because she rarely cried. She wasn't an emotional person by nature."

My stomach sours, because I know something awful is coming. I remove a hand from his face and place my palm over his heart. His chest pounds beneath me, but a moment later, his body begins to calibrate to my calming touch.

"Ad—" He chokes, his head dropping down, chin to chest, deep sobs wracking his chest, shaking his shoulders. I take his head in my hands and press kisses into his hair over and over, showering him in affection until he lifts his head, beneath his nose is shiny; his cheeks stained.

"Addie," he says, his mouth stuck slightly parted after the name is free, like just saying it has pierced him all over again. His dark eyes come to mine. "I haven't said her name in years. But her name was Addie. Addie May Steele."

"A beautiful name."

His nostrils flare as fresh tears paint his face. "She called and said Addie is okay, but I'm shaken up. And I calmed her down and got her to tell me. The kids were swimming and it got wild, Addie slipped out of her life vest. Valerie was there, and pulled her up. It hadn't been more than thirty seconds, or a minute, I don't know, not long, she said."

I don't know what any of these people look like, yet I can see the scene as clear as day. A sandy embankment scattered with neon buckets and plastic shovels, towels and floaties strewn about, the smell of sunscreen and blooming trees filling the air. An orange sun pinned far off in the distance, laughter and splashing the perfect soundtrack to a perfect summer day.

"She swallowed a bunch of water, even though it had only been a minute or so, she panicked. She was only four, so she tried to scream but… she just kept swallowing water."

A chill licks my skin as I imagine the piercing screams, Valerie's panic, the way a beach full of life would suddenly go silent and concerned, everyone edging in around them, looking.

"She vomited a ton. Valerie said she vomited water for five minutes, and then she was crying, and clinging to her." He swallows. "They were shaken up, but she was okay. She was alert, speaking, saying that she was hungry… *we dodged a bullet,* Valerie said on the phone that night. I remember that. I remember her using those exact words. I don't know why I remember that part but I do.

But Valerie was so shaken up. Just… beside herself, really. Couldn't believe it happened, and Valerie was an attentive mother. Some would even have accused her of being a heli-copter parent. It was just… *an accident.* But she was shaken and she said instead of driving back, she and Addie were going to stay at her sister's for the night. And in the morning, when she had recovered, she'd drive home with a level head. No emotion, no more tears."

"She woke up in the middle of the night, sweaty, she said, burning up. She got up and got a glass of water, but her nerves from the day were still running rampant, so she decided to check on Addie." His lip trembles, and mine does too.

"Oh, Cohen."

He closes his eyes, and I wait for him to come back to me.

When his eyes reopen, bloodshot and wet, he picks up at a different place, skipping the things he's unable to say. "Secondary drowning," he rasps, "the paramedics said it was a secondary drowning. The... the..." his voice shatters into a trillion pieces, coming out broken, low, wrecked. "Autopsy said she had water in her lungs, and her body made fluid to protect her lungs from the water." He sucks in a breath. "Pulmonary edema," he says. "That's what it's called."

Finally, I wrap my arms around him, and he loops his around me, and our bodies come together in a crushing hug. I hold him, I stroke my fingers up the back of his hair as his silent tears melt over my skin, his pain burning me, changing me.

"I'm so sorry, Cohen. I'm so, so sorry you lost your daughter. I'm so sorry," I repeat, my words watery and broken. His heart races beneath his heated skin, and I want nothing more than to steady him, be his place of calm, the one who takes his weary and broken and makes him whole again.

"I should've done more. I should have looked up things to look for after swallowing water, I should have insisted she take her to the Emergency Room just to be sure. I could have done so much more, but I didn't. I was too fucking busy working."

"Cohen," I say weakly, both of us fatigued from the tears. I take his face in my hands, our noses and foreheads almost touching. "You had no control over the situation. It wasn't your fault. Sometimes, bad things happen. Bad things that forever change us. Bad things that are so terrible, we become new people, because the us before the trauma can no longer survive. So we morph into something more stoic, someone stronger, a person shut off to the idea of love, because we know the pain of loss." I bring my lips to his and he kisses me, pressing into my mouth with fervor.

Our kiss breaks. "Can you be with a man who lets his child die? Who lets his marriage fall apart because of the loss?" His nostrils flare as he chastises himself with sharp, cruel words. "Can you fall in love with such a failure?"

On our knees before one another, the room so dense with emotional charge that a single spark could ignite us, I take the risk. I pinch his face in my hand. "You are not a failure. You did not let her die. Bad things happen to good people. You are not to blame."

He shakes his head.

"You are not to blame."

After a moment, he nods. "My therapist has been saying that for years. And I don't know if I'll ever believe it. I don't know that I'll ever believe that I did all I could. But he's right about one thing," Cohen breathes. "I stopped living for the last four years and look," he raises his bare, empty palms between us, arms and hands trembling. "I didn't bring her back."

I shake my head. "You've been fighting so hard," I breathe, now seeing the lines near his eyes as scars from his pain, not marks of age. The weathered look in his eyes isn't aloofness, it's the look of a man who has survived. Survived something no one should live through.

I link my hands with his, and start getting to our feet. I guide him down the hall into my bedroom, and ask him to get in bed. He stands at the foot, both of us still completely naked, moonlight casting slivers of gold through the blinds, all over the room. The nudity is symbolic now, our hearts stripped completely bare with nothing to hide.

"Thank you for telling me," I whisper, pulling the covers down to expose the bottom sheet. I crawl in and pat the space next to me, and still, he doesn't move.

"Do you see me differently now?" he asks, voice hoarse from the exertion of his story.

"Come," I say, my tone wrapped in velvet as I order him to bed.

He does, and I pull his head to my chest, feeding my fingers through his hair, softly stroking him. Slowly, his breathing shifts from short, shallow inhales to something slower, calmer, softer.

"I see you more clearly now. And... I want you more than ever," I whisper, thinking aloud so no part of my thought process is left unknown to him. If I learned anything at all from my time with Dr. Evans, it's that communication is the core of relationships. I trace the lobe of his ear with a fingertip and he wraps his arms around me, even fishing one under me, holding me close to him. The weight of his head against my chest feels so good. Holding him, helping him calm, bringing him the safety he brings me, it's fulfilling. "But I want us."

"Me too," he says, voice rough, his hot breath licking at my nipple. We're naked and he's so close to my breast, and even though my core thrums with need, that's not what tonight is. "And I understand we have intimacy... issues. That it may be hard for you to be physical. And it's been four years for me... I don't—"

I interrupt him. "Was Valerie the last..."

He nods. "Yes."

"You know, when I said you could say red, I meant that about anything." I want him to know that if he's had too much emotionally, we can stop. "Safe words aren't just about sex. They're meant to protect you, period."

He nods against me, holding me tighter. "I know." He drapes his leg over mine and my body goes rigid. His heavy, warm cock falls onto my thigh, and my awakening seizes me, my body silently crying yes, *take him, have him. You're ready.*

But I know I have to move slowly, because the last thing this man needs is a woman to have a panic attack mid sex, thrash and attack him, and leave him worse than he was found.

We have time, we'll move slow, and honor all that we've been through as we grow together.

"I'm so tired," he says against my body, his soft lips against my flesh making my nipples hard.

I cup the side of his face with one hand, stroking him. "Sleep. Sleep well with me. I have you," I whisper, knowing the drop he must feel after unburdening himself to me. "I have you, Cohen. Just sleep."

His breathing evens out, and when I know he's asleep, my mind wanders back to his story. My heart aches for Valerie, the woman who had him before me, and the life they had and lost. Anguish and sorrow flood me when I think of her. Addie. The beautiful little girl they both lost. I squeeze my eyes shut, feeling the sting of tears dripping down my temples.

No one should have to go through that. I hold him closer though he can't feel it.

I hold him close because the idea of letting go is too painful.

eighteen

· · ·

cohen

I'm yours, Scarlett

Morning is here, I can feel it with the way my brain is stirring, despite the fact I don't want to open my eyes. The room around me is cool, but inside the bed I'm warm. Carefully, I untangle my legs from hers, wondering when and how we got in this heap of heated, naked bodies.

We're naked.

My head throbs as if I spent the night drinking, but as I sit on the edge of her bed, looking down at my bare feet on the apartment floor, I remember last night, and know why my head hurts.

Addie's face, full cheeks with emerald eyes, flashes in my mind. The ringing phone that night. The way I jolted up in the bed, Valerie's stilted breaths and incoherent words.

I told Scarlett everything. Things I've never told anyone other than my therapist, and Augustus.

Peering over my shoulder, I glance at Scarlett, the sheet positioned over her torso perfectly, hiding everything that I have yet to earn permission to gaze at. Her blonde hair is fanned out around her, reminding me of Alphonse Mucha and his beautiful women.

We slept together, in each other's arms, all night. I slept soundly. I didn't dream, or more importantly, I didn't have a nightmare. She clutched my head to her chest and being in her arms and under her care last night felt so much better than any hug I received at the cemetery, any card or phone call that came in those following weeks, any speech from my therapist. Being in her arms seemed to calm me and give me hope, and as much as I have avoided voicing my history and letting people see my pain, I'm glad I did.

It felt good to say her name again, as much as it also hurt. Addie. She was my gorgeous, sweet, bubbly, smart daughter. We'd wanted to make her a big sister, too. After the summer came to an end, when things slowed down at the theater, we were going to try for another.

We didn't make it to fall.

Quietly, I take myself to the bathroom and close the door. It's when I'm greeted with the sight of my morning erection in the mirror that I realize not only am I naked but I have no clothing here. I came over in a towel.

Bracing my palm against the wall, I relieve myself, closing the toilet lid to muffle the flushing noise. While washing my hands, I notice in the mirror that my morning wood is slow to fade, and there's a pulling sensation, low in my belly, like I could wrap my fist around my length and find pleasure. Find release. Somewhere in my brain, awakening from a deep slumber, synapses fire off and the urge to do it, the drive to touch myself, watch my cock twitch and thrum as I stroke until release—it's there.

I dry my hands on the small towel near the sink, and make my way down the hall, to the living room. As quietly as possible, I unlock the door and slip out into the breezeway, the icy bay morning taking care of any burning going on below the belt. My balls climb right up into myself as I bolt to my door, twisting it open easily.

I didn't lock up last night. My mind was in chaos. All logic was gone. I was driven to go to her, do anything I needed to do to have her, win her, earn her, prove to her that being with me wouldn't be a mistake.

It's the first time I've been reactionary and spontaneous. The first time since that night that I did anything impulsively. I thought I'd lost the ability to be impulsive, to feel urges so wild and frothy that I can't keep a logical thought.

She brought that back to me, too.

I leave my door open as I jog to the bedroom and pull on a pair of sweats, turning around to immediately go back to Scarlett's.

I know she's a grown woman but the idea of leaving her alone in that apartment where I know *he knows she is* drives me wild with anger.

Quietly, I close the door and put all of the locks back in place. Leaving the lights off, the light of early morning peeking through the windows enough to let me see, I pull open her fridge. She'd gotten groceries at some point, and discomfort slithers around inside me at the idea of her going around the city alone, knowing he's out there, too. Quickly I survey the items in the fridge, and make a mental note to reorder those things and have them delivered to her in a few days.

At her stove, I pull out her saucepan, digging through her

cupboards quietly to see if she'd purchased any pans yet. If she got groceries, maybe she got other things, too. But after finding a bundt cake pan and a mini rolling pin and not much else, I decide to make do with what I have. Using the broiler in the oven to toast bread, I scramble eggs in the bottom of the saucepan, stirring constantly to evenly distribute the heat. I make us each a cup of coffee, and slice up the blueberries and strawberries in her fridge, butter the toast, and plate everything.

"Good morning," Scarlett greets through a yawn, her voice thick with sleep. She appears in the kitchen, also no longer naked. In an oversized hoodie, her bare legs are exposed, long blonde hair twisted into a bun on the very top of her head. She smiles, coming my way until we're toe to toe. She loops her arms around my waist and presses her cheek to my chest.

"Good morning," I greet, letting my eyes close. Morning with her feels like I'm watching a movie, one where the main characters are so in love that you get irrationally jealous. I want this forever, and I want to wake up with her on Saturdays, I want to sleep in with her on the Friday after Thanksgiving, I want to wake up in the middle of the night to check that the door is locked and come back to bed... to her.

She kisses my bare chest, then brings her hands up, cupping my face. After she flashes a smile, she tugs me to her, pressing her mouth to mine. Her hands slide around my head, pulling me even closer as the kiss intensifies. I moan into her mouth, feeling this kiss everywhere, wanting to put space between us.

"I was thinking we could eat breakfast and talk," I say as she rocks to the heels of her feet, blotting at her bottom lip.

"Yeah?" she peers at the two plates full of food then looks back at me. "Cohen, how did you do this?"

I scratch at the back of my head, not wanting attention for making breakfast. "Do you normally eat breakfast?" I prod, realizing that if she has no cookware and has been here for two months, she's likely not feeding herself. Not well, at least. I don't like that. Then again, I haven't treated myself much better.

She pinches a bite of scrambled eggs, tipping her head back to drop it into her open mouth. I hold up a piece of plastic cutlery from the counter. Her cheeks pink as she finishes the bite.

"You're probably grossed out that I just did that instead of using the fork," she guesses as I come to her side, poking her eggs with the plastic tines.

I bring the fork to her lips, and our eyes tangle in silent heat for a moment. She swallows hard, the noise like a spark between us. Her lips part, and I slide the eggs inside, my chest rising with pride at the way she closes her eyes, savoring it.

"It only makes me want to feed you myself," I reply, my voice unusually husky, bearing both depth and lightness, reminding me of... how I felt waking up with happiness in my heart and a purpose in my soul. I tip my head toward the couch. "Let's sit."

We sit hip to hip, and I have her hold the plate as I drag her legs into my lap. Setting the plate on her legs, I collect another bite, and feed her. She chews as my hand slides up and down her calf.

"I swim in the mornings, before work. I don't know if I told you that already," I say, pushing the eggs around as I procure another bite for her.

Her tongue licks at the corner of her mouth. "You did. You told me when we had coffee."

I nod, bringing my eyes to hers, bringing another forkful

to her lips. "I..." I start, not realizing until this moment just how supremely dark my actions have been. In my mind, in all that water, with no noises or humans, it made sense. She opens her mouth and cleans the tines, keeping her eyes on me. "I would hold myself under, hold my breath for as long as I could, and stay down as long as I could stand the burning pain of not being able to breathe."

"Cohen," she whispers, taking the plate from my lap to lower it to the floor.

I turn my head away, embarrassed but also determined. If I find sympathy and sadness in her eyes, I may break. "I didn't want to kill myself, but I didn't know how to live either."

"You told yourself you didn't deserve to live because she didn't," she whispers, seeing my broken reasoning so clearly.

I nod, forcing the rock of emotion down to my belly, making room for words. "I never wanted to escape that sinking, choking feeling until now." She reaches out and takes my chin, twisting my face to hers.

"You deserve happiness. Do you understand me?" she says, tone unwavering, focus on me unrelenting. "We both do. Together."

"Together," I say. "Is that what we are now?"

"Lie back on the couch," she whispers, placing the plate of food on the counter. When she returns, she straddles me, knees pinned around my hips. She grabs the bottom of her sweatshirt, smiling at me. The sunlight swims around her head, specks of dust glowing as they dance. The house smells like breakfast, and her warm body on top of mine feels like home.

"Hands up, behind your head."

I do it, and in return am greatly rewarded with her satisfied smile.

"I'm going to talk, you're going to listen, and you're going to look," she rasps, then yanks off her sweatshirt, tossing it to the floor.

Twisting my head, I look at the crumpled sweatshirt, seeing it for what it is. I face her again, still just looking into her eyes. "I respect you, Scarlett. It's why I keep my eyes on yours, it's why I'm not pushing you. I want you to be comfortable, and ready for me. I don't want to get physical too soon and damage things. I care about you far too much for that."

Leaning forward, she takes my face in her hands, something I've grown to need because it feels so fucking good. Being cherished by her feels like being knighted, something holy and special only for me.

"Look at me, look at me and let me see how much you want me, even if we're not ready," she rasps, releasing my face. She rocks up, and my eyes follow her hands as they pull down my chest and over my belly, then come to her thighs around me.

Against her center, my cock rises, eager and fat, and I can't stop him. But I don't want to scare her or trigger her. "Scarlett," I husk, "you're beautiful and I haven't... It's been a long time." I don't know what else to say or even what I'm trying to say, but she seems to understand.

A soft smile lifts her lips as she brings her hands to her breasts cupping them. "We'll go slow, for both of us, but I need to feel that you want me. I need to see it, Cohen."

She drops her hands, and my eyes fall to her full, bare breasts, pale and beautiful. Her nipples are hard, her areolas puckered. My mouth was on that breast last night. An inch away from being able to lick and lave that tiny little nubbed peak. From between my legs, my cock grows angrier, thicker, more eager. She looks down, and the sight of her naked in my lap, watching me get hard for her, it makes me fucking feral.

I want to flip her onto her back and slide inside of her, latch my mouth to her breast and enjoy everything her body gives me. Sustenance, energy, confidence, power.

But my eyes find her core, and lower to her pussy, shaved completely bare. "I know I told you but I want you to know what a big deal it is, Cohen; you gave me back my orgasm," she admits, wrapping one hand under the waistband of my sweats. Her knuckles against my belly have my cock straining for freedom, seeking the deep, wet warmth between her legs.

"What?" I question, realizing what she's admitted.

"Cohen," she interrupts. "I'm going to touch you and if you want to stop, you'll tell me, okay?" She leans down a little. "Remember, red."

I nod then add, "I do what pleases you, always."

Our eyes idle together, my words bearing so much subtext that we need a moment to process. *I'm here to serve you, I want to serve you, you are the only thing that gives me life. Let me have you, let me belong to you, let me make you happy.* I can't say those things now, but I hope she knows I feel them.

She lowers the waistband of my sweats, and the cool air licks at my cock, sending a shiver down my spine. My stomach clenches and my pulse spikes, and an unexpected anxiety roars to life in my veins. "Wait," I breathe. "I want you to be ready. I'm... I'm afraid you're doing this for me, because you think I need this to want you. But I want you, Scarlett, I want you in whatever capacity I can have you. And if you aren't ready, don't do this. Don't do this for me. Do it for you, do whatever is right for you."

Her eyes drop to my cock, and I watch her take me in. Watch as her eyes widen then grow hooded, how she tips her head to the side, then traces my balls with the tip of her finger. I shudder at how good just one fingertip feels against my heavy, long neglected sac. At how good it feels to be naked and hard with someone who wants me, to regain the ability to be vulnerable.

She wiggles over me, and then I feel it. Her bare, wet pussy resting on my cock, forcing it down against my belly. She rocks her hips, gaze holding mine, her cunt so wet that I let out a groan.

"Scarlett," I breathe, straining my head from the couch to look between our bodies. Her lips are spread, my cock prodding between them as she rocks back and forth, her glistening heat smearing along my shaft. Her pussy is so perfect, lips swollen and pink, clit engorged; my lips tingle at the idea of going down on her, discovering her cunt with my tongue, filling my mouth with the sweet taste of her. The weight of her thighs on my shoulders. The feel of her heels digging into my back. Her nails grating my scalp as she begs me to make her come. The flood of sweetness and saltiness as she grinds my face, coming hard for me, *because* of me.

"I trust that you won't hurt me Cohen," she breathes, dropping her head to look down at where she's grinding me. I look right in time to see her fingertip trace the dark slit in my cockhead, collecting precum, bringing her finger to her lips. Her eyes roll shut like she's sampled heaven, and my cock spits at the sight.

"Fuck," I groan, looking down at the clear rope spit along my belly. She collects it with the pad of her finger, using it to trace the hard peak of her breast, leaving shiny arousal on her flesh. My arousal. "I would never hurt you," I choke out, my mind a battle ground. Do not fucking come. Four years or not, if I come right now, I'll be humiliated to have reached that point before her.

She comes first, I serve her before she serves me. *That's how it goes.*

Like she knows what's holding me back, she reaches for my arm, and brings my hand to her pussy. Rocking over my length, grinding me in hot, wet strokes, she gives a single command. "Rub."

I place the pad of my thumb over her clit, my cock throbbing at how soft and swollen it feels as I stroke it. Arching her back, her head tips forward, watching my thumb make slow circles on her needy bud. She's wet, and by the way her hips move faster and her moans get breathier, I know she's close.

"Sit... sit up," she pants, her cheeks flush, eyes hazy. I sit up and bring my lips to her nipple, but look at her for permission. She nods and feeds her fingers through the back of my hair, bringing my mouth to her breast.

My world floods with light as I suck her nipple, the abrasion of her nails against my scalp making me moan into her body. She steals herself away, commanding me to sit upright. I do, and my cock joins, rising up from my lap like a flagpole. She brings her beautiful body back to me, leaning her knees against the couch, partially standing, her bare cunt over my cock.

Her hand falls to her pussy where two fingers stroke against her clit. "I couldn't come, for over a year, I stopped being able to orgasm. I thought I never would be able to again," she breathes, a single drop of sweat gliding between her luscious tits. A thread of clear arousal stretches from my cockhead to my belly, and it's been so long since I've seen myself like this. I almost can't believe this is real. She's real.

Scarlett takes my cock in her hand, and both of us moan from the depths of our bellies when she does. It feels so good to be touched by her, to have my cock in her hand. I look at her delicate fingers wrapping my shaft, the way she holds me and uses the hand that stroked her cunt to trace the wide slit. Notching me at her entrance, she sinks down until her cunt swallows my crown.

"I masturbated thinking of you. And I came. I came like crazy, Cohen."

"Scarlett," I rasp, too close to the edge for comfort. I look at her cunt eating up my head, and the way her delicate fingers return to stroking her pert little clit. "I-I was content with celibacy," I pant, our admissions making me drunk and dizzy, the truth of them pulling us together, binding us invisibly but powerfully.

She rises, and my cock slips out, bobbing with weight between us. I'm so hard and so full of years of release, when she grabs me again and brings the head to her entrance, I let out a warning groan.

Grinning, she sinks down onto just the head again. "A crown for your queen," she smiles, her fingers returning to her clit. Her eyes close, and I watch the erotic movie play out before me.

Her arm shakes as she rubs and a moment later, she's unraveling over my cock, her cunt spasming around my head, contracting in fast, rhythmic waves as her hips move.

As if she knows my body better than me, she reaches down and fists my shaft, taking my cock from her warmth. My head is nearly purple and she lowers her mouth to it right as the tidal wave of heat whips through my core, centering my groin. My mouth falls open, sweat slicks my forehead, and I watch as she slips her mouth from my head, the first shot of long awaited release streaking over me. I groan as she runs her finger tip over the slit with such light pressure that I grit my teeth, the next rope coming stronger, thicker, and the next even faster. I come so fucking hard as she plays with the head of my cock, watching with wide eyes as I coat myself in what feels to be endless ropes of long held back release.

I want to jerk up off the couch, worried that with this amount of cum, there's no way it's not going to get all over.

I want to.

But my body is suddenly so goddamn relaxed. Every single tense muscle has released its grip on stress, my chest is open and light, my mind free. I stare at Scarlett, catching my breath, watching her as she drags her finger from my collarbone to my belly button. Her eyes are wide, staring at the mess, and I'm hypnotized by her playing with my cum.

A moment passes and our eyes come together over the heated mess between us. "Thank you," I tell her, my voice husky and unfamiliar.

"I'm sorry I couldn't..." she trails off... still playing with the now drying mess. I catch her hand, stilling her, and shake my head.

"You lead, remember? And anything you give me is perfect. And that was..." I look down at the sea of cum on my torso, drying now but still visible. "Well, look at me," I laugh, and she laughs, too. And we both just laugh for a minute or two, tears forming in the corner of her eyes, my lungs burning as I struggle to breathe.

My laughter ceases and I bring my hand to my chest, draping it on my heart. My cum is sticky against my palm and Scarlett watches the movement, laughter draining from her face.

"Are you okay? Was it too soon?" she panics, pushing off the couch to her feet. She kneels at the side of the couch, running the back of her hand down the stubble on my cheek. "What's the matter?"

I shake my head. "It's just... my lungs burn because I'm

laughing so hard, and I haven't felt that in years. At the pool, I feel it there. I cause it there. I invite it there. But this is…"

"A good burn," she finishes before leaning over and pressing her soft lips to mine. Then she's gone, running water in the bathroom down the hall, returning with a towel. Straddling me, she pulls the wet terrycloth through my release, cleaning me up. I watch her with affection, and in comfortable silence, she takes care of me.

When she's done, she brings our breakfast plates back and I pull her into my lap. I continue feeding her, and then I eat as she curls into my chest, snuggling me while I do.

My chin on her head, her warm breath tickling my chest, she asks, "Did your celibacy extend to self-pleasure?"

She pulls away, blonde hair sticking up, cheeks still flush from our excitement earlier. She's never pink like this after scenes, and it dawns on me that's because with me, what we just did, everything was real. Nothing was acting.

"Yes," I admit, almost disbelieving of myself. "There were… inadvertent releases," I say, recalling the dozen or so times I woke up in a sticky, wet mess, my cock pulsing, my release clinging to my skin and the borrowed sheets. "But my mind could never really go there. I lost… all interest."

She nods, her lips turned down in sweet sadness. "Do you take anything?" she asks, and I know despite the fact we're talking about orgasms, she's asking about my depression. Because loss of interest in the things you love, like sex and orgasms, is a clinical sign.

I clear my throat, wanting her to know everything, but also not wanting her to see me as weak. Lifting my chin just slightly, I nod. "Yes. I have been on an antidepressant for four years. I actually changed my dose about a year ago."

"Up or down?" she asks quietly, curiously, trailing her

fingers over my chest in a way that makes talking about anything feel possible.

I swallow thickly. "Up."

She nods.

"Is what you said true?" I question, my voice still rumbly.

Sliding off my lap, she drifts down the hall, reemerging in a robe tied loose at her hip, and a blue bottle in her hand. Sitting next to me, she drapes her legs over my lap and slowly turns the bottle around between her hands. "I was in the grocery store, buying the steaks and salads for our dinner. You know, the night we got Italian," she starts, and I nod, imagining her long blonde hair trailing down her back, hands wrapping the red cart handle as she garners stares from everyone in that store, housewives included. She's so beautiful, and I'm protective of her and that beauty.

"We should shop together," I state, "I don't like the idea of you going out alone. Not while he's still trying to contact you."

She smiles. "I'd like that." She flips the lid up on the bottle, and brings it under her nose, the beachy fragrance making it my way. "I saw this," she says, cheeks flooding with pink, bottom lip pinched between her teeth as she casts a shy, seductive look at me. "When I left my old place, I only took what I could in a day. I only had a day before he'd realize I was leaving, so Aug and a few others came over, grabbed the boxes I'd packed, and that was that. I only took a few things, and a few documents."

I nod, transfixed by the bottle between her hands, wondering what one thing has to do with another.

"I hadn't wanted to touch myself in so long. And at work I'd just be acting, forcing the orgasm face, pretending to experience pleasure. But the truth was that after the last time Pete had told me I wasn't cut out to be a mother because—"

I curl my fists at that, and her eyes flit to my balled hands before coming back to my eyes. "Something shifted. My brain just... shut off to pleasure. And the scene I did after that, I didn't come. Didn't even come close. And I figured it was just my mood that day. But then one scene turned into a few, and a year later, I believed I couldn't orgasm anymore. That I was so psychologically fucked up that my body just... wouldn't do it."

"Could you have an orgasm alone?" I ask, getting a flash of her touching her clit while swaying over my cock. Another erection begins stirring, and my heart stutter steps a wild beat in response.

Her eyes are unwavering on me, and her response is clear, sun piercing through heavy clouds. "Not until you."

She holds the bottle up. "I couldn't stop thinking about you, and the way you treat me. You're such a gentleman, but so strong and caring and..." she lets out a heavy but comfortable sigh, and I feel it in my belly. The release of shame, the sharing of information, the bonding through words. It feels good to finally admit things, share things, and I imagine she feels the same.

"If you can believe it, I don't actually have any toys. When I left P—like I said," she corrects, leaving his name in darkness where it belongs. "I only took a few things. And anyway, why does a woman with a broken vagina need sex toys?" I tug her legs, bringing her closer.

"You're not broken."

She holds up the bottle. "No, I'm not. But I needed to meet you to realize that."

That's a powerful statement, one I share. "Do you mean that?" I ask, feeling insecure in needing to hear her say it again, but my ego needs it. I need to know my queen needs me in the same vein that I'm hungry to serve her. Nearly

215

obsessed with her at this point, which only slightly terrifies me.

"I do." She puts the bottle between her thighs, and plays with the lid as she speaks. "I had that feeling in my stomach," she whispers, pressing her other palm low to her belly. "And I was wet, I got wet thinking of what it would be like to take such a good, solid man, to have you inside me, to feel you pulsing and throbbing, to have your sweat on me, your body pressing against mine."

Jesus fuck. My sweats tent.

"You started to unpack my groceries that day, do you remember?"

I remember. I remember because she asked me not to help, so I didn't. As much as I wanted to help her, more than anything, I always want to obey her, give her exactly what she needs so she never doubts her voice matters, never wonders where she stands with me.

I nod. "I remember."

"You left, and I took that bottle, and I went into my bedroom, and I pulled my panties down, and I fucked myself with my eyes closed, wanting it to be you." With a loud click that makes my shoulders jump, she snaps the lid closed and looks at me. "And I had an orgasm. The first time in… over a year."

To an outsider, the question may sound silly, but between two people with our baggage, I know she'll understand the complexity of my question. "How was it?"

She sighs, and a strand of blonde hair sails up in her exhale. I reach out and tuck it behind her ear. "It was intense, physically it was intense. I was trembling, it was… explosive." She places her palm against my chest. "Not unlike yours. But it was also… life-changing. Knowing that I could still, knowing that I wasn't broken. That he didn't get the best parts of me. It gave me hope." She slides into my lap, straddling me, our faces a breath apart. Taking my face in her palms she whispers against my lips, "You give me hope, Cohen."

I slide my hands up her smooth, bare back, and pull her into me, gripping my wrist with my hand, holding her so goddamn tight. Our hearts beat wildly, rhythmically, together.

"Can I tell Aug about us?" she asks quietly. "Can we officially be an us?"

I grip her by the shoulders, push her back so our eyes align. "I'm yours, Scarlett."

nineteen

. . .

scarlett

He's beautiful and flawed, but perfect. And mine.

It's been a long time since I've been happily exhausted from work. But as we wrap the final voiceover for the Loved by Lucy promo, I'm thrilled to be, from the inside out, utterly exhausted.

I've worked so hard today and it's been so rewarding.

Vienna pulled me in for another casting, showed me her final prototype, and then I had three back-to-back solo scenes, each with a completely different set, costume and vibe. It was so much fun, and the best part?

I actually orgasmed.

It reminded me why I love what I do so much, how good it feels to give the viewer exactly what they came for—and more. And to bring the honesty and intention to the scene like I want to—that feels so good, so real... so me.

The old me, at least. Although, I was only happy and free and enjoying my work as Lucy Lovegood for a year before things took a turn, and even then, I wasn't as happy then as I am now. Despite the fact I was top billing for nearly every role, and was gaining notoriety in the community as a star, still, Pete's darkness was always there. Like a hand muffling the cries of a victim, his predatorial side was always present... just faint, lurking, something I could almost convince myself wasn't really there. But I felt it in my gut, I was just too sidetracked by promises of money and the life I desperately wanted.

I slip the headphones off, and carefully place them on the table, draped in thick, fuzzy, sound-absorbing fabric. The engineer ushers me out and I head straight to my dressing room, eager as ever to get home.

It's only been a week since me and Cohen have been an official item. Though in truth, our connection began weeks before that. The first time he showed up for me, driving me home then checking on me the next morning. He went out of his way with no expectations, and from that moment on, he's been at the forefront of my brain. Wiggling into places in my heart that I told myself would never be invaded again.

Now my arms are open, and I want everything he has to give me. I trust him, and I believe that together, we'll heal, more than we ever could alone. There's something about sharing pain, and starting to heal fractures that unites souls. That can't be denied.

Pulling on my very favorite pair of sweats, I quickly braid my hair to get it off of my face, and slip my feet into my slippers. Normally I'd never wear slippers to work in the event that my car broke down and I'd have to get out and walk— slippers are not the walking through the city vibe.

But Cohen is picking me up.

He told me he'd stay on set with me until we were finished, we were running a couple of hours late, and I did not want him to waste his evening waiting. The only way he'd leave is if I agreed he could pick me up.

After saying goodbye to Lance, who is lingering in Augustus's doorway, I push through the heavy metal door and my heart does backflips at the sight.

Cohen leaned against the back of my car, ankles crossed, those lace up boots and black jeans he always wears, paired with his favorite long sleeved flannel, have bumps rising up on my skin, heat slipping down my hoodie. A smile lifts his lips as he looks up, spotting me. He crosses the lot and takes my bag from my shoulder, looping a strong arm around my waist.

Cedar and sandalwood engulf my senses, mixed with shampoo and toothpaste, and being in his arms after a beautifully long and rewarding day feels like the perfect end.

I can see myself ending all of my days with Cohen.

His lips press soft kisses on the top of my head, along my hairline, then find my lips. From my bag, my phone rings. Cohen ignores it, walking me to the car, opening the door and waiting for me to sit inside. When I do, he leans in, kissing me again, pulling the belt across my lap. With one hand on the hood, still eating up the doorframe, he says, "I'm so glad you're done now. I missed you."

"It's only been a few hours." Still, I feel the same way. "I missed you, too."

I watch as he walks around the front of my car, dropping his hand subtly inside my bag. He stands with his back to the driver's side door, my phone pressed to his ear. I can't hear his words, but I do hear his tone. Deep, unrelenting, but he's not loud. A moment later, my phone is back in the bag as he places it in the backseat and gets inside.

I know it was Pete.

He's called all day. And since Otis has given him the brush off after being used and played, Pete's been a little frantic this week.

More calls.

And according to the super, more showing up at my apartment, banging on the door, shouting and in general, being the piece of human excrement that he is.

Neither Cohen or I have been there when it's happened, and I don't understand how Pete wouldn't realize midday I would be at work. Or, for that matter, why *he* isn't at work. I can only say I'm grateful filming and promo work has been so busy this week. And in the evenings, I've been so wrapped up in Cohen that nothing else exists except us inside one of our apartments.

It's the most beautiful thing I've ever experienced.

"My place or yours tonight?" I ask as we climb the cement stairs to our apartments, Cohen's hand at my lower back for support. I won't fall, but I know his protective and guiding touch is there.

We stand in the landing between the doors, looking back and forth. "Whatever you'd like," he says, adjusting my bag on his shoulder.

I point to my door. "I really need to shower. Maybe I can do that at my place and then we go back to yours?" I look down at my sweats and up at him. "I haven't done laundry in a week. I'll have to put this back on."

He unlocks the door, and holds it open for me. We head inside and only after I'm a few feet into my dark and cold apartment, do I turn around and face him. "Maybe I can shower at your place?" I know our bathrooms are exactly the same. We have the same apartment. But still, something about this place, especially after knowing Pete's been here off and on all week, banging on the door.

"What do you need to take back to my place?" he asks, lowering my work bag to the floor, bringing with him my phone and keys. "Toiletries?"

"Yeah," I say, tapping my chin. "And clean panties. Those for sure I have," I say with an embarrassed shrug. "But I may have to run down to the laundry room tonight and start a load. I don't have anything clean to wear after." I press my palm to my forehead, frustrated with myself for forgetting something so basic.

Cohen lifts my chin with his hand, winking at me. "I got a stackable unit delivered to my place tonight, so I can wash your clothes at my place. Got a few other things delivered, too. Let's go to my place, I'll run you a bath, and wash your clothes while you soak." He kisses me, and warmth blooms in my eyes. He's so considerate and thoughtful... and calm. I never knew how much I adored calm until Cohen.

With his hand wrapped around mine, he leads me across the hall to his apartment, and when he closes the door behind us, I'm overwhelmed.

I face him. "You cooked," I breathe, taking in the scent of marinara and spices.

"Arms," he says, and I lift in response. He peels my hoodie off, then crouches, peeling my sweats off, too. Taking my hand again, he guides me the remaining few steps to the bathroom, and flicks on the light.

Along the counter are blue and purple bottles, one bubble bath, one body wash. *Rainfall scented.* I pick it up as Cohen starts the bath, then pulls a freshly washed and still warm white towel from the rack above the toilet.

"You shopped," I say, winking at him as he spots the blue bottle in my hand.

Reaching around my head, he slowly pulls the hair tie loose from my hair, and runs his fingers through my scalp, causing my eyes to flutter shut. Taking your bra off after a long day feels good, but having a head massage after having a ponytail all day feels better.

He bends down, testing the temperature with two thick fingers, and as I watch him swipe through the water, my pussy clenches. I take off my bra and panties while he adds bubble bath to the tub, and when he turns around, a low groan erupts from the depths of him. He shoves a hand through his hair, pushing out a breath.

I press my hand to his chest, over his flannel, and step so close that my nipples rub against him. "Thank you for running the bath for me."

He holds his hand out, and I place mine in his to hold steady as I step in. Cohen keeps his eyes on the surface of the water, and it's not the hot water I'm sinking into that has me hot. His discipline and the way he respects my body, waits for me to invite him, it's fucking hot. That's where I'm at in life; seeing respect and care as hot.

But it is.

"Cohen," I say to his back as he's walking out. He stops, and turns partially, gripping the door frame with both hands as he turns his head over his shoulder, looking at me.

"Will you be naked with me again tonight?"

I watch the silhouette of his Adam's apple slide beneath his collar. "Laundry won't take too long. The drum is small. I can have a load washed and dried in less than forty-five minutes."

I swish my hand between the foamy bubbles. "I want to be naked with you all night."

He faces forward, sighing, before turning completely in the doorway, facing me in the tub.

"I want you to be ready, Scarlett. I don't want to move too fast." The way he grips the doorframe, knuckles white, strain in his neck, I know he wants me, too.

"I know you do." My voice is gentle, smoothing his sharp, defensive edges. "You take care of me. Now let me take care of you," I practically whimper. Beneath the surface, I'm touching myself.

I keep replaying how he erupted violently over himself, a release so big, I'll always remember; it was so fucking hot. I want to please Cohen, but more so, I want to show him all the things he deserves.

"Cohen," I say again, sure that I want him, unsure that he'll let me have him. He's protective of me and his cognizance of my needs, balanced with his awareness of my trauma only makes me yearn for him more. And while I know his hesitance comes from reason and a place of safety, I feel ready.

I come to a decision on a way we can each get what we want and need.

"What did you make for dinner?"

He looks confused for a moment, then scrubs a hand down his face. "I made ziti, and roasted vegetables, and I stopped by Rise and Grind and grabbed some pastries, too."

My stomach rumbles and the aroma from the kitchen seems to intensify now that I know what I'm smelling. I sit up in the tub, the air chilly against my soapy, bare breasts. His eyes drop to them, and his grip on the doorframe intensifies.

"That sounds amazing. Can you keep it warm for another twenty minutes?" I lift a leg, watching as clusters of white foam drip off me. Cohen's watching with bated breath.

"Yeah..." he says, voice raspy, stirring up loose embers in my belly. "Enjoy your soak."

I reach between my feet and pull the drain. "I'm done."

He looks a little puzzled. "That was only five minutes."

I push off the edge of the tub and reach for the towel, wrapping myself deliberately slowly, letting him feast on me.

Before I have to ask, Cohen extends a hand to me, helping me step out of the tub. He adjusts where the towel is tucked into itself below my collarbone, and his hands brushing my damp flesh have me certain of my plan.

Leading him around the corner by the hand, we stand in his bedroom, one that mirrors mine. Our apartment floor plans are identical, however, laid out opposite. It's comfortable being in a room that looks and feels like mine. His scent is everywhere, and paired with the heady aroma of homemade food, my chest expands.

The status of his room isn't unlike mine either, with a boxspring and mattress centering the floor, no bed frame in sight. Since I've last been here, everything looks the same, and I wonder when we're not together, how things are for Cohen. His bed doesn't look slept in, or else he makes it every day before work.

I turn to face him, and it takes him a moment to take his eyes off my ass. I'm warm and wet from his gaze. "Do you make your bed every morning?"

His head volleys, a cross between a nod and a timid shake. "I do, but I haven't been sleeping in bed."

"No?" I ask, leading him to the edge of the mattress by our linked fingers. "Take off your boots and socks. Now."

He sits on the edge of the bed, his fingers sweeping down the intricate brown laces of his boots until they're unlaced. Toe to heel, he kicks them off, and peels his socks off next by the toe. Sitting up, his gaze idles on me, waiting for instruction.

"Where have you been sleeping?" I ask, knowing that two of those nights he was with me, but the other nights, we made the choice to sleep apart. I don't know that either of us wanted that, but we came to the agreement that it was likely a smart choice. Because I'm falling for Cohen hard and fast, but I also know I fell for Pete that way, too.

I need to pace myself this time, be so sure before I tie myself to someone else.

"On the couch."

When I came in, I noticed he'd moved his couch from one wall to the opposite, now facing the rectangular window facing the breezeway between our places. I assumed he moved it to better capture the morning light and evening sunset.

"You moved it," I state, then add, "Stand up and take off your pants."

He rises without question, hands working his belt with a clank as he says, "I slept on it facing the window, in case Pete came back."

A warm shiver wraps my spine, the type of burning tingle that comes with new affection. My voice is quiet when I say, "Take your shirt off, too."

A moment later, Cohen is standing before me with nothing but boxer briefs on. With the tips of my fingers, I trace the hard ridge of his cock before grabbing it, lifting it off his thigh to position his cock to standing. Tugging the waist of his briefs down just slightly, I adjust him as he groans, releasing him when the crown of his hefty cock is exposed. I tease the tip, tapping the slit on his head, loving his gasps and grunts and the way his spine lengthens as he battles his body for control.

"Get on the bed."

His voice is raw. "You need to eat, Scarlett. You worked 14 hours today."

"I need you to eat first." I point to the center of his bed. "Get in the center, please. And lose the boxers."

"Are you sure?" He asks, though he asks while positioning himself in the middle of the tufted, buoyant mattress.

"Lie on your hands," I reply, ignoring his question. "And remember, Cohen, if you want to stop, we can stop at any time."

He nods but I need to hear his understanding. I need him to verbally acknowledge that I'm not pushing his boundaries, or taking advantage of him because I know how much he likes to please me. As he slips his boxers off, I tell him, "Say it, please, I need to hear you say that you know I would never go further than you're comfortable with."

"Let me be clear right now Scarlett," he growls, his cock leaving a smear of arousal on his belly as he slips his hands beneath his lower back, obeying me. "I want you in ways I've never wanted anyone. I want to fuck you and fill you and absolutely fucking devour you. I want to know what every inch of you tastes like, and I want you every day. But I respect you and what you do, and I want you to lead. I want you to show me *what* you're ready for and *when*. So know this, if I say red, it's because I want *you* to consider what we're doing, not because I don't want it." His nostrils flare with his passion. "I haven't made love in four years. I haven't *wanted* *to* for four years. But now I have you, and all I want to do is make up for lost time." He inhales slowly and exhales heavily. "But only when the time is right."

I nod, biting back the sting of tears. Who knew consideration and kindness could be an aphrodisiac. When this thought came to me in the tub, I wondered if I should move faster, take it further. But as I stare at the meaty length of his hard cock and the red hue of his swollen, shimmering head, I realize moving slowly doesn't have to be just a way to respect my trauma.

Teasing and edging one another until we're ready for the next step can also be the best foreplay and so much fun.

I climb onto the bed, straddling his hips, my knees dipping into the mattress. I drag my nails down his chest, admiring how his muscles stay defined and knotted even while lying.

"You have such a beautiful body," I breathe, admiring him. I find his face, and my hands still when I see him turned away from me, eyes hovering on the wall. "Cohen," I breathe, but he doesn't look. With my palms flat on his pecs, I slide my groin over his, calling for his focus again.

"Cohen."

Why doesn't he want to look at me? "Look at me, Cohen." Slowly, he faces me, pain is his eyes. Immediately, I know I'm in deep. Because his pained expression sears through me, leaving angst and sadness in its wake. I lay one hand to his cheek, pressing my thumb to his lips. "Tell me how you're feeling, or say red."

His swallow is slow, and he takes his time with his words. And in his lap, his hard cock notched at my bare core, I wait.

"I don't deserve you, I don't deserve this," he finally breathes, emotion thick in his voice, making it weak and unsteady.

Oh. In my journey of self-awareness to honor and respect my trauma, I selfishly forgot to consider that Cohen's celibacy wasn't necessarily intentional or by choice. What happened in Michigan, the tremendous loss he's suffered, he's still battling blame and the belief that because of what happened, he doesn't deserve happiness. A new life.

A second chance.

"You are my deserving, sweet, most beautiful man, do you

hear me?" I ask now, gripping him by the chin, piercing his eyes with mine. "You deserve every happiness this world has to offer. What happened to you was awful. Terrible. Horrendous," I gasp, my chest heaving as anger and frustration course through me, strengthening my grip on his chin. "You had no control over what happened, and it wasn't your fault, and you deserve this Cohen." I slam my lips to his and do my very best to absorb his sadness. When I pull back, my eyes fall to his cock, beautiful, thick, weeping for us.

I swipe through what pools on his belly, and suck his essence into my mouth. "Ready?" I ask, my eyes flitting between his.

He looks down at my cunt splayed over his groin, groaning at the sight of his cock head, fiery red with need. "Sit on my face and fucking smother me, *now.*"

Jesus Christ. Those filthy pleas coming from my loyal and courageous protector... my pussy clenches in eager anticipation. "If you need to safeword out, free your hands then give two taps on my ass," I warn as I shimmy over him, letting my knees slide along the fabric until his mouth is smothered.

Warm lips and a hot tongue surround my clit, and his moans vibrate through me, making my entire core rattle with need. With his hands still beneath him, I rock my hips as he licks and kisses, my orgasm builds urgently, toe-curling need sweeping through me.

I rock and sway over his face, loving the way he nestles into my wetness, lapping at everything I have for him. And it is for him, and so I tell him as much.

"I'm so wet for you, wet because of you. God, I need you, I need you so much it hurts," I moan, dropping my hands to his hair, tugging as he sucks my clit between his teeth.

He nibbles softly as my hips slowly sway, riding out a slow, sweet orgasm.

As the clenching and tightening subsides, while my breathing is still hectic, I slide down on Cohen, only slightly. Exposing his swollen lips and red nose, colored from the friction, I lock eyes with him.

"Thank you," I tell him, as I reach behind me, between his thighs, and take him in my hand. I stroke him, and praise him. "Sweet man," I whisper, our eyes idling, my hand stroking. "Taking care of me in all ways," I tell him, swiping my thumb over the rounded tip of his cock. He's sticky and slick, and I want more than anything to notch him at my entrance and sink down on him, and fuck him until he believes he deserves it.

But he's not wrong in his caution.

I love what we just did, but his hands were behind his back. Had his hands been free and discovering my body as I writhed on his face, would I have been completely okay? Would I have freaked out? I want to believe because of the connection I feel, I wouldn't be triggered and that my ability to orgasm wouldn't just evaporate. But I don't know, and I'm scared to risk it.

"Now it's time to take care of you."

He doesn't protest, but I can see in his timid expression that he's not sure he deserves it, but the way he's made me see I deserve more, I'm determined to do the same.

I release my hold on his cock and slide down until I'm positioned between his legs. With both palms atop his thighs, I begin slowly kneading his muscles, easing the tension. As I rub him, inner thigh and quad, even up to his hips, his cock perks up. It jumps on his belly when my fingertips skim the underside of his sack.

"When you put your hand on the top of my foot that day, before that scene," I recall softly, his eyes fluttering open to watch me speak. "That was the difference between me doing the scene for the contract and me doing the scene because I actually enjoy my job."

Slowly, I bring my hands to his balls, wrapping one around them at the base, and use my fingertips to gently drag my nails over the hot, bumpy flesh. "You made me remember how much I love my job," I clarify, loving how his breath hitches in reaction to me playing with his balls.

Along the curve of his hip, precum drips, and I look to his cock to find the head resting in a large pool. I sweep my finger through the mess, collecting it.

"You're so messy for me," I breathe, my nipples hardening. His eyes go to the mess, then to my hands, then to my breasts before he squeezes them shut.

"Scarlett," he groans. "Touch me, *please*."

Suddenly, I have an idea better than making him come from ball play. "Come on," I whisper, "come to the bathroom."

He blinks at me, caught between almost ejaculating from the foreplay and the urge to obey me. I raise my eyebrows and he swings his legs off the bed, using those big hands to hold his cock and balls as he walks to the bathroom with me.

I turn on the light and find us in the mirror, sweaty and pink-cheeked from the passion.

He dwarfs me in height, his hips nearly a foot above mine, and as I nudge us forward, his balls come to rest atop the bathroom counter. He hisses from the cool tile, and I place my palms on his belly and chest, pulling myself to his back. His entire body deflates with relaxation. My breasts press into him from behind, and his eyes pinch on my hands in the reflection, watching the way I soothe and calm him. His long cock bobs above his big, heavy sac, and my pussy clenches when I see the precum strung between his head and the sink basin.

He's so ready.

My poor, beautiful man has been celibate for years. This perfect, most amazing cock has been shelved and unused for *too long*. My hands traverse the ridges of his carved muscles, and take almost all of his sac in one palm, wrapping the other around the base of his shaft.

"Keep your eyes open, and watch me give you what you need," I tell him, raising to my toes, calves burning as I lean into him. His posture melts from the heated moment, allowing me to rise up enough to rest my chin atop his shoulder. He turns his head slightly, and I watch his reflection as his eyes flutter closed, taking a long inhale with his nose in my hair.

"I love your hair," he says, voice rough.

"Hmm," I humm, relishing the way he nuzzles into me for comfort, the way he lingers in my scent like I'm the best thing that ever happened to him.

He faces forward as I tighten my grip on his balls. Round, full and heavy, I don't know if it's just because they're Cohen's and I'm quickly reaching the place in our relationship where every single thing about him turns me on, or if these are just really amazing balls. Whatever it is, my mouth waters. I ache to drop to my knees and feel his hard cock rest along my face as I suck and lick those glorious things until he unleashes a load on my face, streaking my hair.

"Cohen," I breathe, staying focused on his pleasure and his pleasure alone. "Watch us."

Fingers splayed along the edge of the counter, he tips his head forward slightly, gazing into the mirror.

I squeeze his balls and his jaw flexes, letting go of only the tiniest moan. I pump his cock, his precum making the best lube. Twisting my hand over his head before pulling it down, loosening my hold as I near the base, I jerk him. Stroke after calculated stroke, I jerk as I squeeze and knead his sac, nearly drooling at the way his abs tighten and his head bobs.

"You're so good," I tell him, realizing that good is a broad statement, but holding him like this, his strong back to my chest, manhood in my hands, I can't think of anything more eloquent. "So good," I moan as I twist my hand over his head, smearing more warm precum down his length.

"Lift your eyes," I breathe at the back of his ear, calves burning as I stand on the balls of my feet. Across from us, our image blinks back, our eyes idling somewhere in the in-between. His lips curl up just slightly on the edge, a semblance of happiness amidst the need. Then Cohen does something unexpected and sweet, making my belly burn with desire, intensifying the demanding ache between my legs.

"Can I come for you?" he asks, strain etching his neck. I bite into his shoulder gently, then kiss the mark I've left behind.

"Put your hand on mine," I whisper, and watch as he does just that. Slowly then, I slip mine out, and release his balls, loving their swollen state in the reflection. "Do it," I tell him, narrowing my gaze, sharpening my tone, demanding his release.

My cunt spasms at the sight of that strong hand gripping himself. Why is seeing how a man touches himself so fucking hot? I like it on set, and try not to look, as I don't want to fantasize about co-workers. That's how hot it is.

And seeing how they masturbate? The way they bring themselves to orgasm—it's so intimate, private, and personal. And so hot. So. Fucking. Hot.

My body literally incinerates from the inside out as his biceps flexes, his arm jutting out as he pumps his length, thumb and tip of middle finger not even touching. His balls jerk.

My mouth waters.

My pussy aches.

My fingers dance at my sides.

Placing my palms on his shoulder blades, I slowly and softly knead his back as he jacks off, staring at our reflection in the mirror.

"And yes, please," I add, my voice hoarse, mouth dry. "Come for me. I want you to come for me."

Before his lids get too heavy to battle, his eyes go doughy, soft and detached as his orgasm roars through him. His hand stops just before the red rim of his crown. His belly tightens, knotted with muscle and a sprinkling of trimmed hair.

His eruption marks the mirror, cum dripping down the faucet, streaking the tile counter. His fist twists around his crown as more release scatters over the sink, dropping with weight into the basin. Cum rolls around the curve of his knuckle, dripping from his fist.

My stomach bottoms out as my kegel muscles seize, my pussy clenching, desperate to be full, achy from emptiness. I press my lips to his back and reward him. "You were so hot. I got so turned on watching you. You're..." I sigh against his back and enjoy the sinking of his shoulders as he relaxes back against me. "You're so fucking good, Cohen. Everything about you is every-thing I've always wanted, and started to worry never existed."

He turns in my arms, forgetting the mess in his hand, his eyes clearly captivated by my words. "Thank you," he says. "Thank you for giving me that."

Then he turns, and twists the sink knob, gushing water eating up the post-orgasmic haze, leaving us in light and clar-ity. "You're welcome."

He turns back once the sink is off, and drops to his knees carefully, bending down. His lips land on the top of my foot, and work their way up my ankle then around my calf. He kisses his way up, getting to his feet, pressing his lips to the top of a hand. He pulls me to him, kissing my neck, then jaw, and finally, my mouth.

His cock twitches against me, and my reaction is a soft smile, and nuzzling deeper into his lips. We break apart, and Cohen asks if he can help me get dressed. I don't have much, so he loans me one of his t-shirts and a pair of his boxers. I let him dress me, loving the attention. Loving how my body warms as his hands graze my center, slipping his t-shirt on me. How the backs of his fingers slide up my legs as he pulls up his boxer shorts.

He dishes up dinner, and fills his new dining table with plates of delicious, homemade food. Two glasses of wine and a bottle are there, along with a basket of warm bread and napkins. With silverware. Hallelujah to no more plastic utensils.

Before we dig in, and because I don't think I can eat without knowing, I clear my throat.

"If I were ready, I mean, if I were to be completely sure I was ready to have... sex with you... would you be ready? Could you?"

His Adam's apple jumps and his nostrils flare just slightly. "Yes." His answer comes relatively quickly, and I wonder if all he needed to end his celibacy was hearing from someone that he's worthy.

He's punished himself for so long, deprived himself.

He needed to know he was worth more than that, because that was the key to moving past his grief. Feeling that there was a purpose for him here.

I feel so much for him, and what he's been through. And I want him. I want to use my body to bring him so much pleasure that he's drunk off of me. Intoxicated, fully addicted to me and only me.

He's beautiful and flawed, but perfect. And mine.

"Are you ready?" he asks, voice strong and steady, like him.

"I'm ready, Cohen. I want you. And you're ready, too." I swallow, and brace myself for a strange reaction, but I have an idea on how we can have our cake and eat it, too. Something I learned at Crave.

"But… to ease into things, there's something we could do where…" I swallow and look down at my plate of warm, homemade food, and something ignites in my chest. I hope he gives this a chance because just the thought has me drenched. "You would be inside of me. But we wouldn't have sex. We'd just… *be*."

His lips twitch.

"What?" I ask, brows dipping. Is he laughing at me? I can't believe Cohen would. Now he's full blown smiling.

"Cockwarming," he says, and Jesus Christ, my burnin' loins and my achin' ovaries. A man like Cohen saying dirty things? I may come right here, right now, swear to God.

"Why are you smirking?" Not that I don't like it, I just don't know what it means.

"I know what it is. You didn't think I would."

I don't disagree. "You're right. I didn't. And you do?"

He nods but his smile is gone, his focus already back on the issue at hand.

"Sit in my lap," he offers, voice rocky and raw, but low, too, scraping the nerve endings from me. My nipples are hard, my skin is covered in goosebumps, the back of my neck is moist from sweat and my cunt is pulsing so hard. "And I'll feed you your dinner." He pushes back from the table, moves his plate aside then leans over, tugging my meal to him. He pats his leg, and I go to him slowly, dragging my nails along the curved edge of the table, my tongue sweeping my bottom lip as I eye him.

"You like the idea?" I ask, my voice unexpectedly smoky.

"I think it's a good way to see how you'll feel," he says, his tone serious. "But I do only what pleases you."

I take a seat in his lap, legs draped over one side. With one shoulder partially leaned against him, he slides his hand up my back, under my shirt. He keeps me steady as he reaches between us, sliding his cock from his sweats. I tug my panties and shorts aside, and let out a whimpering moan as he notches himself at my wet hole.

I want to feel his cum tear through me, hot and potent. I want him to leave me so full of his cum that I leak into panties all week. I want him to drill that big dick of his so fucking deep that when he pours his cum into me, that perfect ass of his clenching, there's no way I'm not getting pregnant.

Fuck. I want his babies. I want him to breed me, carry his child. Bring a life that's from him into the world.

"*Jesus Christ,*" I utter as I sink down, down, down, like Alice down the rabbit hole, until his wide crown nudges my g-spot and my pussy feels so full, I can hardly move.

But that's the point: *not* moving.

My mind shrinks down to a singular focus: *do not clench your pussy.* If you clench all around him, you're going to either come immediately and ruin this, or start bouncing, because his dick is thick and long and so fucking hard. So perfect.

Shit.

I'm a porn star and I've never called a cock perfect.

My focus is stolen, relaxing my cunt as he drives a bite of ziti into my mouth, after blowing to cool it. I moan through the bite, the warm ricotta creamy, the noodles the perfect soft-ness. His voice is smoky against my ear when he asks, "Does it taste good to you?"

I nod. "Very."

He gives me another bite, and as I swallow, he thickens inside me in a few pulsing waves. I see in his eyes determina-tion, and know he's fighting an orgasm. We both are.

But we're going to do this.

Cohen pokes at the ziti with the tines of the fork, bringing another bite up to my lips. Before he serves it up close enough for me to take, he stops short. "If there's a meal you want, tell me and I'll make it, okay?"

I lick my lips, and my heart tickles my ribs. "I like the ziti."

He nods. "I know. But I will make you anything." His cock flexes and I bite my bottom lip so I don't start milking him. My pussy feels so good, I no longer have control.

"Thank you," I say, in awe of this man who genuinely wants to serve me. But it's not just food. He wants to pleasure me first, he wants to open my doors for me and hell, he fixes things in my apartment and the other day he bought me vita-mins. His kind heart and penchant for protecting me have me so deep in this. So ready for more.

But for now, keeping him hard inside me is something I can do. And I am lucky enough to do so.

His breath is hot against my neck. "We don't come like this. I feed you. I make sure you're full, and you enjoy every bite. And then I take you to bed, and make sure you get rest because you've had an extremely long week, and you need it."

I lick my lips, both hating and loving those plans. I want that orgasmless intimacy, those vulnerable and deep moments.

But I want to be worshiped by him in equal measure. I want him kneeling at my feet again, kissing his way up to my bare cunt and feasting on me until I collapse in sticky pleasure.

But his way is better, and exactly what we need to bridge the gap.

"Another bite," I tell him.

He feeds me, taking turns to feed himself, and like that, we work through both plates together. He adjusts me a few times, asks to be kissed a couple of times, too. But at the end of the meal, he leans forward and I steady myself on my feet, letting him slide out. I reach out, grabbing the edge of the table to adjust to the emptiness. I almost whimper, I swear.

His hand presses to my lower back as he guides us... first to the bathroom, where we talk about our favorite desserts ever—because that's what you do after you eat a good meal, you dream up a delicious dessert.

He turns down the bed, and waits for me to slide in.

Cohen joins me in bed but pulls me all the way onto him, stacking his chin on my head. "Thank you," he says, adding, "you changed my life."

I blink into the darkness, heart running wild, pulse hammering. He kisses the top of my head and says, "Goodnight. I'm here if you need anything."

And I want to pull apart those words—*you changed my life* —and really jump into how beautiful and completely romantic of a thing that is to say but I feel so pleasantly warm in his arms, and my body relaxes and goes limp.

And I fall asleep before I can think of anything else.

twenty

. . .

cohen

She comes first, always.

Waking slowly, my eyes are slow to adjust to the room around me, but already, my brain is replaying yesterday and last night. I stretch my feet through the sheets, curling myself around her, remembering it.

Her laugh makes me smile, and yesterday, I found myself smiling midday on set for no other reason than the fact I feel happy and lucky.

I smelled her on my clothes, and my heart raced a little faster, and my thoughts about lighting and boom arm position fell away, going only to her, and how I was going to make her happy. Because she is the sole reason for my life returning to me. And all I wanted to do yesterday was praise and worship her, prove to her that her past is her past, that she deserves everything and then some.

The day was filled with me staring and dreaming, and fuck did that feel surreal. I'd planned to fall to her feet and give her anything she needed last night, but instead, she gave us slow, caring intimacy. And it was perfect. It was a night I'll never forget. Then again, all of the time I've spent with Scarlett is unforgettable. She's the breath that conquered my slow suffocation, and now that I'm breathing, I'm seeing color again.

At some point while we slept, she stripped from her jammies and sent them to the floor, and as I stare at them with groggy eyes, I remember how she cuddled back into me, whispering through sleep how she needed us to be skin to skin. I happily obliged, and I can safely say, she's a goddamn genius because waking up naked and tangled with Scarlett is the best way to wake up.

Far better than an alarm and cold pool water.

With her slender frame folded over mine, my hand stroking up her back, morning wood tenting the sheet as she sleeps... her phone vibrates. It skitters across the new nightstand several times before she stirs, and rage floods my veins. Rage at our moment being interrupted, at him not leaving her alone, at all the pain he caused her. She can't even make love without fearing she'll be unable to enjoy it, fearing she'll be triggered to close her body off and disappear in her mind. He did that to her, and I want to fucking kill him.

But anger and rage, big hate and loud voices, those things would be for me, not her. Scarlett gets anxious around those reactive actions and behaviors because, surprise surprise, they take her back to her time at Jizzabelle, and her time with Pete.

As much as I want to curse and yell and, quite frankly, find him and beat him fucking senseless, I remain calm, cool and collected. Her loyal, calm presence, devoted to her and her needs.

That means, when I reach over and take her phone in my hand, I keep my voice low and calm as I relay to Pete that Scarlett does not want to speak with him. I grind my molars but keep my face free of strain or anger as she rolls back into me, blinking up at me with sleepy, sated eyes.

I don't tell her that Pete says he's going to fucking kill me and her both.

I don't believe him, so I'm not worried, and as soon as I end the call, I turn her phone off, and pull her against me.

"I thought he'd stop. The calls were… I don't know, dwindling I thought," she says as she captures a yawn with her hand. But instead of diving into Pete and the past, she smiles up at me. "I'm getting used to sleeping in your arms."

"I am too," I reply, stroking my fingers through her silky hair. "What's your schedule like today?"

She pushes up, stacking her chin on her fists atop my chest, and it's such a simple thing but it feels so casual to do while we're naked. Talking like this, in bed, about the mundane details of our day. I want to wake up everyday with her body against mine while we sort out her schedule and plans.

I ignore the tightness in my chest. Waking up with her, falling deeper for her, being part of her life. It's exactly what I thought I'd never have again, and everything I've always wanted again.

I just never let myself consider it.

"I have therapy this morning, so Aug scheduled me for a later shoot."

"Are you done with promos for Loved by Lucy?" I push a strand of honey hair from her face and slip it behind her ear.

My morning wood seems to be aware that she's here, because it's harder and more aggressive than ever.

Ignoring it, I tuck a folded arm behind my head to better focus on her answer.

"Yeah, done with promos. Today's shoot is actually a menage." She looks down at my chest, but I can tell she's not seeing much.

"What's the matter?"

She volleys her head. "You know I love what I do, and even with all the shit Pete forced and tricked me into doing, still, at the end of the day, I do love making movies that make real couples more likely to explore their sexualities and kinks. And I know that's what Crave does, and I love it. I love doing it. I do."

I give her half of a smile as my cock still throbs. "I know you do. I also know, and want you to know, that when you're with me, you don't have to be worried about what comes after the *but*."

She arches a brow, pushing up to sit cross-legged next to my hip, exposing her luscious nude body to me. It's now that she notices the tented sheet. Wrapping her hand around my cotton covered cock, she returns her focus to me.

"After the but?" she questions with a serious curve in her brow, as if she isn't jerking me slowly over the fabric.

"Uh," I clear my throat and keep my eyes on her, despite the fact I want to tear this sheet off, put her on her back and slide inside of her sweet, wet heat and make her forget everything that's ever made her feel bad. "I could sense a but coming, and I want you to know, that's why you have me. For everything after the but."

She gives my cock another tug. "Okay," she exhales, taking a moment to gather her words. Still stroking, she says, "At first I thought I was broken, you know, well, *obviously* you know." She pumps again and a dark spot forms on the sheet where my cock weeps for her.

"But now that I know it was more of a psychological block than anything, I feel like I have some clarity. I guess... I'm glad everything happened with Jizz and Pete because now I realize exactly what I need and want from life."

I swallow hard, my mind swerving between *oh god I'm going to come soon if she keeps this up* and *please tell me your needs and wants and for the love of anything holy, I hope I'm in there somewhere.*

"What do you want, Scarlett?" I hope I can give it to her, whatever it is.

"The same things I wanted before it got really bad with Pete." She looks over at where she squeezes and strokes me. "I want to finish school, and I want to code. And... I want to be a mother."

She doesn't look my way, but pulls the sheet down to expose my pink, eager dick. With her palm, she gives my full sac a gentle squeeze. "And I want to work at Crave, but I want that to come second to my first dream. I really want to finish school, Cohen."

"You can have and do it all, I promise you. You want to stay at Crave but go part-time? I have no doubt Aug will understand." I close my eyes to gather strength, but her hand works me expertly, and the warm glide of my own precum isn't helping my resolve.

"I'll help you re-enroll. Or start somewhere new in the city. And as for..." my words trail off as she twists her palm around my crown, that dangerous way she does, the way I'm learning is probably a trick of the trade. I fucking love it. But after four years of ignoring hard-ons and blowing in my sheets, the move is intense.

"Scarlett," I reach for her, stopping her hand. "I'm..." I

shake my head a little, but she grins at me, blue eyes glittering in the morning sun that fills the room.

"Going to come? I know. That's the point."

I knock her hand away, and silently ask God if he saw that, because come on. "I don't ever want to come before you. Understand?" I sit up. "Let me give you an orgasm. Please, let me be the lucky man that feels you come on my mouth first thing in the morning. *Please.*"

"Can we come together?" she asks, filling her hands with her breasts, her lashes fluttering as she peers down at herself. Fuck she's gorgeous. It doesn't surprise me in the least bit that she's the top performer. I'm sure she's great in scenes— fuck me, she's great in real life—but I think the number one draw is her sweet sensibility and delicate features. She looks like someone who would make you happy, and she looks like she'd feel like goddamn heaven.

And I'm the lucky fuck that knows she does.

"You come first," I repeat, because the truth is, nothing gets me harder, fills my cup, and makes me sleep more soundly than giving to her. Providing for her. Caring for her.

Her hand wrapping my crown is a pretty close second. Though I can only assume the hand will be usurped very quickly once we have sex.

"Lay your head back, do as you're told and I promise, I'll come first," she says, getting to her knees on the bed.

I trust her. I don't make her repeat or explain her promises, I simply take her words and roll with them, lowering my head back down on the mattress.

"No pillows," she orders, nodding to the row of stacked down feather pillows behind her. With a sweep of her arm she knocks them off the bed. She slinks over me like a predator, on her hands and knees, then drops an unusually raw and rough kiss on my lips before turning around and lowering her perfect pussy to my face.

"I'll let you make me come first," she announces, looking back at me over the smooth curve of her back. "But you better hurry, because my mouth is watering."

She turns back, and drags the tip of her tongue along my slit, and I can't help myself. I let out a loud, breathy moan. As I kiss her clit and trace her opening with my tongue, reality twists tightly around my spine, making me so fucking aware that I can have more than my past.

"Put a finger inside me," she guides, telling me what she needs to feel good. I love that about her, and I don't know if it's the adult film star in her or the girlfriend in her, but the way she communicates her physical needs and plans—I'm never left guessing.

My cock bobs as she licks up my shaft, and I bury my groan in her cunt, slippery and swollen. Sucking and licking her clit, I slide my index finger inside of her, and practically come when she seizes up around me, clenching my finger like a cock.

"Mmm, Cohen, yes," she moans into my cock head like a fucking microphone, the subtle graze of her lips and her hot breath making me clench my ass. It feels so good and she hasn't even sucked me into her throat yet. "Another finger."

I slip in another and at the same time, she sucks my head into her mouth, sealing her lips beneath my crown. She sucks me like she's trying to siphon out my cum, and god damnit I'm close.

But she comes first, always.

"Another finger," she begs, after popping off my head. She licks up and down my shaft again as I give her one more finger, my abs tightening at how good she feels. How tight she is.

"I can't wait for you to fuck me, Cohen," she breathes, wiggling her bare ass over me before sinking down on my face so deep, I have to turn my head to take a breath. I suck in a big one, preparing to feast and finger fuck for as long as I can.

She bobs down on my length, and when my cockhead slams against the back of her throat, my toes curl. Precum slips out, I can't fucking help it, but I focus on my meal, suckling at her clit, making her tremble all around me.

She pops off. "You're going to spread me wide, fuck me hard and fill me deep, aren't you?" she breathes, her voice trembling, her back concave as she sinks into me further. "I want you to, Cohen. I can't wait to feel you pump all that cum inside me. Empty yourself inside me. Give me everything you've been holding back. Give me every last drop." Her hips sway as I pump my fingers in and out, lapping at her clit frantically as she stills over me.

"You're so good, you're going to breed me so good, aren't you? Pump me full and leave me round, make me yours," she moans dizzying promises.

And on that sentiment, she comes. Writhing, wiggling, moaning, she fucks my face and sucks my cock until I see goddamn stars. I can't even warn her I'm about to erupt because she doesn't stop riding my face and filling my mouth with her sweet release, coming, shuddering, shivering.

I can't hold back. I fucking can't. With my mouth full of sweet, swollen pussy, I growl my relief as my cock throbs and pulses, releasing long, thick streams of cum.

I come so hard my back crescents along the mattress, and my nose drives into her ass as I lift off the bed in orgasmic contortion. Her tongue curls the top of my cock, and my head is pinched at the back of her throat, caught in her swallows.

It's the most erotic, addictive feeling ever, coming and being swallowed at the same time.

Never felt that until now.

Smoothing my palms around the globes of her ass, I keep kissing and licking at her now sensitive cunt as my body drifts down from its orgasm high. She sucks and licks, cleaning my cock as I soften, and there's something intimate about that, too.

Climbing off me, she drifts into the bathroom, returning with a damp cloth. "For your face," she says, outstretching the washcloth to me.

I lick my lips. I was never, in my past life or otherwise, a lick your lips after eating pussy kind of guy. I was never a 69 guy. I was never a guy who came from being told how good I could breed my partner, either.

Scarlett sets me free. She makes me need things I never knew I wanted.

I use the washcloth to instead cool down my forehead, which makes her giggle. The sweetest noise is her soft, buoyant laughter, bouncing around the room full of morning sunlight, the air thick with orgasm.

"This is the perfect morning," I tell her, wanting her to know that even without having sex, our time together is everything to me.

Her smile wanes as her eyes drop to the floor, searching for her pajamas. She tosses me some sweats and I watch with my limp cock draped along my belly as she covers herself. Pulling her hair out of the collar of her pajamas, she looks at me, cheeks flush, but not from exertion.

"What's the matter?" I ask, sitting up in bed, reaching for my pants.

"That thing I said," she starts. "About…" Her forehead falls into her hands and she moans, the sound full of embarrassment and… regret. I don't like that. "About you breeding me," she says, still not giving me her eyes.

"Scarlett," I say, getting off the bed, clambering to my feet, only to drop to my knees at hers. I bring her foot to my thigh, and knead it with both hands. With a dip of my head, I press my lips to the inside of her ankle and calf, and kiss her until she's stroking a hand through my hair.

I look up and find a small smile lifting her lips.

"Don't be embarrassed." I place a kiss on the top of her knee, and close my eyes as she sifts her lithe finger through my hair, nails grating my scalp. Her touch centers me.

"But you know I know it's just… bedroom talk, right? I don't really expect you to, you know, have a baby with me or anything."

I bring her other foot to my thigh, and give it the same treatment. "I know." I kiss the words into her calf, sliding a hand behind her leg, outstretching it. I smooth both hands up her leg, letting my fingers drag down slowly, attempting to soothe and calm her.

Her eyes droop and her hand slides to my cheek, cupping my face. "I just… I don't want you to be weirded out or anything."

"I liked it," I admit as I layer kisses over her warm, velvety skin. "In my past," I say, toeing into new territory but nonetheless, a land that deserves dual exploration. I think I've got the gist of how things were with Pete, but I want her to know how it was with Valerie. For no other reason than to know me. Because I think it's real with Scarlett, and our foundation has to be solid. Knowing each other is that foundation. "Well, Valerie was my first. We were college sweethearts, but we actually knew each other in high school. I guess I kind of saved myself for her and didn't really know my needs, so I wanted what she wanted, and that felt normal. And it… well, it was. It worked for us. We were happy. We weren't adventurous but we were happy."

She takes my face in both hands. "Thank you for sharing. I know talking about your past is difficult." She strokes her thumb along my bottom lip then dips down, pressing her soft lips to mine.

"And never be embarrassed about anything you say when chasing an orgasm," I say with an uncharacteristically big smile, which earns me a beautiful grin in return. I push blonde hair away from her face and kiss her again. "Because I heard myself make some noises that I'm not exactly proud of."

She laughs at that, and just like that, levity is restored between us. Getting to my feet, I weave our fingers together, holding her hand so tightly our palms kiss. "Let's get you fed before work," I tell her, realizing as we walk down that hall that... I've missed my morning swims for the last week.

I pull a newly acquired barstool out for her and take her hand as she climbs on, positioning her feet on the lower bar.

"Coffee," I say, with a wink, knowing I have a surprise. Opening the fridge, I pull out the pink box I nabbed yesterday. "I walked to Rise & Grind after work. I got you some things."

I slide the box to her and busy myself with filling the carafe with water, then scoop fresh ground beans into the hopper.

She peels the tape back and opens the box, moaning at the sight. I got one of each. Of everything.

Cruller, a brownie, a cupcake, a slice of apple pie, a cheese danish, a pineapple cream cheese pastry, a slice of bacon and spinach quiche, a bran muffin and a chocolate chunk cookie.

"I can't eat all this!" she laughs, wiggling her fingers over the open box. She freezes, her eyes pinching in on me as I hit start on the coffee and pull out two brand new mugs. Amazon for the house-filling win.

"I'm trying to think what's going to digest loudly, and I'll save that for when I'm not on set," she muses, peering back down into the box. She plucks the cruller, and takes a huge bite, icing at the corners of her mouth as she chews.

"Cohen," she says around the bite. "Clean up my mouth."

I love how she's so sweet but on a dime, turns into a commander, knowing just what she needs and wants. And the best part is, she knows that I'll be the one to give it to her.

I slip around the counter and come between her open legs, taking her face in my hands. Our eyes lock, and her sweet breath hails down on my senses, making my chest grow tight and my cock thicken. Slowly I bring my mouth to the corner of hers, first kissing then leisurely licking the glaze away. When I'm done, I move to the other side, and heat slides down my spine at the little whimper she does as I lick off the rest of the cruller glaze.

When she's kissed and licked clean, I pull away, finding her cheeks pink. She licks her lips. "Thank you."

"Anything for you," I breathe, an electrical shock zipping down my core at the reality of those words, and how I mean them with every inch of me.

Her eyes hold mine as we both process just how much I mean it. "After work," she says, her voice weak. "Do you want to go furniture shopping again?" I look around the space, and it's much fuller than before, but still severely lacking.

I nod. "Yes, I do." I swallow around my nerves, suddenly lodged in my throat. "I want to sleep with you again tonight, Scarlett. In truth, I don't see myself wanting to sleep without you anymore." I look down at my bare feet, considering how powerful that statement was, realizing it may be… too much. "But I know it's—"

"I want that to," she buzzes, eyes brimming with excitement, the sadness all gone.

"Okay," I nod, slipping from between her legs to return to the kitchen. I pour her a cup of coffee and one for me too, then gather ingredients from the fridge.

"What's your favorite thing to eat for lunch?" I ask as I assemble a salad in a glass container, dropping pre-sliced carrots onto the bed of spring greens.

She watches me as she says, "Honestly, I pretty much like everything. Why?"

I drop cherry tomatoes onto the salad, and open a tupperware of grilled, sliced chicken, adding that, too. Pulling a brand new knife from the drawer, I slice cucumbers and add them as well. "Because I want you to eat lunch."

Her brows pinch together as she wraps a hair tie around her hair, leaving a messy bun atop her head. Fuck that's hot. "I eat lunch."

I place the knife atop the cutting board and brace my hands on the counter, leveling a stare her way. "Scarlett, we work at the same place, remember? An apple and protein bar isn't lunch."

For the last few months, I've tried my best to not look at her. To not notice her. But my eyes would veer her way every so often, and when I'd see her at lunch, I noticed she never had a real lunch. I hated it then, but didn't know why I cared.

"He ingrained that in me," she says, sipping her coffee, picking at the cheese danish in the box. "And he wrote a weight clause into my contract and I guess… even though I'm at Crave now and can look however I please, it's just… perma-fried into my brain that I need to lose weight, or should watch my weight, at the least."

I reach into the box and set the cheese danish onto a napkin and slide it to her. "You're mine now, Scarlett. And that means you eat what you want, when you want. And if you want to eat this whole box of sweets, you do. And you don't question yourself. You don't devalue your body in any way, not in front of me. Because you're beautiful and perfect, and I won't hear a word otherwise."

I have to tamp down the anger and rage that run rampant through my veins when I picture that fuckface telling Scarlett she needs to change.

She brings the danish to her lips and takes a satisfying bite, moaning around the sweet pastry. While she eats without guilt, I continue making her lunch, bringing out a loaf of wheat bread.

"Condiments?" I ask, wanting to get it just right for her.

With her mouth full she says, "Any, all, none. I'm easy. Honestly. And I like all the veggies, all the meats and all the cheeses." She pauses, then adds, "I haven't had cheese in a year. Pete always said I could do without, so I felt guilty eating it."

Body shaming piece of shit. I slide on an extra slice of cheese, and add a slice of provolone for good measure, then give her a small wink.

She sips her coffee, tracing the rim with her fingers as she hedges into conversation. "Back in Michigan," she starts, taking time to be intentional, which makes me respect her so much. "Did you cook a lot?"

I freeze with one palm pressing into the top of the closed sandwich, my knife stilled too. "I didn't," I reply slowly, painful bursts of my life exploding behind my eyes. Memories long repressed, because the simple happiness of our existence seemed too painful before.

Now, though, discussing that time doesn't immediately

turn my stomach and make me crave the pool, yearn to hold my breath and wait for pain, hope for darkness. In Scarlett's company, sharing details of my past feels like honoring something that's been ignored too long.

We lost her. But we were happy, and to pretend we weren't is devaluing my daughter's short but happy life.

"I worked a lot," I admit, "and Valerie took care of everything." I slice her sandwich and open the remaining tupperware. "I should have done more. I should have done so much more." I place the sandwich inside and put the lid on.

"Hindsight," she says quietly, gathering my eyes with her soft words.

I nod and grab an apple from the produce bag and retrieve the nylon lunch bag I ordered her. I put everything inside, and zip it up.

She's finishing the pastry with a smile on her face, and this simple moment in the kitchen has me feeling more pride and value than I have in years.

We divide after that, Scarlett going back to her place, the both of us getting ready for work. And then, because it makes sense, we take just one car.

I've been here for years and never felt the urge to stop work to watch a scene. To watch anyone perform for that matter. Have I seen them perform? Of course. But I've never really *watched*. I've been so detached. My eyes see but my brain could give a shit less. I'd never even gotten hard at work before, and I'd always been proud of that fact.

But I'm falling so hard for Scarlett. I don't use *the* word, not even to myself, because it's too soon. But I know I am because she's all I think about, every thought I have now is how can I please her, add to her life, simplify her life, make her happier. And after our night, and the way I easily and surprisingly opened up to her this morning about my life in Michigan—I know.

I know as I stare at the silk robe she drops to her feet.

I know as Alexa swipes lipstick across Scarlett's full lips.

I know as Otis strokes lube along his shaft, and Maxi readies herself.

I want her forever, even if neither of us are ready for that. And I also know, watching her hold Maxi's head steady as Otis impales her throat, all while Lucy Lovegood offers sweet words of encouragement.

Lucy Lovegood is *mine*. And right then on set, with a boom arm in my lap and duct tape in my hand, eaten by the shadows of the set, I get hard.

I get so unbelievably, achingly hard that I have to excuse myself.

Locking the bathroom door, I grip the edge of the sink, my heart racing a million miles a minute. This has never happened before. Ever. And that's not what has my goddamn mind spinning.

I'm not just getting erections, but I *want* to masturbate. I want to unzip my pants and choke my cock until it spits into this sink, and I want her name on my lips, the taste of her cunt on my tongue.

It's the first time I've really wanted to be... a normal man again.

I won't do Crave that way, though. Coming into the sink at a porn production company has Jizzabelle written all over it, not Crave.

I adjust myself and splash water in my face, and return to my spot in the corner, in the dark, and work on the boom arm as the scene resumes.

When the slates clatter, my eyes veer from the broken boom to Lucy. The tips of her fingers are lost in Maxi's hair as she grips her, keeping Maxi steady.

Otis surges forward, his cock disappearing into her mouth, and both of them make noises of approval.

"Good girl," Lucy breathes, leaning down to whisper the praise into Maxi's ear. It's a reverse cuckold scene, with Lucy and Otis being the couple, Maxi being the third brought in to pleasure Otis. I've heard this scene run several times over the years, because viewers like cuck and reverse cuck.

But today, I can't fucking look away.

I don't want a third, but watching her work has me like a goddamn brick. She is so good at this, she makes everything feel real. I watch with bated breath, knowing it's nothing more than a scene in an adult film, but I'm buying it. I'm seeing Lucy give permission to Otis, I'm seeing them go through women together at a bar until they stumble across Maxi and make her their third. I see what's not there, because she's so fucking good at what she does.

"Cohen," Lance interrupts my thoughts, and I make sure the boom arm is over my lap so my hard dick is hidden.

"What's up?" I ask, pulling my gaze from her.

"Two of the surveillance cameras in the back lot are shattered. The replacements are here. Can you get them installed before you go? We asked the building manager but he's out of town. I know it's not your normal task—"

I cut him off. "I'll do it now," I say, needing fresh air but also immediately on edge. I want those cameras more than ever since Pete showed up here not too long ago. Those cameras keep us all safe, but they also keep us aware, and awareness is key when you've got a fucking loser clinger ex hovering around.

I follow Lance to where the boxes are stacked, and grab them, and my tool belt and head outside. The San Francisco breeze licks at my neck, and it's just what I need to kill the hard-on between my legs. I respect Crave and Aug and everyone here far too much to be that guy.

But I install those cameras with a smile on my face, because I never thought I could be that guy.

"What brings you two in this evening?" the salesman asks as Scarlett and I walk into a little furniture store shoved into a small shop on the corner not far from Crave.

I watch her fingers stroke over the back of a leather couch, something neither of us need as we purchased couches a month back. But ever since I got hard watching her work, everything she does is making me hard. And I don't want to feel fucking creepy about it, but I'm relieved, and I want to bask in it. *Just a little.*

"We're kind of hunting for a few things," she muses, looking around the small shop that has every square inch of real estate packed with things, tags hanging off all of it. The carpet is maroon and dingy, and the lights flicker, but the furniture looks just the same as something from a department store. And there's a very real part of me that wonders how long we'll have the things we purchase here tonight.

How long will we live in two separate places?

I know it's only been a few months, but I don't see my life without her anymore. *Holy shit.*

I grab the edge of a tall dresser, steadying myself as that thought nearly wipes me off my feet. Fuck, I want to cry a little everytime I realize I am finally moving forward. Tears of relief that I won't be miserable forever, tears of joy to be happy again… and tears of grief and pain, because moving on feels like I'm pushing them away.

I think of Valerie right then, as Scarlett lifts a lampshade off a lamp, asking the salesman about different styles and colors. My eyes follow the binder he pulls out, full of worn pages of lamps and rugs, but I tune out their small talk. My mind is back there.

We couldn't survive the pain together. It made us angry and irrational, we pointed fingers, we called each other names, and then one day, I just couldn't do it. I couldn't stay in that house where love used to live. I couldn't exist inside the ghost of the life I lost.

I told her that. And she felt the same. She cried tears of grief and I held her, and then we both cried tears of relief, in each other's arms, because we knew that separating would sadly bring us both a tiny sliver of solace.

Where is she now? Does she hold her breath in the shower? Does she slide below the surface of the tub and torture herself, the same way I did? Does she still put flowers out every single week? I don't know. I've never wanted to know. Ever.

Scarlett places her hand on my forearm, and blinks up at me through her thick dark lashes. "Cohen, are you okay?"

I smile, shaking Valerie and my thoughts away. "Yeah," I reply, nodding at where the binder is spread open. "Is that the one you like?"

She wrinkles her nose. "No, I think I'm going to get the two here in store." Concern weighs her shoulders, and she slumps a little as she blinks up at me. "You sure you're okay?"

"Yeah. I'm good. What else did you say you wanted to snag tonight?" I dig my phone from my pocket and open it to the notes, and hold the screen for her to see. "I forgot—I made a note of what you mentioned you wanted the other day."

Her eyes fill. "Y-you did?"

I lean in and steal a kiss from her cheek as she looks down and sees the note. I slip my hand in hers and turn to the salesman, ready to ask where the bathroom cabinets, end tables, and TV stands are.

But his eyes are on her breasts, and in a matter of a second, my happiness transforms into a physical, palpable anger. I stare at him until he finally looks up at her, then me.

I give him a warning glance. The kind of look a man gives another man who's checking out his wife. The kind of look a man gives another man to warn him that he just got his first, second and third strike. The next time his eyes hover on her anywhere, we're going to have a problem.

I don't break his gaze when I soften my tone and grip her hand tighter, lifting our joined hands to our lips to press a kiss to the top of her palm.

"I see some things in the back that you may like," I tell her, and we keep moving, leaving the salesman behind us. Standing in front of a large media cabinet, wood painted white, rich florals etched with precision, Scarlett lowers her voice.

"Your nostrils were flaring back there," she whispers with a giggle in her voice. She wraps her other hand around our linked ones, and strokes my thumb.

Her affirming touch calms me. "I didn't like the way he was looking at you," I admit.

She sighs, dreamy and light. "People look at me all day. On set, online," she muses, poking me to clarify what's different between that and this.

"I respect your work, and I know that Otis and Tuck and Maxi—and all the actors at Crave—are working. And when people watch your movies, you bring them pleasure, that's what you do. You make people feel good and happy." She sits on the edge of a mattress near the media cabinets. I find myself naturally dropping to a crouch at her feet, placing my palms on her knees, kissing her there. "But we're in public, you're mine. And I don't appreciate some sleazy salesman thinking he has any right to what's mine."

She flushes, capturing my hands on her knees, weaving both of our hands together. "I'm yours," she states dreamily before leaning down, bringing our mouths together in a scorching kiss.

Right there on my knees at her feet, I feel overwhelmed by the urge to share. "I watched you on set today, for the first time."

She arches a manicured brow. "For the first time?"

I nod. "And I wanted to jerk off."

She understands the weight of those words. "Is that the first time you've had *that* urge?"

I nod again, because my mouth is dry.

Scarlett glances at the media center again before fishing

her wallet out of the bag slung across her chest. "Let's pay, and then let's go home."

Home. Do I have one of those? I did. Before. Do I now? She holds her hand out, and I know what she needs. I take it, and she gets to her feet, using me to steady herself.

Wherever she is, that's my home.

Back at her apartment, where we go to place her new lamps and side tables, Scarlett collects a few things, and asks if we can sleep at my place. She chews at the inside of her cheek, as I unplug the lamps and grab her multivitamins from the counter. I got her these last week, because she's always so tired. They've got iron in them.

"Do you think they're helping?" I ask, shaking the bottle as I flip off the light over the kitchen sink, preparing to head across the breezeway.

She volleys her head, still chewing her cheek, her eyes glazed, focus faraway.

"Are you okay?" I pace to her, and pull her into me, holding her until she's ready to share. After a few peaceful moments, she nods and I step away, giving her space and room to speak.

Vitamins still in my hand, I blink down at her, hoping to God or whoever, that this isn't going to be bad, or about us.

"I'm just... I'm thinking about what you told me earlier.

About wanting to touch yourself, and how that's the first time you've really felt that since…" she trails off, and I'm relieved it's not bad news, but I'm still unsure.

"I'm here for everything after the buts," I remind her, trying to make open communication as easy as possible. I learned that in therapy, a few years too late. But I won't make the same mistakes twice.

I will protect the woman I love, and protect the life I'm building, and I will communicate my needs, my pain, all of it.

I won't fuck up my life again.

"I want to have sex with you Cohen. So fucking bad. I mean, neither of us knew if we could even fuck before we started dating," she breathes, her words and energy gaining momentum with each toppling thought. "But I want to talk to my therapist first, because… well, I think I'd be okay, but… I care so much about you. I just don't want to fuck it up, you know?"

I nod. "I know exactly."

"Sooo," she says, a little smile twisting her lips. "I was hoping maybe you could just… be inside me for a while tonight." She steps closer and her breasts press against my chest, and I turn to steel behind my zipper. "Like before."

I groan. "Yes, we can do that."

"You groaned," she points out. "Tell me about that."

I pull a hand down my face with a heavy exhale. "I may need about forty seconds in the bathroom first," I admit, "because of that scene today. You were…"

"*Lucy* was," she corrects, cupping the back of my head with her hand, rising to her toes to kiss me. "And if you like Lucy… you should see what Scarlett has up her sleeve."

Jesus fuck.

"And no bathroom time without me. Be strong," she teases, walking her fingers up my chest between us, still holding me by the back of my head, fingers swimming dreamily through my hair. I'm so hard already. "You'll make it. Just... *don't come*."

I lick my lips as I look down at her. "I won't." She doesn't want me to, I won't. It's as simple as that.

"But first..." she says, peeling off her clothes until she's naked and I'm aching. "I thought I could help you make dinner. At your place."

"I don't mind cooking for you. You had a long day. If you want to take a bath or relax, I'm happy to cook," I let my eyes roam her perfect body, loving every soft curve, all the carved slopes. "If you haven't figured it out, serving you pleases me." I shake my head, because that's not quite right. "Serving you *fulfills* me."

She reaches out, cupping my erection with a grin. "Your servitude will be rewarded." Leaning in, she presses her lips to mine and holds them there, speaking instead of kissing, "My devoted man."

Something about those three words, what they bear and their intent—I pull her naked body into me, pressing my hand to her lower back. "That's it, Scar," I say, having never simplified her name into any personal or intimate term, but loving how it sounds, and what it means. "I'm here to serve and protect you." *And love you.*

Her eyes fill, and I realize I went from silent and stoic to emptying my bag of feelings, but this is better, this is healthier.

"You've freed me from the darkness I thought I'd live in forever. Do you know what that makes you?" I ask, my voice hoarse. She drags her fingertips up my cock, eyes still on me as she shakes her head silently.

"It makes you my queen." I scoop her up, bumps lifting on my neck as she squeals against me. I get her phone and keys with one hand, and move through the breezeway between our places in just two steps. Once she's inside my place, I lock her lips, then I lock us in.

Her hair cascades down her back, light and shiny, the extra pale strands picking up the dull overhead light. She turns the lights to gold, like every room she's in, she makes the small, poorly-lit apartment kitchen better, more beautiful. Worth being in.

"What do you want to eat?" I ask her, trying to focus on the fact that I'm going to cook a meal. Not on the fact that she wants to just feel me inside of her even though she's not ready for sex. Jesus fuck, I'm dripping in my briefs at the four-second flash of it in my mind.

"You know I like pretty much everything," she muses, her fingertips sliding along the edge of the counter. I think I'm harder than that tile countertop right about now. Her ass moves so gracefully, hips swaying so subtly, I've never been a man who's fantasized about asses or anal sex but I think I'd make a deal with the devil right about now just to get my face between those cheeks.

"I have some chicken that's already cooked. How about a protein bowl? Quinoa, chicken, some white beans, diced veggies, stuff like that? Sound okay?"

She beams and places a palm on her belly. "So good." Her smile slides into a sultry pout, her tone dipping. "Will you feed me?"

"Yes." A groan bounces around in my chest, but I contain it because if I'm going to feed her and give her what she needs, I'm going to need a lot of self-control.

Being celibate for years did nothing for my discipline; I never had to exercise it because I was without urges. Now, though, my drive has returned and my dick is excited.

I keep my back to her as I make the food, talking to her the entire time. Asking her about the scene today.

"You like working with Otis?" I ask, stirring the heated cannellini beans into the cooked quinoa.

"I do. Actually, that's the weird thing I'm still getting used to. There's not a single person at Crave I don't like. I mean..." she pauses, and I can almost guess what she's going to say. It's a common theme. "Lance can be a bit of a cold fish sometimes but... I still like him."

I think of Aug and how no one at Crave knows my story but him, and that's because he's kept his word. He's not shared without my consent, and so I pay him the same respect, despite the fact that I wholeheartedly trust Scarlett. My trust for her has nothing to do with his personal life, so I choose my words carefully. "Lance is great, but he's working through a complex situation in his personal life. That would make anyone edgy, I imagine."

There's silence, so I turn and look at her as I drop pieces of sliced chicken into the bowls. "You imagine?" She rises from the barstool and saunters toward me, looping her arms around my waist. Looking down at her, all blonde hair and hard nipples, wide eyes and toothy smile, I question if I can keep my word tonight. I want to be inside of her so bad, but I can't get what she said earlier out of my head. "Cohen, you've been going through something complex, too."

"Yeah," I admit. "Lance is great, though, I know that for certain." I slide her the bowl. "Hungry?"

Her eyes dip to my cock, with the subtlety of a steam roller. "Famished."

I didn't know when I bought the small dining set that I'd be so glad I had it, but as I take a seat at the table and Scarlett stands over me, unzipping my jeans, I'm thanking God.

She smiles when she finds me hard and eager, my cock

coming willingly through the open fly hole. "I need your precum for lube," she says, dropping to her knees between my spread ones. "May I?" she asks, blinking at me for permission. Permission for what, I don't know, but I nod my head yes without a second thought.

"I'd suck your balls if you were naked, but since you're fully dressed—which, by the way, is super hot—I'll get it a different way."

Never did I think I'd be sitting at my dining room table being milked for my precum, but she had me jacking off into the sink so I shouldn't be surprised. Using the pointed tip of her tongue, she gently laps at the underside of my cock, over and over. It's ticklish at first, but quickly becomes intoxicating and dizzying.

And it works well.

I groan at the sight of clear liquid bubbling up on my cockhead, curving down my head, slipping down my shaft. Scarlett stacks her fists on my shaft and pumps, giving me a sweet little smile. "I'm so wet just thinking of how full you make me, I didn't need the precum. I just wanted a reason to lick your cock."

Fuck. I close my eyes, suck a long breath in through my nose, and push it out through my lips. My cock is still pulsing, precum unstoppable at this point, so I take one more deep breath before opening my eyes.

She's released my dick and is standing now, positioning our bowls of dinner at the table. She gets us two glasses of water, and then, it's time.

I'm excited. I'm fucking very excited in fact. I could fucking hammer nails with my cock right now. But I'm also nervous.

The more I'm with her, the harder I fall. I've been falling for a while now, the rabbit hole getting deeper and deeper. I don't think I'll ever find the bottom. But being inside her, knowing she wants what I want—to be at Crave, to have more, and to be a parent—it changes things, intensifies them.

Naked, she comes to one side of me, and slowly lowers herself into my lap, aligning my swollen and angry head at her slick, tight hole. Her arm loops my neck and her other hand braces the tabletop as she sinks down on me.

I groan like a goddamn porn star when her wet cunt tightens around me. She sinks down further, moving slower and more seductively, and my balls ache and thrum, pressure building low in my gut. Then she's sitting, my head sweeping her g-spot, spongy and ripe, just begging for me to prod as I fuck her.

But not now.

Instead, I reach out and clutch the fork, staring into a piece of grilled chicken. Collecting a bite, I bring it to her lips and become tantalized by the slow opening of her mouth, the pouty curve of her lips as she moans around the delicious bite.

"I'm glad you like it, but please, Scar, baby, don't moan like that." My cock throbs inside of her, begging to rip the cord and release, flooding her with so much cum that her thighs will be sticky for a week.

But no.

She swallows the bite, I take one, then serve her another. After she chews and swallows, she asks for a drink of water. The condensation on the glass cools my palm as I raise it to her lips. They curl around the end, and her swallow has me thinking of when she swallowed my load, and I don't even know if I can give her a drink of water tonight.

"I'm thirsty, Cohen," she says, and like that, I give her another drink, bringing it to her lips again, tipping it back.

She adjusts herself just slightly in my lap, and I scoop another bite of food to divert my brain. Then I feel it.

Her fingertips sweeping over the place where we're joined. Her fingers touching her clit, then my cock, right where I disappear inside of her.

"Scar—" I warn, "I want to give you this, I want you to have the intimacy. But you're not ready for more, and I'm... I need to come. Your pussy is so tight, and I need you."

"You need me?" she breathes, leaning into the fork to steal the loaded bite. Sweat beads on my upper lip and my flannel shirt seems like a really fucking stupid choice right now.

I nod. "I need you."

She smiles. "I need another drink."

My hand is practically shaking as my cock throbs between her walls, but I bring the glass to her lips and tip it. Water slips from her mouth, gliding in smooth beads down the curve of her throat, over her collarbone, rolling down her breast.

"Do you need a drink?" she offers as I return the glass to the table. She taps her breast where the water rolled off, a faint streak of moisture left behind.

I nod, because I'd agree to anything to get my lips on her tits right about now. My groin clenches and the pressure low in my belly builds to nearly undeniable. She feeds her hand through my hair and drags my mouth to her breast. Her words are a command, but a quiet one, laced in tenderness and adoration. "Then lick."

My tongue follows the streak of water all the way to her mouth, and we share a slow, heated kiss. Our lips move together, and when I cup her face, my palm partially on her throat, her pulse beats hard against me.

"I'm still hungry," she says against my lips before turning her head, waiting for me to feed her another bite. Thick and steely, my cock stays hungry inside her as I continue to feed her until the bowl is gone, alternating a drink with every few bites. Then I finish my meal, while she plays at the ends of my hair, nips at my earlobe, and plucks at her nipples, keeping them hard, torturing me.

When I've eaten every bite—not even because I'm hungry, but because I knew once that bowl was clean, this would be over—she tells me it's time for bed.

Carefully, she lifts off me, leaving me to stare at my very hard cock and the streaks of arousal she left behind. I reach to shove myself away, to take the sight of what I had just moments ago from me, she grabs my wrist.

"Let me," she says, tugging on my erection. I get to my feet, and like a leash, she holds me and takes me to my room. "Let's get naked, and go to bed, okay?"

I nod, and wipe drool from my mouth. Between her thighs, her skin shimmers and my cock weeps as the sight of her smeared arousal.

"Cohen, I love the feeling of you inside of me. It burns, but I've never felt so full, so good."

God damn this is hard. "Uh huh. Me too." That's all I can say. If I even verbally acknowledge her pussy, my control will slip.

"Fall asleep inside me? Please?" She sticks out her bottom lip in a pout.

"What?" I ask, despite the fact I heard her just fine.

She works the buttons on my shirt and tugs it off, arm by arm. "I want to fall asleep with you inside of me. You can slide out of me once I'm asleep, but the way I feel with you deep inside me," she whispers, the filthy word on her lips chipping healthy chunks from my resolve. "Please, *please*."

I'm unlacing my boots while bending down around a

painful erection, yanking off my shirt and sending my jeans careening into the new hamper.

"You're fast."

I arch a brow. "Don't say that."

We share a laugh that only partially cuts at the tension in the air. Not emotional or conversational tension, either. Sexual tension. But I'll fight the urge, because she needs this to feel good.

She needs me.

"Lie down," I tell her, and watch the dark slit of her ass open as she crawls onto the bed on her hands and knees, finding her spot. I get a look at the dark ring between her cheeks and touch myself just once, a long, thick strand of precum dropping between my feet.

"Get in your favorite sleeping position," I advise, climbing onto the bed. She gets on her side, pillow fluffed and tucked beneath her head, then gazes back at me over her shoulder.

"Is this okay?" she asks, hesitation in her voice. Her toned back drips into a narrow waist, ballooning into a gentle sway, her hips so fucking grabbable I almost can't stand it.

"Perfect," I reply, voice hoarse with strain. I'm using all my energy to not make her back a canvas.

Positioning myself behind her, I peel her ass cheeks apart and groan something fierce when her tight little hole winks at me. Closing my eyes, I press my lips to her shoulder, muffling my entry moans. I drop an arm over her waist, and pull her back toward me.

"Thank you for being you," she breathes in a yawn.

We get comfortable, but not without her asking several times if I'm sure I want to do this, or if I can. She even reminds me of a safe word, and that I can always change my mind, no matter what.

I wave her off and enjoy the feel of her warm body in my arms, my dick buried deep.

She dozes off in just a few minutes, and I visit the bathroom after she does, painting a masterpiece in the bathroom sink before getting back in bed and dozing off, too.

twenty-one

· · ·

scarlett

And we haven't even had sex.

It's funny, I'm a porn star. Through and through. I love my job. I love porn. But it wasn't until I got with Cohen that I truly understood some of the kinks I've acted out for years.

The first time I heard of cockwarming I thought it was more about torture and edging. And yeah, I would say both of us were pretty tortured last night. But the truth is? It's about intimacy. There's something bonding about trying new things together, things that involve giving your most private part of yourself to exploration.

Now I know, cockwarming is so much more than showmanship for a porn orgasm.

It's real. It's about edging and connection, teasing and bonding.

I really do find what I do at Crave to be so much more

enriching now that I know what it translates to in a healthy relationship. Taking these ideas and concepts from scenes and carrying them over, giving them a twist to make them ours, shaping them so they work for us, it's pretty amazing. I believe in healthy pornography even more now that I have Cohen in my life.

We're healing together, and I don't think we'd be able to do it so intimately and beautifully without knowing and believing in exploration of kink so well.

"Scarlett," Dr. Evans smiles, propping her office door open by her hip. A pencil peeks up from the top of her coiffed hair, and her pink lipstick is wearing already, telling me she's either hit the coffee hard or had a challenging few sessions before me. For her sake, I hope it's the first thing. "Come on in," she smiles, stepping back, making way for me.

I slip past her, and take a seat in my favorite chair. Now I notice… this is the only chair. Dr. Evans sits across from me, adjusting the pad and pencil in her lap as she smiles.

"You only have one chair, I just noticed. Does that mean you never treat couples?"

She surveys the room the way only therapists do, where they look at their own surroundings as if they've never explored them, her gaze traveling back to me full of questions. "I guess you're right, I've only made the space comfortable for one, haven't I?"

I blink at her. "You just rearranged what I said," I tell her, because I do like to give her a hard time here and there. And she's the type of therapist that plays along, and that makes me like her even more. It's comfortable, and that's one of the main things you have to have with someone if you're going to be honest: comfort.

She laughs. "Well, to answer your question, no, I don't treat couples." She scribbles something more for her than me,

I can tell by the way it's off in the corner of her notepad. "Why? Were you hoping to have a session with Cohen?"

"He has his own therapist," I say immediately, because the thought of Cohen coming here, in my private healing space, I don't know. He and I do our healing together, but this space with Dr. Evans is my clandestine corner. "But I did want to talk about Cohen."

She writes something else, this time, in the center of the page. "Let's talk."

I chew the inside of my cheek and look down at my clothes.

I'm wearing black jeans, and they're new. Cohen saw me browsing online and when I was taking a bath, he ordered what I'd left languishing in my cart. When they arrived he told me, "You left nearly everything behind when you started over. It's not frivolous to replace them. There's nothing wrong with self care, Scar."

Paired with my jeans are new sneakers, and a fun, flowy silk blouse. My hair, which Cohen brushed out for me this morning as I ate breakfast, is down and even curled. I'm wearing makeup. And I have earrings in. I thought those holes closed up until I reached for a pair of diamond studs, one of the only things of value I managed to take from my old place.

"I feel so… ready with him, you know?" I ask, though I know better because Dr. Evans doesn't answer questions that way. Therapists never really give you answers, they more so guide you to the stream. You have to teach yourself to drink. I rephrase my question into a statement she can work with. "When I'm with him, I don't think about anything but the future. I want to plan. I get excited. I see the life I thought I'd have before, only now it's not blurry. It's clear. Every detail. Every smile. I see it with him."

"That's good. I'm happy to hear you two are moving on together positively."

I chew the inside of my mouth again, finding it a little sore and somewhat raw. "We haven't had sex yet. But I have been able to orgasm again, and that's new, you know? I couldn't for the longest time, my brain was just... Shut off to the experience. But he's awakened that part of me."

"But you're waiting for sex?" She asks, her tone flat, leaving me antsy.

"I actually wanted to talk to you first." I let out a breath to gather my thoughts, taking a moment. Glancing around her office, I see a gold plated clock ticking away, completely unaware of the stress it bears. Time. Timing is everything. My eyes come back to her. "I feel ready, but I just don't want to try it too soon and like, have my body shut down or something. Because I know if it happens, it won't be because of him. It will just be because of past trauma."

She nods as she scribbles on her notepad. With her focus on the long stretches of cursive across her paper she asks, "Have you felt those anxieties on set lately? The ones you shared with me before?" I know what she's asking. I'd said before I felt like a cheat on set, because I'd been faking orgasms.

I shake my head, honestly. "I haven't. Even when Pete calls, I have no anxiety. I just feel... fatigue."

She lifts her gaze, leveling concern my way. "Pete is *still* calling?"

I nod. "Yeah. But it's becoming more and more sporadic." I really do believe we're on the cusp of a breakthrough, and that he will return to the shadows where he belongs.

Dr. Evans crosses her legs at the ankle, dropping an elbow to the arm rest, hand cradling her chin. "If your anxiety is under control, and you've felt good with Cohen, what's your real fear? Is your real fear that once you're having sex, you'll lose the progress you've made? Or is there something else?"

Well fuck. Heat scatters across my skin as sweat pools in my armpits and slips down my spine. "I mean, I don't want to think I'm ready then have underwhelming sex," I say, knowing how bullshit the words are as I speak them, and Dr. Evans knows, too. She remains silent, waiting for what she knows is bound to come.

The actual truth.

My eyes grow moist and warm. "What if he realizes he doesn't want me, either? Just like Pete?" My bottom lip trembles with the sour, bitter, ugly truth. "He loved me once, I know he did. And then... he didn't."

Her lips fall into a flat line, her eyes serious, making my insides roil. "He loved himself, and only ever loved himself. Let me make that clear," she says of my ex. "And ask yourself this, when it was good, how good did *you* feel?"

I wipe under my nose, remembering the first night we spent together in our apartment. The first night in a new place as a couple living together should be exciting, celebratory and hot.

We argued.

He wanted me to do an anal scene with Chip, one of the particularly well-endowed male actors at Jizz. And I didn't want to. In fact, I never wanted to do anal on camera. And then I tried to please him by offering anal to him.

I shake my head at the memory, almost disbelieving *that* Scarlett was me. I was bargaining with my body, and that's not healthy.

"It was never really good," I admit, voice quiet with embarrassment. "I don't know why I stayed."

His words wash over me. *You'll get enough money to pay for that degree you so desperately want, and we can have a baby. Then you'll get back to work. We all win.*

Except, that never took account for what I'd do with that degree if I actually earned it, but he knew he had me. Being a mother and finishing school were the juiciest, fattest carrots he could dangle, and I chased them.

"In any relationship, you risk pain. But if there's no risk, nothing on the line to be gambled, you wouldn't want it, would you? Because it wouldn't make you scared. Things that are worth chasing and having, they're scary."

"I'm in love with him," I admit, having known that little truth already. For some time, even. But saying it aloud makes it real, turns it into an actionable item, something he needs to know. So we can move forward, or back, if he doesn't feel the same.

But... I think he does.

"We've both been broken, in different ways. And we're both healing, and ready to move forward. I just... I want to protect us both, I guess. I'm scared that if it doesn't work, neither one of us will make it."

That truth fills the room with uncomfortable silence for a moment.

"You survived Pete. You can survive this too, but Scarlett, what if it's not a survival situation? What if you thrive, and live the happiest, most fulfilled life ever? Don't let fear drive your life. Grab the wheel."

Grab the wheel. I want Cohen.

I want sunsets and dinners out, I want grocery shopping and fixing ripped screens. I want movie nights and trips away. I want... to be picking out a crib and changing diapers with him. I want to slide a ring off my finger for work, only to eagerly await putting it back on.

I want to make love to Cohen. I want to feel Cohen fill me

with cum, I want his lips on my breasts and his fingers inside me, I want to be bent over a table for him, riding his lap, upside down off the edge of the bed with his cock in my throat.

"Grab the wheel," I snicker, despite the fact my heart appreciates the analogy. "A little corny," I tease.

She sees through me but lets me have the moment, smiling. "A little. But I am a vegetarian."

I grin. I love Dr. Evans.

We finish our session by discussing Crave and how I'm still finding it to be such a great place. She asks me if I've still not heard from my parents and I tell her the truth—that I've made peace with life without them. And half an hour later, I'm sliding on my sunglasses and driving to work.

My pulse rockets at the thought of seeing him, slipping into his office, into his arms, and inhaling his soap and cologne.

I'm so in love. And we haven't even had sex.

My phone buzzes the entire drive to Crave. I know it's Pete because I glance down at it once or twice, just to make sure it's not Cohen or Aug. When I pull into the parking lot, I sit in my car and play through the ten voicemails he's left... just today.

Listen you little fucking cunt. I own your ass. Your contract may have been up but—

Scarlett, why do you test me like this?

You fuck—

I skip through the rest and delete them all, acutely aware that there is no uncomfortable twitch in my belly, no spike of my nerves, no sweaty palms.

His grip on me is gone. Now if only he'd let go.

Entering the building, it takes a moment for my eyes to adjust to the low light. Cool air filters between my legs and arms, and I know an intense scene must've just wrapped. Aug blasts the AC after the spotlights have been on, because they're hot as hell and we'd be too sweaty without the thermostat set to 65.

But when my eyes adjust to the darkness, they settle straight on him. My Cohen.

His back is to me, arms up, extension cord strung between two hands. Lance is with him, handing him things as he staples the cord onto the piece of wood. He's likely building part of a new set, and as much as he gets to watch me work, I realize right now that I'd love to sit and watch him work.

Peering over my shoulder, I take in the elaborate set splayed out. This one is meant to mimic a library. Yep, they just shot some librarian reverse age-gap naughty college boy fantasy, but aside from the storyline, I can't believe the set. An onlooker would think a film was shot here, they'd have no idea it was an adult film.

Wall paper and crown molding add a touch of reality, complete with electrical switches and plates, with a Tiffany lamp plugged into the faux outlet. Four worn wooden benches rest behind weathered desks, each with books and pencils scattered across each. The ground is blue, tight knit carpet, much like an actual library, and there are even card catalogs in the back of the room.

It's beautiful and requires so much thought and attention to detail.

I look back at Cohen, who is done stringing up the cord, Lance having disappeared. He's smiling at me, and my heart thumps at the sight. He never used to smile. And still, when I think about it, he doesn't smile at others.

Only me.

I close the distance between us and rest my cheek on his chest, soaking up the affection of his long fingers stroking through my hair, his lips on the top of my head.

"How was therapy?" he asks, just like he asks after every session. My attentive, kind man.

"Good," I reply, knowing that inside me I'm bearing very good news. Dr. Evans thinks I'm ready, and in truth, I know I am. I know I need to lower my shields, the fear of hurt and abandonment must be pushed aside if I really want him.

And I do.

But, I also don't mind the idea of drawing it out a little more. Having him inside of me those two times, just existing comfortably with his big, aching cock filling me—that shit was hot. Hotter than any scene I've ever done at Crave. Because real life is so much hotter than even the hottest art.

"You want to get some lunch?" he offers, as we put a foot of space between us, only out of necessity. If I could have a conversation while buried in his neck, I would. But we're at work, so we honor Crave and Aug by keeping a level of professionalism. Kinda.

"You made me lunch, remember?" I stroke my fingers down the buttons centering his chest, always loving the way he looks in his uniform of dark jeans and a flannel.

He shrugs. "But if you feel like getting out and talking

about how your appointment went, we can do that." He places his hands atop my shoulders, both grounding and soothing me. "We can stay here too. Whatever you want."

Whatever you want.

He means that. I know he does. But not just about lunch or the couch or clothing or vitamins. He means that about everything. And not in a weak, tagalong way, either. The way Cohen Steele loves is with his whole being, and his act of love is a form of unquestioning devotion.

The fact that he exists and is mine makes my head spin.

When I look up into his eyes, I can't say no. I don't care about lunch, I just want him. I just want to reward him for being so good, so caring, so... loving.

Does he love me?

I know I love him.

"Wanna run home for lunch?" I ask, glancing very casually at the watch on his wrist. I lift a shoulder and let it drop as I say, "Or whatever."

His eyes narrow, the corner of his mouth lifting. "Yeah," he draws out, nearly stepping inside the response he spreads it so thin. "Let's go."

I enjoy how the word home belongs not necessarily to either of our apartments, but moreso, to wherever we are together. On the drive back, we hold hands, but I keep our linked palms in my lap, against my thigh. He's not done anything sexy today, not overtly. He hasn't grabbed my jaw and stolen a kiss. He didn't grind into me against a wall and tell me how I make him feel. There have been no whispered words of adoration in the darkness.

It's just him. Being him. That's what has me drenched and aching the entire drive back... home.

We end up going to Cohen's, though both of us have groceries now, thanks to him. He writes our lists, plans possible meals to make sure we both have things at our place, and takes us there. Can I shop for groceries and meal plan? Yeah, I can. But the fact that he wants to do it, and make sure the week is filled with the right meals? It makes me feel so taken care of, so... treasured.

He locks the door and bends down, running his pointer finger beneath the laces of his boots. Once his shoes are off, he peers around the apartment a second before his eyes come to me.

"Well, we could take a nap?" he offers, then glances at his watch again. "I could set an alarm. We could nap for twenty, eat for twenty, then head back?"

His plan sounds really good. A midday nap can be the difference between a meh afternoon scene and a fire one. And I find myself really wanting to give Crave my best.

"This afternoon is actually a scene with Uma, Maxi and myself." I walk toward him and cling to the front of his flannel like I'm saying goodbye to my soldier. "So right now, all I want is you."

He steps back, sifting one of those large, capable hands through his silken, somewhat messy hair. "Scarlett," he says, tone slightly warning. "We're waiting—"

I could tell him I'm ready. Tell him right this second, and push away the last barrier between us. Because despite his years of celibacy, Cohen is clearly ready. He got it back the moment I brought him to orgasm, and I think we both know I'm the one holding us back from more.

But I interrupt him to tell him we aren't doing that.

I don't tell him we can, because I know if I do, restraint and control will go from hard to damn near impossible. And I want our first time to be... Jesus, I can't believe I'm saying this. I'm a porn star. But... I want our first time to be slow and beautiful. I want it to be perfect.

Sex is never perfect, and I know that more than most. Your body can make weird noises doing a natural act, air goes in places it shouldn't, wet skin slapping wet skin isn't always hot, and a lot of awkward things can happen.

I don't mean perfect in that sense. I just mean perfect in the sense that we have time to take time, we have the time to do, be and explore everything together. I don't want our first time to have a forty-minute time limit.

That's just not enough.

"Yes, we are. But right now, I want you. And I need you to give yourself to me, Cohen." I word my demands in a way I know he can't refuse. Because my man lives to please me.

His hands are on his belt, eyes on mine. "What do you need?"

I lick my lips.

"Get completely naked and sit at the table, in a chair." His fingers fly down his buttons and I get undressed too, both of us catching excited glances of one another as we strip. My heart is racing. I wonder if that goes away? Or if the belly flutters and heart leaps are always there when you're about to be physical with your person?

I hope I get to find out.

He's naked, his long cock draped up on his belly, resting as he waits. He's half hard just from looking at me, and that feels better than a million views on any video ever will.

"Do you still have the rope from the furniture store?" I ask, peering around the kitchen.

He doesn't even question me when he says, "Yes, it's under the sink. I saved it."

The urge to call him a good boy is on my lips, but instead I stroke my fingers through his hair and step between his spread knees. I bring my breast to his mouth and let my eyes fall closed as he showers my hard nipple in soft kisses, and before we both get too carried away, I pull back.

Grabbing the rope, I return to him, now fully hard. So hard that he stands tall from between his legs, and keeps his hands on his thighs, like he knows he's not supposed to touch himself without my permission.

"Remember, if you ever want to stop," I say, and though I'm the one bearing trauma when it comes to intercourse, I still repeat his options to him, because you don't need to have a history of pain and hurt to have healthy, communicative sex. If I'm in charge at this moment, he needs to know that it's a role, and that in truth, our power is equal. And his words have more power than any of my actions. "Red, or a double tap, okay?"

He smiles. "I'm a little nervous now."

"Put your hands behind your back," I advise as I walk around the chair and crouch. I tie his wrists together tightly, even weaving the rope around the back of the chair, to keep him in one spot. I've done enough shibari scenes in the past to know how to tie the common knots, and feel confident that the one I've tied will both keep and be easy to disengage.

"You always say you need me to come first," I say, straddling his lap while standing over him. He's so thick and tall, standing so erect for me, that the head of his cock is merely inches from my bare, swollen cunt.

This won't take long.

I bring my fingers to my clit and begin stroking, short, small strokes. "Watch me. Don't look into my eyes. Just watch my fingers," I command, with the softest tone. His loyalty isn't loud and overbearing, therefore my power must be calm and docile, too.

"Jesus," he mutters, his Adam's apple sliding down the

curve of his throat as arousal beads atop his cock. "I can smell you, Scarlett."

"Mmm," I purr in response, my insides suddenly starving for fullness, aching to be crammed with hard throbbing cock. *His cock.*

Knowing that's not what we're doing, and forcing myself to remember the reasons, I continue petting my clit, this time dipping a single finger inside. I run the slick digit along his bottom lip, and ask him to taste me. Slowly, as if savoring the sweet chocolate or the richest wine, his tongue sweeps along his bottom lip, a dark rumble moving through his chest.

"You say I saved you," I moan, rubbing my clit faster than I'd planned. But it feels so good. Cohen motionless between his thighs, his perfect cock pointing to where it belongs—all of that makes not coming so fucking hard. "But you saved me, too," I tell him, pausing my strokes to pull myself open and lower down, so his head is a mere inch from my spread cunt. But then I stand again, teasing him, teasing us, and start to rub.

"Can I show you how that makes me feel?" I lean down and lick his lips. He tries to catch my tongue with his mouth but can't, and I smirk down at him as I resume my playing. "Can I show you what I do to myself when I think of you?" I work my clit harder, the noise of my wet cunt bouncing around the apartment walls. I'm literally so fucking wet, so wet that my arousal slides down my thighs.

Suddenly, I have the urge to fill myself in front of him, to show him what we're both waiting for, to tease him and torture him before we both explode. Throwing a leg back, I move off his lap and wander into his bathroom, eyeing him over my shoulder.

His erection bobs, his chest heaves, and his eyes are tamped on me. Just how I want him.

In the bathroom, I open the shower door. We do shower together, but Cohen washes me. He washes my hair and conditions it. He shaves my legs, kissing the tops of my feet and ankles as he crouches to do so.

I look at the row of bottles, the items we've used together to get clean that I'm unaware of. A smile curls my lips when I see it. The blue rainfall bottle. I snatch it up and wash it under the sink and return to Cohen, who looks like heaven with his arms pinned behind him, biceps twisted, muscle defined on every visible inch of him.

I hold it up. "Did you buy this or is this from the other apartment?" I don't even bother saying *my* apartment, because both of the spaces feel like ours.

He shakes his head, his voice raspy as he struggles with words, his eyes dancing across my hard nipples. "I saw it at your place. You, you told me about it. Then when I got groceries, I saw it. And I got it because it makes me think of you."

I have access to sex toys like crazy. I can get anything I want from Debauchery. Hell, in a month, Lucy Lovegood will be a sex toy herself. A pocket pussy.

But right now, the bottle is absolutely perfect.

I straddle him again, standing right over his cock. I move the cool, slick bottle against his length, loving how he weeps at the touch, the clench of his jaw, the knotting in his belly.

"I fucked myself with this bottle, you know?"

He barely nods, his voice a husky whisper. "I know."

"And I thought of you."

"I know."

I press the rounded lid at my opening and push it inside me, unhurried, loving how his eyes lock to it with a single command. I slide the bottle inside with ease, taking a few inches right away. My head tips forward, my eyes locking to his cock bobbing beneath the scene. His head is so pink, I push the bottle inside deeper at the sight.

"Scarlett," he rasps, a little delirious and far away sounding. "God, I can't wait to be inside of you," he says, keeping his eyes on where the bottle slides in and out of me, slick and wet.

"If this were you," I tell him, holding the bottle still while I lower down onto it again, sinking it fully inside of me. "I'd be moaning your name and begging you to pound me, hold yourself deep inside, and unleash everything you have for me." I reach down with my free hand not shoving a body wash bottle in my pussy and squeeze his balls. He growls and curses, but keeps his loyal gaze on my cunt.

"I want you to fuck me deep, Cohen," I tell him, feeling unable to stop saying his name. I just love it so much, and the fact that he really is mine. "I want you to come so deep inside me and I promise, I'll keep every precious drop," I pant, my arm growing fatigued as I fuck myself with the bottle, faster, deeper. Each pump of the blue bottom between my thighs, every glance at his weeping, hard cock, and I get closer to the edge.

"I can't wait to ride you," I tell him, then bring my lips to his as I position the bottle as deep as it will go. Then I admit something to him that I hadn't really considered until now, but want more than ever. "I can't wait for you to push that huge cock of yours into my tight ass." I kiss him again and stand up straighter, my cunt directly above his eager, bobbing dick. "You'll be my first by choice, and you'll ruin me for everyone else. I'll only be yours. Once you come in me," I pant, my own fantasy taking me to the edge. I can't even bear to look at the glistening mess on his groin, I'll come. "I'm yours. Ruined for anyone else."

"You're mine now," he growls, fighting the restraints but

not winning. "You're mine, Scarlett." His tone is almost angry, but that's his protective territorial side, and I fucking love it. My hand stops as an intense wave rolls itself up my spine, the pressure low in my belly coming to a peak, right between my legs. My pussy clenches around the bottle as my orgasm takes hold, but there's still so much pressure as I begin coming, so much fullness. I slide the bottle out, ready to eagerly fuck myself over him as I spasm and moan, torturing him with the knowledge that his favorite pussy is orgasming an inch from his cock and a foot from his face.

Except when I pull the bottle out, warm liquid splashes out, coating his thighs and cock beneath me. For a moment I think the body wash must be open, because what is that? Then Cohen lets out a soul shaking, bone rattling, gut clenching moan.

"Scarlett," he moans, like a warning, like a praise, I don't know.

I look down at the bottle and his cock, following his advice when he says, "Put it back in again, put it back and pull it out."

I impale myself on the bottle again, and the pressure and fullness returns, making my belly ache and clit pulse.

"Out," he pants, "out, out."

I pull it out and another rush of warm liquid spills from my lips, raining down on him on the chair.

"*Fuuuck*," he groans, wiggling in the chair like he'd do anything to have control of his hands. "I wanna grab your hips and slam you down on my cock right now so fucking bad, Scarlett. I want to bury myself inside you, let you drench my lap as I flood your insides."

Jesus Christ. My breeding kink strangles me, and the rest of my orgasm grabs hold, causing my eyes to shut right as my spine starts to quiver. I fuck myself faster, harder, more and more liquid gushing out of me, bringing relief and calm with each drop. After what feels like forever, my arm burning from use, my cunt sated but pulsing, I finally look down into his eyes.

"You," he breathes, unable to catch his breath for a moment. "Did you know you could do that?"

I shake my head. "I've never done that before, ever." I drop to my knees between his, letting the bottle topple to the floor, used and discarded. Wrapping my hands around his shaft, loving the striations of veins and the heat of his erection in my palms, I pump him.

"Scarlett, you're so goddamn beautiful. That was so hot," he breathes, his arms twitching. "I'm close."

I stack my fists and pump him again, appreciating that his cock is one of the most beautiful I've seen. Long with veins, thick with the power to please, his balls tight beneath his shaft, heavy and turgid. Ready to come.

"I got you messy," I breathe, sounding more like a porn star than Lucy ever has. "Now get me messy." I angle his crown to my bare chest, glistening with sweat. "Get me messy, Cohen. Come on me. I want to feel your warm cum all over my body. I wanna rub it in and wear it all day."

I've never said it but as I do, I realize it's not just dirty talk. I really do want to rub it in, wear him like a badge of honor. His spine goes rigid in the chair, his hefty thighs flex, and I stop moving my hands.

The first shot of release streaks up my chest, curling my shoulder. I feel the warm slide of cum down my back as the next shot jets over my breast, this time coating my nipple, dripping down between us. He moans my name as his cock pulses in my hands, spewing rope after rope of thick release. His cum is everywhere when he's done; on both of my breasts, my chin and lips, my belly, the floor, his legs—literally everywhere.

I fucking love it. I lick my lips as his lazy gaze takes me in, a slaked expression on his handsome face. I rock back onto my calves, sitting between his legs, still holding his softening cock in both hands.

"I have to tell you something," I say before either of us has even caught our breath yet. I don't even give him the chance to acknowledge that information is incoming. "I'm ready. I'm ready to have sex with you." Nervously I remove my hands from him, the stickiness drying.

His voice is thin and hoarse as he breathes, "Untie me."

I do, and both of us move to the bathroom together, slowly, so as to not make a mess of the floor more than we already have. I wash my hands and wet a washcloth, turning to bring it to his groin, but he stops me.

He begins wiping my orgasm from him in small swipes, all while still looking at me. Still paying attention to me. "I want you to be sure, because I don't want to hurt you."

"I realized I wasn't afraid of what I thought I was."

He grins. "Dr. Evans?"

I smile, because he knows therapy, too, and I like that. We can be broken together, but we can heal together too. "Yeah." I breathe, wiping most of my body free of his cum. Leaving some around my nipple. Even post orgasm, I really do want to rub some of him into me, and wear his cum proudly. A badge of love I wear proudly.

"I think I was worried you'd get tired of me. You'd change your mind. You'd have some epiphany that didn't include a future with me."

He takes my hand and brings it to his chest. I find his heart to be racing. "I have no future without you."

We haven't shared those words or made promises to each

other, so I rock to my toes and seal his words with a kiss. Back on my feet, I rub the drying cum into my hardened nipple and look up at him. "I want you on me for the rest of the day."

His groan tells me he approves. We redress, with Cohen kneeling at my feet to help me get into my jeans. There's something about the calluses of his working hands on my feet, the way he tenderly touches me and looks up at me for direction, it makes my insides all melty and mushy.

But I think that's just what real love feels like.

"Cohen," I start, watching him toe into his boots, bent over to lace them up. He strains his head, still tying, while looking up at me. *I love you. I'm in love with you. I...* "I just want you to know, you're so worthy of happiness. You deserve everything. And I hope when you're with me, you realize that. That you don't punish yourself anymore."

He rises, one boot tied, the other not. Blinking at me, the air between us heavy from the weight of my words, he swallows. I hear it go down, I hear my own heart thudding in my ear drums. Reaching out, his calloused palm cups my face. "Thank you."

I watch as he bends over again, returning to his boot. My eyes fill but I blink away the sting, and just watch him. What he's been through is horrendous and unimaginable, and while going through my shit, he's seemingly shelved his trauma. And before I say those words, before we commit physically, I have to know he realizes I'm right. That he does deserve, despite the lies his grief told him before, everything good.

"You know that, right?" I ask, my voice quiet and unsure. We had a great time on lunch. My body did things—for him —that it's never done for any person or camera before. We shared orgasms yet again, and this one was just as powerful, if not more, than the last. Each experience with him becomes more binding and intense.

"I'm working toward accepting that." He takes my hand and brings it to his lips, the scruff of his unshaved face sending bumps up my arm.

The conversation settles there as we flit between the apartments, making sure both are locked up. As we take the stairs down to the car, I hear my phone ring in my purse but I don't check it.

I'm with the only person I want to talk to right now. But Cohen glances at my ringing purse a few times, stroking a hand down his chin, then pulling at the back of his neck, elbow out.

I drape my hand on his thigh the entire way back, and his demeanor shifts back to calm, and he even smiles at me as we pull into the same parking spot we abandoned earlier.

We're going to be okay. We may look different than other couples, but low in my belly, I feel it—we're going to heal. We're going to make it.

Together.

twenty-two

. . .

cohen

I miss her, too.

Tonight, Lucy Lovegood is hosting a mixer for investors at the Crave & Cure studios. I could be there, hell, she begged me to stay.

But I had therapy tonight, and going to a drink mixer after a therapy session isn't something I'm looking to do.

I've been in therapy for years. And it's not like the sessions are as rough as they used to be. Oftentimes they're positive now, but still, I know I have heavy shit on my mind and a social function won't blend well with that.

Back when I started seeing Scarlett, I told my therapist that I'd met someone. And we worked through the expected emotions of moving forward. He told me that moving on will bring a fresh wave of grief, like I'm really abandoning my old life and the memories, and that it was to be expected.

I did feel that. I did. Those feelings of guilt are what kept me tied to the past for so long.

After that passed, he'd told me, I may still feel undeserving. Because guilt is a conditioned emotion. It keeps me protected from emotional distress. And as soon as I was able to take apart that guilt and break it down brick by brick, I saw he was right. I saw all that emotional distress waiting, rushing toward me, wrapping around me, reminding me that she died and I didn't save her.

I wanted the guilt back, but swam through the emotional distress as advised, surprised to see I didn't immediately sink and drown.

Tonight's session was interesting though. I came with a lot on my mind, and emptied the contents of my brain right out on the table as soon as the door clicked shut.

I told him that while things with Scarlett and I are progressing and while she is also making strides in her therapy, that I sense we're coming to something pivotal. A choice will need to be made.

Can I be with her? Because she wants a full life. Can I do that? Am I ready to recommit?

I know that I am ready, in my heart I know I want her and a life with her.

A family.

I was a family man then, and at heart, still am, but locked that away in self-defense, because who the fuck wants to marry and have a child with a man who had that all once and let it slip away?

My therapist gave me the nudge. Told me that her wanting to be with me was her choice, not mine, and that I'd have to let her decide. He also directed me to the pool.

The place where I went to hurt everyday for years. Where I thought of them. Her. *Tortured* myself thinking of her.

He said go there, and hold yourself under water, and think instead of Scarlett. See what happens, see how I feel.

So after therapy, I went back to my apartment—which feels weird and lonely without Scarlett—and grabbed my trunks. I hadn't gone to the gym pool in weeks, because I never wanted to take morning time away from her. I didn't want to leave her alone, if I'm being honest, because Pete is still calling. So I didn't go.

I was avoiding facing the pool, because I knew the pool would help me figure out where I was at in the closure process. If I could move on. I was terrified if I got in the water and felt my chest seize and my brain go blurry and my heart crack that I wouldn't be able to move forward with Scarlett. That I'd realize I was still stuck with them.

Avoiding the pool seemed like the solution. But that's why I'm an art director and not a therapist, because apparently avoidance is not the solution.

I went to the gym, put my things in the locker room, and headed to the pool. In the room, despite the fact it's evening instead of morning, is the same father and son I met all those weeks ago. The heavy metal door slams closed, drawing their attention to me. The man raises an arm and shouts an echoed hello as I lift my hand and wave in silence.

I drop my towel near the edge and stand with my toes on the bullnose, looking down into the lazily rippling water. The chlorine burns my nostrils, smelling stronger than it ever did before. Maybe they just treated the pool? I don't know. I rake a hand up the back of my head right as the boy calls, "*Cannon ball!*" and plunges into the other side, sending slow ripples and waves my way.

I take the opportunity to jump in, and I let the weight of my body pull me to the bottom, bubbles all around me clouding my vision. I blink through the chlorinated pool, the chemical and heat stinging my eyes. I press a hand to my chest, searching for the throb. Trying to find the pinching pain.

It's not there.

And as my breath runs out, my body and mind beg for the surface. Yearn for a lungful of air. No part of me wants to stay below.

Not anymore.

I do as the Dr. said and think of Scarlett for a moment, waving my arms to stay below the surface. As soon as I see her blonde hair around her face, wide eyes and charming smile, as soon as I imagine her in my lap, fingers in mine, feeding her bites of pasta and sleeping with her in a mess of tangled legs and twisted sheets, I brace my feet on the bottom and push off.

Breaking the surface, I find the little boy and his father are there, looking at me. His dad throws me a look of caution.

"My boy tells me you like to hold your breath." His eyes ask me if I'm okay, the way they soften at the edges, the crows feet disappearing, his pupils searching mine.

I look at the boy, who looks moderately concerned. I wink at him, something I've never really done.

"He's right," I say, returning my focus to his father, who is running his palms along the surface of the pool. The three of us stand in the middle of the pool, this pool that I've swam in way too many times, more times than I've ever swam anywhere, even the lake back home in Michigan. But now, it feels like I don't belong. "I used to. But I've seen how far I can take it. I'm done testing myself now," I admit, knowing it's quite the loaded statement, but relieved they are unaware. To them I'm just a loner odd ball at the public pool.

The boy leans in, as if there are children nearby he's

protecting from this grown up talk. I almost laugh, because he himself is a kid. But he's so serious, I go along with it.

"That's good. It was kinda weird how long you'd stay down there."

"Yeah, you're right. And holding my breath just isn't that useful of a skill. I'd rather be doing things above the surface, than alone below." I clap a hand on his shoulder and he looks at me with pride. "So I'm done with that."

He beams over at his dad, who looks much more comfortable now. I swim a few laps then get out, feeling so detached from the pool. It was a dark, inviting hug before. My home, the place where I sickly felt I belonged. A place where I could inflict pain on myself.

It was just a place where I was treading water in misery, and I know now that was wrong.

I shower quickly in the locker room, getting redressed in the same thing I went to work in. I text Scarlett that I'm on my way back to my apartment, and she texts back that she misses me.

I miss her, too.

Coming back to my apartment, there's a small brown package on my doorstep. I peer down at the label to make sure it's mine and not Scarlett's. The label reads my name, and I know immediately what it is.

I found it online a few weeks ago when I was at work, and couldn't stop thinking of her. Couldn't bring myself to schedule light bulb orders and paint samples when there was something out there in the world that she wanted, that she needed.

I had to find it for her. I had to bring her back that singular item that bore so much emotional security and sweet memories. Scooping the box up, I kick my apartment door closed and flip on the lights.

More than ever, I feel like telling Scarlett about my swim tonight. Not even the therapy but the swim, because that's where I realized that no matter what I've taught myself I deserve or don't, I want her, and all I want is a future with her.

It's one thing to realize you're finally going to live again. It's another to realize that living again means potentially losing again, and then I'm reminded of them. And my failures.

My therapist says one day what I perceive as failures will look different with perspective, because I didn't fail. I had no control of the things that happened. Still, I feel compelled to remind Scarlett, to lay all my cards out, fall to her feet and hope. Hope that she wants me, because I'm ready to have her, fully.

I hop in the shower, taking my time under the heated stream, my head a bleary mess. The front door, which I left unlocked, thuds closed, and I know she's here. I pop open the shower door, and peer into the endless steam. She appears, and the world settles onto its axis, my brain shifts, everything slows and… I feel better. I feel okay. I feel like it's all possible.

I turn the water off, and step out. She hands me a towel, wearing her post-shoot sweats, her blonde hair in a braid down her back.

"Hi," she says softly as I quickly towel off, eager to talk. And being naked in a room with Scarlett is quickly training my cock to get excited, but tonight, I have to tell her.

"Hi, are you hungry? How was work?" I greet her. As much as I want to sit her down and tell her all about the pool and what I want, I have to take care of her first.

She smiles. Beams, really. "It was fun. The triple F shoot went so well. It was super fun. I wish we had commissioned more of those." I take her face in my hands, pruned and damp, and bring her lips to mine. I need her kiss, I need to taste her for a dose of courage.

"And yes," she says when I finally release her and lift her under her knees and around her back to carry her to the kitchen. She drops her head to my shoulder comfortably, and her hot sigh flanks my neck, making my heart race. "I'm hungry."

I lower her to the kitchen counter, and find my hands... shaking.

Jesus Christ, Cohen, get it the fuck together. I clear my throat as I grip the edge of the counter, leaning down to steal a breath. Her hand falls across my wrist in a gentle grip, wordlessly commanding me to pay her attention, give me her focus.

I look up through bleary eyes. My scalp tingles from excitement, fear, everything.

I spot the box, and exhale, reaching for it. I put it in her lap. "This is for you."

It's not what I planned. I wanted to talk. I wanted to pour my guts out. But with shaky hands, I think I need more time. I don't want to rush things. I want control, and right now, pleasing her with this gift is what I need.

She slips her finger beneath the tape, loosening the edge enough to tear it off. Rolling it between her palms, she balls the tape until it's ready to toss, and I take it from her, dumping it in the can beneath the sink. Slowly, she peels open the box and blinks down at the contents. She doesn't look up at me for a minute—the longest minute—and when she does, her eyes are wide, mouth open with silent awe.

"Cohen."

Then I realize what tonight is for. Maybe it's not to share what I learned in the pool. Maybe it's to share a little more of me, and see how that settles.

"Addie had one like you described. I think maybe even the same exact one. And I've been looking for one just like it, too."

"Addie," she whispers, drawing out my daughter's name like delicate lace filigree, cautious as ever.

"My daughter. Addie." I'm qualifying her name for me, to say it aloud, and Scarlett knows.

Tears slip down her cheeks without hesitation, and I fight the knot centering my chest. I work around it, pushing it down, forcing more words out, knowing that this is what this moment is for. Honestly, depth, and connection.

"I didn't keep anything of hers. I regret that now. I was in so much pain, I just..." I swallow hard, wondering how long I can stave off the pain searing up my throat, clinging to the backs of my eyes like fiery torches. "Anyway, I've been looking for this music box. I wound it every night when I tucked her in. It was... our thing."

I drop my head between my shoulders, hands still gripping the counter's edge. I let heavy tears of pain and grief drop to the old linoleum, because I don't want her to see me this way.

"Look at me," she commands, her tone strong but soft. And as much as I don't want to break for her, I look up, because... she owns me.

My lip trembles as Addie's sweet face flashes through my mind. I can hear the splashing of water as if I were there. The piercing ring of my phone that night echoes in my brain. I hold the counter more tightly, my knuckles draining of color. My head whirrs. "I should have kept it. I knew as soon as I came here, I should have kept it. So I've been looking for one since." I swallow hard, watching her face mirror mine, tears coating her cheeks, pain coloring her cheeks. "When you told me you were looking for the same music box, I just... I knew I had to find it. For you."

Her small hands retrieve the music box from the packaging, and it falls to the floor where we both ignore it. She turns it between her palms, the pink ribbons hand-painted on it, the gold clasp, the tiny drawer in the bottom. It's exactly like Addie's.

I choke, and drop my head again at just the sight. I hear the box slide onto the counter, then her feet are next to mine, hands collecting me. With one hand on each side of me, holding me by my ribs, she peers up at me, not trying to slow her tears.

Those are for me, for my daughter, and it doesn't do much to stop mine.

"You keep it," she whispers. "Keep it and think of her. Please, Cohen."

I shake my head, words challenging around the emotion clogging my throat. Husky, I rasp, "No, Scarlett. I found it for you. I want you to have it."

She glances back at the box then to me again, wearing a soft expression. Not a smile, not sadness, but somewhere in between awe and pain. "We'll keep it. Together." She raises to her toes and sifts her long fingers through my damp hair.

Her touch is so comforting, and feels so good, I let my eyes close. I let tears slip free. I let my chest heave and wrack with cries of grief and loss. And I let her hold me, pull into her. Feel her hands slide up my bare back, soothing and caring.

"Thank you for sharing with me." She finds my eyes and holds me by the chin, sealing her praise with a kiss, and I'm flooded with relief. Like telling her was cathartic, and released me from some level of guilt and pain I didn't know, amidst it all, I'd been holding back.

"Cohen, I'm ready to be with you, and I think tonight, maybe it would do us both good." She reaches into the towel and holds me. I'm soft, but I still crumple into her, feeling good from the intimate asexual touch. "Give yourself to me tonight. I'm ready. And I want you to have me, too."

"Scarlett, I want you to be sure. I need you. I know it now but I need you. I can't hurt you. I can't hurt another woman I love."

By the hand, she leads me to my bedroom and motions for me to sit on the edge of the bed. I do, but not before she pulls the towel free, leaving me naked and exposed. I'm soft, soft everywhere. No part of me is flexing or clenching. I sit there, emotionally drained, but also somehow sated after our exchange.

"I can't believe we were looking for the same thing," she whispers, and I don't know if she's talking about the music box or us, but I agree with both.

"I know," I say, watching as she peels her clothes off slowly, creating a heap on the clean floor.

"Crave tests us regularly," she says slowly, cautiously, watching my eyes for a wordless reaction. I have none. Because I know how Crave cares for their actors, and their health is top priority.

I also know where this is going. And nerves seize my stomach, tossing around the limited contents. Her eyes move along the curve of my arm, clenching the bed. I've been inside of her bare, but I've never come inside of her. Not yet.

"But we're going to save that," she says, referencing what I know we're both thinking about. "And tonight, I'm going to take you, I'm going to fuck you, Cohen, and make you feel everything. Because we need that." She steps closer, dropping a hand between her legs, fingers spreading her pink lips apart. "I'll stop if I need to, and you'll stop me if you need to, won't you?"

I nod, and slowly my cock comes to life as she feeds her fingers up my thighs, pushing them apart.

"Have you ever been a bottom for a partner?" she asks, her eyes on my thickening dick.

I swallow hard, and her question fully steers me out of the emotional tangle from moments ago. A bottom? My ass clenches as I repeat the question in my head aloud. "A bottom?"

Her eyes veer over the terrain of my naked body and come to my eyes. "Being a bottom isn't just about anal sex," she says, but not with condescension or teasing but... to explain, to educate.

My throat is dry and sticky but I manage to say, "I... I don't understand."

She wraps her hands under my knees and tries to tug me down lower but because she's much smaller than me, I don't budge. "Slide a bit lower," she says, and I do. I bring my knees towards my chest with legs still parted and she straddles the backs of my thighs, planting the soles of her feet on the mattress next to my hips, and I can't help it. After years of not looking, all I want to do now is feast on her body. My eyes fall to the way her cunt opens for me, puffy and pink, begging to be filled. My bottom lip tingles as saliva pools beneath my tongue at the sight.

"Bottoming for me right now means that I'll hold the control, the dominance. And I'll take you this way," she says, reaching down to collect my fully erect cock with her hand. Positioning my crown at her center, she surges toward me until my entire head is swallowed in her warm tightness.

I look down at where I'm barely inside of her, my abs knotted with strain, suddenly all of my body tensed. "You feel so good," I admit, even though I'm only barely in.

"To prove to you I'm okay and I'm ready for you, I'll take you like this. I'll fuck you, I'll control it. And then, I'll get off while you... get off."

I liked all of it until that part. I like the idea of her fucking me. Her being in control until we both know she's okay to do this. That I won't trigger anything, that she'll be able to orgasm—all of it, just to make sure. The idea of sharing that intimacy only to end with pulling out... I understand it. I want more of her, but I understand her need to wait.

We aren't ready for me to come inside of her. We aren't.

I nod, my body ready for the pleasure, ready to lose myself to her. "Okay," I agree.

She reaches her arms out straight and wiggles ten fingers at me. "Hands," she orders. I reach for her and we weave our fingers together, and I'm glad I'm already inside of her. I throb and leak a little from the feeling of connection we have.

She rolls her hips into me, and it's the fucking strangest and best sensation. My legs open, our linked hands keeping my knees spread. I feel so vulnerable this way, but it's freeing, too.

I like relinquishing control, knowing it gives her comfort and peace, and makes her feel good. Selfishly it makes me feel good, too.

Hips jutting forward, my cock pulled back and up toward her as she fucks herself on my cock. The position is new and hot; I'm on my back with her straddling my thighs and simultaneously spreading me open so I can see her tits swaying. Our moans escalating as my cock slides in and out of her, at her will.

I can't take my eyes off the sight of my veiny dick disappearing inside of her, over and over, her swollen pink lips hugging my shaft with each needful stroke.

I've never had sex this way, with a woman fucking me and herself on my cock? I don't even understand but I stop trying. My head cranes from the bed, my back sweaty against my cool sheets.

"You feel so good," she breathes, her eyes rolling closed. She pumps herself on me a few more times before telling me to keep my hands on my knees and my legs open and apart. Hearing her say that was fucking hot. Sliding her hands down my calves, she grabs my ankles. Her ankle digs into my hip as she moves faster and faster, my cock sliding in and out of her more urgently. I can see myself in her position, fucking her on the edge of the bed this way. I never considered a role reversal in this position, with her fucking us both on my cock, but goddamn I love it.

Sweat coats her belly and her hands slide along the hair on my ankles. I feel everything. Every bent hair, every roll of sweat, every bead of precum that spills into her with each aggressive thrust.

My orgasm cyclones my core, tapering down to my groin, rocketing up through my shaft. My voice is hoarse but I call her name in warning. "Scar."

She sinks all the way down, clenching and spasming, her heated orgasm spilling out around me in warm, wet waves. It's messy and fucking perfect. Her eyes close as her pussy seizes around my length, and the sight overwhelms me. Her orgasm threatens to milk me with how tight she convulses, the breathy little moans she releases into my space.

"Scar," I try again, clenching my ass and core, letting her use my cock, letting her finish. Her pulsing slows and her eyes open, finding the urgency in mine immediately. She rises to the balls of her feet and slides me out of her, my cock slapping down on my belly.

That belly slap, and the sight of her engorged, well-fed cunt send me over.

I reach down and grab myself just as my cock lifts with a twitch, sending the first rope of release sailing along my belly and pecs.

She knocks my hand away as my head falls back, stroking me slowly, rolling her thumb over my slit as I burst.

When I'm nothing more than a hollow chest, a canvas of white and am utterly speechless, she appears above me. Lips against mine, she whispers, "That was perfect. You're so good to me, Cohen, so good."

We share an unhurried kiss and I realize how much she needed the first time to be in her control, how she needed to prove to herself that there is still safe sex. That I can give her that.

"How are you?" I ask, cobwebs hanging in my voice. "Are you okay?"

She presses her naked body to mine, and cum smears hot and thick between us. I don't hate it. Her little moan tells me she doesn't either.

"I'm so good, because you make me feel so good." Our mouths come together, and her tongue sweeps along mine. She pulls back and our gazes meet. Her lips part, eyes studying me so intensely my stomach knots. My heart pounds in my ears.

But before she says anything, she slides off me, calling back to me that she's going to get a towel.

The spell is broken, and if she was going to say something weighty and profound, she waited. The same way I waited on what I wanted to say earlier. I respect her timing, and while I want her to say those words to me, I let her clean me and tell her all about the dinner we have waiting in the crock pot on the counter.

After another shower, one where we share the hot stream of water and soapy sponge, taking care to wash each other. I lock the door and close the blinds as she gets comfortable in my bed, and when I slide in and she draws my head to her chest, I find myself asleep before I can even stress about what's left to be said.

Because we had sex.

And that's a big step for us both, and enough for tonight.

"I can't Cohen, seriously, I'm so full," Scarlett whines, sitting topless at the small dining table. Well, not just topless. Completely nude.

When I asked her if she likes being naked because it's comfortable, you know, because of the porn star role, she shook her head. She said, "I like the way I feel when you look at me. I feel so good, and I just want that feeling all the time."

I told her I look at her the same with clothes on, and her

response? "But you get hard looking at me naked, and I like looking at you hard. It's a win-win."

Talented and smart to boot. Can't argue with that.

"Are you sure you don't want a little more?" I ask, sifting the spatula around the pan of scrambled egg whites. Scarlett lived on protein bars and God only knows what else when she was with Pe—not with me. I no longer want to speak his name.

What we did last night feels like the next step, despite the fact I'm well aware there is a lot of ground to cover in the conversation department.

She waves her plate away, pressing her hand to her belly, which I can't see. "I'm stuffed."

I arch a brow. "What's on the agenda for today?"

She leans back in the chair, and you'd think the weird positioning and partially reclining in a hard dining chair wouldn't be hot, but Scarlett looks hot. I think I'd get hard at her flossing. "It's actually a solo scene today and I'm looking forward to it." She plucks a piece of strawberry off the plate, tipping her head back to drop it in. "Okay," she cautions, "that was the last bite."

I finish packing our lunches while she gets dressed, and while I dress, she does the dishes. I don't want her doing the dishes, and when I appear in the kitchen as she wipes her hand on a dishtowel, I let her know as much.

"I do the dishes," I say, my tone unwavering. "You eat, you enjoy. I cook, I clean."

Our eyes idle. I reach out and take her by the front of her throat, my thumb aligned perfectly with her pulse. "I want to take care of you in all ways, Scarlett, and I want you to let me. Will you let me?"

She swallows, and blinks a few times. I'm on the brink of

rewording myself, making sure she knows I'm not trying to control but please. Only ever please.

"Okay," she breathes. "I just don't like being useless."

I'm glad I didn't release my hold on her yet. "Is that something he said to you? Is that something he made you believe? That you're useless?" I have to really control my anger, because rage sears up my throat, burning my mouth.

She nods, and attempts to drop her gaze, yet another thing she likely learned from being his fucking beaten down dog, his punching bag.

I drive her face up to mine, pressing my thumb into the underside of her chin. "You are not useless. And not doing dishes or folding clothes does not make you useless. If it did, a significant proportion of the male population is, by that definition, useless." I crash our mouths together, surprising both of us really. "Understand? Understand that cleaning a house doesn't define a single fucking thing about you?"

She nods in my grip, and it's the last time I ever want to feel her throat slide against my palm if we aren't in bed.

I let go, and we walk to the car together, heading to work... together.

Words are waiting, this I know. But we are, for all intents and purposes, together. And I've already come farther than I ever dreamed, because of her.

The scene is hard to ignore, because when you're dating a beautiful on the inside, gorgeous on the outside adult film star that silences a room with her soulful solo scenes, ignoring is very fucking hard.

But so is my cock if I watch.

So I busy myself away from the set, the set I built for her, and work on the open electrical panel on the back wall, beneath the security feed. Out of the corner of my eye, in my faded and fuzzy peripheral vision, something on the monitor moves. There's movement in one of the many squares on screen, but it's mid-morning, and cool out. Breezes and rains carry all sorts of things through our parking lot, but for some reason, this morning, my soul goddamn full to the brim and my gorgeous girlfriend acting her heart out just feet behind me, I look up.

I look up and let my gaze scatter over the squares, and I don't know why.

But then my happiness drains, my face falls, and at my sides, my fists ball. I bring my face closer to the grainy surveillance but the thing is, this isn't the nineties. Even grainy, these are pretty fucking good quality. But I wouldn't need the high definition or 4k bullshit right now anyway.

I'd recognize that pathetic gait, that revolting presence. He paces at the steps to the back door, mouth running silently from the screen.

I lift my hand to my waist, unclipping the utility belt I wear here daily. I don't let it drop to the floor and disrupt everyone. Instead, I drape it over a metal guardrail near the exit door, and very fucking quietly, slip out back.

He stops. He looks at me. I've got four cement steps on him, but I'd rather it be as fair as it can. I jog down the stairs and step right in front of him, a few feet of space between us.

His snort is vile. "So you're him, huh?"

"I'm him," I reply, because whatever *him* he's fucking referring to, I'm it.

The new boyfriend? The guy who answered the phone? The man who takes care of her? The man who will fucking kill anyone who tries to fucking harm her? I'm him.

He snorts again as realization settles into me. I really want to hurt this man who hurt her so fucking badly. And I've never been violent. Even in the aftermath of Addie, when I was so angry with Valerie, I was never violent. Stupid and cruel, yes, but violent, no.

I'm thoroughly different now given everything that's transpired, and I feel that now, in the rapid pulsing in my throat, and fiery anger that races through my veins. She's changed me, and I'm no longer the same man. I've dragged some of my past, carved something new, and she's added onto that and now I'm a different man than before.

I am hers, and I will stop at nothing to protect her.

"You're just a fuckin' placeholder," he laughs, the noise making hairs of awareness lift off my neck. "You're just someone she's using for cum like the whore that she is."

In that moment, those vile words rolling from his lips, my world goes white. Anger wraps my brain and covers my eyes. All I can see is my own seething rage.

I clench my fist and am about to rear it, cock it, and drive it forward fast into his face; when he pulls a gun.

I look down at it, spotting the carved ridges on the slide and the smooth barrel. The grip is nubbed and worn, and when his hand falls sideways, I can see the safety. It's off.

My eyes go to his, and I study him. They're dark but bloodshot, and he can't take the eye contact, and looks to my chest.

"If I'm a placeholder, why do you have a gun drawn on me?" I ask, my voice completely even and unwavering.

He's been calling her non-fucking-stop. He showed up at her apartment, even. He fucking played a long con on Otis just to get back into her life.

He smashed her music box.

I take a step toward him, so full of rage that it easily usurps my fear. I wrap my hand on the barrel and bring it to my chest, aligning the muzzle to my sternum.

"I'll give you five seconds to shoot me," I breathe, nostrils flaring. Pete's hand shakes with indecision, and I count to five in my brain before the gun is in my hand, and the butt of it is coming down across his face.

Scarlett doesn't like violence. It's triggering, and harmful to her mental health and her healing. But beautiful, sweet, loving, gentle Scarlett is inside, behind the protection of these steel doors, kept safe by friends, locks and cameras.

So I shove the gun in the back of my pants as I collect his unhinged ass by the collar, and drive my fist into his face again. I let go, and watch him stagger around like a drunk, stumbling, his hands braced for impact around him. Miraculously, he doesn't fall, and he brings one hand to his forehead, pressing on the rupture where blood flows freely.

He comes close to me, still looking unstable. And somehow he fucking clocks me.

I falter, and my back connects with the metal railing lining the back door. I don't leave my feet, but I wasn't expecting to be hit and take a moment to feel the pain swirling round the socket of my eye, pulsing in my temple.

I blink through the pain, seemingly unaffected. His mouth falls open, the blood streaming down his head curling his lip, into his mouth. He spits and I take that time to hollow his gut with a hefty punch, sending him backward several paces.

The back door swings open, but I don't turn. I don't risk taking my eyes off of him.

"She only wants you to fuck her so she can get what she really wants. A baby. You're just a fucking sperm donor." He spits more blood and it's then I remove the gun from my waist and lower it to the ground, kicking it to Lance behind me. I know it's him because I hear him utter, "Jesus fuck," and call for Aug.

"Don't talk about what she wants like you know or fucking care," I spit, sweat sliding down my forehead and I move toward him, scared for us both. Because it's been a long time since I've been angry at anyone but myself.

I grab him by the shirt and yank him to me, relishing the cuts and damage I did to his face. Piece of shit deserves worse. "You're right. Killing you isn't worth it. She's nothing more than a useless whore who can't keep her own baby alive."

That can't keep her own... My mind spins. Aug appears, worming his way between us. He presses a stern palm to Pete's chest and drives him back.

"Get the fuck out of here, now." His tone is heavy but quiet, and it's then I realize if Aug is here, the scene is over.

She's likely looking for me. She does that now after every scene.

"I'll fucking call the cops. You assaulted me," he says.

"You pointed a gun at me," I hiss, my chest connecting with Aug's back as I surge forward, my rage driving my reactions.

Aug cuts us both off. "Pete, I'll call the police. I'll delete the footage out here. No one will know what happened. But you have a history of stalking and harassing. And Cohen has years of perfect employment, without so much as fucking parking ticket to his name."

Pete steps back, balling the sleeve of his shirt to bring to the wound gaping on his forehead. He spits, he snarls, and then he walks the fuck away.

We wait for him to disappear out the gates and around the corner until I let my shoulders sink. Aug turns around and faces me, placing his hands on my shoulders. His vision dips, analyzing my face from every angle. He pats my bicep.

"You're alright, right?"

I nod but glance back at the door. Lance is standing there, on the top step, hand wrapped around the handle, keeping it closed.

I look between the two of them. "She hates violence," I say quietly, swiping the trickle of blood from beneath my nose. "I don't want her to see this," I add, looking around my feet at all the dark drops of blood scattered against the asphalt, telling a story of struggle and pain.

"I'll hose it off now," Aug says, his voice carefully treading.

"I'm going to go," I say, becoming anxious, my mind a complete mess. Pete did deserve it, he did, but she would hate this. This scene would make her sick. And she doesn't want to be with another violent fucking man.

Can't keep her own baby alive.

I hear those words on loop, and I don't know what they mean. As I walk out of the parking lot, in search of a stalled Uber or waiting taxi, I try and pull them apart, jump into the space between them and understand how they fit.

She's never said she's had a child. I think of her body, and remember the marks of growth and change along Valerie's abdomen. Even her breasts bore those marks. I recall every mark on Scarlett's body, and I didn't see any of that.

But everyone is different.

Fatigue clings to me as I slip into the backseat of a cab, and mumble our address.

Her address. I gave him her address. And I use the key she put on my ring to get inside. I don't know what I'll say to her, I can't seem to control my thoughts enough to solve anything right now. I'm still circling on those words and what they mean.

I lock the door behind me once I'm inside, but don't use the chain. I lie on her couch and stare at the ceiling, frozen in the unknown. But I have to be here. With Pete angry and on the loose, I can't risk her coming home and him being here or trying anything. Even if I'm just across the hall.

Guilt engulfs me realizing that she'll have to drive home alone. We went to work together after a perfect fucking morning, and we should be driving home together, too.

I close my eyes, trying to let the confusion and anger settle, trying to find a sliver of calm and understanding before she gets back.

It seems like now is the time for that talk.

twenty-three

· · ·

scarlett

He does so much.

My hands don't want to work with me right now. My robe has slid from the wire hanger three times, and I've dropped my phone and keys once, too.

The scene was great, and I felt fantastic. When the lights flicked off, and Aug was up from his chair passing me compliments, I looked for him.

Cohen doesn't watch my scenes, he never has, only now he assures me it's for entirely different reasons altogether. And when I found him hard as nails in his office one day, reciting famous baseball games and tapping his foot, I knew what he meant.

It's his place of work, and we both respect Crave far too much.

But he didn't even have his back to the scene, working on something else, like usual. I went straight to his office, I almost rushed there. But it was empty. His utility belt was slung over the railing by the back door, and spotting it brought relief. He's here just... probably busy with something else.

He does so much.

Now in my dressing room, after a crucial shower, I stumble through my jeans and nearly trip, and finally, after a healthy battle with my purse strap and the straw from my tumbler, I'm ready. I head out into the dark hallway, and lay eyes on Lance and Aug, near the backdoor.

Their faces are shrouded in the shadows from the back of the set, but their voices are low, tone vibrating with gravitas. I'm slow to approach, but they both spot me right away. Aug steps forward and I know something is off.

"Scarlett," he starts, which is never good because a normal conversation very rarely involves a person's name at all. "We need to talk."

I look at Lance, whose gaze is pinned on Aug's profile.

"Pete came here this afternoon," he starts, gathering my focus from Lance.

"Where's Cohen?" I breathe, suddenly beyond anxious to lay eyes on him, especially after knowing *he* was here.

"He's okay, he just... he went home," Aug says, his eyes darting between mine. He's clearly waiting for relief to wash over me so he can breathe, too. But why was Pete here? Why did Cohen leave? We came here together.

"Why?" I ask, not sure which question I'm attacking first. "Did Cohen talk to Pete?"

Aug glances at Lance, a nonverbal passing of the *this is fucked up* baton.

"We're going to delete the footage," Lance says carefully,

his intense gaze imparting the subtext. They love Cohen, and if they're deleting footage, it's to protect him.

My stomach twists, and my heart beating in my ears is all I can hear when I ask, "What happened?"

Deleting the footage. I reach out and grab Lance's wrist. "Have you deleted it yet?" I turn to face Aug, willing him to look at me. Finally he does. "Show me. Show me, Augustus, now."

That's fucking right. I want to see it and I don't want what I need to be steamrolled ever again. I know Aug is likely protecting me, but I want to see it. Hell, Cohen is the reason I'm standing up for myself.

"I don't know if he'd want you to," Lance says softly, in the kindest tone he's ever used with me.

"Show me," I say, practically snarling my teeth. I need to know where Cohen went. I could give a fuck less about Pete. I don't bother asking about him.

I follow behind Aug, in front of Lance as we go into his office, where he's holding the recorded feed hostage. He pulls his office chair out for me, and I take a seat. None of us speak as he starts up the footage. It's silent so I turn and face him.

"Can you turn on the sound?"

The way he looks at Lance before answering makes me feel like maybe the sound being off was a last ditch effort to protect me, but whatever it is, I want to know.

"Fine," he says, reaching down to take control of the onscreen mouse. He clicks, and noises spark up from the speakers.

Pete appears, and he's pacing, talking shit, talking nonsense. I really don't even consider what he's actually saying, I merely tune him out and grow angry and tired as I watch him pace.

Maybe that's why Cohen left. Maybe Pete showing up

overwhelmed him. I can't say I blame him. Afterall, he's been making emotional headway in being with me. The last thing he needs is my asshole, narcissistic piece of shit ex to add stress to him.

I let out a low exhale as Pete continues to pace on screen. I can talk to Cohen, we can talk through Pete showing up. Fuck, at this point, I would get the restraining order. Especially to keep Cohen in the right headspace.

The door squeals open and I drop my eyes to the bottom of the screen.

Cohen is there, taking the steps with speed and ease, immediately standing in front of Pete.

"So you're him, huh?" The hair on my neck and arm lifts with his pinching tone. I look at the back of Cohen's head, wishing I could see his face, wishing we had one more angle of this to watch from.

But it's just Cohen's heaving back, and Pete's stupid fucking face.

"I'm him," Cohen says, stealing the breath from my lungs, making my head go warm and fuzzy. Nothing real has been said here, and yet, a lot has been conveyed.

I almost can't breathe.

"You're just a fuckin' placeholder. You're just someone she's using for cum like the whore that she is," Pete laughs, shaking his head as he spews the hateful bullshit. Once again, here he is, using the thing I want most as a fucking weapon. A tool. A device. Just using, using, using any fucking way he can.

I press a palm to my stomach, and from the side of my eye I see Lance watching, but I don't take my eyes off the screen.

Pete reaches back, and my heart nearly stops. Because I've seen movies and TV shows. I know what the reach back is for, especially in the middle of a goddamn fight. He pulls a gun on Cohen, who doesn't even move an inch. It's silent between them for a moment as my eyes fill. I know he's okay, Aug told me as much, but for him to have to go through this for me?

I feel sick.

"If I'm a placeholder, why do you have a gun drawn on me?" Cohen steps closer to Pete, bringing the end of the gun even nearer to him, completely unafraid. The gun shakes in Pete's hand as Cohen takes it by the barrel and brings it straight to his chest. "I'll give you five seconds to shoot me," he breathes. I gasp, and my hand flies over my mouth, the other still pressing deep to my aching belly. Why the fuck is Pete like this? Cohen does not deserve this shit. This trauma.

I count. I fucking count. Even though I know Cohen is okay, I count.

There is no pop or blaze at the count of five. Instead, Cohen yanks the gun from Pete and slams it across his face, forehead first. I blink at the screen, the violence unfolding in front of me making acid claw at my throat.

He stashes the gun in the back of his pants, takes Pete by the collar and strikes him with a curled fist. Pete stumbles but doesn't fall and crashes into Cohen with his fist, connecting with his eye and the bridge of his nose. I gasp, both hands now curtaining my shocked, open mouth.

Lance appears at the back door, surveying the scene cautiously. I chance a glance at him, and he's still studying me. I watch as Pete comes nearer, feeling confident after landing a strike.

"She only wants you to fuck her so she can get what she really wants. A baby. You're just a fucking sperm donor."

My lips curl at that. Cohen knows I want a baby. He knows. Because we've discussed the important things. Yet fear worms through me, leaving me shifting weight on my feet.

He knows, but not *everything*.

Tears roll down my cheeks and Lance's hand comes to my back, between my shoulder blades. His small token of affection causes my tears to intensify.

I was going to tell him.

I just… I hadn't yet.

"Don't talk about what she wants like you know or fucking care," Cohen defends me on screen, and I feel a million times worse. I know now why Lance's gaze is lingering.

I think I know why Cohen went home. And I don't know if it had anything to do with the punch or the gun.

"Oh my god," the words rush free from me. Cohen told me about his trauma. "Oh my god," I breathe, the office closing in around me. He told me about his deceased child, his marraige's end, he told me everything with tears in his eyes, no fear of being vulnerable or anything. I collect my head in my hands before it smashes against Aug's desk.

I keep my eyes lifted to the screen, because I have to know what Cohen knows.

This isn't about Pete at all anymore.

"You're right. Killing you isn't worth it. She's nothing more than a useless whore who can't keep her own baby alive."

My elbows slide out from beneath me as my vision goes dark, just for a moment but long enough for my head to slam against the desk. Aug and Lance smother me, bending down to rub my head and ask me if I'm okay.

"I'm… it's fine," I breathe, still dizzy and sick. My eyes are still on the screen. Until Cohen isn't on that screen, that's where my focus is. But Aug pauses the recording.

"That's pretty much it," he says, pointing to the bottom of the picture where he's entered the screen. "He threatens to call the cops, I tell him to leave and Cohen walks out of the lot to get an Uber."

"Wh-what"—I can't get my words to do what I want—"What did he say when he left?"

They know I mean Cohen. They know Cohen is all I care about. "He didn't want you to see the blood on the ground," Aug says. "He didn't want you to know there was... violence."

Lance's voice is so quiet I can hardly hear it over the fear and embarrassment coursing through me. "You didn't tell him about the miscarriage." I don't know if it's a question or a statement, but I look up from the chair at him.

"I was going to. I just... We were progressing. Dr. Evans said I should. And I was going to but..." I look between him and Aug. "I didn't want it to cause him any more pain."

I can't tell if they know about Cohen's past, but it doesn't matter right now. All that matters is I get to him. I push away and grab my keys. "I'm going home."

Aug follows me out. "I'm driving behind you until I see you get inside." He levels his gaze. "We don't know where Pete could be."

I don't give a fuck about Pete.

"Fine, let's go."

I dig my phone out of my purse while I drive, unable to sit

behind the wheel without moving. I check the screen but I have no missed calls, no text messages waiting. I try to imagine what he must be thinking. What he pulled from those words, because I certainly know it sounded terrible.

What happened was terrible. But it's not at all how Pete portrayed it.

Aug's headlights shine in my rear view as I pull into the parking spot in the complex. I slam the door and jog across the lot to the bottom of the stairs. He idles nearby, squinting up at me. From the breezeway, I crouch and give him a thumbs up. He waves me off, and then I stand there between the two apartments, hoping to fuck, for once, that he's not home.

I want him to be at my house so goddamn bad, for so many reasons.

I put my key in the lock and turn slowly, opening and closing the door the same way. As soon as I have the door relocked with the chain on, my vision pulls to him, sitting on the couch, looking… like shit.

One eye is marred with maroons and pinks, swollen. Dried blood is beneath his nose and his hair is mussed. I'm on my knees between his feet, his face in my hands, in a frenzied moment. He places his hands over my palms, and tears fill my eyes. He stands and I clamber to my feet to stand with him, too. Then he puts an arm under my knees and around my back, and collects me, pressing me to his chest as he guides us down the hall.

He lowers me to the edge of the bed, the way I placed him last night. And he, my good protector, my sweet man, he falls to his knees at my feet. His soft but faithful grip on my ankles has heat burgeoning up my thighs. I bring my hands to his face, inspecting the growing knot, the discoloration, the trickle of pain left behind.

I lick my thumb and swipe the remnants away, and, with a tremble in my bottom lip, face him.

His head falls but I raise him up again. Looking down at this man who held a gun to his chest for me, I know what he wants to hear.

"I wanted to tell you," I breathe, not needing to quantify or clarify. We know which of Pete's words are currently haunting us both. "I just... I don't know. I felt ashamed."

He rests his heavy palms on the tops of my feet, and the touch infuses me with strength, knowing that he's here, waiting, caring, listening.

"Share with me now, Scarlett," he urges, thumbs tracing the arches. "Please."

I swallow the bobbing lump in my throat, and give him every iota of my attention. "I got pregnant the second month we were together. And it was then that I realized just how much of a priority it was to me to be a mom. And Pete assured me I could have both. Jizz and motherhood."

His palms wrap my ankles, thumbs now smoothing circles on my shins. More warmth, more security.

"I can't say for sure what happened. It was early. Women lose babies early all the time. But... we had an argument. I was only eight weeks. We fought over, God, I don't know. That's how stupid it was. I don't even remember."

His grip on me intensifies, and the man at my feet transforms, anger left behind. "He fucking put his hands on you?"

I shake my head. "No, no. I mean. Yeah, he shook me a little but... the fight left me fucked up emotionally. I cried so much that my belly ached. Then I cramped. Then I miscarried."

His hands smooth over my knees, up my thighs. The weight of them there brings me comfort through the discomfort.

"When I told him, he held me. He seemed to care. And I took that as my opportunity to roll forward, keep trying. But then he just saw it as a tool, an opportunity. And when waving it in front of me failed to work, he'd play that final card he had stashed away. He'd... tell me I can't even keep a baby alive."

Cohen's hands come to my waist before he drags his palms over my belly, resting them there as he waits for me to ready myself for his gaze. Tears fall and I take a deep breath.

His eyes are soft with grief and understanding. "You miscarried. A lot of women miscarry and go on to have thriving families. You are not at fault for a miscarriage. You have no control over your body."

"I know," I breathe, pinching my eyes, feeling silly for believing what I know isn't true. But something that doesn't hurt on its own will hurt if given repetition.

"Do you though? Do you know?" He grabs my hips, rising, taking me with him off the bed. My legs wrap his waist as his hand fishes up my back, holding me by the neck. Our foreheads come together. "You are not at fault."

My throat and eyes burn. "Neither were you."

He lowers me to the center of the bed and stands at the foot. We share a silent moment.

"He isn't worth losing your job at Crave or getting arrested."

Cohen steps closer to the foot of the bed, eyes trained on me. "I wouldn't lose Crave." He works his jeans. "Lance deleted the footage." He goes to work on the many buttons on his black and white flannel. He steps out of his boots, toe to heel. "And it doesn't matter to me. I would take responsibility for what I did to him because he deserved it. No one fucking talks about you like that, not anymore."

My chest is heavy, vibrating from his caring, protective

energy. "He isn't worth the risk," I manage, practically choking on held back tears.

I told him now, and he's accepting. I should have told him before. I felt so ashamed and here he is, showing me I have nothing to feel ashamed about. And that he's here no matter what.

Reaching behind him, I watch as he yanks his black t-shirt off and drops it. Hooking his thumbs in his boxer briefs, he gives those a tug too. He's fat and long between his legs, and my body flushes from the sight.

"It's never been about what he's worth," he growls, crawling on the bed over me. He unbuttons my jeans, and shimmies them down my legs. "It's about you, Scarlett. It's always about you and what you're worth. You are worth risking everything for."

His hard cock presses against my body as he straddles me, rocking me forward to pull my sweater and t-shirt off. The feel of his fingers at my spine as he unclasps my bra has my pussy clenching. Resting me carefully against the pillows again, I reach down and wrap my hand around his erection.

"It's about you," he says, his voice husky. He pushes my thighs apart as he positions his face at my cunt.

I reach out and fill my fingers with his hair, stilling him. My voice cracks like crazy, but I don't hide it.

"Why are you so good to me?" I ask, my chest rattling, eyes wet. He catches my palm in a kiss.

"You brought me back to life," he says, voice rough.

twenty-four

· · ·

cohen

And tonight, I'm in control.

Everything that happened today leaves my mind. I don't even have to force it out. As soon as we're alone together, and she's told me everything she was scared to say, it's just us. And tonight, I'm in control.

I want to show her how special she is and how much I care about her in ways I never have with anyone else. I want her to know she's not at fault for what happened, that she's not useless, that she's the opposite of everything he ever said to her.

She's mine now, and today, I want her to feel it. Know without any doubt that despite the fact we don't yet wear rings, she is fucking mine and I will do everything I can to protect her. Anything in my control.

I bring my mouth to her pussy, inhaling before I taste. She

brings her other hand to my head and strokes through my hair, not guiding my head but touching me praisingly. No matter the state I'm in, her touch is the key, the solution, the thing that grounds me. She's realigning every disjointed piece of me.

"Scarlett, you saved me," I tell her, needing the words to soak into her skin and be absorbed fully by her consciousness. He broke her down but I will devote every moment of my life to rebuild her, show her she's strong and perfect.

"You saved me," she whispers, voice rocky with emotion.

God only knows what she thought driving over here. Aug texted me and said he was tailing her home for safety. He also let me know that she watched the footage.

She knew what I heard. While I waited on that couch, I turned it over in my mind, studying those words from all angles. And I realized that I know Scarlett. I know her well. And I chose to believe that there was a reason she withheld.

I chose not to fight. Not to run. Not to accuse.

I chose to hear her out. Hold her and listen to her, and stay to love her. Which is what I plan on doing.

"Move in with me," I whisper against her clit before lapping a few times, making slow, long strokes. She plumps to my tongue, and her grip on my head tightens. "Live with me. Sleep with me. Shower with me. Let me make your meals and plan trips away. I want to see you grouchy, and take care of you when you're sick. I want to bicker about shoes on the floor and clothes not in the hamper," I whisper, slipping two fingers into her. She seizes around me, her spine arching slightly as she moans. "Let me be yours, Scarlett. Let me in, and let me stay."

I suck her clit into my mouth, sealing my lips to her cunt. She moans beneath me, fingers splayed across my scalp. I blink up at her over her velvety mound, finding her breasts in her hands and her eyes on me.

Curling my fingers, I flick her clit with the tip of my tongue, pressing my other hand into her lower belly with a bit of pressure.

"Cohen," she moans, her hands coming down over her eyes, then dragging down her face. With a pop, I pull off her pussy, pressing a kiss to her bare, slick cunt. Our eyes lock. "Yes," she pants, and our grins imply an accepted marriage proposal, not just moving in.

I think we both realize where we're headed. I know I can't envision myself without her.

I bring my arms under her legs and settle my mouth against her seam. My cock throbs against the mattress, weeping at the sweet taste of her. I make slow passes between her lips, stopping to run tight circles around her clit, sucking it in, nibbling, then dropping my thumb on it as my tongue circles her cunt.

She calls my name, and my flesh burns when she does. Her breathy moans for more, the way she mewls her pleasure, and calls my name is so incredibly hot, but it's even more than that.

Just the two of us finally, tucked away into a room, a single bed, all of our problems spread out, laid bare. We're chasing our happiness now, with nothing left to poke and prod us. Challenges lie ahead, and every great relationship feels like a rollercoaster sometimes, too. But we're done with unwrapping our baggage.

It's onward now, just the two of us, and the thought of that brings me so much happiness that I want to gorge myself on her cunt. Use my mouth to make her come, then, if she's ready, slide inside of her, pin her to the mattress and give her every aching inch of me until neither of us can breathe. I want to fulfill her, give her the filthy words she loves right in her ear. Work my hips over her until she tells me she's ready, until I have her clenching and milking me. That's when I'll let go of my control and take her pussy the way I want; deep and slow. I dream of coming deep inside of her, watching her face as my cum floods her insides, turns her warm, stuffs her.

I imagine rolling her onto her side, her pregnant belly too big for missionary. I spread her legs and feast on her extra sensitive cunt from behind, plunging my thumb in her ass as I do. She comes hard and my head jerks up, at the real Scarlett, my fantasy falling away.

I just envisioned her pregnant.

And I didn't freak the fuck out. It made my cock harder, it made me feast on her deeper, licking her more, wanting and needing her like crazy.

I move the tip of my nose along her clit before latching on again, sucking her slow and licking her softly. She writhes and I drive my fingers into her deeper, holding her tighter to taste more and more of her. Bring her to the brink.

"Cohen, Cohen, Cohen," she pants, her thighs trembling as they close around my head. Sound goes as she tightens her legs, and I sink my fingers deep into her thighs. I love my senses being smothered by her. I let my thumb take over on her clit as I fuck her with my tongue, nearly spilling when she tosses her feet onto my back and digs her heels into my ass.

My groin thrusts against the bed as she strangles me with her beautiful legs, her wet warmth flooding my tongue as I fuck her with my mouth. She stills, her hands slap at my shoulders, clawing at my flesh as she moans my name, praising me as she clenches all around me.

"Cohen, yes, Cohen, I'm coming. You're so good, fuck Cohen, good, good, good," she chants, her body immediately breaking into a trembling mess, core shaking right along with her legs.

I climb on top of her, dragging my dripping length over her supple curves as I find her mouth with mine. "Can I kiss you?" I ask, my lips brushing against hers.

She seals her mouth to mine without question, and she moans at the taste of herself, and *Jesus fuck I love this woman*. I love her free spirit, her strength, her big heart and—

She drives a palm into the center of my chest, pushing me up. "Cohen, do you really want to live with me?"

The fact that I mentally just admitted my love for her has me grinning.

She slaps my bicep with a chuckle, still sort of catching her breath, the orgasm still in her cheeks. "What? Why are you smiling?"

I kiss her again.

"Cohen, were you serious or do you have post-nut clarity and regret it? Because—"

With my forearms, I push myself to my knees, my body hovering over her. She swallows as her eyes take in my steely cock, and she bites her bottom lip at the sight of my swollen balls. I don't know if they're actually swollen, but goddamn do I want to empty them.

"Oh," she says, a smile curling her lips as her wide blue eyes glitter up at me, orange sunset painting her edges. "You don't have post-nut clarity yet."

She flips over, peering at me over her shoulder. "Fuck me like this," she purrs, "then come on my back. Please."

Fu-uck.

She brings her thighs together, and Jesus it's been a while since I've had to last for a long time, and I know she's already come but still, she needs to come again. Everytime my cock is in her, and we're not warming, she's fucking coming.

I'm a man on a mission.

I lower myself onto her, and she moans at the feel of my weight at her back.

"You're so warm and hard against me," she whimpers, turning her head to give me access to her ear and cheek. I press my lips to her ear, and give her all the clarity she needs.

"I don't need post-nut clarity. I want to live with you, Scarlett." I press into her, feeling her wince at the wide intrusion of this angle. With her legs pulled together, she's even tighter, making my already thick cock spread her somewhat painfully.

But very quickly, I'm seated fully inside, my groin smashed against her ass as we take a minute to calibrate. "You feel so fucking good, Scar," I breathe, squeezing my eyes shut, turning my head away from all that silky blonde hair, and the smell of the studio on her skin. I love that fucking slightly sweaty, mostly sweet, fresh air scent she brings home after work. It makes me hard.

"Yes," she pants, agreeing in moans to everything I'm doing and saying. I watch her back muscles flex as her spine curls with pleasure. One cheek pressed into the pillow, her face is flushed, eyes shut, fingers clutching the mattress like we're fucking flying. "I want you to come for me," she whimpers before adding, "you earned it."

I don't know why those three words wrap themselves around my balls like an oiled palm but Jesus. "Scar, I want you to come again, can you come again for me?" I coax, rolling my hips at a new angle, touching places inside her deep and spongy. Her fingers release the bed covers as she lets loose a chest-hollowing moan.

"Ohmygod," she moans before turning her head, pressing her face directly into the pillows. I reach down smooth a palm up the back of her neck, my thumb tracing one ear lobe.

"I wanna hear you come again," I say, and she turns her head for me, giving a tiny, out of breath nod. "I wanna feel you."

"Right there," she guides as I press into her deep, my cock throbbing, groin full of pressure.

I grit my teeth, I hold my jaw tight, and I dig deep. Fucking her in deep, slow strokes, she unravels, her tunnel seizing around me, tightening, milking, gushing. Her warm release coats me, and the rush of her arousal makes me harder.

I pull out, and my cock slides perfectly in the split of her ass. I push my thumb down, bridging the two perfect globes, and fuck the space between her ass and my thumb. I roll my hips as she pleads for my release, begs to feel my hot cum all over her. A few pumps and I'm stopped, stomach clenched as my cock pulses beneath my thumb. I cover her back in threads of white cream, and when she peers over her shoulder at me, barely getting a glimpse of the scene, I have the strongest urge to take her photo.

To remember this erotic experience we're having.

But she's on camera so much for work, I don't suggest it. But I do peer down at her a moment longer than I'd like, soaking up the sight.

"I've never done that," I admit, knowing she has. I'm not sour that she's more experienced than me—only excited to explore together. "You look incredibly hot, laying down like this, with my cum all over you."

She snickers. "I mean, I'm into it. I think it's super hot, too. But I've always wanted to know..." she trails off as she cautiously lifts her chest from the mattress, propping herself up on her elbows. Some my cum rolls off her back down her ribcage, and I react, surging forward with my palm to collect it before it gets on the sheets.

"What's your question?" I ask, awkwardly trying to bring the stray drops to join the rest, sliding my hand up her side.

She laughs again. "First—what are you doing?"

"There's so much, and I don't want to get your bed dirty."

At that, she's quiet, and I reach out with my other hand, losing the battle to the slippery fluid. As I'm looking around for a towel, she says, "Rub it in."

I look down at the drying load on her back. "Rub it in?"

With the one eye visible to me, she winks. "Why not? I liked having it rubbed into me the other day. It was like... our secret."

I'm unsure as I stare down at her painted back. My cock thickens between my thighs at the idea of rubbing my cum into her. But a little drop rubbed into her nipple is different than a completely saturated back. I mean, I remember waking up to a dried, sticky mess in the sheets many times.

"Are you sure?" I ask, because if she wants it, I'm in. But I want her to be certain. Always.

"I'll shower before I leave the house tomorrow but... for just tonight, having you on me... why not?"

I run my hands through the mess, some fresh, some already dried, and knead her back, staring at her shoulders. "I've never done this either," I admit, loving the way her skin has a sheen after my hands make a pass. I've never actually rubbed cum in, but the act is... strangely sensual and hugely erotic.

She feels me harden against her ass again as I drag my fingers down her sides, making all the white disappear. "See? You like it." She peers back at me with one straining eye. "And you were hesitant."

I slide off the bed and, with my sticky hands, help her up. "You're my guide to new things, I think," I say as my eyes hover on her lips, my mouth tingling for a kiss.

She crashes into my chest, wrapping her arms around my neck, bringing her mouth to mine, giving me exactly what I need. How she always gives me what I need before I even know it, I don't know. But I'm hooked.

We wash our hands together, and my groin tightens when she slips a shirt over her cum-soaked skin, keeping me rubbed into her for the evening, just like she said.

So fucking sexy.

For dinner, we stay at her place, and I whip up some salmon and rice, and as I'm squeezing lemon onto the fish, moments away from plating our food, Scarlett runs her hands up my bare back, clinging to my shoulder. I lean back and she tips up, and we share a quick kiss.

"Smells good, looks good, too," she hums from behind me, looping her arms around my waist, pressing her cheek to my back. "I was thinking..." she starts, her sultry tone telling me this isn't about dill or tartar sauce.

"I like when you do that, I always benefit," I tease, discarding the drained lemon into the trash.

"I'd like you to be inside me when we eat. Like we did before. Just... to feel close," she says, her voice softening as the sentence goes on. Almost like she's unsure if I'll say yes or unsure she should want it. I spin to face her, my back butting up against the oven handle at the stove.

"I like that idea," I say, pushing a golden lock from her shoulder, letting my fingertips trace the delicate curve of her throat. "Can I ask why *you* like doing that?"

We've done it less than five times, but it's a unique thing to be inside of someone so intimately while not actually fucking. Most people likely never do it, and we're gearing up for round three. "I'm just curious," I admit, adding, "I fucking like it, but I am curious."

She smiles, but it's lopsided, sadness weighing one side

down. "I like feeling so close to you, and since we're not actually, well, you're not finishing inside of me," she says uncomfortably around the topic we usually so easily discuss.

I bring my curled knuckles under her chin, and tip her face up, bringing her eyes to mine. "We haven't talked about that."

Our bodies are so close, but the unspoken subject throws a massive silent divide between us. One we need to squash right now. "What do you want, Scarlett? Have you thought about what you want with me? Between us? Life?" I don't highlight the part of our story that says we've only been together a handful of months. Instead, I focus on how far we've come together, and how far into the future with her.

"I know what I want." She licks her lips. "I want what I've always wanted. To finish school, to stay at Crave while I do and maybe even after, and… " her eyes flit between mine, nervous and wide. I know what's next. And I despise the way he made it hard for her to say. "I want to have a baby. I want to be a mother."

I study her features, take in the hope in her expression, the lift in her brows, the way her eyes search mine. She wants this, but she wants me to want it, too.

And I fucking do.

"You want to live with me," I say, earning me a look of confusion. "And," I add, "usually after people live together, they get married and then they have kids."

Still, she looks confused. I smile down at her, taking her chin with my curled knuckles and thumb. "I want those things, too. But we don't have to go in that order, you know that, right?"

I realize after the words leave my mouth that it may seem like I don't want to marry her. "I want you to finish school before we do anything, because that's important to you, so now, it's important to me, too."

She smiles, eyes misty. "See, I don't know if I'll ever get used to that. You really just... caring about me, genuinely, truly."

My throat constricts, and my chest does, too. And I know it's the time.

"I love you, Scarlett."

She nods, a faint smile warming her lips. "I love you, too."

And after those words are exchanged, conversation slips to casual. We sit together at the table, Scarlett taking her spot on my lap. She adjusts herself, then me, and with my happy cock deep inside her, I feed her bites of salmon from my fork.

When we've both eaten, she carefully lifts off my lap and puts away the food as I clean the kitchen. By the time we're in bed, her body melded to the side of me, her hand on my chest, mine in her hair, I'm soft again.

Spending time with her while I'm inside of her is... fucking intense. And then having a platonic night after—it's the ultimate fucking edging. And I like it.

I fall asleep content knowing the woman in my arms wants me.

Loves me.

twenty-five

. . .

scarlett

I'm exactly where I want to be.

Cohen stands over me, slicing a banana into my bowl of hot oatmeal, and I smile up at him. "Thank you."

He winks, and my empty pussy clenches in hunger. Back at the counter, stirring around the rest of the cereal, Cohen clears his throat. "How much school do you have left?"

I don't need to count units in my mind. I know just what's left, and am proud it's not more. "Only one year, so, two semesters and potentially a summer school course."

He nods, stirring, steam clouding his expression. Twisting, he turns the burner off and slides the pot to the back of the stove. He scoops his oatmeal and I watch, because my stomach is tight in anticipation for a reason. I can feel it.

I know that sounds crazy, but it's just one of those

moments in time that, without rhyme or reason, you know just what's going to happen.

Pouring coffee into two mugs, he asks, "Do you want to use birth control?"

Something tumbles through my torso, ending up in my stomach, wings fluttering, making me light headed from excitement. "I know the logical thing to do would be wait. Wait until I'm done with school and have a job but..." I sigh, prepared to act like I didn't think this through and it's all coming off the cuff, casual and simple. But the truth is, I have thought about this. A lot in the last few weeks. "Life is too short to always be waiting for a better time. I have a year left." I swallow, taking a leap of faith. "I'm okay with having a newborn when I graduate, or, likely, a little bit after. I'm okay with it. And honestly, I like doing life differently with you. Because it wasn't working for me before."

"I will wait as long as you'd like, but I want you to know, I'm sure about us. And I may not have a ring on your finger this second, but... it's going there, Scarlett. I promise you. It is." He takes my hand, curling my knuckles before kissing them. "I love you so much."

I swallow, my eyes suddenly blurry from an onslaught of happy tears. Happy tears are a thing.

I really didn't believe that until now. Then again, I thought my ability to orgasm was broken until Cohen, too.

He's changed everything. *Thank God.*

"I'm ready," I say, practically panting at the idea of Cohen plumping and pumping inside of me. To feel his hand skirt along my low belly, whispering words of encouragement, both of us waiting for more. "And I love you."

We settle in at the table, sipping coffee as we each roll through our phones, checking schedules and plans for the day. As I'm scooping the last bite of oatmeal, Cohen sits up a little straighter in his chair.

"You okay?"

His eyes veer to mine, a somewhat playful expression on his face. "Otis just texted in the group thread that he needs a place to live."

I wrinkle my nose out of pure shock. "You're in a group chat with Otis? And who else?"

He shrugs. "I don't know, some of the guys from work."

Surprised, since Cohen is more introverted than anything, I smile. "You are always surprising me."

He locks his phone and looks up at me. "He can move into your place and take over the lease. We can move into my place."

I blink. "Jeez, that really worked out well, huh?"

He volleys his head, expression pinched. "Well, he... he needs the apartment by next week. And if that's too fast for us, you can move in here and I can get my old room back and—"

"Cohen, you are not moving back into a family home with strangers in a single bedroom." I sip my coffee. He makes it stronger than I used to drink, but I like it better. "Let's do it. Let's move me into your place."

"If it's too soon—"

I lift my leg, bringing my foot between his spread legs beneath the table. I nudge his cock with my heel. "I said it's not too soon. It's what I want."

He looks at his lap where my foot fondles him, and I take another sip of coffee. "Give me what I want?"

"Always," he says, capturing my foot with his hand. He draws his thighs together, trapping me there, and we finish breakfast while I massage him.

I haven't worn a swimsuit for a long time. It's true, I'm naked at work a lot of the time. Or scantily clad at the very least. But still, something about tight, stringy nylon is so uncomfortable. I pull the fabric from my ass crack for the umpteenth time, but it slides right back in.

Cohen hands me a towel, and we stop before the big, rusted metal door.

He asked me to come to the pool with him, and while I realized there was some significance there, I don't think it hit me until now.

What happened to Addie... Cohen told me he swam here every single morning for the last four years, until he met me. I don't know why I didn't string together the logic.

He punished himself here, and now he's bringing me.

I reach for his hands, and weave our fingers together. "Thank you for bringing me."

A rush of air leaves his chest, like he's relieved I've realized some significance, like putting words to the occasion may break him. And I hate that no matter what we build together, he will always bear that pain. "I know what this place was to you, and it means a lot that you'd let me in."

It's just a gym, a pool in a shitty old gym in the city. But it's also so much more. The place where he tortured himself, relieved the pain, rewrote history, making it all his fault. He pulls open the door and a wall of hot, chlorinated air hits us, stifling my lungs for a moment.

The door closes behind us, and when I step to Cohen's side, I realize the place is empty. And kinda creepy, the way the encased fluorescent light flickers from the roof.

"I came here everyday," he says, but I don't think he's really speaking to me as much as he is just surveying the past landscape of his life. "I thought... It brought me closer. I thought it... I don't know, I thought it was what I needed to do."

I clutch his hand, my voice quiet but the words important, the question critical. "Did you ever want to hurt yourself? Did you come here to do that?"

His shoulders rise and drop in one fell swoop. "I don't know. I mean, I did want to hurt. But I don't know if I wanted to die. Maybe, I don't know."

He looks down, his eyes suddenly reassuring and soft. "I'm not healed and I'm not all good, but I'm much better off than I have ever been before. And I don't want you to worry."

We walk toward the pool's edge and Cohen drapes our towels over a faded brown beach lounger.

Outstretching a hand to me, I step into the pool, watching the surface gently ripple from my presence. He joins me, and we stand in front of one another, the room temperature water and the scent of chlorine stinging my senses.

He stares at his palm floating on the surface as he skates it across. Eyes on the water, he says, "I didn't want to die. I just didn't know how to keep living."

I nod my head because... I understand that. "I get that."

Another swipe across the surface, and he says, "I wanted to come here to see if it still has power over me," he says, stepping closer, water squishing between our bodies as he hugs me. His muscles are slippery but his hold is comfortable and tight.

"What?" I ask. "The pool?"

His chin grates my head as he shakes his no. "The past."

I swallow, relishing the way his heart thuds against me. "And does it?"

We peel apart and he gives me serious intensity in his gaze. "No. Not at all."

"Good," I reply as the metal door swings open and a dad and son saunter in. They both lift their hands and Cohen returns the gesture.

"C'mon, let's go home." He wraps a towel around me after helping me out of the pool, and kisses our linked hands the entire drive. And when we're back he turns to face me. "I... I really want to come inside you right now."

I smile. "You can." I'm so glad we talked about this.

But he faces the windshield, staring at the overgrown shrub spilling over the cement barrier. He drags a hand down his chin as unease wiggles through me. "What's the matter?" I ask, hoping the pool didn't trigger some trauma, hoping that he doesn't think we're moving too fast because I'm on board with this pace.

"Before we do that, I want to call Valerie."

My brain loops around the name a few times before I realize he's talking about his ex wife. Lifting his gaze to meet me, he adds, "And I want you to be there."

I nod and take his hand back, weaving our palms together. "Of course."

Knowing he wants me there for a very difficult but healing conversation? My heart literally beats for this man. "Of course," I say again, and then we go up to his apartment where we do nothing but eat popcorn and snuggle on the couch. It's as if we know when we need a night to decompress, and with the important phone call on the horizon, a restful night is just what we need.

I'm exactly where I want to be.

twenty-six

. . .

cohen

There are no accidents

"Are you sure?" I ask again, because the way the stack of boxes sway in Otis's arms has me nervous about the contents. "Because I don't mind—"

"I got it, I got it," he banters, taking the first two stairs cautiously. He gains confidence and starts to charge up and I watch in what feels like slow motion as the top box teeters, a flap lifting in the commotion. Otis barrels forward, and the box slips backward, tumbling onto his head before clunking down each concrete step, the contents being spewed everywhere.

I reach down and start collecting things as Otis drops the boxes that made it to the ground in the breezeway. "Fuck," he groans. "Why didn't you take the top box?"

He grins as I snatch baseball cards and elementary

school trophies from the lawn. "You have a lot of, uh, momentos," I say as I climb the stairs with an armful of his crap.

We've been moving him for the last two hours and for a single guy, the man has a lot of... trinkets. I've seen boxes of Playstation games, boxes full of new sneakers, one plastic container that looked to have toys in them and when I questioned, I was promptly corrected that they are collectibles.

Yet he has no bed, and no furniture.

"You sure you guys don't mind me using Scarlett's stuff?" Otis asks, fishing a hand through his sweaty hair. "I mean, her shit looks new and nice." He winces. "I ruin things. I spill a lot and I'm not very careful."

I clap a hand on his shoulder. "I appreciate the honesty but, she's sure. She's... living with me now. She doesn't want that stuff anymore."

"He's right, I don't care at all," Scarlett says from the open apartment door. I turn and take her in, wearing cropped jeans and a flowy black shirt exposing one silken shoulder. Her blonde hair is twisted on top of her head, and her feet are bare. She looks so much healthier and happier than when I first met her.

"Want me to Venmo you for 'em?" Otis asks as he moves the stacked boxes from the breezeway to his apartment floor.

She wrinkles her nose, pushing a stray piece of hair back into her bun. When she does, her belly is exposed, and my mind shifts from moving boxes with Otis to having sex with Scarlett.

My mind has been on sex a lot, obviously, but not just because I was a monk for four years prior to her. Mostly because we decided we'd... not use protection. It's not actively trying to have a child, but it's not actively stopping it either.

I'm a firm believer there are no accidents, and I think we both know what we hope happens sooner than later.

But I need to talk to Valerie first. Because no matter how hard I try, I need that last piece of closure. The piece that levels me up and allows me to really give myself to the future.

"Don't, Otis, honestly. I don't care," she waves her hand down, then wiggles her brows between the two of us. "And anyway, my first royalty check and my signing check for Loved by Lucy comes in this week, the day of the party." She looks down at us over her nose, playfully. "I'm about to be one-hundred and twenty five grand richer."

"More than that, that's just your signing, isn't it?" I ask, because she showed me the contracts and everything else. When she started moving her things in, that included transferring mail. She showed me her contract, and all the numbers that came with it.

I'm proud of her for leaving Jizz, and thriving at Crave despite the fact she had every reason to shut down. She fought through her trauma, she's still in therapy, and amidst it all, she inked a deal with Debauchery. This week, the final toy is launched and Crave is having a party in her honor.

Tucker Deep offered to host, but I told him that we would.

The first time having people over together, the first time for people to really see us as a serious couple. We don't hide it at work, but we don't go hard on it either. And I think that's to respect Crave but also so I can walk. Because a kiss from Scarlett makes me think of all of the places on her body that I'd like to kiss.

"Yeah, but, you know where the rest is going." She wiggles her eyebrows with excitement, but Otis misinterprets it.

"Implants, huh?"

I turn to face him, disapproving dad written on my face. "She's got a year left on her bachelor's degree," I deadpan, to which Otis responds by showing me his palms.

"Otis, we're about to have a quick shower then dinner. You wanna come eat with us?" she peers into his open door across the hall. "Looks like you don't have much."

Otis waves her off. "Naa," he says, "I ordered pizzas. Tuck and some of the guys are coming over. We're gonna play some Diablo on the Playstation." He catches my gaze and extends an invitational arm. "Wanna come chill dude?"

I shake my head. "Thanks, but I need a shower and we're making sushi."

I walk backward toward our place as I say goodbye to Otis, and my entire body fills with pins and needles of anticipatory excitement when she loops her arms around my waist from behind, peering at Otis around me. I place my hands on hers and even though I'm sweaty as fuck from helping him carry boxes of crap upstairs, I love the feel of her cheek against my back.

"Have a good time, though, and hey, we're neighbors now so… keep it down," I say with a wink. Otis levels me a serious gaze.

"He's kidding," Scarlett clarifies, which makes Otis let out a relieved sigh, draping a palm on his chest.

I lock our door and slide the chain on. When I turn, she crashes into me, settling against my chest, sweaty shirt clinging to me.

"I started on the sushi without you. It's probably a lot uglier than when you make it but… I wanted you to have extra time tonight." She lifts her gaze, her chin resting on my chest as she peers up at me. "I thought after your shower but before we eat, we can call Valerie. Together."

Nerves stir up inside me, bringing the dormant parts of

me to life. It's not going to be easy but I want to make the call. I want to move on.

"Okay," I reply, dragging my fingers through the sides of her hair, wanting to touch her everywhere but not wanting to mess up her bun. "That's a good plan."

"Yeah?" she asks, like she wasn't sure of the proposal.

I kiss the tip of her nose. "Yeah. I want to do it, so we can move forward." We both know what I mean by that, that I can't freely make love to her like we both want until I can free my mind from that last piece tethering me to the past.

Her eyes veer around the room with unease, and I realize then that she's nervous about this call, too. I do what I know calms her, but in truth, I know it will calm me, too.

"Come sit," I say, feeding my fingers through hers, walking her to the couch. She sits and I lower to my knees at her feet, placing my palms on her. My thumbs stroke the arches of her bare feet, then I move to her calves, kneading, worshiping.

"Can I tell you what you mean to me?" My voice is raspy and raw as the emotion building for the impending call surfaces. I don't fight it. I don't fight anything with her, or she with me.

She nods, but doesn't speak, her eyes a little misty.

"You made me see that I can be happy, and that..." my voice breaks as my head droops between my shoulders. The words still don't feel like the total truth, but that's part of why I have to make the phone call tonight. "That I deserve to move on, to find myself. To love again. To live again."

Scarlett takes my head in her hands, planting a soft kiss to my hair. She cradles my face in her palms. "You deserve so much. I wish you knew before we met, but I'm glad you know now." Her thumb strokes my cheek bone and everything in my torso warms at her touch. "You deserve it all, my wonderfully kind man. And I'm going to give you everything I can."

At her feet, I make a decision. "Let's call now. I'll shower after."

It's possible I'll need a moment alone after, too. Because I haven't heard Valerie's voice for so long. And it's rare for me to speak of Addie aloud. I think about her all the time, but outwardly, I keep it close to the vest. I know it's going to be hard.

I take a seat next to her on the couch, searching Valerie's name on my phone. Scarlett watches me type my last name after Valerie's first, and her voice is quiet when she asks, "Do you think she still goes by your name?"

I shake my head, because I have no clue. When I left Michigan, I never looked back. Everything important to me was underground or in my heart. "Not sure."

A number comes back belonging to Valerie, showing her living in Michigan, a town a few away from where we lived together. Closer to her sister, whom I believe will never leave her lakeside bungalow.

I click the number, and put it on speakerphone, and my heart leaps into my throat as the ring bounces off of the apartment walls. Scarlett rests her forearm on my back, letting her fingers play at the ends of my hair, pressing kisses to my bicep.

The call, which I've thought of making no less than a thousand goddamn times, feels much more possible with Scarlett next to me. *Fuck*, life does too.

"Hello?" Valerie's voice is soft and calm, but I'm still jerked back to that night, to her panicked voice at two in the morning. My stomach swirls but Scarlett drops a hand to my knee, squeezing to remind me she's there.

"Valerie," I say, the word almost sounding new on my tongue at this point.

The line is quiet, the ether between us loaded with pain and grief.

"Co-Cohen?"

I look over at Scarlett, and her soft eyes urge me on. "Yeah, it's Cohen." I pause, because I hadn't thought of this in detail and I'm not sure where to start. "How... how are you? How have you been?"

Valerie swallows, and there's some rustling that leads me to believe she's going somewhere private. "I've been... a lot of things. But now, I'm good." She sighs, and I feel the weight of it from here. "How have you been?"

She's so calm, and there isn't even a trace of anger in her voice. I don't know how she couldn't be filled with rage. Something terrible happened to us. And I blamed her, then myself, and then fought with her, picked on us until we were nothing, and then I left.

I'm a fucking asshole, and a second wave of undeserving guilt washes over me.

"I'm sorry," I blurt out, eager to get to the point. I didn't call for small talk, and she knows it, too. "I'm sorry that I didn't stay and do therapy with you like you wanted. That I didn't fight for us. I'm sorry that I blamed you and blamed myself and did everything fucking wrong. I feel responsible for so much, Valerie, and I just wanted to tell you that I'm sorry. Very."

Scarlett's hand slides up and down my back again, soothing and calming. My eyes sting and there's a lump in my throat, but through the struggle I hold it together.

"I know Cohen. I know you're sorry. I'm sorry too. We aren't bad people, we just had something really bad happen to us."

"I shouldn't have left. I should have fought for us," I say, reliving moments in my mind. Arguments, tears, slammed doors, broken hearts.

She lets out another weighty sigh. "I could have done things differently, too. We were just... really messed up. And we did what we thought was right at the time."

"I fucking left," I spit out, remembering how I didn't even go to the cemetery one last time. My skin itched, and all I could do was run. Run, go, disappear.

"I would have left you if you didn't leave me. I knew you blamed me—"

"I didn't. I mean, *fuck*," I sigh, raking a hand down my face, battling anger and sadness, completely aware of Scarlett's soft stroking up my back. "I did blame you, but after I stopped blaming you, I blamed myself. I should have gone with you on that trip, I should—"

Valerie takes over. "Stop. We didn't do anything wrong, neither of us. Hindsight, you know what they say. But years of therapy have me sure of one thing: we didn't do anything wrong. Sometimes bad things happen to good people. The only thing we can do is keep living, living so we can remember her. Our Addie."

I choke on a sob, not trying to hold it in, not trying to be brave for Scarlett right now. At this moment, I need this. I need this final break so I can be rebuilt for good. And as Scarlett leans against my shoulder, holding my arm as I cry, I know she'll be the one to do it. For the rest of my life.

Pulling my shit together, I finally ask through a sniffle, "Are you... are you happy now?"

Valerie's voice is gentle, like she knows I could be shattered and she's handling me with care. God, I don't want to be broken anymore. I really don't.

"I am." She clears her throat. "I recently remarried. We have a one-year old."

I swallow that information, trying to imagine Valerie in a white dress with another man, holding a baby the same way she held Addie in her arms.

I can see it. And when I turn and look at Scarlett, I can see that for her, too. Only I'm there. And it's our wedding, our baby in her arms.

"I'm happy for you, Valerie," I say, truly fucking meaning it.

"Are you happy, Cohen? Are you with someone?" she asks. I slide my hand onto Scarlett's thigh, pulling her leg tight to mine.

"I am. We aren't married, but... we will be one day."

Her happiness rattles through the line. "I'm glad, Cohen. I hope you're happy, and we can always remember her. That's where you and I exist now, in the memories we share of Addie."

"Yeah," I agree. "Valerie," I say, holding Scarlett's leg way too fucking tight but God, just her warmth near me is making this call so much more palatable. "Thank you for talking to me."

There's quiet, and I think we're both deciding how to end the call. Make offers to stay in touch? I don't think either of us want that. Finally, she says, "You're welcome. Take care of yourself, okay?"

"Okay," I say, then add, "Goodbye, Valerie."

"Goodbye Cohen."

I know as the call evaporates from my screen, Valerie ending it first, that we just had the last conversation we'll ever have. And the most healing.

I face Scarlett, eyes stinging from the heaviness of that call. "I needed to do that."

"I know," she murmurs. "I'm proud of you. And I love you."

"I love you, too," I say, meaning it more than I ever have. I wouldn't have been in the place to seek out closure from Valerie if it weren't for her. "Shower with me?" My body pulses, craving closeness, starved for her comforting touch.

She weaves our hands together. "Of course I will."

Sushi is eaten with Scarlett in my lap, with my very eager cock stretched out inside her.

What started as something to bridge the gap between discomfort and comfort, has now bled into something intimate and erotic. Tonight, she sat in my lap after sucking my cock to get me full mast, which took under fifteen seconds. Then she told me she wanted to feel me inside her as I fed her, while she fed *me* things she believed I needed to hear.

That she loves me.

That I'm worthy.

That she can't wait to be full of me.

She focused on my worthiness, smoothing out the jagged edges left behind by the phone call. But I feel good and more ready than ever as we turn off the apartment lights, check the door, and head to... *our bedroom.*

We undress without preamble, stripping in comfortable silence. She'd changed into a skirt to sit in my lap during dinner, and the skirt alone was a cruel form of foreplay. When we're completely nude, she drags her nails down my bare chest, slightly pinching both of my nipples.

"You're going to fuck me," she says, enunciating the f in a way that makes my balls ache and my stomach clench. "And bury yourself as deep inside me as you can," she breathes, my nipples so fucking sensitive that her warm breath against them has me reaching for my cock. "And then, when your balls are hot against my ass and you're so deep that my belly hurts," she says, walking her fingers up my chest as my fist makes a mindless stroke down my aching shaft. "You're going to come. And come, and come, and come," she drifts off, her promises light and airy, but erotic and piercing all the same. Her tongue sweeps her bottom lip as she pushes two fingers into my mouth, onto my tongue. "And when you're done filling me with every single drop of you, you're going to stay inside me." I stroke again, but release myself when I realize what a bad idea it is.

Everything she's just described has me drooling around her fingers.

"And then, when you're getting soft and my pussy is all slippery and wet with your cum," she breathes, the sentence stretched out, slow and seductive. "You're going to dig deep, and give me another."

My ears ring as I struggle to swallow, my throat dry, my mouth cottony. "Another?"

She pinches my nipple then presses her lips to the stinging flesh. "Yep. You're going to give me more, and fill me up all over again."

"Okay," I murmur, moving my hand to her pussy, sliding two fingers through her lips. She's wet and swollen, her body already preparing for tonight. Anxiously, I move for the bed, taking her by the hand to bring her with me. But her feet don't budge. A crooked smile hangs from her lips.

"That's not where we're starting, though."

I'm at the point in the night where my brain is just a lawn ornament inside my head. My cock is heavy and eager between my legs and I need inside of her, and I need it now. "Okay," I say, because honestly, whatever gets me inside of the woman I love.

She turns, opening the top dresser drawer she claimed for her panties. With something hidden behind her back, she licks her lips, taking on a familiar air. Lucy Lovegood. I don't think of her as Lucy, not even when we're fooling around. She's always been Scarlett to me.

But when she brings her hands to her stomach, in them she's holding the Loved by Lucy proudly, a tipsy little smile appears on her lips. She's excited.

"I'm gonna fuck you with *me*," she says, "and then you're gonna fuck me."

"Twice," I say, remembering how she coolly yet powerfully laid out the terms of the night. *You're going to dig deep, and give me another.*

"Twice," she agrees, then brings the toy up between us, the bare cunt looking just like hers facing me. "First, describe this to me."

Oh Jesus. This is some mental fucking edging, or torture, or pleasure... or all of it. "It's..." I stop myself and look past the toy, into her eyes. She's so fucking sexy when she's in control of me, and I fucking love it. I have the strongest urge to drop to my knees and worship the most beautiful woman I've ever known, but she wants me to describe this replica of her cunt, and I want to give her just what she wants.

It's my sole purpose in life.

My eyes veer back to the toy, and my cock weeps when I

focus on it. "God, Scar, it looks just like you," I breathe, getting harder and fatter at the thought that men around the world will also get to pay homage to her perfect, sweet little cunt.

"Tell me how?" she baits me, biting delicately into her bottom lip, waiting.

"Your lips are the perfect size for you, and when I'm lying between your legs, your cunt opens just slightly, giving me a tiny glance at heaven, just like the toy." I swallow and ignore the way my cock lifts, twitching with need. Her eyes are hazy and her nipples are hard now, too, like mine. I go on. "When I lick you, lick small circles around your clit, you bloom and swell, and everything gets pink and puffy, and it's so fucking hot." I lift my hand and drag a finger down the faux labia. "Like this."

With a bottle of lube from the dresser, she fills the toy, eyes on me. Raising her fingers, the ones just plunged on my tongue, she turns the toy to her, driving them inside.

I groan, unexpectedly, but loud, making my entire spine shake. This is quite possibly the hottest thing I've seen. *Jesus Christ.*

"I feel good, don't I?" she asks, and while I know it's rhetorical, the answer spills out of me.

"So fucking good." I clutch my cock. God I'm hard.

She removes her fingers but brings it to her mouth, driving her tongue inside the pink, flesh-like canal. I watch and stroke, my insides burning. After a moment, she lowers it, spit glistening on her chin from the way she lapped at herself.

Her eyes lock to mine as she brings her silicone pussy to my cock. Wrapping her hand around my base, she feeds me inside of the toy with her other hand, inch by glorious fucking inch, and I groan the entire time.

She pumps the toy around my shaft, telling me how she can feel every vein, every aching pulse of me in her palm.

"Does it feel like me?" she questions, pumping me hard enough to make her full breasts sway. My face tingles as I focus all of my remaining brain cells on her question. A lone drop of traitorous sweat slips down my neck, giving away my weakness.

"Yes," I grit, my voice broken and raspy with desperation.

She stops pumping me, loosening her fist. My hips move forward of their own volition, seeking out the comfort of her cunt. "Be good and don't come," she warns, "because if you do, you'll still owe me two more."

Resuming the movement, she pumps me again a few times before saying, "I'd prefer your cum deep inside me, but if you'd rather breed a knock off than the real thing—"

"Stop," I grunt, my chest rising and falling more urgently now. That lone drop of sweat has given way to many more, and I'm officially teetering. "I need you," I admit, not afraid to show her what she does to me. "I need to be inside you." I swallow, summoning courage to say what I'm feeling, because they are words I've never spoken before. Not aloud. "I need to empty myself deep inside you, I need to fuck my cum into you so hard, it's all I can fucking think about."

Cohen Steele has never been a dirty talking man. But goddamn, it feels good to say what I really need and want. It's so freeing.

"Then do it," she bites back, yanking the toy from my cock, then spinning me around by the hips. "Wait," she says, crawling past me to get on her back in the center of our bed. The sheets are dark and forgiving, but tonight, I hope there's no remnants left behind. I hope every drop stays deep inside her, to bring us more.

From the middle of the pillows she shakes her head only

slightly. "Come fuck me already." Her grin makes my stomach flip, and in my fist, my cock leaks. I knee my way onto the bed over her, positioning my hips between her open legs. I press my head to her wet hole, and sink my hips forward, dipping into her center.

She's so wet, I slide in easily despite the way she winces from the burn. Once she gets comfortable with the way my girth stretches her. She loops her arms under mine, placing her palms on my shoulders.

"When I'm in your lap," she pants, her mouth spilling filthy words as I rock my hips back and forth, nudging her deepest spot with each stroke. "And your cock is inside me, this is what I'm thinking of. And I play this game with myself." She pants harder, stealing a moment to moan and catch her breath. "I try not to clench around you, I try as hard as I can. Because I know if I just move a little, clench a little, your perfect cock will unravel me in an instant."

She wraps her legs around me, and drives me deeper with her heels driving into my ass. "What do you think about when I'm in your lap, and you're nestled deep inside me?" she asks, the question's last syllables riding an outstretched moan, breathy and beautiful.

I look down between us where my cock is disappearing inside of her, and knowing I get to stay inside of her when I come is nearly killing me. The orgasm clawing up the backs of my legs, the twist in my chest that ties me tighter to her, it's all building and pushes the words from my mouth. "I think about breeding you. Having you underneath me, and fucking you into my bed so hard, coming so deep that nothing fucking slips out. And I fuck you like that, every day, until you're giving birth to my child, and then I'm doing it all over again. Keeping you well fucked and full."

For a moment, her femme face falters, and I see Scarlett,

the gorgeous loving woman who longs to be a mother, I see her turning those words over in her mind, and melting for them.

But I'm not even trying to make her melt; breeding her is all I think about when she warms my cock.

"Fuck me, Cohen," she whimpers when she snaps back into the moment, driving her groin off the mattress, trying to get me even deeper.

"Look at you," I whisper, "so hungry for my cum," I tell her, lowering my mouth to her earlobe for a bite. I feel like despite the fact we've had sex, we've been intimate in all sorts of ways, getting to take her to completion tonight is the most profound moment between us.

"Yes," she gasps out, "I am. Starved. So please, pin me down, fill me up. I wanna feel you throbbing inside me." She lifts her head off the pillow to plant a messy kiss on my lips. "I want to know what it feels like to reach down and dip my fingers into my pussy and feel your cum, warm on my fingertips."

Fuuck.

"Scarlett," I growl, my chest burning and tight, but with a new feeling. Not struggling to breathe or fighting against taking air but filled with heat for this moment. For her. For everything we've already experienced together, and for everything ahead. I can't hold back a second longer. The thrumming pressure pooling at the base of my spine bleeds into my groin, filling it with a familiar, undeniable ache. She jerks off the bed, sealing her body to mine, my balls pressed against her ass so hard that the added pressure only adds to the intensity rocketing through my cock.

"Take it," I groan as the first pulse moves through me, firing into her, hot and thick. "Take it, baby, take it," I whisper, my voice husky and raw as my cock pulses repeatedly, her little cunt clenching all around me, taking more and more.

"Oh god," she moans, dropping a hand to her low belly between us, putting pressure on herself. "Fuck your cum into me deep," she breathes, and I thrust into her again, harder, sending the last few ropes as deep as they'll go.

She moans, telling me I'm so warm, her cunt is so full. I release the lock in my arms, draping myself over her, panting as I try to catch up.

"You like the dirty talk," I breathe into her neck, sucking up her soft, sweet scent.

"I do," she says, stroking a hand up my sweaty back, using her nails, leaving goosebumps lying in their wake. "So talk dirty to me, Cohen."

I push off and look down into her eyes, my brain still a little spinny from that intense orgasm. She smirks something sinister. "Give me one more."

My dick perks up, those four words wrapping around my balls, urging me to groan and move my hips.

My cum slides around inside of her, slippery and still warm. I fuck her, and feel a tingle run through my cock as I plunge deep. Grinding my groin against her clit, my cock expands inside of her cunt, regaining his girth as she milks me.

"There you go, see? You can do it," she encourages, reaching down to filter the split of her fingers around my cock where I'm currently stuffing her. "There you go, give me more, Cohen, give me another."

Sweat litters my back and slips down my forehead, landing on her beneath me. She takes her hand from my shoulder and swipes at the drops of sweat on her breast, bringing them to her lips. Her tongue juts out, and her eyes fall closed, and Jesus fuck is that hot.

Shifting my hips, I look down to see I'm long and hard again, fucking her with the same tight strokes as before. I can't really believe it. I've never come like this, back to back. I didn't think I could because *refractory period*. All thoughts of expectation get shoved out the window as she holds the tips of her fingers out, teasing my balls each time I pump into her.

"More, Cohen, I need more of your cum deep inside me. So give it to me, give me another." She brings her wet lips to my ear, straining from the pillows when she says, "Fuck it into me, baby, right now."

Slippery and sticky, I crash into her one more time and just as I'm about to fire another one off, she seizes up, her walls tightening on my length.

"Come with me, come on," she coaxes, though I don't need it. The orgasm is already throbbing, and a moment later, I'm spewing inside of her, filling her so full that it oozes out onto my base, smearing against her pussy lips. "Yes," she purrs, tilting her hips off the bed, sealing her body to mine. We writhe like that, my cock still twitching inside of her, warm and cozy in a pool of my own cum. She's so tight and hot, I can't help but lift up and find her eyes.

"I can't believe I did that," I say, still out of breath, minutes later.

She smiles, eyes shining, blonde hair strewn about the pillow in a post-fuck mess. Fucking gorgeous. "Now, roll over and let me lie on top of you. But please," she says, her eyes intense on mine, even in the new moonlight her intensity roars. "Stay inside of me."

I manage to give her what she asks for, and we end up falling asleep with her slender body curved into my bigger one, my cock soft but big enough to not slip out. And that's how we sleep, my cock buried at home.

twenty-seven

. . .

scarlett

Take it off with your teeth

I do yet one more spin in front of the floor to ceiling mirror, wondering if this is the dress. I don't know why I'm so nervous, it's going to just be everyone from Crave and a few heads from Debauchery. Still, as I survey my body in the third dress I've put on tonight, I find myself nervous for the Loved by Lucy celebration at our place tonight.

I put my hands on my hips, head tipped to the side, debating as Cohen appears in the mirror behind me.

He runs his thick fingers through my hair gently, freeing the tangles that formed during outfit changing. Last week, he asked me if he could braid my hair. Since giving up swimming, he's developed some secondary anxiety simply due to not having a place to dispel that extra energy. We did yoga one morning, and that quickly devolved into sex. And now, day seven, he's working on his braiding skills.

Lifting the brush from the dresser, he carefully runs it through my locks. My eyes follow him in the mirror, and my pussy pulses at the tender way he watches the comb slide through, making sure not to pull too hard.

The way he takes care of me never fails to put me in the mood. I spin in his arms but find a serious look waiting for me. "Can I give you a braid?" he asks when we find each other's gaze in the mirror.

I nod.

"And trust me, after everyone leaves, you can give me that look all you want. But right now," he says, slipping his fingers through my tresses, quickly sectioning three pieces. His elbows move and his eyes pinch as he works. I can't help but hide a smirk at how sweet it is. "Right now we're celebrating Lucy and her toy." He ties the elastic at the end, then curves his hands to my hips, gripping me. "You look beautiful in this dress."

His compliment eases my stress. "Thank you."

He follows behind me as we head into the living space, and a moment later, the first knock comes. The apartment is full of Crave & Cure in less than fifteen minutes, and later in the party, when things felt crowded and people got warm, Otis opened up his place across the hall, and people moved between both apartments, even lingering in the breezeway for a private moment and quiet talk. Vienna presents her toy, which is me but definitely more credit to her—and everyone applauds. Cohen whistles, and my lips tingle when I catch him doing it.

The night rolls on, and just as I'm getting tired, Aug pulls me aside. "Where's Cohen?"

I look around, finding him taking a sip of an amber liquid,

a smile on his face as he nods along to some crazy story Tucker is telling him. His hair is styled tonight, a neat coif of shine, and his jaw is clean shaven. His eyes are bright and his smile is wide. I'm about ready to slip away and grab him but once my eyes are on him for more than a moment, he looks at me, winking.

I lift my hand in the air, motioning him to us. He nods to Tuck, and heads toward me. His strides are long and confident, his trim physique owning his mud colored pants and white button up shirt.

"Can I talk to you guys somewhere quiet?" Aug says, head moving between us.

"Our room," Cohen offers, leading us that way. My body vibrates from the way *our room* sounds and I traipse in behind them, pussy tingling.

With the door closed, Aug turns to face me. "The toy is a hit. They want to sign you for another design, but they also want you to be more proactive in the advertising campaigns. It will be more money but much more time, too."

"The toy isn't even officially launched yet," I say, disbelieving that my replica is that sought after.

"The soft launch essentially set fire to the expectations and built a skyscraper in the ashes," Aug says, his tone even, eyes locked on mine.

I look at Cohen, because he knows that I actually had hoped to talk to Aug this week. He nods, because he knows there's no time like the present. I face Aug and give him a smile that screams "sorry, no thanks."

"I was going to ask you if I could go part-time, actually. I know my contract stipulates I'm full, but… I'm going back to school. I had almost completed my computer science degree. And I want it." I stand straighter, feeling empowered by my choice. I glance at Cohen who wears a proud smirk.

"Well," Aug says, without missing a beat, "When you get that degree, I'll hire you."

I blink, my heart racing. "I mean... am I fired?"

Aug laughs, but not before rolling his eyes. "No, Scarlett, you're not fired. Of course you can go part time. We can change the contract. It's a piece of paper." He smiles at me, and it's knowing and soft, and suddenly the moment grows serious. I swallow. "I'll hire you as the head of IT, and you can manage and oversee web and app development. Debauchery'd likely hire you, too. We're trying to step out of the past and up our online presence."

I shake my head but pinch my temples with my fingertips. "You would really hire me as the head of all of that? What if I suck?" I'm in disbelief of his kindness.

"You won't suck. You're disciplined, hard-working, and generous. I believe in you. You won't fail. And if there's one thing you've demonstrated since you started, it's that you're dedicated to Crave's ethos," he says, and he sounds more sure of me than I do. I caution a glance at Cohen, who is wearing a sexy smile, then winks.

"Okay, I won't say no to that. And thank you for letting me go part time." I don't know what else to say, I'm scared to say the wrong thing and have it taken back, that's how good it is.

He slices a horizontal palm through the air as if to say no worries, then turns to face Cohen. "And you're getting promoted. You're already doing the job of the in house engineer. What do you say you add it to your title and get some more money?"

Cohen shakes his head. "I don't need a title change or more money."

Aug snorts. "Don't give me that *I'm just happy to be here* bullshit, Cohen." He grins. "You're gonna build a future now, aren't you?" He motions between Cohen and I, and my stomach floods with warmth, my limbs tingling. I'm proud to be acknowledged as his, and that's a first for me. "So you're taking the title jump to get the pay jump because you earn every fucking cent and I won't hear another word."

Cohen brings his hand to his forehead, giving Aug a silent salute. Aug turns to face me. "Congratulations on the toy."

We share a handshake, and he's slipping out of our room, leaving us to grinning at each other. "Come to me," I whisper, holding my arms out.

He stalks toward me, head down, so fucking handsome. "I'm so proud of you. Look at what you're doing, finishing school, already securing a great job. You're getting everything you deserve, Scarlett."

My face is in his hands and he's crashing his lips against me in a hot instant. Before I can fill my fingers with his hair and get a taste of his mouth, he pulls away. "I am so proud of you."

"You just said that." My heart is racing so fast, my cheeks hurt from smiling.

"I want to make sure you know exactly how I feel," he says.

"And you," I whisper, "you got a promotion."

He shrugs humbly. "I already do the job."

"You're incredible," I whisper, everything inside my panties growing warm from the tingle that overtakes me. He smells like sandalwood and soap, and maybe a touch of bourbon, and it's everything I want to smell on my pillow for the rest of my life.

"I'm excited for tomorrow," I tell him. We're going to register for classes, and the semester is starting in a month. Now that I don't have to worry about asking Aug to go part time or having to quit, I'm really excited for registration. And to do it with Cohen.

"Me too," he says, dancing his eyebrows as his hand slides around my waist. He slips his fingers between my ass a few times and I moan. "And I like this dress."

I press a palm to his chest and give him a gentle shove back. "Take it off me later."

He nods as we walk toward the bedroom door. I yank it open and turn back, stopping him one more time. "Take it off with your teeth."

twenty-eight

. . .

cohen

I'm her desperate, loyal, leaking fool.

"A little more," Scarlett coaxes as the sheen of sweat on my forehead slips into my right eye. Blinking and giving my head a shake, the sweat goes splattering and my focus is restored. A little more, she said.

I clench my ass—something I found myself doing a lot these days. Scarlett is a huge fan of edging and in the last two weeks, I'm well acquainted with the art of staving off for a big release. It's torture but it's... fucking heaven.

My hips piston off the bed, and a little more of my cock slides between her soft pink lips. "Bring it closer, please," I beg, straining as far as I can with the restraints on my ankles and wrists.

She smiles at me, stroking her fingertips in lazy circles around her pebbled nipple. Fucking teasing me, and it's working. My groin sears with need as I jerk my hips off the mattress again, desperate to slide inside another inch. Hell, another fucking centimeter.

"How about a little less," she teases, withdrawing the pussy from the head of my cock. She brings the toy to my face, her tits grazing my sweaty bare chest as she does. "Lick me," she whispers with a sultry smirk. With *Lucy* at my lips, I do what she wants and lick. I move my tongue through her soft folds, tasting my salty precum, but not caring. Because Scarlett moans as she takes me in, licking her counterpart, driving my tongue into her tight canal.

After a moment, she draws it back, and tosses it to the floor. "Thanks, Lucy," she says, her mischievous eyes idling mine. "Now, are you ready?"

Very little blood circles my brain at this point, since she's been teasing my cock with her mouth and her toy for the last... well, it feels like forever but it's likely been around forty five minutes. My wrists and ankles burn from struggling, but the restraints are safe, wrapped in velvet. I've fought them so hard that I'm exhausted, and I know whatever she's going to do to me now will be very hard to fight.

"You struggled so much," she says, dragging a pointed nail down the center of my chest. My nipples perk up and my cock bobs with eager energy.

"You're driving me crazy," I breathe, watching with rapt attention as she brings her long hair to one side, collecting it on her shoulder. I love the way her hair feels looped around my fingers when she's got her mouth on me, and it's almost all I can think about until she straddles me. Hovering over me on her knees, she grips my cock with her bare hand for the first time tonight.

"Fuuck, Scar," I groan, my spine lurching from the bed as much as it can before the restraints jerk me back down.

"Now here's what you have to do," she says, smiling as she sinks down on my cock with—

"Holy shit," I grit out, teeth clenched, stomach knotted as she feeds me inch by inch into her tight asshole. We've never done this. I've never fucking done this. "So tight, so fucking tight," I pant, my ability to form full sentences fading away with every inch of me that enters her.

"You're going to give me a creampie," she says sweetly, voice dripping with honey, nails sliding down my chest so delicately that it makes me a little crazy. She winces as she sits down a little more, easing me into her slowly, so slowly that I think I may snap.

"Fuck, slower, slower, slower," I growl. She cocks a brow.

"If I can handle it, so can you." And then, she sits down completely, her eyes snapping shut, bottom lip pinched behind her top teeth as she takes a moment to calibrate to my extreme size stretching her tightest hole. I throb, I pulse, and I think about when Miggy Cabrera hit his 500th home run back in 2021. I picture my Detroit Tigers ball cap. I think of a pen cap. I think of a captain on a ship. I think of anything but my cock splitting her tight ass and the way her body clings to me.

I'm a fool, but a brave fool, so I ask, "Can I touch you? Can I make you come?" I don't know what this is doing for her in terms of finishing, because even though something can feel good doesn't necessarily mean it can make you come. Women are more complicated creatures than men, and whether I'm playing back my favorite episodes from It's Always Sunny in my mind to not come or not, she has to come first.

It's my responsibility.

"Unhook my hand and I'll rub your clit," I promise, sounding desperate, feeling desperate.

She giggles then drops her hand to her clit, smearing

two fingers around and her eyes hold mine. "I'm going to come, and you're going to come, and then I'm going to clean you off," she says, eyes fluttering closed as she finds the spot that feels good. She wiggles on my cock, sending me somehow deeper, and my eyes jump to the ceiling, where I read the model of the smoke detector over and over.

"Clean me off?" I try to understand the subtext but again, a beautiful woman whom I love bouncing in my lap with my dick in her ass. "Clean me... off?" I stumble, sweat sliding down my temples, seeping into my tousled hair.

"Then you're going to give me one more, deep inside me," she leans forward, working herself on my cock in quick, small grinds. "In my pussy."

I swallow thickly, and when I get the courage to meet her eyes, my orgasm pulsing in my balls, my cock practically vibrating with need. "Oh thank God," I breathe, seeing her eyes flutter closed, her mouth in the tell tale position—parted and panting. "Come on it Scar," I coax, dying to feel her clenching all around me, dying to let that take me over the edge.

Her hand moves against her clit, fingers rubbing my groin, and the friction, and watching her face plus the tightness. My stomach clenches and my spine curls. *Fuck. Fuck, fuck, fuck.*

"Yes," she moans, and right as the first pulse rockets from me, she seizes all around me, her orgasm wrapping my cock. Our hips rove in sync and I come in abundant, overwhelming waves as she does too, her body sealing all around mine, drawing out every single drop.

When she's panting and her fingers have slowed on her clit, she slowly lifts off me, rocking her hips over my cock, which rests along my groin and belly, glimmering from us.

Cum leaks from her dark hole, falling in slow, thick drops along my used shaft.

"Look at all of that," she coos, and even though I just came, her sultry dirty talk and pink, abused cunt waving around in front of me is enough to get me hard again. "Now, you're going to give it to me again, where it counts," she breathes, slipping to my side, leaving a trail of cum along my thigh.

With a damp towel, she lovingly and tenderly strokes my cock, taking care to clean and wipe every inch. And when she's done, all the jostling and care has me hard as nails again.

Keeping me in restraints, she turns around in my lap, and I watch in rapt delight as her long hair spills down her back. She notches my cock at her wet lips, and takes me in all at once, sinking down completely.

"Fuck," I groan.

"Cohen," she praises, wiggling her hips to feel my cock push around inside of her. "How'd you like taking my ass for the first time?" she questions as she begins rocking, her groin rolling over my cock. I watch myself slide in and out, fill her, empty her, impale her, tease her, all at her control.

"Good," I breathe, "so fucking good. So tight."

"Mmm," she breathes, a slow trickle of sweat slipping down the hollow of her spine. "You'll have to tell me which is better," she pants, riding me faster, slamming her cunt down on me with more force, more urgency. "Filling my ass, or breeding my cunt."

Her hips stop and my cock is pulsing with urgency in her warmth, begging to let go. "Don't stop," I beg, not recognizing the desperation in my voice but not caring how bad I sound. I need her and she knows it. I'm her desperate, loyal, leaking fool.

"What do you think?" she asks, peering at me over her shoulder as she grinds her groin to mine. "Do you think it feels better to pump my ass full of cum, or to dump all of it in my cunt?"

Fuuck. Fuck. Fuck. My balls thrum and my thighs twitch. My cock aches inside of her as she resumes her hips roving over me, her cunt jerking me like a fist in tight, slow strokes. Dizzying strokes.

"Give me another, Cohen, and tell me which is better."

She slams her hips down on my cock, my head pressing into her spongy center. She whines, tipping her head back, clawing at my flexed thigh muscles, clawing at anything as her cunt spasms all around me.

Fuck yes. "I'm coming," she announces, but I already felt her. Tighten and release, her cunt milks me as her hips undulate and her shoulders roll, her body dancing to the pulsing waves of her orgasm.

"Now, Cohen, tell me now," she whines, writhing on my cock, her pink lips spreading all around me. I look down at where I'm filling her, and lose complete control.

"Your pussy," I groan as the first rope of cum slips out, eager and fast. "I love filling your pussy, breeding your cunt, leaving you full," I breathe as shots three and four pulse from my slit, flooding her insides with my warm, thick cum. She rides out my orgasm, using her pussy to coax the final drops of release from me, her ass winking at me, wet with cum.

A moment passes where we just… breathe. Coming back from the chasm we delve into when we're together this way. The entire world falls away when I'm inside of her and she's using me how she pleases.

She slides off, pressing the expended towel between her legs. As she leans over me to release my wrists, her breast hovers above my lips, and I lift my face to fill my mouth.

She moans as I suck her breast, and steals it from me to reach over, releasing the second restraint. "Surprise," she smiles above me, placing a quick kiss on my lips before moving to the foot of the bed, releasing my ankles one at a time. Without hesitation, she drapes herself over me, bare chest to bare chest. Stacking her fists beneath her chin, she stares down at me. "I was nervous about taking you *there*, so I thought having control of the situation would make me the most comfortable."

I nod. "That was incredible and unexpected, too," I admit, because I know she'd said she wanted to save anal for off-screen moments, but in truth, I never gave it a second thought. She thoroughly pleases me all the time, so asking for more is never a thought that comes into my brain. Ever. "Thank you," I tell her, because it feels important for her to know that I appreciate the way she gives her body to me, the trust she shows me, the intimacy she surrenders to me.

"Now," she says, stretching her legs between mine, her cold toes skimming my inner calves. "You sure you wanna?"

My mind returns to where we started this evening.

Scarlett had a big shoot today, and because I try my very hardest to stay away from her when she's filming for reasons obvious and already discussed, she brought some of the edited scene home for me to see.

When she told me she asked Lance if it would be okay, a little wave of embarrassment wiggled through me because he most definitely knows why she wanted it. I mean, we're not watching her tapes like game footage, revising the game plan, and he knows it.

But the embarrassment quickly dwindled when she told me it was a shoot with her, Otis and Tuck.

"Aug was different about this one. And he had Lance sit and watch, and yeah, Lance is normally there but he doesn't usually watch so intently. Aug wanted him to, that much was clear," she says, waving a hand through the air as she queues the video on the TV hanging from the wall. "Bluetooth," she smiles, wiggling her phone.

"What kind of scene was it?" I ask, because when I peered at the schedule it just said *AUG'S CHOICE*.

She dances her eyebrows as we slide up on the bed, pressing our backs to the headboard. "A three-way pet thing."

I don't judge, but confusion scores my brows because I don't think I know what that means. "That's new to me," I admit, finding her hand in her lap, closing mine around hers, fingers woven together.

"Me too," she admits as the scene appears in vivid colors across the screen. She turns in my arms, her blonde hair tickling my bare chest. "Your set is beautiful, Cohen," she says, placing a kiss on my mouth.

We face the screen, and I take in my work, the set designed to replicate a bedroom. Obviously, I do a lot of bedrooms, but Aug was specific with this one. Usually I get the basic information and create the rest. That's... my job.

This time, I was given such specific instructions, down to which side of the nightstand the phone charging cord falls on. Seriously. It's only now though, as I watch Tuck and Otis sit side by side on the bed centering the space, reality snatches me.

I look over at her profile, studying the way her lips curl as she watches her two friends share a slow kiss, Tuck's hand possessive at the back of Otis's neck.

"What do you think this scene is about?" I ask her, letting my vision bounce between the scene and her.

She rolls her lips together, nodding at the screen. I look and see her entering, wearing something close to what she normally wears. Jeans, a cropped little hoodie, her blonde hair in loose beachy waves down her back.

"I think, from my perspective, it's about two lovers who can't quite make it fit just the two of them. They're... together but stretched thin trying to stay that way. I think it's about the third joining them, and the three of them becoming the relationship each of them needed. Despite the fact it's non traditional."

I nod. "That's... I think, insanely accurate."

She shrugs as the scene flickers against her shining eyes. "Well, I mean, we'll never get to know for sure, but I think so, yeah."

I look back at the screen and why it only occurred to me now, watching it on TV, I'm not sure. But I've been to Aug's place. When I first started at Crave, one of the monthly mixers was there. I got lost looking for the restroom. I stumbled into his bedroom.

"Aug's room looks just like that," I say quietly, spreading the secret out between us, making it ours instead of mine.

She hits pause as her head whips toward me. "What?"

Then I tell her exactly what happened that night at the party. How I had a few too many drinks and needed to take a leak and splash some water in my face. I stumbled down the hall, pushed into the bedroom and saw... "Pretty much that exact thing," I say, motioning to the set on screen.

She drapes her hand over her collarbone. "Interesting."

We sit there for a moment as she stares at the frozen image on the screen and then her gaze veers my way again. "Lance," she breathes, putting things together. "Aug? And Lance? I suspected there was more going on with them, but I wouldn't have liked to guess." She looks back at the screen and back to me again. "Who am I in this scenario?"

I laugh and shake my head. "I don't know, but *I definitely think you're someone.*"

She shakes her head too, like there's too much rattling around in there and she needs to settle it. She grabs her head with her hands. "Aug and Lance..." she trails off.

I take her hand again, bringing her back to me. I kiss her knuckles. "Whatever is going on with them, I'm sure they'll work it out."

Her eyes are wide. "Wow." She flips the scene back on and we watch in rapt silence as she settles between the two of them, guiding Otis's hand to Tucker's cock, and Tucker's hand to Otis's. With her palms wrapping theirs, she ski's until they're both spilling over, and the scene ends, the screen going dark.

"That was hot," I tell her, my cock lifting from beneath the sheet despite the fact I've just had her twice. I point to the hard ridge and the dark spot on the sheet. "This is why I keep my distance on set."

She wiggles her brows. "Well, we're at home now, so you don't have to stay away. In fact," she says, yawning and she nestles against me. "Put it in me, Cohen, and keep me full and warm until I fall asleep."

"Big day tomorrow," I say, feathering kisses along her jaw as we get comfortable on our sides, her the little spoon. She lifts her leg, opening herself, and I slide inside, groaning at the warm, comfortable feeling of her pussy.

With my chin on her shoulder, her blonde hair wrapping my senses and tickling my nose, I grip her hip and talk softly in her ear. I'm getting so used to just being inside of her without coming, it's so intimate and strangely romantic. "You ready?"

She's been in classes for a couple of weeks now, and tomorrow is her first test since she's been back. It's an Information Securities exam for her Computer and Network Security class. She's had her head in her laptop for nearly two weeks straight. Well, in her laptop when it's not in my lap, or under the lights at Crave.

"I'm ready," she yawns, "and I'm ready to have it behind me, to know if I revised the right way."

My dick twitches as her cunt flutters around me, her body growing soft with her sleepiness and comfort. She turns her head back to me over her shoulder. "I love you, Co." She yawns again, and I capture it with my lips.

"Love you, too, baby. Sleep well."

She reaches back and fills her palm with my bare ass. "I always do."

I close my eyes, running down the list of things to talk to my therapist about tomorrow. First thing? How full of hope I am, followed by reduction of my antidepressant doses. But my eyes grow heavy and Scarlett is so comfortable next to me, that I drift off, knowing I'll sleep well. Without question.

twenty-nine

. . .

scarlett

I'M PRACTICALLY VIBRATING AS THE SLATES CLACK, AND THE scene ends. Maxi outstretches her arms, and the back of my nose grows warm. If I speak right now, I will full on cry, so I give her a wide smile and fall into her hug.

"Your last for three months!" she says, her cheek pressed tight to mine.

"I know," I say quietly into her hair, holding her a moment longer to get control of my emotions. I don't know why I'm so emotional—I'm not quitting Crave. I'm still part time and will be part time when I return. But my Algorithms and Artificial Intelligence courses really fucking reared their heads on week four, and I found myself behind and panicked.

One night, while sitting snugly in Cohen's lap, crying my frustrations and fears that maybe I couldn't finish, that maybe it was all just too big of a dream, he suggested that I take a small hiatus from filming.

Loved by Lucy has been exceeding sales projections. Not

only is my position safe at Crave as a part time film star, but Aug promised me, when Cohen took me to him the next day, that I'd have a place here as long as I wanted. He also assured me that I could shape that role, be it IT or acting. That's when I said I needed a small break. Just a couple of months to get back into the headspace of deep, critical thinking. Hours of going through lines of code is challenging to anyone, but after a two year break, it felt impossible.

"I am coming back though, I promise," I say, sniffling the burning feeling away with a smile.

Around me, a silk robe comes down on my shoulders, Cohen smoothing his wide palms down my biceps. "It's after noon," he says into my ear, after pressing a kiss to the edge of my jaw.

I spin to face him, blocking out the set and bright lights behind me. My exam results should be posted at noon, and I'm dying to know how I did. It feels a lot like this first test will tell me if I can do this. Cohen says no matter what the test result, I am meant to do this and he believes that with his entire being.

It's crazy that I believe in him believing in me more than I believe in myself.

He drops to a knee, putting my fuzzy slippers out in front of me. Carefully and slowly, he drapes a palm over one foot, and looks up at me as he slides the slipper on. "You can do anything you want," he says, voice husky. He switches feet, and the grate of his calloused thumb along the arch of my foot has wetness burgeoning between my thighs. He slips the other fuzzy slipper on, still looking at me when he says, "And I'm here to support you while you do."

Then he stands, but smooths his fingers and palms up my bare legs as he does. A sudden shiver wracks my shoulders as he pulls me into a hug, smoothing his hand around my back in comforting circles. "It's pulled up on my computer, if you want to look."

I waffle our fingers together. "Let's rip off the bandaid."

We head that way, my mind racing. I think I did well on the exam, I mean, I studied a ton. And when the anxiety of studying that much seemed to swallow me up, Cohen pulled me into his lap, slipped himself inside of me, and I wiggled on his cock while sifting through my notes yet again.

Something about him being inside of me makes me release my death grip on anxiety, and the more comfortable I feel, the better I learn.

Though I can't lie, sometimes when he's inside me, casually sketching set designs on his iPad, hair a tousled mess, the comfort turns to heat, and I'm bent over the kitchen counter, begging to be bred.

Closing the door, Cohen pulls out the office chair, and I sit to find my university portal on screen, my username stored. Sometimes between scenes, I'd slip into his office and use his computer for online assignments.

"It's pass or fail," Cohen notes, reading the banner as I enter my password and student identification number.

"Yeah," I breathe, running numbers in my head. "With only fifteen questions, I need—"

He dips down and presses his lips to mine. "It is what it is, so let's check, okay?"

I sigh, leaving my fears outside of my body. He makes me brave, and I don't know how, but he just does. "Okay," I smile. He reaches over me, his big hand dominating the mouse easily. A few clicks later and the screen is loading, the results of my hard work and long-standing dream all coming to a proverbial head. I know I can fail and retake, but I don't want to.

Cohen's hands come down on my shoulders and he's

spinning me around, collecting me from the chair like his rag doll as soon as the word PASS appears on the screen, green letters making my eyes warm.

"You fucking did it, Scar, you did it, baby," he breathes, pressing kiss after kiss to my cheek, my nose, my lips, kissing me everywhere. I love it. My entire body thrums with pleasure at making him proud.

I shake my head. "And today was such a good day on set, too." I squeal a little, because goddamn it, I have a reason to be squeal worthy. "And now we get to go home!"

He laughs, holding my face, his eyes shiny. "Yes, we do. So let's go home and celebrate how fucking phenomenal you are."

I don't argue with that. Cohen hangs his utility belt and answers an email, then shuts his computer off and goes to my dressing room to collect my things. When he's through, we walk out of the building hand in hand, and he stops us on the back stairs.

"Hey, I know it's not new, and I've said it before, but when I realized you had feelings for me too, I made a promise to myself to let you know everyday just how much you mean to me, you know, in case."

I know his *in case* has nothing to do with breakups and everything to do with sudden losses, the kind we're both unfortunately so familiar with.

"I'm proud of you," he says first, and I cling to his flannel, holding myself steady as his deep timbre pours sweet words all over me. "And I love you so much." He doesn't seal it with a kiss. He just smiles, then leads us to his car where he opens my door for me, and buckles me in the seat.

My mind is running with excitement and plans as we drive to our place. Because I've been busy with school and my new schedule, and Cohen's taken on more hours at Crave designing more sets, neither of us have really had a moment to acknowledge that we've been having unprotected sex now for almost a full month.

We're off work early today, though, since Aug and Lance are bringing in their new film school mentee for some sort of orientation or meeting. That means we have the whole afternoon and evening to indulge in our love of fucking bareback.

God do I love it.

I also like the excitement that comes with being filled by him. Not knowing if in a few weeks from now, our raw and unfiltered passion has grown into something more.

"I've really enjoyed the last few weeks," I tell him as he opens then closes the apartment door behind us.

"What do you mean?" he asks, sliding his keys onto the counter, toeing off his brown lace up boots after snagging the laces free with a hooked finger.

"No protection."

He stands, and starts on unbuttoning his shirt as his eyes idle with mine. Finally he says, "Me too."

My voice is quiet when I ask, "Are you hoping?"

We stand there, my question hovering between us. The answer should be easy, but after what we've been through, it's also terrifying. He swallows. "Yes."

I smile at him. "Me too."

And before we get too mushy, he shrugs off his flannel and drops a kiss on my cheek before turning the corner to the kitchen. "I'll make you anything you want so tell me what sounds good," he says, reciting the same thing he says almost every night. Except now, whatever he makes, he makes sure to include fertility friendly foods.

"Honestly, Co, anything. Everything sounds good," I tell him, ready to strip out of my jeans and put on literally anything but. Because even the best fitting jeans are still jeans.

"Hey," he calls after me, bottles of condiments rattle in the fridge door as he yanks it open in the distance. "I redid the tulle on the ballerina's dress, by the way. I didn't know what color yours was as a kid," he adds, and his words lasso me, bringing me back to the hallway where I stop. He turns from his spot in the kitchen, smiling. "I did her dress in pink tulle. Addie's ballerina had a pink skirt," he says, his chin lifting slightly.

He's trying to talk about her more, and I've urged him to do just that. He's shown me some photos, and even talked a little bit more about that weekend. I know it's hard but I can also see it does bring him happiness to remember her.

"Cohen," I say softly. "Thank you. And I'm sure she'd love that the skirt was fixed."

He waves me off, pulling a black styrofoam tray of steaks from the fridge. "Anyway, I hope pink is okay."

"Pink is perfect."

I leave him cooking, and give him the moment I'm sure he needs after talking about her, and head into our room. I'm anxious to peel out of my clothes and into something like sweats or nothing at all, but now that I know he's worked on the music box, my heart pulls me toward it.

With a flip, I send the gold latch to the top of the box, and pull the lid open. Centering the pink velvet is the ballerina, the brown paint of her hair wearing, but her painted unitard is as crisp as when it was made years back. Her dress is pink tulle, and sewn perfectly to reflect a real ballet dress. I think he's even fed some wire through the bottom, to get it to hold its shape.

I run a finger along the edge, and twist her once, to see how she looks. Bringing it off the dresser, the box shifts weight in my hand as I make the dancer come alive. But when I do, something in the tiny drawer toddles around inside. I set it down and slide the drawer open.

Inside is a diamond ring, and in the doorway is Cohen.

"We don't have to go in order, but the sooner you're Scarlett Steele, the better." He closes the gap between us as the air in my lungs rushes out, and my heart literally stops beating as the world locks into place around me. Oh my god. He's proposing.

He falls to a knee at my feet, and I exhale thick and heavy, shaking me from the inside out. He's so handsome at my feet, and he's so good to me. "I love you so much," I manage, before the waterworks starts.

"Marry me, Scar. I don't care when and I don't care where. All I care about is making you my wife, and having you forever."

I pull the ring from the box and pass it to him with a wet laugh, running my wrist under my nose. Women in movies who get proposed to are gorgeous and full of life.

My mascara is running and I have a total snotty nose.

But it's real, and it's perfect.

He slides the ring up my finger and drops his hands to my feet. He lowers his head between his shoulders, looking down as he says, "I promise to take care of you, to worship and love every bit of you forever. My beautiful girlfriend, my future wife, my queen."

epilogue

. . .

cohen

"B<small>UT</small>," <small>HE CONTINUES, SUCKING IN A VERY DEEP BREATH THAT</small> tells me he isn't even close to wrapping this up. "If I add the molding and we decide to cut shots, it's all for naught. And it's a decent part of my wall budget and without the molding, I could do wainscoting, which essentially gives the same vibe, but is more time consuming. I mean, it would be on camera more unlike the molding, which could, in theory, be rough cut."

I clap a hand to his shoulder because it's 4:55 on Friday and I'm just about out of sagely, mentor advice.

Two years ago, we had a film school student assigned to Aug as a protege for her last semester. It was at that time, Aug decided he didn't want to be alone in having a puppy trail his heels, because misery loves company, I guess. He got *me* a protege named Sam, and Sam is… a golden retriever.

High energy, excited for everything. The only place he differs is that he overthinks everything. Like now. He's creating his first set all alone, without my guidance (read: he asks me so many fucking questions that I've essentially, by proxy, made all of the choices for this set) and we still have four days until shooting.

"I'd say go safe, because details don't do much if the scene is cut or the angle changes. Wainscoting will be in the shot unless they change locations, in which case you're making a new set anyway." I hold his eyes, because if I look away too soon, he'll trail after me, asking if I'm sure. "I'm sure," I add, "go safe."

He nods, mumbling his next steps under his breath as he heads toward the computer in his office. My old office, and sometimes I poke my head in there and simultaneously bask in the history of memories painted invisibly on the walls. So much loneliness, so much swallowed grief. But happiness, and understanding, too. Her hands moving through my hair, her words of praise in my ear.

I have a new office now, and it's even better.

Scarlett and I share it. And at some point during year one, Aug had a sign made. STEELE OFFICE. I still get a halfie when I see Steele after Scarlett's name.

She's my wife.

Wife seems limiting at this point, because she's more than the parameters of that title. She's my life partner and lover, yes, but she's my savior, she's the reason I laugh, the reason I live and breathe, the reason for it all.

I'm about to head back into our office and see her when Tucker sidles up to me. "What's up?" I like Tuck, but I'm ready to get out of here with my wife and get... home.

"Do you watch the SF Seagate on channel 6?" he asks, invading my space by coming a foot too close. But his voice is private, and my interest is fully piqued.

"The news show?" I ask, scratching under my chin,

finding my face itchy. Back in November, Aug, Otis, and a couple of other guys and myself started a no-shave month. Scarlett is enjoying the burn between her legs and at the back of her neck, so I now have a beard. So does Aug, who passes by at that moment, digging at his cheek with a pen. Bearded men don't tell you how fuckin' long it takes to get used to it.

"Yeah," he nods. "Do you?"

"No," I shake my head honestly. "I hate the news."

Tucker swallows, nodding more to himself than me, then steps even closer. Close enough to know he's been drinking coffee. "Pete Bryson got arrested last week. And it's... serious."

I blink at Tucker, and stare at the way his hair stands up awkwardly, likely having had someone's hand running through it the last hour. I'm not seeing his hair though. I'm remembering the last time we heard from Pete.

He showed up at Otis's, not knowing it was Otis's. And because Otis felt some type of way about being duped by Pete in the first place, he made sure Pete saw his way down the stairs.

Pete never found out we live just across the hall, and while Scarlett ultimately changed her phone number to avoid the unending calls, he never showed up at Crave again. And I never felt like it was good enough. I never thought him being able to slither away into obscurity was punishment enough for how he treated her, the things he said to her.

I smile at Tucker. "Good."

His eyes dart between mine before he cracks a smile. "Yeah, man, it is good. I just didn't know if you'd heard."

I loop an orange cord around my elbow and over my palm, wrapping it up. Tuck stands there, watching me. I freeze with the end of the cord still on the floor. "What?"

"I don't know what happened between him and Scarlett,

but I wanted to tell you in case you wanted to break the news to her."

I shake my head, missing the understanding of why this even matters. "She hasn't thought about Pete in a long time."

He nods a thousand times if he does it once. "I know, I know, it's just... he killed his girlfriend. Well, allegedly."

"Jesus," I mutter, letting the length of the cord drop to the floor. "He what?"

"I don't know how that information will impact Scarlett, or if it even will. I don't know. But I wanted to tell you because... well, we're glad she got out. And I think I speak for all of Crave when I say that."

He outstretches his hand to me and I shake it. "Thanks, man," I tell him.

I head back to the office, knowing I'll find my wife there, and I'm processing what Tucks just said. I don't know if she'd want to know, but it feels like something I have to share. Not because I want to talk about Pete and what a piece of shit he clearly continued to be, but because we're married. Withholding information like that would be wrong.

I close the door behind me, and lock it, too. I glance at my watch, knowing not many people are left in the studio, and the ones that are, won't be looking for us. From behind her computer, Scarlett lifts her head.

"Hey, babe, you wanna go? I can wrap it up in like, five minutes. Just waiting for my download to finish," she says, spinning in her office chair as I come around the side of her desk. She slides her feet out of the high heels she insists on wearing, and I crouch at her feet. I kiss the top before I drive my thumbs into the ball, spreading and kneading her sore and tired feet like I do everyday. It's not a foot thing, it's a Scarlett thing.

"Ahh," she moans, "that feels so good." Her eyes close as

she sinks deeper into her chair. I look up at the download bar, monitoring the progress. It seems to be moving slow, so I clear my throat as my eyes fall to her business card. Scarlett Steele, Head of App Development and IT, Crave & Cure Productions.

"Scar," I start, still kneading stress from her feet.

"Hmm," she murmurs, lost in the attention and affection.

"Tucker just told me Pete was arrested. It was on the news."

Her head lifts from the chair and she offers one peeking eye. "Yeah?"

I level her a serious look, and she opens her other eye. "Tuck says he's allegedly killed his girlfriend."

Her eyes go wide, and a medley of emotion runs through her face in the span of thirty seconds. Shock, horror, sadness, sickness, and finally, acceptance. Not for the life lost but for the harrowing news. "That's awful," she says finally.

We sit in silence as we process what's transpired. The man whom she lived with, who ran her life and was almost part of her life forever, he killed someone. When our eyes finally collide in a heated gaze, we know we're thinking the same thing. It could've been her.

She leans down to me as best as she can, and takes my face in her hand. "And you say that I saved you."

I grab her fuzzy slippers from under her desk and slip them on her feet before rising, her heels pinched together in one hand. I get our things ready while she waits at her computer and amidst the comfortable silence she says, "You saved me."

I turn to hold her gaze, and my chest splits as I process her meaning. It was out of my control when it came to Addie. I wasn't there. And it was an invisible attack, one we couldn't control. But I saved Scarlett, and there's a sliver of redemption in that knowledge. And she knows it.

The download slows considerably, and Scarlett's lumbar was aching, so what started as a back rub has, as the history of all backrubs would tell you, turned into sex.

Hot, slow, intentional sex. On all fours she rocks for me, naked and whiny. I feed my fist through her hair, and pull her head back slowly, leaning forward to kiss her neck.

We broke the rule about having sex at Crave about a year ago, but we made sure we did it after filming hours, in our office, with the door locked.

We've christened the wall, both desks, the floor, the couch and both desk chairs, too. And these days, Scarlett wants it more than ever.

It's the hormones.

I inch inside of her, and rock her up, to just her knees. My hips saw at her back as I fill my palms with her round, heavy belly. Smooth and warm, I run my hands all over it as I thrust into her from behind, her center hot and wet.

"Please, Co, please," she moans, grabbing her tits, bringing them together. The way she touches herself is so fucking erotic, the way she plucks her nipples with force, only to smooth the underside of her breasts with her open palms, slow and gentle.

Heat rattles my spine, and while I'm already close, I also know just what she wants. It's been new with pregnancy, but I hope it stays after the baby is born, because it's insanely hot.

She wants me to get close to the edge, then pull out and face fuck her, rough and sloppy until I'm giving her a throat full.

"Okay, okay," I promise softly, slowing my hips. As I'm sliding out of her, hands still holding her beautiful belly, a rush of wet heat coats my cock, thick and fast, immediately dripping from my balls.

"Fuck, you came already? Baby, that's hot," I say, pulling out completely. But when I do, there's a slow trickle from her gaping pussy, lips swollen from friction.

"I didn't," she says, turning in my arms so we're face to face. She looks down and quickly back up at me. "Oh my god, Co," she breathes, eyes wide, nostrils flaring. She clings to my shoulders, since we're naked she has no shirt to grab.

"What?"

"My water broke."

And just like that, the next part of our lives begin just how we started; at Crave.

The end.

if you liked this story...

Leave your review on Amazon! I'd love to hear your feedback.

Thoughtful, comprehensive reviews are the best way to help Indie authors grow, both their skill and their business. Next to reading our books, reviews are the next best gift!

If you have time, I'd love to hear your opinion.

And thank you again for reading!

Sign up for my newsletter to keep up-to-date with my projects, deals on books, sneak peaks, and much more.

about the author

Daisy Jane is an indie author writing contemporary romance with kink. In her stories you will find small towns, ordinary people and extraordinary sex lives.

When not writing romance, Daisy enjoys reading, finding new ways to eat peanut butter, black coffee, funk music and cool cover bands, Yosemite, browsing Reddit, true crime, and so much more.

She lives in California with her husband of fifteen years, their two daughters and three cats.

facebook.com/DaisyJaneAuthor
twitter.com/authordaisyjane
instagram.com/authordaisyjane

patreon

I write erotic novellas over on my Patreon. So if you like my writing style but want something shorter in length, I release a chapter every week.

Also, you'll get access to commissioned NSFW art featuring your favorite heroes and heroines from my books, Men of Paradise and Wrench Kings included!

You'll get access to everything in my one and only tier. Quarterly merch coming soon!

Come on, hold my hand.

Patreon.com/DaisyJane

(Content ages 18+)

also by daisy jane

Series:

Crave & Cure (3 Books)

Stuck With Tuck / male porn star / MF / Book 1

Cohen's Control / subtle femdom / MF / Book 2

Wrench Kings (3 Books)

The Wild One / a reverse age gap romance / MF / Book 1

The Brazen One / a grumpy/sunshine romance / MF / Book 2

The Only One / a femdom romance / MF / Book 3

Men of Paradise (3 Books)

Where Violets Bloom / a stalker romance / MF / Book 1

Stray / a femdom romance / MF / Book 2

With Force / a CNC romance / MF / Book 3

Oakcreek (2 Books So Far)

I'll Do Anything / a bully femdom romance / MF / Book1

After the Storm / an alpha MM romance / MM / Book 2

The Millionaire and His Maid (3 Books)

His Young Maid / an age gap boss/employee romance / MF / Book 1

Maid for Marriage / an age gap romance / MF / Book 2

Maid a Mama / a surprise pregnancy romance / MF / Book 3

The Taboo Duet

<u>Unexpected</u>/ an age gap Daddy figure romance / Book 1

<u>Consumed</u> / a Daddy kink romance / Book 2

Standalones:

<u>The Other Brother</u> / dual POV / MF

<u>The Corner House</u> / single POV / MFMM, MFM, MFM with an HEA

<u>My Best Friend's Dad</u> / age gap instalove novel / MF

<u>Waiting for Coach</u> / age gap novel / student teacher / MF

<u>Hot Girl Summer</u> / a taboo step sibling romance / MF

<u>Pleasing the Pastor</u> / an age gap virgin romance / MF

<u>Release</u> / a taboo MMF, MM, MF romance

Raleigh Two / a taboo MFM romance / MFM

The Man I Know / a married couple romance / MF

Novellas:

Cherry Pie / very taboo why choose / MFMM

Printed in Great Britain
by Amazon